# THE
# LAST
# ROMANS

# THE
# LAST
# ROMANS

JOHN STEWART

ARCTURUS
PUBLISHING LIMITED
LONDON

Published by
ARCTURUS PUBLISHING LIMITED
1–7 SHAND STREET
LONDON SE1 2ES.


This edition published 2000

ISBN 1-84193-021-0

Typeset by Christopher Smith Design.

Printed and bound in India.

In memory of
Sheila Rosenberg

My grateful thanks to Mary Allen for her untiring
help in typing all the various drafts; to Joan
Crammond for help with the early drafts and
publicity; to Arthur Farndell for proof reading and
to Ian McLellan, my publisher and agent for his
unfailing support.

The general framework of this novel is historical
but the character portrayals are fictional.

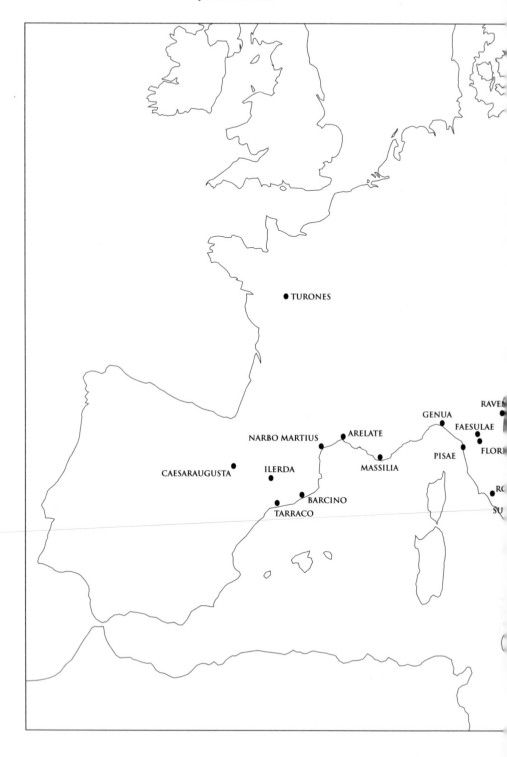

TURONES

RAVE·

GENUA

FAESULAE

NARBO MARTIUS    ARELATE

FLOR·

PISAE

MASSILIA

CAESARAUGUSTA    ILERDA

RC·

BARCINO

SU·

TARRACO

UM

● SIPONTUM

● BARIUM

● BENEVENTUM

● BRINDISIUM

● DYRRACHIUM

● PHILIPPI

CONSTANTINOPLE ●

● EPHESUS

ATHENS ●

● DELOS

# CONSTANTINOPLE

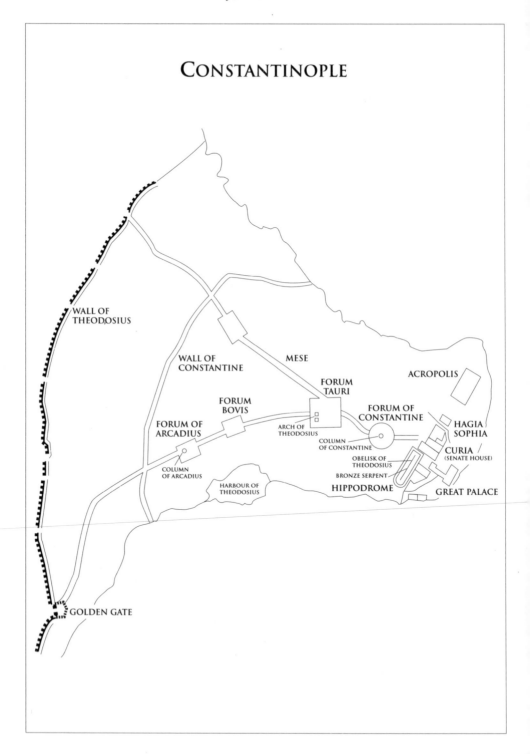

WALL OF
THEODOSIUS

WALL OF
CONSTANTINE

MESE

ACROPOLIS

FORUM
TAURI

FORUM
BOVIS

FORUM OF
CONSTANTINE

HAGIA
SOPHIA

FORUM OF
ARCADIUS

ARCH OF
THEODOSIUS

COLUMN
OF CONSTANTINE

CURIA
(SENATE HOUSE)

COLUMN
OF ARCADIUS

OBELISK OF
THEODOSIUS

HARBOUR OF
THEODOSIUS

BRONZE SERPENT

HIPPODROME

GREAT PALACE

GOLDEN GATE

# CHAPTER ONE

# CLOVIS

The Roman road was arrow-straight, but Rome had ceased, long since, to care for and maintain its surface. Scrub grew close to its side and ate into its foundations. Even in her declining years Rome would never have allowed such negligence.

A lone man, clothed in the manner of the northern tribes, stumbled over the worn paving. Absently he turned from the road onto the rain-softened ground and, in a sudden movement, fell to his knees.

'God,' he exhaled.

Hunger and exhaustion had brought him to the limit of endurance, yet stubbornly he struggled on. For days he had vainly sought some human help in what appeared to be an endless desolation, for fire and sword had ripped across the land with wanton licence: a bitter reminder of the smouldering embers that had been his own established villa secluded well amongst the rolling hills of southern Britain.

He had hoped to find Gaul safe, especially in the west, but disillusionment had come quickly, strengthening an old resolve to visit Tuscany, the land of his ancestors and, what was more, to see the once mighty capital, Rome herself.

Marcus Valerius Tullus Britannicus was a living anachronism. His name, his Latin and his behaviour were the habits of another age. In Britain his family had lived and ruled their large estates for generations, during which the close family circle of the Tullus household had maintained the old traditions.

Now on the bleak deserted road no one would have guessed at the Roman heart beating beneath the barbarian rags – indeed the perfect disguise in a land infested with banditry. Again, no one would have guessed at his thirty-five years, but he knew his childless years. He, the last Marcus Tullus, knew too well.

On hearing distant voices echo down the surface of the road he was suddenly alert. With practised caution he hid himself within a thicket adjacent to the ancient road and there, perched well above the ground, he waited.

In time two men came into view: brutal-looking men, their swords swinging much too low from ill-fitting belts – no doubt stolen. They were followed by a broad, rough-hewn figure, indeed a formidable character. He was teasing a young girl, or so it seemed, but it soon turned out to be coercion. The girl was of gentle birth, that was evident from her pleading; while her tormentor was typical of the present anarchy – a brutish brigand unrestrained. He wanted his enjoyment, and her misery only added to his lust. Fiercely Tullus gripped his vine-rod staff, his knuckles white, but he felt powerless.

They were opposite his hiding-place when the girl looked up, with that instinct which a woman has for watching eyes. Despite her obvious distress she looked attractive. Sensitive, Tullus judged, the type of woman he was drawn to. Boiling with frustration, he drew his thumb across the sharp point of his staff. Then he braced himself. He had always been good with the javelin.

There was a sudden rush of air and, much too late, the girl's tormentor turned. The vine-rod staff had struck and with a chilling yell he grabbed his shoulder. Blood pumped between his fingers and the girl, now free, ran frantically towards the trees that flanked the far side of the road.

It had all happened quickly and without calculation. They would discover him, of course. He felt exhausted, almost indifferent, feeling that his last reserves of energy had gone.

Swearing continuously, the girl's tormentor screamed at his companions, to seek him out, no doubt. Tullus listened, intent on every sound. They were under his very hiding place. Strange, he mused wearily, why are people so reluctant to look up? They would, in time, and soon an end would come.

Tullus remained statue-still, his breathing soundless, until another presence, like a distant thunder, gained his whole attention. It came from well beyond the trees across the road, a valley hidden from his view. Slowly the thundering drew nearer, until he recognised the sound of horses smashing through the undergrowth. All at once, it seemed, horsemen were straddling the road, and in their wake a stream of soldiers gathered in a round, informal mass. They stopped, a scheduled meeting place, perhaps; maybe to await their general. For the men before him were an army, a motley army when judged against Rome's cohorts, but nonetheless an army.

The girl's tormentor and his two companions were apprehended and held at swordpoint. Blood still seeped from the brigand's shoulder, but his captors treated this with cold indifference, and when he tried to speak a brutal blow brought silence.

The ranks parted. An important officer had arrived, the army's general, Tullus guessed, judging by his special ring of guards. There were churchmen too. Suddenly it came to him. This was Clovis, monarch of the Franks and a recent convert to the Roman Church; hence the numerous clergy, clothing the ambition of their new-found convert with the aura of a holy war.

Clovis was no ordinary man, that was clear enough. He vibrated with energy, its rawness spilling over in the torrent of his orders. His ambition ruled and on that selfish altar all would be a sacrifice.

The three men held at swordpoint were quickly brought before him and he, still mounted, was instant in his judgement. A choice was offered them – the army or the sword. Tullus felt the difference would be marginal. Then it was the girl's turn. Obviously she had fled straight into the advancing soldiery.

At once Clovis grew gracious – the posture of a Christian prince – but his true intent was written on his face. She would add some pleasure to the brief night hours. In this Tullus was a realist. The mistress of a king was better than the plaything of a brigand. At least she would be housed and fed.

Still mounted, Clovis nudged his horse close to where Tullus was hiding. All attention was on the King, but it only needed one alert and roving eye to spot the crouching form, shadowy in the tree above. Tullus was at peril, his fear reflected in the pounding of his heart. If caught, he would be seen as an assassin, when the cleanness of the sword would be a luxury.

Suddenly the King's restless energy exploded into action. Dramatically he raised his sword and pointed to the south.

'Give me your support,' he shouted, first addressing the churchmen and then the surrounding ranks of soldiery. 'Give me your support and the Arian heresy will be as straw before our horses' hooves!'

The soldiers bellowed their support and once more Clovis pointed vigorously with his sword. With that the massed ranks moved forward.

So that was Clovis, Tullus mused, his tensions easing, the new unstoppable power in Gaul; the great convert to Roman orthodoxy. He smiled cynically. Gaul had been worth a change of faith.

They had seated the girl upon a mule. Her shoulders were hunched and her blonde hair hung listlessly as if reflecting her dejection. Pity rose in Tullus, but he could do nothing, absolutely nothing!

After waiting for some time he ventured to the ground and at once began to search for food. There was hope, for swarm armies such as that of Clovis could be careless. He scoured the area with growing desperation until, astonished, he came across a pack-horse grazing unattended. He approached it gently, talking all the while, and the horse, unheeding, kept on grazing. It was used to human kind. Deftly Tullus gripped its reins with one hand, while the other delved into the baskets strapped across its back. His spirits soared, for they were packed with dried fruit, cheese and bread.

Making no attempt to mount, he led the horse away, not daring to stop until he felt the army to be safely out of reach. Then at last he halted by a stream, where he ate, and drank his fill. Now he needed shelter and a place to rest.

It was late spring, and in northern Gaul the nights were often cold. To find some dwelling that was dry was now his dream. He was fortunate, for as he topped the next incline he saw a farm-house nestling in some trees. But he ignored the impulse to rush forward until he felt completely certain that the place was empty. He had a fear of army stragglers, who could be unpredictable and brutish.

The farm dwelling, its roof partially collapsed, had been abandoned for some time. Judging by its size and structure, Tullus guessed its owners had been prosperous, but nothing remained of value. The place had been fired, so Tullus guessed the occupants had fled.

It was five hundred and seven years after the birth of Christ and typical of the time. The order of the Western Empire had collapsed, and in its place was Clovis, battling with the aid of sword and church to force a unity.

He led the pack-horse into the high-roofed structure of the dwelling where the owners and their animals had enjoyed a common shelter. There he tied the docile creature to a sturdy post, after which he pulled some grass and laid it at its feet.

'At last,' he said aloud. 'At last a chance to sleep.'

ooo

The blonde girl that Tullus had pitied was a widow of twenty-two. Her husband had been killed when his estates were overrun. The servants had fled and she was spared to be the plaything of the plundering warlord. By pretending compliance, though, she tricked him and escaped, only to end up at the mercy of a lesser brigand. A miracle, it seemed, had saved her from his clutches. Who had been the shadowy figure in the thicket? She would never know.

Since her husband's death, survival had grown to be her full-time occupation. She had been forced to view despair and grief as luxuries and the present need, to eat, to find some place to sleep, had focused her attention. That, and her determined aim to join some distant cousins in the south, kept her on the move.

She had been educated well and was not flattered by the prospect of the King's attentions – indeed, it filled her with aversion. So, slowly, she allowed the mule to slacken pace and fall behind, but this was quickly noticed. When admonished, she responded listlessly, disguising her intention.

After some time they halted, when she found herself within the privileged circle of those about the King.

Clovis lifted his hand and commanded immediate silence.

'We are now within the lands owned by the monastery of the Blessed Martin. Know this well: we will abstain from all foraging – only grass for the horses and water from the streams are permitted.'

So saying, he grandly turned to the churchmen.

'Two of you will go before us to Turones and offer prayers to the memory of the holy saint. Ask his blessing on us, we who are the staunch protectors of the one true faith!'

The King continued to eulogise the memory of St Martin. In the young widow's opinion it was gross and overdone, yet those about her seemed to relish it. Their faith was simple. She, though, doubted the sincerity of Clovis, yet he played his part with convincing vigour.

The army had hardly started up before there was another halt. The reason was soon evident. A soldier, an innocent-looking man, was dragged to face the King, accused of taking hay from a local peasant. Hay was grass, the soldier pleaded desperately, but the monarch's face was black with anger.

'What hope have we if we offend the blessed Martin?' he exploded, and at that the man was cut down where he stood.

'Arria.' The young widow mouthed her own name. 'This company's not for you.' She was horrified and incredulous at the murmurs of approval that surrounded her. Then it came to her that she could use this fervour to advantage. Impulsively she jumped from the mule and threw herself before the King.

'O King, may I seek the blessing of St Martin? May I join the pious ladies of Turones?'

For a moment Clovis showed annoyance. He had been cheated. Even so, he quickly showed his grace. He had no alternative, but what was done in public could be soon undone in private.

'Escort the lady to Turones,' the King commanded, to the general chorus of approval. He had acted prudently.

ooo

Tullus spent four days resting at the disused farmstead. He washed daily in a nearby stream, a pale reflection of Roman luxury, and in the manner of solitary men he chattered to himself and to his horse.

On the fifth morning he headed south, following a crude but obvious path. The sun was warm and about mid-morning he came upon a wayside shrine. *Twenty miles to Turones* was carved upon its stone. Shelter for the night, he thought hopefully.

As he journeyed on, he could not help but notice the prosperous nature of the countryside. The hamlets of the peasants were bustling; a sharp contrast to the desolation he had recently experienced – not least in the deserted farmhouse. The key was given by a peasant that he talked to on the mud-caked road.

'These lands are owned by the monastery of the good St Martin of blessed memory. God protects us.'

The peasant had praised the goodness of St Martin. The brigand would fear his wrath. It was a world of faith, and any leader anxious for the backing of a powerful church would be careful to refrain from violent trespass on the lands made sacred by the memory of the saint.

Tullus had grown up in what had been a Roman world. Then had come the chaos of the raids and pillage, and then his desperate flight to Gaul where, contrary to his hopes, he had failed to find the old familiar world. Instead there was a new and potent force, the force of faith that seemed to turn its back on reason. He thought of Clovis. Could his fervour be sincere? It was certainly real enough amongst his followers.

It was late in the afternoon when he sighted Turones. Dismounting, he crossed the old, neglected bridge that spanned the Liger. No one bothered to question the rag-clad figure, so he plodded on until he found himself amidst the encamped army. He should have known, but it was too late. He would have to brave it out. The horse! – they might recognise the horse! He kept going, for there was nothing else to do, and no one stopped him. He was just another peasant.

Tullus always offered some service in exchange for food and shelter. His literacy in Latin was usually welcomed, especially by the Church, and the monastery of St Martin was no exception; indeed, in their case they were more than pleased. The King, they said, was putting an impossible pressure on the scribes.

The King! Tullus froze – but why? Clovis did not know him. He laughed, the first time he had laughed for what seemed an eternity. The brothers eyed him strangely. Tullus noticed that one of them had no teeth at all. It was not uncommon, but the monk was very young.

The monastery church was dark and permeated with the smell of incense. There was little peace, though, for the presence of the King was like a whirlwind.

Ever impatient, Clovis did not trouble with the detail of his letters; he merely gave the outline and Tullus found himself composing proclamations and despatches of the highest import. It soon was crystal clear to him that war was imminent with Alaric, the Arian and Visigoth King, and it was also more than clear that Clovis welcomed the prospect.

There were those, of course, who urged restraint; the most prominent being Theoderic, the Ostrogothic King of Italy. Indeed, a mission had arrived to press his case. Theoderic made it clear that he would aid his brother Arian and he had the backing of the Roman Senate. Alaric was not without his allies, yet this did not seem to trouble Clovis. Rome and Ravenna were a long way off.

Clovis, Tullus imagined, had few scruples. He was clever, charged with energy and confident. His single-minded will had spurned his own tradition, for, by his conversion to Roman orthodoxy, he had broken with the family-like circle of Arian kings that dominated Europe. He had chosen the church of the people and, in Tullus's opinion, the winning side.

For two days Marcus Tullus worked within the frenzy that spun about the Frankish King. Clovis was impressed and asked, if not commanded, that Tullus join his secretariat. Tullus refused. The King's close aides were incredulous and Clovis just managed to control his fury, for he was careful not to violate the house of Martin. Tullus, of course, had been prudent, couching his refusal in appropriate terms.

'Noble King,' he had said respectfully, 'I have made a vow of pilgrimage to the blessed city of Rome before high summer and a sacred vow made in holy Church cannot be broken.'

Tullus's earlier dislike of Clovis had mellowed. Even so, he had no wish to spend his substance in the service of a ruthless warlord, however great. So when the Frankish army moved he stayed behind at Turones.

For two days he rested at the monastery, and with the payment for services to the King he bought new clothes. He persistently enquired about the blonde-haired girl, but to no avail. And at the house where rumour said she was, he was received with cold resentment.

At the monastery, however, a certain camaraderie had grown up between him and a number of the monks; those who had been picked to serve the will of Clovis. At supper they talked and on the final evening of his stay he introduced the subject of Arianism. What exactly was it? He asked.

'They deny the divinity of the Son,' said one, the words sharp like arrows.

'Yes,' another supported, 'they say the Christ is not an incarnation of the Father, but rather a man filled with the power of the Father.'

'As far as I'm concerned,' Tullus responded, 'when Christ said, I and my Father are one, he meant it!'

'Well said,' was the chorus return, and at that the conversation quickly changed. Clearly the monks were not at ease with a subject they believed to be a devilish perversion.

Tullus had never doubted the divinity of Christ. The belief was deep in his family history. Indeed, the family legend maintained that the first Marcus Tullus, a centurion, had met the Christ in Galilee. His grandfather had learned the tale from his grandfather. How much had been added in the telling was another story.

It was certainly a romantic tale, how he, the first Marcus Tullus, had married the daughter of a patrician senator named Valerius; that the marriage had been blessed by one of the disciples of Christ and of course, as all such legends go, they had been blissfully happy. Tullus never scorned the story.

'I wonder where he is.' someone asked, jerking Tullus from his thoughts.

'You mean the heretic Alaric?' asked another.

'Yes.'

'No one knows.'

'Clovis does! He has spies everywhere.'

'What about Alaric? He's not a fool.'

'He hasn't the Church on his side.'

'Will the Frank win?' Tullus cut in.

'If praying wins him battles, yes, he'll win. He's forever asking the blessing of St Martin.'

Tullus was amused at the cynical turn in the conversation. He smiled at the last speaker, a round-faced man whose laugh revealed a few remaining teeth like standing stones.

'Do you fear Alaric?' Tullus asked pointedly.

'We don't want him here,' was the reply. Fear was abroad in Turones; it was obvious, for no one welcomed, however distant, the presence of warring armies.

'Alaric cannot be close, otherwise he would have stopped Clovis crossing the broad waters of your river Liger,' Tullus suggested.

'You're right, friend from the north,' the round-faced man returned with some relief. 'Here, drink up; we don't want you to complain of our hospitality.'

Tullus did not refuse.

The next day disappointment came early when he found his horse was missing. Clovis had taken all the horses, he was told. It was a bitter blow, but as Tullus knew, the King had only claimed his own.

Abruptly he turned away, heading for the road that ran eastward and north of the River Caris, with the Liger to his left. Behind him was Turones bounded by the two converging rivers. He looked back at the basilica and the finger of the old Roman bridge, in disrepair yet holding firm against the river's flow. Then he thought of the fair-haired girl. Her forlorn image haunted him. Where was she? Was she there amongst the cluster of the town? He sighed, turned to the road in front of him and continued on his way.

ooo

Clovis had not taken all the horses. One had already left its rickety stall, led by a figure in the habit of a monk. There were no challenges, for the army of the Frankish King knew better than to trouble any member of the church, especially in a place made sacred by St Martin. No one had seen the blonde hair beneath the monk's cowl and no one had recognised a woman's faced grimed purposely to avoid detection. Arria had made her first bold move, but when she saw the massed ranks of the army spread out to the east she panicked and turned off the road. By chance she found an empty yet well-constructed stable and there she waited, both fearful and frustrated, hoping, as the rumour went, that Clovis would soon leave. Luckily she had ample food and there was fodder in the stable too. Water was a problem but it was close at hand. She did not try to hide, but she could not nerve herself to face the concentrated mass of soldiery up ahead. She chose her times to venture out for water, times when there were few about; but no one troubled or attempted to approach her. The mantle of the monk was her protection. Day followed day until at last, without her knowing it, the army had departed.

The next morning she left at dawn, her fear receding as the town grew distant; but new fears were now in waiting, the perils of the open road. She was grateful, though. She had escaped the bed of Clovis and the icy bleakness she had felt within the Church's house for strangers. She had sensed a jealousy, but did not know the reason. Perhaps they had been told she was the mistress of the King.

Clovis, in fact, had forgotten about the blonde girl with the delicate features until the final hours of his stay and, when one of his attendants had tried to tell him she had disappeared, the busy monarch was inaccessible. Thus the matter merged with the chaos of an army on the move.

# CHAPTER TWO

# NARCO

Rarely, if ever, are armies free from the prying eye of the enemy, and the host of Clovis was no exception. Not only Alaric, but all of Europe was watching, and one leader in particular, the uncrowned king of the Arian alliance, Theoderic, Lord of the Ostrogoths and master of Italy.

It was assumed, and correctly, that Theoderic had spies at the court of Clovis, for no king worth his salt would have neglected such precautions. Clovis, though, was careless of such interlopers. Few men knew his will and in any case spies could be fed fictitious rumour.

One spy, the servant of a Roman, but seconded to a high-born Goth hoping to impress Theoderic, had been present at Turones. Recommended for his cunning and determination, he had noted all the scribes who worked for Clovis, especially Tullus; and now that Tullus was without the court's protection it was a lead he was determined to pursue. Here was his chance to prove himself, to be rewarded, and hopefully one day to be a well-paid servant of the state; but he did not act immediately. He waited. Time and place would soon arise.

ooo

Four nights out of Turones, Tullus awoke with a knife at his throat. He froze, his eyes quickly scanning the dim interior of the shack where he was resting. It was early dawn and the faint light revealed two men, one lean-faced, the other large and heavy. The lean man spoke. 'Not a word – or' He drew his hand across his throat.

Tullus said nothing. Initially he guessed that Clovis had decided to employ him. Such recruiting methods were not uncommon. He quickly changed his mind when, with his hands and feet bound, he was roughly pitched into a farm cart. This was not the will of Clovis. His agents would never maltreat someone that their master wanted to employ, certainly not a scribe.

A heavy rug was thrown over him, blotting out the sun and then the cart jerked forward, not towards Turones but eastwards.

'Born to be a slave,' he grated to himself. What other reason could his captors have? Beneath the rug the last Marcus Tullus shuddered.

After a short distance the cart left the road, bumping violently on uneven ground. Tullus could do little to protect his body. Then at last they halted and the rug was thrown back. What now? he thought desperately.

Blinking from the sudden glare, Tullus was hauled into a sitting position. The lean-faced man smiled thinly.

'Well, my friend,' he began, 'I want information, real information. You scribed for Clovis – talk!'

'Is that all?' Tullus exploded. 'Why not simply ask? Why this?'

'Speak!' The smile grew thinner.

Tullus responded plainly.

'The King outlined some of his diplomatic messages and I filled them out. I know that what he said was by no means what he thought. What more can I say? It was ...'

A vicious blow brought blood to the corner of his mouth.

'You call that information!' The smile had an obvious look of relish. This viper, Tullus thought, got pleasure from inflicting pain. Anger, not fear, began to burn within him.

'I want news, hard news!' Like the knife-thin smile, the voice was mean.

Another blow jerked Tullus's head to the side.

'Is Clovis ready for battle?' the inquisitor hissed.

'All the signs suggest it.'

'I'm not interested in signs!'

The knife of the inquisitor scratched Tullus's neck and beads of blood began to trickle downwards.

Stubborn and angry, Tullus said nothing. Then suddenly it was over and he found himself beneath the rug once more.

'Either he knows nothing or he's a fool, but we'll soon find out,' the inquisitor shouted to his burly companion as the cart bumped back towards the road.

Tullus had little doubt that torture lay before him and he knew that his tormentor would enjoy his misery. The man loved cruelty, his eyes had told it all. Once more Tullus shuddered. He was at the mercy of a mind that hated pain yet loved inflicting it.

The noise of the cart wheels on the uneven paved road continued, and after something like an hour of pained discomfort it began to rain, the water running down beneath the rug and soaking both his back and legs. Then, when frustration had grown to screaming point, the cart swung over to the right and stopped.

He expected the rug to be hurled back but nothing happened; instead, he heard receding footsteps. A door opened, followed by the sound of laughter – an inn, perhaps. Here was a chance, a breath of hope. Struggling desperately, he pushed his head above the rug. It was an inn, one of the lowliest kind, and it looked as if his captors were the only callers.

Awkwardly he raised himself to a sitting position and there, the rain beating against his face, he waited, frantic with impatience. There had to be someone who could help, for at any moment his tormentors would return.

At last, in the distance, he saw a horse and rider approaching. They were maddeningly slow. He could not wave his hands, but when the rider drew close he shouted with repeated urgency, alas to no avail, for the traveller, a monk, rode on, his head bowed against the rain. Too timid and afraid, Tullus concluded hopelessly. At least his captors had not been alerted.

As he slumped back the rider turned and, all at once, it seemed, a knife was sawing at his bonds. Desperately he urged speed while anxiously watching the hovel inn. In the hurried effort the monk's hood fell back, revealing the blonde head of the girl he had seen on the road to Turones.

'It's you,' he reacted, for the moment stunned by the coincidence.

'What do you mean?'

'Later, later. Let's get far away from here!'

They ran across the road into the tree cover, with Tullus leading the horse. Tight-lipped, Tullus continued on with frantic urgency, unheeding of the constant stream of questions. 'Why were you bound? What have you done? You said, "It's you." Do you know me? Who are you?!'

Suddenly he turned to her.

'You've just saved me from a nightmare,' he began, breathing deeply with relief. 'I've a lot to explain, but first may I ask you a question. Who threw the wooden staff at the brigand? ...'

'You were the ...?'

'Yes!'

'You were hidden in the trees.'

He nodded.

'But who are you? Do you come from Rome?'

He smiled and shook his head.

'My family have lived in Britain for generations. Marcus Valerius Tullus at your service,' he added, bowing playfully.

'Your name! – it's from the histories – from Tacitus – but what happened? Who bound you?'

He told his story and she believed him totally.

'And I almost didn't stop!' she reacted, shuddering with aversion. 'Thank God I did. It was your voice that held me. It was so obviously Roman – thank God! I've found a real Roman. – I've got some food,' she burst out. Then she added quickly, 'Will they follow us?'

'I doubt it, they're creatures of the road, but we'll have to be careful.'

'We?!' she questioned with pretended naivety.

'Well, you're certainly not travelling alone.'

'Where are we going? You don't mind me asking, I hope?' She could not suppress the smile lighting her face.

They laughed.

'Will Rome do?'

'All roads lead there, so we're told!'

'So we are – how is my travelling companion named?' he asked, continuing the banter.

'Arria.'

'An ancient name.'

'Enough of the ancient. At least I'm not pre-history, like a certain Marcus Tullus!'

He was just the right height, she thought subjectively, and he was strong, though not brutish in his strength. She liked his nose.

They ate and drank at a nearby stream before continuing through the rich but neglected countryside, but as they progressed doubts began to trouble Arria. Who was he really? Had he told her all the truth? 'Don't be stupid, Arria,' her better part returned. 'Be grateful you've got someone to protect you – and a high-born Roman too.'

Peasant generosity was their boon as they proceeded. There were religious establishments, of course, though these were an infrequent luxury. Seven days passed, then fourteen, and soon it was a month. All Arria's doubts had disappeared. Tullus was a man of honour; too much honour, she was wont to think. They were attracted to each other and at times desire arose, obvious and awkward. Yet at no time did the will of Tullus bend. He could neither protect her nor provide if she were with child, for as it was the sheer effort of survival fully occupied their waking hours.

It was when they least expected trouble that it came. They had reached Valentia on the Rhodanus, and were enjoying the luxury of rest within the confines of a small religious community. The community had been generous in payment for some scribing and Tullus was securing food bags on the horse's back when he heard footsteps behind him. He half turned, expecting Arria or one of the community. Instead, a blow felled him instantly.

He came to, spread-eagled against the stone wall of an ill-lit room. His arms were tied to iron rings and his feet, bound together, barely touched the floor. He could ease the biting pain by standing on his toes, but this in turn brought pain. His head thumped from the blow.

'Dear God,' he mouthed.

Someone was coming. The worst had happened, he thought desperately, turning his head in the direction of the sound, and there before him was the familiar thin smile of his tormentor.

'You thought you had escaped, my friend – no one escapes from Narco!' The same narrow, gloating voice. The nightmare had returned.

Narco, as he called himself, spun about and left, only to return abruptly with a red-hot iron rod. He approached slowly.

'No one escapes from Narco,' he repeated.

Tullus winced. Life was precious and, strangely, so was death, a friend to end the nightmare.

'Watch the pain – don't become it,' he whispered intensely to himself. Then he saw the slight figure of Arria, desperately gripping an old rusty sword – he had seen it lying just inside the community building.

Narco, gloating with perverted pleasure, continued to approach and, being so preoccupied, he did not sense the presence just behind him. Slowly Arria lifted the sword with both hands and suddenly, with all her might, she slashed at Narco's arm. The blunt, rust-covered sword hacked deeply. Narco screamed, the red-hot bar rang against the stone slab floor and blood, it seemed, was everywhere. Shouting for his accomplice, he fled from the room, and Arria, close to panic, sawed at Tullus's bonds.

'The sword's too blunt,' she moaned.

Tullus said nothing. He could only watch. At last one arm was free. Desperately she sawed at the other side, perspiration streaming down her face.

There were sounds at the door.

'Dear God, it's too late.' Tears welled in her eyes.

'There they are!' Narco's voice was high-pitched and screaming. 'Arrest them! Arrest them!' Blood was pumping through a rough bandage on his arm.

'Servant of Cyprian, hold your tongue!' The voice came from a high-ranking soldier, a tall, fair-haired, powerful man. Behind him more soldiers spilled into the small, stone-walled room.

The officer stood for a moment, reflective. His eyes missed nothing.

'Take the servant of Cyprian to the surgeon,' he snapped, ignoring Narco as he left, complaining still.

'And the Romans call us barbarians,' he muttered, looking at Tullus. 'Release that man!'

The officer waited silently until Tullus and Arria were before him.

'My name is Thulwin. I am a general in the army of the noble King Theoderic of Ravenna.'

Tullus was impressed. The man before him had substance.

'And, sir, my name is Tullus, and the lady, my companion, Arria.'

Again for a moment Thulwin was reflective.

'Tullus, your case will be justly heard. 'His voice was measured, his Latin often hesitant. With deliberation he turned to one of his senior aides. 'See that these people have leisure to refresh themselves. I will receive them within the hour.'

With that Thulwin left, and immediately Tullus and Arria were escorted to a house and the luxury of palatial quarters – requisitioned by the army, Tullus guessed.

As soon as the door closed behind them they were in each other's arms.

'What a brave, courageous lady,' he whispered.

'Oh, Marcus, dear Marcus, I could hold you for ever – we're safe. I know we are – Thulwin is a Goth, isn't he?'

'Yes,' he answered quietly.

OOO

CHAPTER THREE

# THULWIN

Thulwin was standing behind a table when Tullus and Arria were ushered into his presence, and when they were all seated he dismissed his guards, a direct, if not remarkable, sign of trust. Tullus wondered why.

For a moment Thulwin sat quietly.

'Your philosopher Seneca said, I believe, that life was the gift of the immortal gods, but living well was the gift of philosophy.' He smiled. 'My Latin is not good, but I persevere.'

Again there was a pause.

'I need no lawyer to tell me if a man lives well. Even so, I need to know the details of your case.'

For a moment Tullus bowed his head before responding. The implied compliment presaged good fortune, but the Goth had some motive. This he strongly sensed.

In reply Tullus spoke plainly and at length and, at the mention of Narco, Thulwin thumped the table with sudden violence.

'He's a cur. Gods of my fathers, who employed him?'

The squall-like fury of Thulwin contrasted vividly with his habitual reserve. Indeed, as quickly as it erupted, his anger waned and once more he was silent.

'Clovis has destroyed Alaric,' he said with sudden bluntness, 'and all the while his hunger grows, fanned by a zealous church. 'Thulwin punched his words with feeling. 'He is a soldier of the Christ and we, the Arian Goths, the fodder for his holy wrath!' He looked hard at Tullus. 'What is your faith?' The question held no compromise.

Tullus felt his stomach tighten, for the deep-rooted passions of belief were always dangerous.

'I'm not an Arian,' he stated plainly, 'but may I add that I love the Christ more than dogma?' Tullus had spoken the truth.

Thulwin looked briefly at him and then at the table before him.
'I can work with you,' he said abruptly, 'and I need you. You are a master of the Latin tongue and the children of the Pope need reassuring that we, the Goths, are tolerant – this is the will of our noble master, Theoderic – and you will be our mouthpiece.' Pausing briefly, he continued. 'I am here to

16

clip the wings of Clovis, and I will,' he said emphatically. 'You will ride with us, but this is no place for a lady. Your days of hardship are over,' he added, smiling briefly at Arria. 'You will be escorted to Rome, where I will suggest you be a ward of the Roman Senate.'

Thulwin assumed compliance and turned again to Tullus.

'Your task will be difficult, for the priorities of church and state twist like a serpent.'

Just then a servant entered the room and approached at the nod of Thulwin. For a moment master and servant spoke animatedly, after which Thulwin sat reflective, his hands stretched forward on the table. He looked up.

'From the distance of Constantinople, the Emperor has made Clovis a consul!'

'A consul!' Tullus repeated. The tone was not complimentary.

'It will be a token title.' Again Thulwin thumped the table in an instant flash of anger. 'Constantinople is jealous of my master and the title of Clovis is meant to cause him trouble, for the purple and the ancient name Augustus are still large in the people's mind. Anastasius is balancing the crusading Frank against the power of Italy – he's a fool – what do you think?' The question was like a javelin.

'Clovis will take the honours of the Empire and use them, but he won't war at the whim of Anastasius. Clovis only answers to Clovis!'

Thulwin nodded.

'How will the Church react?'

'The Church,' Tullus responded slowly. 'The Church is surrounded by the passion of the people and the people will applaud their champion.'

'You're right,' Thulwin exploded in response. 'I knew I could work with you.'

Again there was a pause when silence seemed to cling to Thulwin.

'In Italy,' he began, 'all men worship as they will. Whether Jew, Arian or the followers of the Pope, all receive the King's protection, but the King is growing old. Sometimes I fear his patience will not hold, for the militant orthodox know no peace but victory.'

Tullus felt that Thulwin's view was somewhat coloured; nonetheless the general point was taken. He liked the soldier before him. There was a grandeur about his dignity and he felt sure that it reflected the stature of the Gothic King Theoderic himself.

Thulwin rose to his feet, signalling the end of the meeting. He turned to Arria.

'I will send a personal message to the Patrician Quintus Symmachus. He is indeed a Roman, and you'll be cared for as befits your former status.'

Arria was stunned by her sudden change of fortune. Her plan to seek some distant relatives had faded in the presence of Tullus, but now her situation was transformed. Yet in spite of her new-found fortune she felt a sadness close about her. She would be parted from Tullus, probably for months. She might never see him again. She shuddered. It was an uncertain world.

That night she pleaded with him.

'If I grow large with child I will be cared for. I may never see you again – I want your child.'

Her tears melted his stubborn will and at once they were afloat upon a sea of tender love.

OOO

The villa in which they were staying was in good repair. Water flowed fresh and abundant and the boilers worked, allowing Tullus and Arria the luxury of hot baths.

Wearing new clothes, the gift of Thulwin, they walked together in the morning air.

'Your white tunic and your sandals – you look like Trajan with a beard,' she teased.

'I hope my nose is not as long as that.'

'No, not that long,' she responded, gently squeezing his arm.

'And you, my dear, the distillation of a thousand Helens.'

They laughed.

'We're talking like Romans, but out there' -his arm swung round – 'out there, there is no Rome! It's a new world, Arria, and I don't understand it.'

As they walked, fear and suspicion were written in the looks of many. It was not surprising, for they were strangers and Thulwin's army was abroad. Last week it had probably been the Burgundians. No wonder there was apathy and decay.

Arria, who was no stranger to distress, was troubled by the frequent sight of listless, unwashed children, so Tullus gently steered her back to the villa.

They had met no soldiers on their walk, for Thulwin's law was strict and harassment of the people was not tolerated. In any case there was little to plunder. But the restless army needed action, and following a noisy night within their camp they left by first light. Despite the night's carousing progress was brisk and, even when the heat began to mount towards midday, the ordered marching did not falter. The Ostrogothic army was not a rabble. Arria and Tullus journeyed with them, she in a modified baggage cart and he, mounted, riding close.

They stopped at Arausio. Once the town had been a Roman showpiece. Its plan, still extant, was painstakingly thorough. Later, with Arria at his side, he stood before the Arch of Tiberius. There the past was strangely real, with the sound of marching and the clipped orders of a centurion close in his imagination.

The next day Thulwin's army reached Arelate. The town's Visigothic garrison had not surrendered to Clovis and the small Frankish force harassing their supply lines scattered at Thulwin's approach.

On entering Arelate there was little rest for the Ostrogothic army. Thulwin immediately ordered the strengthening of the walls. Tullus, too, was quickly put to work, his first task to make contact with the Roman bishop.

He found the leader of the Roman congregation at the basilica, and was at once made welcome. The churchman, dressed in a long white tunic with light brown overdress, listened quietly to the formal words relayed by Tullus and accepted all with a disarming grace. He would, he said, be more than willing to grant an audience to the Count Thulwin, general of the generous Theoderic, King of Italy and Viceroy of the Empire.

The tolerance of the Bishop contrasted vividly with the crusading passion of the clergy surrounding Clovis, and at once Tullus warmed to the gentle Bishop of Arelate. Then spontaneously, for he had no plan in waiting, he asked the Bishop if he would bless his marriage to Arria. The Bishop assented without hesitation and the audience continued easily. Tullus talked freely of his background and that of Arria. Their circumstances had been very similar: both had lived in an isolated community of order, while surrounding them the Roman system was collapsing.

The interview was rounded, completed by a natural measure, and as the kindly Bishop escorted his guest to the door Tullus felt a peace, blessed by the living sanctity of the good man walking at his side. Suddenly he tensed, for at the edge of his vision was the unmistakable figure of Narco, with his right arm in a sling. The hateful presence was brief, for Narco quickly slipped away.

'What is Narco doing here?' Tullus asked, his sharpness obvious.

'Seeking sanctuary from your general. We're treating a nasty injury he suffered – he didn't mention how,' the Bishop said calmly.

'I bet he didn't. There's no need for sanctuary. He's free to travel.'

'I can't refuse Christ's sanctuary to any man. He's troubled, and many devils twist within him. Yet even so, he's vowed to serve the Christ.' The

Bishop smiled, looking up at Tullus. He was short in stature. 'We are told to love our enemies,' he added quietly.

Tullus made no response, and at the door they parted graciously. He was angry, though, for Narco would exploit the goodness of the Bishop.

Back at his quarters in the circus fortress, Tullus told Arria that the Bishop had consented to marry them. He did not mention Narco.

'You didn't ask me!'

'Ask you what?'

'You are a man, I know, but don't overplay the role,' she returned, looking at him quizzically.

For a moment he hesitated.

'Of course, my dear ... I'm sorry ... I didn't mean ...'

She did not allow him to finish.

'Dear Marcus, you're forgiven a thousand times.'

Tullus and Arria were married within seven days by the orthodox Bishop, and with the Bishop's permission the Arian Thulwin was chief guest.

OOO

As the days passed, Thulwin's force was augmented by the remnants of Alaric's defeated Visigoth army, but there was no trouble from the numerous soldiers in the town. Thulwin's rigorous training programme saw to that, making the Arian force a powerful instrument of war.

As time progressed the friendship between Tullus and Thulwin deepened, for as well as scribing the general's despatches. Tullus had become a close advisor. But the intimate family-like circle of the Ostrogoth was barred. This was a world Tullus could not enter.

Tullus had also grown close to the Bishop and was a frequent visitor at his palace. He had a strong affection for the good man and they talked, it seemed, for hours. The Bishop knew his scripture well, but Tullus received no answer to the deep enquiries of his heart. Some day he would meet a teacher, a real teacher. In this belief he had an inexplicable confidence.

The marriage of Tullus and Arria, bonded by the weeks of hardship they had shared, was happy. Arria's playful wit amused Tullus greatly and she, for her part, gladly saw a new strength growing in her husband – his former state, she guessed, knowing that his flight from Britain had had a bitter toll. From his detailed illustrations she had conjured a picture of his former villa – about ten miles from the sea, he had described – and there, no doubt, he had managed his estates with ease. Arria's respect for her husband grew steadily. Humbug was foreign to his thinking and his view was wide, but it was his presence, gentle in its way – for he was not assertive – that impressed her most. Marcus was a man of substance, and it seemed quite natural that he and Thulwin should be friends.

At Thulwin's headquarters scouts reported daily on the movements of Clovis and his allies, the Burgundians. Thulwin feared a union of their forces for, despite their clashing pride, such a combination would be dangerous. Certainly he had no wish to provoke their merging, at least until he had been given further reinforcements.

Thulwin's concern was the security of Italy and the Visigothic kingdom to the west and south in Hispania. He aimed to contain Clovis rather than destroy him; and by establishing a buffer state stretching from the Pyrenees to the high mountains east of Valentia he would do just that. In the meantime, how should he employ his small, well-disciplined force? A brief punitive strike against Clovis was a possibility. Strategically it would achieve little, yet the political advantage would be desirable, for the King, his master, needed a victory, not only to impress his own, but also the court at Constantinople.

Tullus was party to all these stratagems. Thulwin trusted him; even so he was uneasy, for Thulwin's Gothic staff resented him. He was an orthodox Roman, a natural enemy of their cause. How could he be trusted? Had he not been close to Clovis? On more than one occasion Tullus had overheard such whisperings. In fact there was a general mood of restlessness within the Ostrogothic ranks and Thulwin, feeling the cause to be their static condition within the town, decided on a move. The time was ripe, for the Visigothic garrison, swollen with the remnants of Alaric's army, was strong enough and well enough provisioned to withstand a siege. Again, he could not risk the winter months within the walls, as his Ostrogothic army was too large to feed, should there be a siege, and much too small to cut a passage through the massed army of Clovis and the Burgundians should they combine. Indeed, to winter safely he needed friendly territory at his back and, having that, he could harass the supply lines of his enemy.

Thulwin's men were glad to leave Arelate, the cool morning air lending them vigour. But soon the heat began to rise and by midday the sun had bleached all colours to a seeming white, yet here and there dark grey-green clumps of olive stood like sentinels.

They kept to the Roman road north of Massilia and, as before, Arria was seated in a covered cart with Tullus riding close. On the morning of the fourth day Thulwin halted. He could now entrust the wife of Tullus to a small, well experienced escort. Her journey to Rome was about to begin.

Tullus and Arria contrived to make their parting private. Arria was tearful. They were close and now they had another bond. Arria was pregnant. Tullus was naturally anxious for his wife, but Rome, though distant, would be safe, and with Thulwin's recommendation she would have expert care. He recalled the name of her proposed protector – Quintus Aurelius Memmius Symmachus – a wholly honourable patrician, Thulwin had assured him.

'I'm jealous,' he said as they held each other closely. 'You'll see the great city before me.'

'Follow me soon, Marcus,' she responded, her voice muffled against his chest. 'Don't keep little Marcus waiting.'

'Or little Arria,' he said gently.

In no time Arria, her fellow travellers and their escort faded in the haze. Tullus watched the moving shapes until they disappeared and then he turned his horse about to join the army's dusty progress. Now the deep blue sea was to his left, and to his right the arid hills shimmering in the heat. Clearly Thulwin was retracing his steps. This was short-lived, however, for after skirting Forum Julii he headed north. The pace was brisk and the all-pervading dust, combined with perspiration, caked all with yellow sameness. Heat danced on every rock and stone, making the temperate, green-cushioned climate of southern Britain rise attractive in his mind. At last Thulwin called a halt and, with the army at rest, the ever-present mantle of dust slowly settled. Tullus dismounted, though, unlike the foot-soldiers, he remained standing.

Being above the settling curtain of dust, he could view the surrounding countryside. It was hilly and parched, a mottled picture of scrub and raw earth. To his right the ground fell away to a valley, equally arid except for what appeared to be a square of green. A well, perhaps, with a row of cypress trees blue in the distance.

The stop was short and soon the marching army and its dust-cloud dominated. Hour followed hour until at last the order came to set up camp. At a nearby stream water was plentiful, and gratefully Tullus washed, before the customary summons to the Ostrogothic general's tent.

Thulwin's scouts had been busy, their reports agreeing that no major concentration of either Frankish or Burgundian forces was to be found west of the Rhodanus. To the east, however, it was different, for the indications were that Clovis was renewing the siege of Arelate.

At once Thulwin's staff were ready with advice, and as ever their general listened patiently. Tullus remained silent, deeming it prudent not to speak until his views were sought. Eventually Thulwin beckoned a response.

'Well, Tullus?' was all the general said.

'We cannot stop Clovis laying siege, but we can harass him.'

'How?' barked one of Thulwin's aides, his resentment undisguised.

'With small mounted units,' Tullus answered.

'Are we an army or a bunch of frightened Romans with no stomach for a fight?'

The Goth's Latin was poor and Tullus pretended not to understand and, as the majority of Thulwin's staff had little Latin, the incident soon passed. Thulwin, like Tullus, ignored the jibe and ordered wine. At once the meeting was informal. On the surface all was friendly, but Tullus knew resentment lay behind the hearty looks. In fact, two of Thulwin's aides were plainly jealous of his closeness to their chief. Such rivalry, though common, was sharpened by the differences of language and religion. In short, they were Goths and he was Roman. Tullus, well aware of his isolation, knew his future largely depended on Thulwin alone.

After two hot, dusty days the army reached the banks of the river Druentia. Three days later, following a march upstream along the east bank and a tedious river crossing, they ended at a hilltop town west of Apta Julia.

Two busy days of fortification were completed when confirmation arrived that Frankish and Burgundian forces were before Arelate. The numbers massing were considerable and well exceeded those of Thulwin's army, but the intelligence gathered by the spies was thin.

The next day Tullus was included in an eight-man scouting mission. This was unusual, for mostly Romans were barred from military service.

'You're a scout,' Thulwin barked, but his trust in Tullus was plainly resented.

The initial plans dictated that the scouting patrol should form a forward position on the rock outcrops ten miles or so east of Arelate and, being on horseback, they achieved this within the day.

The view from the towering outcrops was dramatic, though limited by the heat haze. Hooding his eyes with both hands, Tullus gazed at the middle distance where a cloud, very like a wisp of smoke, caught his attention. Its source seemed to be moving; a troop of horse, perhaps, with its attendant pall of dust, but they were too far distant to be sure of anything. He looked down, the sheer drop making him step back involuntarily. Then, looking out again, he scanned the distance.

He did not sense the figure close behind. It was more like a nudge than a push, but it was quite enough to make him lose his balance. He was falling. Fear gripped him, yet he made no sound. His mind was racing. Had he been pushed? He had been given a partial command – jealousy? Arria!

Her face was vivid before him. Would it be a boy or girl? Only seconds to live. Then suddenly he was watching his body. Peace flooded through him, and time, it seemed, had grown to eternity. But when his body hammered through a jutting mass of scrub, fear instantly returned. Another bush protruding from the rock face further cushioned him before he hit the ground.

He came to with a strange, rag-clad figure bending over him. He felt himself being lifted and then cognition faded in a tunnel distance.

OOO

# CHAPTER FOUR

# ARRIA

Arria's thoughts were often centred on her husband. Their union had been forged on the anvil of distress and hardship. They were very close. His life was her life, yet not in any slavish sense. Each gave the other space to live, for their natures differed; he tending to be contemplative, she vivacious, with a ready wit that much amused him. He could be forgetful round the house and she would tease, but always with affection.

Where was he now? she often wondered. What was he doing? Scribing for Thulwin, answering his questions. She did not see him in an army role and therefore did not think of him in danger. She had had a sudden feeling once that he was in peril – their party was approaching Pisae at the time – but she dismissed it: a practice she had followed in the times of her distress, a defiance in the face of fear.

So far her journey had been hot and uncomfortable and the stopping places crude and noisy, but Arria, always full of interest in both town and country, kept her spirits buoyant. The still enduring evidence of Roman greatness filled her with awe, though with her companions it seemed to be the opposite. They, the Visigothic messengers, the two Roman traders, the orphan girl assigned as her companion for the journey and the Ostrogothic soldiers all displayed what seemed a total lack of interest. Perhaps it was familiarity; they had seen it all before. Yet there was something else. Something was eluding her, for her companions were not generally apathetic. In fact, their enthusiasms were vivid, especially in matters of religion. Arria could see that Roman prejudice and Arian resentment flared at the slightest pretext. Only the overriding force of Thulwin's will and the mutual interest in an expeditious journey kept the peace.

Even in Italy the main Roman roads were neglected. Here and there paving stones had been plundered, something that the lurching cart made all too obvious.

After passing through Pisae, they followed the coast. They were now on the great Via Aurelia, which would take them to the heart of Rome – quickly the journey was drawing to a close.

Nothing she had read or heard fully matched the scale and grandeur of the city now before her as she crossed the Tiber by the theatre of

Marcellus. She could see the temple of Jupiter on the Capitoline, which was on her left; on her right the temples and palaces of the Palatine. It was awe-inspiring, yet a sadness rose within her, for the general sense of negligence was very evident. The great temples were pagan and thus ignored.

Turning into the Via Sacra, they travelled on, past the Basilica Aemilia and the huge basilica of Constantine, towards the arch of Titus. There the massive Flavian amphitheatre dominated. In Trajan's time what a place this city must have been.

The journey was almost over, and her mind turned to her destination – the villa of Symmachus. What awaited her? How would she be viewed? Would she be welcome? Doubts rose but were quickly countered. The friends of Thulwin would be honourable.

Bearing left at the temple of Venus and Rome, they headed for the Esquiline and soon they were before the austere façade of the Villa Symmachus.

Arria was escorted into a large and tastefully decorated vestibule, where she waited briefly for the lady of the house.

'You are very welcome,' the lady said in greeting. She spoke beautifully, Arria noted. 'We received a letter from the Count Thulwin detailing your circumstances. My dear, you have suffered much, but now there will be rest and peace.'

Arria was impressed by her easy grace. They were about the same age, she guessed.

The lady smiled warmly.

'Now I must introduce myself. My name is Rusticiana – and these are my two sons,' she said, patting the heads of the two small boys clinging shyly to her dress. 'As you can imagine, they're not always so shy.'

'I can imagine!' Arria returned, matching the humour of her hostess.

'Now, I'm sure you'll appreciate the baths after such a tiring journey, but before I leave you in the servants' care I must apologise that neither Boethius my husband nor my noble father is here to greet you. Father will be here soon, though – he's at the Senate. Boethius, alas, is at the court in Ravenna, reporting to the Gothic King, Theoderic. It may be days or weeks before he's back.'

Arria was escorted to her room, feeling all the while that she was floating in a dream. Yet the facts were real; she had escaped from destitution to the loftiest heights of Roman society. Some hand was guiding her, for the meeting with Marcus, followed by the patronage of Thulwin and now this present fortune did not seem like chance.

OOO

The Patrician Symmachus arrived late from the Senate.

'Quibbling and triviality,' he told his daughter with a sigh. 'And Cyprian – I wish I could believe his Gothic posturing.'

'Will he be admitted to the Senate?'

'In time – his father was.'

'He has many Gothic friends, I'm told.'

'The worst kind. He flatters them at every turn.'

'Father,' she said, abruptly changing the subject. 'We have a guest. The lady that Count Thulwin mentioned in his letter.'

'Oh yes, I remember. What's her name?'

'Arria.'

'A Roman name.'

'Yes, and she's had a Roman training – some pocket of undisturbed tradition.'

'Well, I trust Thulwin's judgement. If all the Goths were like him they would be unstoppable. – Let's have no delay. We'll see the lady now.'

The patrician Senator had the sturdy look of a soldier, but it was self-discipline, and not an army past, that held his body straight. Again, it was duty that persuaded him to endure the tedium of the Senate. He stood up as Arria entered.

'Sir, I am grateful for your kindness in ...' she began, but the Senator waved her words aside.

'My dear, you are a charming asset to our household. Now you must tell us all about yourself.'

Arria's story held her new-found guardian and his daughter in rapt attention.

'Remarkable, remarkable! How brave you are!' The Senator's grey head moved in rhythm with his words. 'So Thulwin looks upon your husband with considerable trust.'

Arria nodded.

'Your husband is fortunate. Few Romans are given the hand of Thulwin's friendship. I'll say this, though – once given, it's for life and ...' He stopped, interrupted by a servant who had entered with a roll despatch.

'What is it, father?' Rusticiana asked, noting his obvious pleasure.

'The light in both our lives is coming.'

'Boethius!' Rusticiana reacted with joy.

The Senator, remembering his guest, turned to explain.

'My adopted son, or my son-in-law – I never know which to choose – will be here before sundown. I know of no one living who follows truth like him. Perhaps I am too proud a father, but I'm not the only one who's named him a veritable Plato, a Virgil and the first Augustus reborn.'

OOO

Arria was a fascinated spectator of the hurried activity pending the arrival of the Senator Boethius. Even his father-in-law, the upright Symmachus, could not disguise a certain tremor of excitement.

'Have you set out the manuscript we discovered on the musical modes?' he asked his daughter.

'Yes, father, and also a summary of the Senate's activity,' she replied.

'My dear Arria,' Symmachus said, turning to his guest, 'we are subjecting you to an unseemly fuss.'

The words of Symmachus were timely, for Arria was beginning to feel awkward.

'You must forgive me if I seem a little quiet,' she replied.

Rusticiana smiled and Arria felt her inner tension melt. She sat back, released from the imagined need for social effort, while Symmachus and his daughter continued with their preparations.

Rusticiana was beautiful. Her eyes were wide apart and her mouth was generous. There was an openness about her which was enhanced by the sensitivity of her face. She was most attractive. There was no envy in Arria's thought, only admiration.

It was just after sunset when Boethius arrived.

Unceremoniously he was greeted by his sons, their enthusiasm unrestrained. Then he embraced his wife. She was alight with joy. He was much younger than Marcus, she noted, as he moved towards his father-in-law and herself, and there was a tangible power about him. She had noticed the same quality in Marcus, but not to this extent.

'My son, we have a guest, the lovely Arria, wife of Marcus Valerius Tullus, a Roman of ancient lineage from Britain.'

Arria was greeted graciously by the young Senator. There was a natural dignity in his speech and movements. It was as if he could not act in any other way. She was much impressed.

At last the two men greeted each other, their mutual respect obvious.

'What was Ravenna like?' Symmachus asked.

'A frustrating place, full of dignitaries lacking dignity.' Boethius smiled wryly. 'The place abounds with smooth Romans parading nimble minds and rough Goths who have drowned their sense in wine. There are good men, but they are few. I fear your adopted son and son-in-law still loves Rome too much, for it grieves me, sir, to see how far our greatness has diminished. In fact, last night when reading Cicero I found a woman's weakness rising to my eyes. I'm growing dismal – a tedious fault. Now, what of Rome?'

'Not yet! Not yet! What of our Gothic lord, the King?'

'Theoderic is a wonder in his time. He strives to be honourable and just, and succeeds to a remarkable degree. He supports the arts, restores the monuments of the past and encourages learning. Few Romans are better friends of Rome than he. Nonetheless, he is a Goth, a Goth to his fingertips. He rules like a father, with a father's emotions, and betrayal or ingratitude are family wounds. Such wrongs, even trivial ones, excite his rage.'

'So like Thulwin,' Arria reacted. She blushed. The words had come without her bidding.

'You know the Count Thulwin?'

Arria found herself relating the story of the past few months.

'You were fortunate in finding Thulwin, very fortunate. He'll be a friend for life, and from what you've said I look forward very much to meeting your husband.'

Again Arria blushed, as praise for Marcus brought him close. It also made his absence sharp, and tears were waiting.

Boethius, sensing her discomfort, changed the subject.

'I had little time for translation,' he complained lightly, 'so Plato and Aristotle rested, but, father, if the truth were known, I talked too much – too many dinners with those of fashionable thought. I enjoy attacking their pseudo-learning, an indulgence I must stop.'

Symmachus nodded.

'Tell me, what of our friends?' he asked.

'We had fruitful talks, for with them there's discipline, as truth remains the aim. Even so, we need to move beyond mere theory. Knowledge is a living thing.'

The conversation had again captured Arria's attention and the surge of turbulent emotion passed. Rusticiana sat silently.

'And what of the Church?' Symmachus questioned. Arria was alerted. It was the first time the Church had been mentioned.

'The Church!' Boethius sighed. 'The Church is full of passion. There are good men, even saintly men, but a wise man ...' He shook his head. 'I know I expect too much; I expect the Church to be a mirror of the Christ.'

'The King still remains impartial?'

'Yes, remarkably so; it's a sight for tired eyes to see the old Arian monarch mediate between the factions. His view is one of common sense, a view well suited to the heat of Church debate. "No man," he growls, "can be compelled to believe against his will." The Arians have their hotheads too, but mostly we're not party to their squabbles. While I was in Ravenna we had one of those recurring riots against the Jews, no doubt incited by some fundamentalist fanatic. The King, of course, was furious – for him not an unprecedented event – and compelled the clergy to rebuild the burnt-out synagogue and compensate the Jews for their loss of property. Only Theoderic could have done it, but such events cause deep resentment. In fact bitterness against the heretic, as they call him, lies hateful and waiting.'

'Well, my noble son-in-law, I do believe it's time to eat.'

'I had begun to wonder if you had invented some new penance – come, my dear,' Boethius added, gently beckoning his wife.

Arria in turn was escorted by Symmachus. Marcus would revel in this company, she thought. Dear Marcus, come soon, she whispered to herself.

'Father, you've been questioning me, but what of Rome? What's afoot?' Boethius called jokingly.

'Today the Greens won at the Circus and half the city is in mourning.'

They laughed in unison.

OOO

CHAPTER FIVE

# THE HERMIT OF THE ROCKS

When Tullus regained consciousness the first sight that met him was a bearded face and two dark eyes, intent and watching; eyes without thought, was his perception. His left arm felt heavy and his free hand moved across to feel both splints and binding.

'Herbs, you must drink,' the rag-clad figure offered.

Tullus nodded and obeyed. He coughed. The taste was bitter. Then there were questions. Tullus struggled to formulate his answers until, exhausted, sleep dissolved cognition.

He was brighter when he next awoke, and he was alone. Slowly he sat up and, careful of his bound left arm, he rose gingerly to his feet. He felt unsteady and his progress to the cavern entrance was like an old man's shuffle. Outside the cave the light was blinding, and at once he sought the cave again, but at the sound of conversation, seemingly near, he halted. He turned. No one was visible and, puzzled, he moved towards the sound's direction, to find himself before a fault in the smooth rock face that towered above him.

Even though they were coming from above, the voices were clear, as if beside him; a baffling trick of sound, he concluded. He listened; the words were easy to follow: two men unused to Latin, yet using Latin to communicate.

'We know exactly where they are, and if we get our timing right they'll be little more than practice for our archers.'

'Yes,' agreed the other speaker, 'speed and timing are the key – you from the south and we from the north – but it will be difficult to organise and control.'

'It can be done. It must be done, for with Thulwin destroyed Theoderic would be much more ready to negotiate and then we would secure our gains. Speed is essential. Another thing, we must stop Thulwin's scouts. Our side will do that.'

'I agree with all you say, but how ...?'

The speakers moved away; even their footsteps were clear, but the voices had grown faint, their meaning lost.

Tullus's mind raced, for the strategy of the invisible speakers was

31

obvious. The Franks would move from the south-west – probably the siege host by Arelate – and the Burgundians from the north. The combined armies would crush Thulwin's smaller force. Again, Thulwin's line of retreat could be hazardous, for behind him was the broad arc of the river Durentia. He had to get word to Thulwin. It was imperative.

Excitement had filled Tullus with a false energy and his plans began to mushroom. He would thank his skeleton-like benefactor, fill his water-bag and set out immediately. There was no point in looking for the Gothic scouting party. They would be far away by now. There was a feverish euphoria in his thinking and it was only when he returned to the cavern entrance that he felt the throbbing in his arm.

'I'll use a sling,' he said aloud, 'but I must move. I must move immediately.'

'You're not yet well enough to travel.' It was his vagrant-like benefactor.

'Are you a hermit?' Tullus asked abruptly. He was clearly not himself.

'People describe me so.'

'What do hermits do?' Tullus spoke like a man drunk with wine yet confident in his sobriety.

'Sir, you're not well enough to talk. You need to rest.'

'No! – I must go – it's vital!'

All at once his energy failed. He staggered, and just in time the hermit caught him. Soon he was asleep again.

The ascetic felt the forehead of the sleeping Tullus and, sensing it slightly feverish, pulled a rug over the recumbent form.

'A pity,' he murmured, 'he should have had more herbs and water. But God's will is never a pity,' he continued, seating himself beside the prostrate body. 'love is everywhere, nothing escapes its care.' And for a long time he sat reflecting on this simple verity.

Tullus slept through the afternoon and the night hours following, but when he awoke the previous day's events came crowding back like some compelling dream.

'Was I outside the cave entrance yesterday?' he questioned as he swallowed another bitter herbal draught.

'Yes,' was the hermit's simple answer.

Tullus stood up slowly.

'Be careful, you're still far from being well.'

Tullus did not respond. Instead, he walked outside into the morning light. The rock fault was exactly as his memory told him. It had not been a dream. At once he returned to the cave.

'I must leave immediately,' he burst out urgently.

'You're not well enough.'

'I assent to that, but I have no choice; my mission is vital – I must at least try.'

'How far?'

'Two days,' Tullus answered quickly. 'But if I buy a horse or mule – or a donkey, for that matter, I could ...'

The hermit shook his head.

'The rocks attract the sword.' He failed to elaborate, and Tullus assumed that warlords and brigands had made the place a desert.

'There'll be something on the way,' Tullus said with casual optimism.

'But you're not fit – you're not fit for such a journey.'

The repeated reasonings of the hermit did not divert Tullus's determination. He would leave immediately, he said, and exploit the cool of the morning.

'It is God's will,' the hermit eventually concluded, and thereupon busied himself providing food and water.

Tullus made it clear he was sincerely grateful.

'It's a joy to serve the Christ,' the hermit responded quietly.

Tullus looked blankly at his ascetic friend and the hermit smiled.

'Christ is in you and in me – Christ is everywhere. Lift a stone, he said, and I am there.'

Tullus bowed his head and briefly there was silence.

'I would dearly like to stop and talk,' he said evenly, 'but duty has it otherwise.'

He set out at a steady pace with his water-bag and a sack of food swinging from his shoulder. His left arm, held by the sling, felt awkward – a minor fracture, the hermit told him. He would progress at an easy pace, he determined, and take things as they came.

It was almost midday when he sensed that someone was following him. It was the same in the afternoon. Whoever it was was keeping a steady distance, but tiredness had made Tullus indifferent. Still he continued, with the same dogged determination that had saved him in his flight from Britain.

The half-arch of a collapsed bridge over a dry river bed offered him some small shelter for the night, though in his exhausted state he cared little where he laid himself. It was enough to stop.

His rest was fitful and when first light came he was on his feet again, but his pace was slower than the previous day. He knew this in a muddled way. Even so, he carried on, holding to his stubborn will, his mind confused with troubled, dream-like thoughts of Arria, Thulwin and the Hermit of the Rocks.

He looked behind him and confirmed that he was still being followed. A vulture waiting for its prey, he mouthed in an indifferent way. He was growing feverish, yet he battled on, his progress pitiful. Just before midday he collapsed. Somehow he struggled to his feet. He did not think to rest and very soon he collapsed again. At that moment the figure following him closed in.

It was a boy's face that Tullus saw staring down at him.

'My name is Martin. The Hermit of the Rocks sent me to watch over you.'

Tullus nodded, his mind at once alert, charged, as it were, with pressing need. He knew that he could never reach the camp of Thulwin's Ostrogothic army. There was only one solution – he would send the boy.

OOO

The Ostrogothic hill camp was four miles or so west of Apta Julia. At its centre was a crumbling Roman villa and there, in the only habitable room, the Count Thulwin paced restlessly. In moments his staff would be before him for the morning briefing.

'My trusted officers,' he muttered to himself, 'and none of them can look me in the eye.'

Tullus had defected to Clovis, they suggested. It was a lie, and their shifty looks confirmed it. Foul play was the answer. They resented his friendship with a Roman stranger and were loth to tolerate anyone who stood outside the fiercely loyal circle of their tribe. This time he feared that they had gone too far. Nevertheless, there was little he could do, for he dared not wreck the unity of his staff in time of war.

'Fellow officers – your reports,' was all that he said to initiate the meeting.

'Our scouts have found nothing new, sir,' said one officer, speaking for the men sent to watch the siege movements before Arelate.

'It is the same for us, sir,' a second speaker added. 'There is no activity as far north as Valentia.'

'And Tullus?' Thulwin asked quietly, his eyes alert and watching. No one answered and Thulwin asked again, but this time sharply.

'As we said before, sir, we feel he may have joined with Clovis and the Franks.' The answer came from the officer who had spoken first.

'For what reason?' Thulwin asked calmly, his eyes cast downwards at the table before him. No one dared to answer, for the studied calm in Thulwin's speech was the known herald of explosive wrath.

'I will answer,' the general continued in the same measured tone. 'You cannot find a reason where there is no reason. The wife of Tullus is in Rome under the ultimate protection of our noble King Theoderic. Would he jeopardise the safety of his wife and unborn child for some cheap advantage gained from the enemy of his wife's protector? I'm not a fool!' His voice was just under control. 'Stop treating me as if I were – you!' he barked, pointing to the officer who had ventured an opinion. 'You will note my words, and what's more, you will mount a further search – is that clear?'

'Yes, sir.' The voice was stiffly correct.

The Count Thulwin looked hard at each of his men in turn. They had accepted the admonition, but that was all. To them a Roman had no place within their councils. He understood their view, for Romans were often devious and lacked the simple honesty of the Goth.

Thulwin sat without speaking, the silence strained, until a commotion outside the room commanded their attention.

'You cannot see the general.' The voice was angry.

'I'll give my message to no one else,' a boy's shrill voice returned.

Suddenly the boy burst through the door, followed by an exasperated soldier.

'Let him speak,' Thulwin ordered.

'Are you the Count Thulwin?' the boy asked with blunt naivety.

'I am he.'

'I've a message from Marcus Tullus. He's sick and can't travel any further – I've learned his message by heart because he had nothing to write with – my master, the Hermit of the Rocks, sent me after him because he was sick.' The boy was breathless with excitement.

'But this can't be. Tullus is …' a voice whispered loudly.

'Dead!' Thulwin fired the word like an arrow before returning to the boy. 'Just sit down, begin at the beginning. Talk slowly – there is plenty of time.'

The boy did as he was told and the general and his staff listened intently.

'You have been brave and resourceful,' Thulwin responded. 'Now tell me, where did you leave Marcus Tullus?'

The boy described an old deserted hut.

'A horse could get there before the midday sun – but he's very sick, sir – I gave him one of my master's herb drinks. That's what my master asked.'

'You'll be hungry after your long walk?' Thulwin smiled.

'Yes, sir,' the boy assented eagerly.

'Theudemir,' Thulwin called, beckoning one of his most trusted officers who, understanding the implied instruction, led the boy away.

Thulwin sat silently, his head bent forward, a posture familiar to his officers, but now one bringing apprehension. Some were perspiring freely.

At last the general spoke.

'Timing will be all-important, for neither Frank nor Burgundian must suspect we know their secret. We must be ready to move quickly, for we cannot shift position until the final moment, as a premature withdrawal would alert the enemy and lose us our surprise advantage. I will need your total co-operation.'

An enthusiastic chorus of support greeted him. It was prompted by relief as the fear of being purged, it seemed, was past. Thulwin, however, had not finished with the subject.

'We all belong to the Ostrogothic family, yet Gothic pride and loyalty must not soil our honour. Let the nobility of Tullus be a lesson to us all, and remember that the fellowship of honour goes beyond the circle of a race. I will say no more.'

At any normal time Thulwin's words would have died against a wall of tribal attitude, but in the charged emotion of the situation they were heard. Thulwin, of course, was hedged about by practical imperatives. He dared not cause division when a clash of arms was due.

The first priority was the injured Tullus, and a rescue party, with the trusted officer Theudemir in charge, set out immediately, the boy their guide.

They reached the deserted hut by mid-afternoon and at once the boy raced through the open door, but Tullus was nowhere to be seen.

'He's gone,' he shouted from the door. 'Someone has taken him away.'

'Maybe he's set out himself,' a soldier said.

'No!' the boy returned. 'Someone's taken him.'

The boy's conviction was not based on fact. It was a feeling, an instinctive feeling that he did not question.

Theudemir, seasoned by many campaigns, sat on his horse, apparently listless, his eyes focused on the boy framed against the doorway.

'It's a hoax,' a voice muttered behind him.

Theudemir sighed wearily before responding.

'I don't believe a boy could act so well,' he said flatly, while casually scanning the scene about him – a sea of dull, parched grass and scrub; in the midst of which a dry earthen track snaked its way to the south.

'I shouldn't have left him – my master told me not to,' the boy lamented.

'You did right, Martin,' Theudemir countered. 'Your master will be pleased with you.'

'Will he?' The boy's voice was full of simple trust.

'Yes, Martin.'

Theudemir was still seated on his horse.

'Men, we'll have some wine,' he ordered, knowing it would keep them occupied.

The soldiers, of course, willingly obeyed and Theudemir slipped from his horse to join the boy.

'Come, we'll have a look inside,' he said, putting his arm round the boy's shoulders. About fourteen years, he guessed, and if a hermit had befriended him he was probably an orphan. 'There may be clues and you have better eyes than me.'

Martin started peering into every corner of the hut's interior.

'There's something scratched on the earthen floor,' he called, 'and it's freshly done.'

'I can't read – can you?' the veteran Theudemir responded.

'Just about – my master's teaching me.'

'What does it say?'

'N A R C ... Narc – just four letters. There's the beginning of another, but it's not finished.'

'Narco!' Theudemir reacted. He had been present when his general had found Tullus trussed for torture.

'The Count will not like this,' he muttered.

'What did you say, sir?'

'Nothing, son – now it's time you rejoined your master. You've done well ...'

'How have I done well? I've lost the sick one.'

'Leave it to us – we'll find him,' Theudemir answered reassuringly.

'I want to stay until you've found him!' Martin protested. He had a boy's persistence, but Theudemir did not bend, and eventually Martin set out for the rocks furnished with a water-bag and food and with a silver coin in his hand.

Theudemir turned to his men. They had been drinking steadily.

'Don't drink it all at once. You may be glad of it later,' he said, not disguising his indifference, and for a moment he stood leaning wearily against his horse. Then, summoning up the energy, he straightened.

'You two,' he pointed, indicating his choice. 'You will return to the camp and tell the general that Marcus Tullus is missing and probably in the hands of Narco. Be prepared – the general won't like it, but tell him we'll pursue his captors. Is that clear? Now,' Theudemir emphasised, 'What is the name you must remember?'

'Narco,' they returned.

Theudemir nodded and turned abruptly to the other soldiers. 'We need to follow these tracks,' he said, pointing at the earthen road. 'It looks as if they had a cart.'

The soldiers quickly obeyed, and only then did Thulwin's faithful aide drink from his wine-bag.

OOO

The Count Thulwin was preparing to break camp when the veteran Theudemir and his men arrived.

'Nothing, sir,' the veteran said bluntly when he faced the general. 'We followed the trail of Tullus and his captors to the sea – a minor village to the west of Forum Julii – but not a trace. The villagers were sullen, but the sight of silver helped their memory. There were eight men in the party, they said: four armed men, two churchmen with a thin man in attendance – Narco, no doubt – and a powerful-looking man half asleep on his horse.'

'Tullus,' Thulwin responded, his voice as weary as Theudemir's. 'The two men you sent back said there was a cart. I imagined the injured Tullus to be in that.'

'It was abandoned, sir – wheel broken.'

'Anything left in it?'

'No, sir. There was one thing, though. Part of the floor had rotted away and had been roughly mended with the side of a wooden box. There was lettering on the box which one of the men maintained was Greek – it may hold some clue.'

Thulwin rose from his chair, walked a few paces and stopped. Suddenly he swung round to face Theudemir.

'I'll wager it's representatives from the Eastern Church returning from a visit to the Frankish court. That fox, the Emperor Anastasius, has been flirting with Clovis, but what do they want with Tullus?' Thulwin paused. 'Torture information out of him and then ingratiate themselves with Clovis – what do you think, Theudemir?'

'Their tracks went south, sir. There was nothing going east or west – it's that rat Narco, Count. He wants revenge!'

'Damn!' Thulwin thundered in a sudden burst of rage. 'They're somewhere on the Great Sea and there's nothing we can do – nothing – Theudemir!'

'Count.'

'Assemble the staff at once. There's work to do.'

However disturbing the news concerning Tullus, the Ostrogothic general dared not neglect the co-ordinated threat from Clovis and his allies, the Burgundians, for his scouts had told him that his enemies were on the move. It was as Tullus had informed him through the boy.

Thulwin had already decided to march against the Burgundians as a first part of his strategy, so when his staff assembled his orders were both brief and simple.

'There's a full moon,' he began. 'We should be ready to march at any time, whether day or night, and when the order's given I'll not expect delay. Are there any questions?'

Thulwin's staff knew their general's mood and remained silent. A fly buzzed close to his face but it did not divert him.

'Pick good men for the vanguard,' he continued, 'stealthy men, men who walk on air, for if we can surprise our enemy, victory will be ours with little loss. Surprise and its companion, stealth, are vital. Impress this on the men.'

Thulwin's army broke camp ten miles' marching time before sunrise, and by mid-morning his vanguard sighted the Burgundians sprawling along a valley that opened basin-like beneath their vantage point. A river, almost dry, cut the valley in two, and here and there a trickle of water sparkled in the sun.

The Ostrogoths smashed through the Burgundians' forward troops with ease and, after a quick assessment of the situation, Thulwin sent his cavalry forward in tight formation to exploit the panic that he saw before him. As ordered, their attack was brief and punitive and followed closely by the mass of Thulwin's foot soldiers.

Caught unawares, the Burgundians panicked and fled in terror for the cover of the woods on either side, but by Thulwin's order no one followed. He knew a fleeing enemy could turn and punish their pursuers who had broken rank.

There were few Ostrogoths among the dead that lay strewn on the valley floor. The victory had been swift and decisive, and over, as it were, before it had begun. Thulwin was proud of his men, still standing in disciplined formation, but he was quick to keep them on the move for the valley, full with the brutal reality of the skirmish, was no place to linger. So, after tending the wounded and loading their fallen companions onto baggage carts, the army climbed to the high ground from where they had descended.

Thulwin looked back, to see ant-like figures already moving about the battleground. The Burgundians were retrieving their dead and wounded. The scene was familiar to his soldier's eye and he turned away, his features fixed as if in stone.

For an hour they retraced their steps towards the hilltop camp before Thulwin called a halt. At once he sought the wounded out, especially those prostrate on litters, the most unfortunate. Usage had never made him indifferent to the brave smiles of the smitten and this occasion was no exception. Notwithstanding, he showed no outward sign of his emotion.

The state of the injured men was better than he had expected and the smell of the dressings, the old tribal remedies known from his childhood, lifted his spirits, and with a new energy he turned to his staff.

'Somewhere over there,' he began, his arm indicating a location west of their hill camp, 'somewhere is a general of Clovis, expectant of glory at our expense. The day is not yet over. See that the men know this. Theudemir,' he added, his sombre eyes seeking out the veteran, 'we need to strengthen the vanguard and also send more scouts ahead.'

They reached the hill camp just as the sun began to set. The men were weary, if not exhausted, and those on watch marched endlessly to keep awake, while those who had remained at base, being fresh, were sent on scouting missions.

One such mission returned at dawn with a prostrate figure on a litter, the moon still bright as they made for Thulwin's quarters.

The Count was dozing in his chair when they arrived. They had found the boy, bruised and beaten.

Martin, wincing, sat up slowly.

'I had to tell them, sir. I couldn't stand the pain. They tied me to a tree. They were going to kill me, but the man they left to do it threw the knife away.'

Enraged, Thulwin wrenched his sword from its scabbard and slashed at a chair before him. It fell to pieces.

'A boy! a mere boy! I vow they'll pay for this.'

'They're half way back to Arelate, sir,' one of the scouts ventured tentatively.

'I can wait. It's autumn, but the spring will come.'

The next morning Theudemir and a hand-picked guard set off with Martin to return him to his master, the Hermit of the Rocks.

Once at the rock mass, Martin ran eagerly to his master's cave but Theudemir, following behind, heard no sound of greeting. The reason for the silence was obvious, for before him was the lifeless body of the Hermit, congealed blood clinging to his rough-spun tunic.

'What mindless brute did this?' he exploded.

The boy looked up at the veteran, his face tearless, almost serene and Theudemir, who believed surprise to have departed with the years, could not contain himself.

'What?! ... Why are you taking this so ... lightly?' he blurted.

'My master did not fear to die. Look at his face – he's smiling.'

'But some fiend's murdered him. Look at ...'

'My master lived with Christ both night and day. He breathed his air. He saw him everywhere. He did not fear to lose his body. He often told me so.'

'You are so calm and so still,' Theudemir persisted.

'My master taught me to be still,' the boy replied. Then, looking straight at Theudemir, he added, 'I know a lot sometimes when I'm still.'

'With your master dead, what will you do?'

'I'll find the sick one,' Martin shot back without the slightest hesitation.

'Marcus Tullus!?'

'Yes,' came the confirmation.

Theudemir shook his head at what he thought was fantasy.

'Come, we need to bury your master's body. Then you can come with us.'

Martin knew the old soldier did not take him seriously.

'I'll find him,' he asserted with determination.

He looked again at his master and this time tears began to fall in plenty.

After a week at Thulwin's hilltop camp the boy's resolution had not faltered. The general, of course, treated Martin's open intent with a fatherly tolerance. The idea was plainly foolish, an obsession that would pass, but one cool autumn morning Thulwin called for his young attendant in vain. Martin had gone and the general did not organise a search.

The next day the army broke camp. Thulwin had decided to winter in Italy.

ooo

# CHAPTER SIX

# THULWIN'S VISIT

After reporting to the King at Ravenna, the Count Thulwin set out for Rome. The pull of his own family hearth was strong; even so, he could not rest until he saw the wife of Tullus. He did not relish the visit, for his news was bleak, too bleak to tell in full, yet it was his duty.

It was close to the celebration of Christ's birth when he arrived in Rome. It was cold, but he and his three-man escort were well wrapped in furs. At the centre of the city, near the crumbling temple of Venus, he hired a guide. Before him was the towering bulk of the Flavian Amphitheatre and to his right the Arch of Constantine. Where were the Romans now? he wondered. Here he was, a conqueror in all but name, prancing through the city that once had been the mistress of the world; whose legions milled their enemies to a dust. Where were the Romans now?

He was passing close to the broken base that once supported the statue of the tyrant Nero when someone hailed him.

'Count Thulwin.' The voice grew louder. 'Rome is indeed honoured,' the cultured voice continued.

Thulwin scanned the busy thoroughfare, to find it was the lawyer, Cyprian. He had met him in Ravenna and did not trust his Roman charm, but the man had pleased the King and he could speak the Gothic tongue. At one time he had served with the army in some capacity. He was very ambitious and, because of this, Thulwin questioned his pro-Gothic enthusiasms, yet they could be genuine.

Reluctantly Thulwin dismounted to acknowledge Cyprian's greeting. Anyway, he could ask about the viper, Narco.

'I met your servant Narco recently. Is he back in Rome?' His voice was casual.

'How strange. I've had four callers asking for him. He's popular! No, he's disappeared as if he'd never been. You should ask the King, for he's in the royal service.'

'Who hired him?' Thulwin barked.

'Your fellow Goth, Triguilla.'

That drunken lout, the general reacted, but he did not speak.

Cyprian continued to converse with casual ease. He had a ready wit, but there was a calculating mind behind the charm. Thulwin distrusted him and he was certain that the Roman would know the purpose of his presence in the city well before the day was out.

OOO

Arria was with Rusticiana when the servants announced the arrival of the Count Thulwin, and at once the colour drained from her face. This was the dreaded call, the bitter climax of her fears, and all too well it could explain her husband's lack of contact. She had blamed him for a cold indifference. She had been angry, especially when she heard that Thulwin had commended his behaviour to the King. She was carrying his child. Why the total lack of feeling? Was there someone else? Then she made excuses for him. He had been ill. Thulwin had been working him too hard. His letter, indeed his letters, could have gone astray. And then the fears, insidious, cruel and always waiting to destroy her rest.

'Stay with me, Rusticiana,' she pleaded as Thulwin entered. 'Please stay.'

The tall, grave general bowed towards the ladies.

'Please stay,' Arria repeated, grasping Rusticiana's arm.

'Madam,' Thulwin began gently, 'your husband is missing.'

'He's not ...' she gulped, tightening her fists until it hurt.

'He was injured, but not seriously, and we believe a party of Eastern Churchmen, returning from the court of Clovis, may have befriended him. The King has written to the Emperor for news.'

'The King has written ...' she repeated, as if uncomprehending. 'Maybe they will land him somewhere on the coast,' she suggested in a hesitating way.

'Indeed,' Thulwin responded quietly. 'Be assured that all will be done to find him.'

The Count went on to explain the circumstances in which Tullus was injured with as much sensitivity as he could muster, but he did not mention Narco; that would have been unpardonable.

'Your husband has shown great courage and loyalty and the information that he passed on through the boy was vital. Our Lord Theoderic is grateful,' he concluded, thankful that a painful duty was completed.

'Please pay my respects to your noble father,' he said, addressing Rusticiana. 'I'm sorry to have missed him and your husband, the renowned Boethius. The work he accomplishes is a wonder.'

'Sir,' Rusticiana replied, 'I hear my father in the vestibule. He will be honoured to receive you,' she added, rising to escort him from the room.

Arria sat alone, bemused, unable to formulate her thoughts in any ordered way. She felt her growing baby move and then she wept.

ooo

CHAPTER SEVEN

# THE HOUSE OF CYPRIAN

On the Aventine the house of Cyprian sprawled large and lavish. It was evening and the servants, busy lighting lamps, rushed from room to room.

Cyprian sat in his study sipping wine and waiting for his mother. It was a habit that they met at dusk. She was late, not an unprecedented event, though on this occasion he knew the reason. Her 'poor boy', as she called Opilio, his wine-soaked brother, had sent two low-priced slaves for her approval. She would keep them, of course, for Opilio could do no wrong. 'Low-priced!' Cyprian snorted. Opilio had got them free from his Gothic cronies and was extracting money from his mother; the only one who could!

'Poor girl,' Cyprian's mother said sadly as she entered. 'The poor girl has lost her memory.'

'And you doubtless took her on,' Cyprian reacted with undisguised exasperation.

'I was sorry for her, son,' she purred, settling amongst the cushions of her couch.

Cyprian knew that there was little point in arguing, for when it came to Opilio, she would gladly hire a donkey as a cook if he sent one over.

Sighing with resignation, Cyprian changed the subject.

'Mother, guess who I saw today?'

'Some dreary saint, my son.'

'A dreary saint who thinks he's Cato!'

'Ah! – they're commonplace.' Cyprian's mother yawned. 'One jumped from the parapet of the Circus Maximus today, cursing our idolatry. It was between the heats and when they started up again they ran him down.'

'Mother – not the races again. How much of our treasure did you squander?'

She shrugged. Her fading beauty had the charm of autumn.

'A trifle – anyway, my son, you like getting and I like spending.'

'To you it's all so simple, mother dear.' The sarcasm was obvious. He sighed, drinking deeply from his wine cup.

'You drink too much!'

'And you, my mother, sport too much. What freedman shares your sleeping hours this week?'

45

'You go too far,' she reacted, fired with indignation.

'Come, Mother – it's Rufus, isn't it?'

'Yes.'

'He's lasting well!'

'He likes me.'

'He likes the gold as well!'

'How dare you!' she shouted. 'Rufus is special.'

'All right, all right.'

She glared at him.

'All right, I'm sorry … Now, before you interrupted me, I was about to tell you who I met today.'

'Your mother waits.'

'A wooden statue on a horse. It bowed, and what is more, it croaked. A Goth who thinks he's Cato – guess, Mother!'

'I cannot guess – who is this savage?'

'The Count Thulwin, general of Theoderic, the viceroy of the Emperor and lord of the warlike Goths,' Cyprian answered, affecting grandeur.

'Thulwin,' his mother repeated cautiously. 'Be careful, son. The Count is a known favourite of our Gothic King and one to cultivate, much more than your other Ostrogothic friends I've seen. What's his business here, I wonder?'

'How would I know that?'

'Come – your late father always knew such things.'

'Give me time, Mother, give me time! There's something, though. He asked about Narco – one of your former playthings, I believe.'

'Narco,' she said slowly, the sensuous tone undisguised.

'Enough, Mother! Narco is a snake.'

'But useful. After all, your friend Triguilla hired him.'

'To be a snake – keep clear of him!'

Cyprian's mother said nothing. But she knew her son was right. Narco was venomous, but part of her was drawn to that very thing.

'Mother.'

'Yes, my son.'

'What if I told you that Thulwin was bound for the villa of Symmachus – there, Mother, I *am* my father's son.'

'You're close – but tell me, what's Thulwin's business with the noble Senator?'

'Like is drawn to like, Mother. Both have never known of life below the level of the neck,' he returned flippantly.

'Cyprian, don't underestimate Symmachus!'

'What – that old magician plays at being Plato. His wisdom is a fraud, for he's no better than the rest of us. Do you really think his wealth was gained by honesty?'

'I think you scorn too much, my son – a little jealousy, perhaps?'

'Mother, I need to be alone,' he reacted sharply.

'Who is she this evening?'

Cyprian did not answer.

'I know, my son, I know – the little flutter from the house of Symmachus, and so convenient. You'll learn the secrets of the Thulwin visit. What a clever son I have.'

'Go, Mother,' he snapped impatiently.

'I'll not be driven from this room by any woman of the street!'

'Oh, don't be tedious – your freedman Rufus will be waiting.'

She rose angrily, but before she left the room, she stopped.

'Do you know what I hear at the circus today?' she said, with mock confidentiality.

'How could I possibly guess?' The note of tedium was undisguised.

'They said Boethius had no equal as an orator. His mastery was praised and praised again – but not a word for Cyprian.'

'Go, Mother!' he spat angrily.

At that she left, or rather glided from the room.

Cyprian sat back on his couch, sipping from his goblet in an absent-minded way. The room was silent. Then, unbidden and certainly unwelcome, thoughts arose about his wife.

'Thank God she's whimpering in the country,' he muttered to himself. It was all his mother's fault: she had only seen an heiress rich in property.

Behind him the door opened noiselessly and a girl passed through with equal quietness. She stood waiting, and instinctively he turned.

'Poppe, my beloved, come to the arms of your adoring Cyprian.'

She ran softly to him.

'My lord.'

The servant from the house of Symmachus had arrived.

OOO

# CHAPTER EIGHT

# SETTING OUT

Martin had spent four summers with the Hermit of the Rocks and in that time he had learned much, for boyhood years are long. The Hermit's teaching had been more by deed than word and had left a deep impression. Martin had learned to trust an inner impulse – an inner voice, yet not a voice. Such was the sudden wish to follow Marcus Tullus. It had arisen when Theudemir questioned him, and to Martin it had felt as if it were the bidding of his master.

Martin knew that no one took his resolution seriously and he could not understand the problems that the adults heaped before him. To him it was a simple thing. His master had repeated many times that troubles only came when Christ was lost through ignorance. What trouble could there be when Christ was everywhere?

At Forum Julii they laughed, the way that adults do.

'Constantinople! – we need silver in our hand for that,' a captain shouted from his boat, followed by a burst of laughter.

'Don't offend him – he may be our next emperor,' the captain's companion joked.

Martin held up the silver coin pressed on him by Theudemir. It was more than ample.

'This is a ship, not a fishing tub,' the captain growled, while winking at his companions.

Why do adults play the fool? Martin thought impatiently.

'Come,' the captain hailed, 'you can be our cabin boy; we'll be honoured by a future emperor!' Again the seaman's laughter boomed as Martin clambered up the plank.

'Do your father and mother know of this?' the captain quizzed severely.

'I haven't a mother or a father,' the boy answered directly.

'The ship will be your mother, then, and we your father.' The rough growl of the captain's voice had softened. 'But see you do as you're told.'

Martin nodded.

He quickly noticed that the captain and his crew all looked alike. The bushy thickets of the beards and hair were similar. Again, their eyes had the same burning intensity.

'You look like brothers,' Martin said with a boy's forthrightness.

'You're right; all six of us.' Once more laughter echoed round the ship.

Martin thought the boat was huge, though to a sailor's eye it was a simple coastal grain ship. Notwithstanding, it bristled with weaponry, and Martin's eyes grew wide with curiosity.

'We brothers own this ship,' the captain responded, 'and nobody'll take it from us – if they try, they'll pay.'

The sea was a new adventure for Martin and he bubbled with enthusiasm. The captain liked him and Martin viewed the big, rough man with awe, for on the bridge he was undoubtedly the master.

Men who are masters of their profession are not necessarily men of reason when it comes to questions of belief. This was so with the captain. Indeed, he was subject to a kind of fearful superstition. It amazed the boy, for the Hermit had never shown such traits.

'My master never talked of luck,' he burst out suddenly.

'He'll be sure of himself, then,' the big man responded.

Martin thought long about the captain's answer.

'Are you unsure of yourself, then, sir?' he eventually asked.

'Hold, boy, don't be cheeky! Who is this master of yours, anyway?!'

'The Hermit of the Rocks.'

'The Hermit of the Rocks,' the captain repeated, his rough voice quite subdued. 'He's done great miracles. I've heard of many that were cured by him.'

'Miracles?' Again Martin was puzzled, but he said nothing.

'Is he still alive?' the captain asked.

'He's dead. Someone killed him.'

'Killed! Who would do a thing like that? A madman ...' The captain shook his head, reflecting disbelief.

'My master did not fear to die,' the boy said evenly. He had said the same to Theudemir.

'There are few like that.'

'And few who know the Christ,' Martin responded.

Next day the captain returned the silver coin that Martin had paid to him.

'I cannot take it – it would offend the Hermit,' he said gruffly. 'Why are you going to Constantinople? You haven't told me.' Because of the Hermit he felt a new responsibility for the boy.

'I'm going to find the man who was helped by my master,' Martin answered.

'Is he a holy man too?'

Martin shifted uneasily, impatient of the captain's questioning.

'I don't know … I liked him … Look there – land!' He pointed eagerly.

'We'll be hugging the coast of Italy for some time,' the captain stated. His old note of authority had returned and Martin felt at ease.

OOO

# CHAPTER NINE

# COMMANDER OF THE GUARD

Justin, the commander of the Excubitor Guards, stood erect in the silver and steel of the Imperial armour. Before him, ivory-covered doors swung open as he strode between the Palace and the Hippodrome. He had just finished his morning inspection and, as usual, the men had pleased his soldier's eye. They were the elite of the empire: the pride of Constantinople.

Justin, Guard commander and Senator in the Imperial Council, felt content. The peasant boy had done well, very well. He smiled, turning to his ever-present aide.

'It's a long time since a certain peasant boy set out to seek his fortune. You know, all I had was a handful of biscuit – and now this – who would have guessed at it?' Justin never concealed his peasant origin. 'Now where is Petrus? – or should I say Justinian?'

'I'm afraid you'll not like this, sir – he's slipped away with the naval force deployed against the current curse of piracy.'

Justin's features crumpled with annoyance.

'I didn't bring him from Dardania to get mixed up in some useless fight. He wants to see everything, do everything and know everything, and all I want's an heir!'

'He'll settle, sir.'

'But when? – I need him here!'

Justin sighed with resignation. He felt old as he viewed the vast space of the Hippodrome. Here the chariots raced in breakneck frenzy. Here, too, with equal frenzy, the emperors were elected, when soldiers, senators, the factions Green and Blue and the crowding common people would battle will for will. Behind the ivory doors the Senate might select, but in the Hippodrome the people could reject, goaded as they were by crowd manipulators. Justin had seen it all.

Again he turned to his aide.

'Apart from my nephew, are there any more headaches to report?'

'No, sir – there is, of course, the Senate Council this morning.'

'That's not a headache; it's a permanent disease.'

The great Senate Council, Justin thought cynically. They would all dutifully assemble with well-polished speeches at the ready – all predictable – and there they would await the Emperor. He elaborated the full title: Autocrator Caesar Anastasius, the Pious, the Victorious, the Just. For all that, the old boy mumbled. Too much muddled thinking, was Justin's opinion. Nevertheless, Anastasius was not a harsh ruler, not at all, but he had one major failing. He dabbled in religion, siding with the fashionable quibblings of the Monophysites. To Justin's way of thinking it was not a practice worthy of the sovereign power. His view was simple. God was in his heaven, and He was orthodox.

'Basil,' he began, once more turning to his aide, 'what is today's Council agenda? I can guess, but you'd better confirm.' He sighed wearily, his eyes gazing listlessly at the empty terraces of the Hippodrome.

'Wall defences, sir; public order – with regard to the partisans' excesses; relations with Theoderic, the Pope and the Senate in Rome; and there's the question of the shared Consuls.'

'They'll talk for hours, especially when it comes to choosing Consuls. Tell me, Basil, what do you know about the young Roman Senator Anicius Boethius? My nephew often talks of him.'

'His reputation is considerable, sir. Apparently he was a prodigy in his youth and, far from fading, his prodigious capacity continues. I believe he's written a brilliant defence of the Nicene orthodoxy.'

'That'll not help him with the Emperor!'

'Boethius is also an undisputed authority on Plato and Aristotle, sir,' the aide added.

'The Council will like that, for Plato was born Greek before he was philosopher!' Justin breathed deeply. 'Basil, why do we waste time on useless titles?' he added, returning to the question of the joint Consuls.

'There were Consuls in the days of Cato and in Cicero's time. There were Consuls when Augustus ruled and in the age of Trajan.'

'Enough ! You have convinced me.'

Justin sat down on one of the many benches that rose from the floor of the Hippodrome. Again he thought of his nephew.

'All that silver on his education,' he grumbled, 'and he exposes himself like a cushion to some chance arrow.' Yet he admired his nephew's manliness. Justinian was not afraid of action.

ooo

# CHAPTER TEN

# JUSTIN'S NEPHEW

The myriad islands stretching between Athens and Ephesus were a perfect playground for the pirate. Even in the great days when Rome was master, the Greek islands had proved troublesome.

The islander turned pirate was a creature of the sea. He knew its moods, its currents and its sudden squalls. Of course, no one would betray his own, so the pirate had security on land.

Towards this island world a squadron of Dromon were approaching, their sails taut in the steady breeze and their ramming spurs, brutal and menacing, exposed from time to time in the substantial swell.

Close to the tiller of the premier ship, Justin's nephew stood scanning the horizon, but he was under no illusion; far from it. He knew too well that any self-respecting pirate would seek the anonymity of his village at the first reported sighting of the Navy. In fact, the sharp punitive action, as boastfully imagined in Constantinople, seemed hollow and naïve.

'Well, at least the islanders will mark our presence,' Justinian said, addressing the squadron commander. The serious note in his voice betrayed no hint of cynicism.

'Yes, there is little we can do,' the commander responded. 'We cannot punish fishermen for fishing, but we have one advantage; indeed, the same advantage as the pirates. For while they often take their victims by surprise we, too, can catch them unawares.'

Justinian nodded, his round face serious.

'Yes, news of our approach may not have run ahead of us in every quarter, though it's not a wager I would wish for at the Hippodrome. It's dark out there,' he added, pointing to the south-west.

'A storm,' was all the commander said.

'Are they common?'

'In the autumn,' came the brief reply.

'What are those islands?'

'We're approaching Delos.'

Justinian's eyes were fixed on the horizon and the darkness that was growing blacker by the moment. Then it seemed the darkness raced towards them. A flurry of cool air played with Justinian's tunic, while all around the sea was calm and waiting.

Suddenly the commander barked an order. The oars dug deep and slowly the powerful galley turned north-west. Justinian, well aware of the urgency, said nothing. Another shouted order strained the rhythm of the oars to battle speed.

'Damn!' the commander swore vehemently. 'It's changed direction and we're now right in its path!' The rising wind snatched at his voice.

Justinian did not answer. He stood squarely on the deck, defiant in the face of the approaching fury.

OOO

CHAPTER ELEVEN

# PRETENCE AND CONFRONTATION

Since his capture, Marcus Tullus had pretended to a greater disability than
he was suffering. Heavy sleep, the symptom of concussion, was real enough
and his desperate efforts to reach Thulwin's camp had totally exhausted
him. Even so, his dull, unseeing gaze was much exaggerated, especially
when his strength began to grow.

After two days at sea he had heard enough to know the nature of the
party who had kidnapped him. They were Eastern churchmen returning
from a mission to the court of Clovis. The question was, why had they
bothered with him? If it had been spontaneous Christian charity, they had
displayed a singular lack of interest. Besides, with Narco present, such
conclusions were naïve. He would have spun a poisoned tale about him; yet
even he had paid him scant regard.

Tullus had been put below the cover of the raised deck close to the
tiller. This provided a roof and, apart from struts and pillars, the area before
him was exposed. Pretending illness, there was little he could do but watch
and listen, a tedious discipline, yet a stratagem to delay interrogation – a
fear made all too real by Narco's presence. He was puzzled, though, by
Narco's strange disinterest. Why had he not at least come close to gloat? –
for it was the nature of the little rat.

As the days passed, the hunger for sleep lessened and the sense of
nausea waned, but accompanying his recovery was a mounting frustration.
Nevertheless, he continued his charade of helplessness, and still Narco did
not act. Why? The whole situation was maddening.

They were nearing the toe of Italy when an explanation came to him.
The Eastern diplomats were churchmen, and open coercion, with attendant
torture, could not proceed within the dignity of their presence, especially
on a crowded ship. They would wait for what they deemed a friendly port,
a Greek port, where Narco could proceed in private and unhindered – but
why? Why would the Eastern churchmen sanction such behaviour? What lies
had Narco told them? Had he promised them revealing information that
would make them look effective in Byzantium?

He, Tullus, had scribed for Clovis and was a confidant of Thulwin.
Thus, for Narco to persuade the churchmen that their captive was a mine

55

of information would be easy. So they had brought the sick man with them to wait for his recovery and the fruit of Narco's methods of persuasion. They, of course, would stand apart, unsullied by direct involvement, and leave the viper Narco free to wreak revenge. The more that Tullus debated with himself, the more he felt his theory to be right. It had the hard, unyielding ring of fact.

With growing certainty he resolved to act. He would affect recovery, present himself to the churchmen in a public area and, hopefully, counter Narco's lies. He would speak Greek, of course. Thankfully, he was fairly fluent, owing to his old-style education. Anyway, the Greek crew hands seemed to understand him well enough.

His opportunity came when the two churchmen were conducting a service in the body of the ship.

Tullus arose and, grasping at the rails, descended to where the churchmen stood. Unsteadily he reached the mast and there, grasping one of the ropes, he waited.

At first the churchmen and the crew, being intent upon the ceremony, did not see him. Then, as if prompted by a common will, they turned.

Tullus bowed towards the elder churchman.

'I am deeply grateful that you rescued me,' he said, his voice resonant and strong, and not at all reflecting his unsteadiness. 'My name is Marcus Valerius Tullus,' he continued, his eyes fixed on the priest. 'I am in the service of the Count Thulwin, general of his Royal lord Theoderic.'

The older churchman smiled coldly. Slowly his mouth twisted with disdain.

'You are well connected.' The note of sarcasm was undisguised.

Still not quite himself, Tullus was the prey of sudden anger.

'How can I rival God's disciple?' he snapped.

The priest was furious. Who was this western upstart who dared insult his dignity?

'You offend the Church,' he exploded. 'Know that I have the power to chain you!'

'What power?' Tullus barked.

'My power!'

'The prince of the world speaks!' Tullus returned defiantly.

'Take him away, away!' the churchman screamed.

No one moved, and the other priest, a squat, round-faced man, began to mumble words of conciliation.

'I'm sure we can settle this ...' He did not finish, and Tullus ignored him. Dithering apologists made poor allies. His hope now rested with the captain and his crew. Somehow he had to gain their sympathy.

Suddenly his finger pointed, its object Narco.

'This man's a snake. He serves whoever pays the most. Last month some Goth within Theoderic's court and now the churchmen here before you – tell them why your arm hangs useless, Narco! Tell them, Narco!'

The words, like arrows, thudded home. Narco stammered.

'You answer well, Narco.' Tullus, spitting out his words with relish, looked about him.

'Who is the master of this ship?'

'I am he.' The answer came from a small, stocky man, his face blackened by wind and sun.

'You've heard all this?' Tullus asked. A certain recklessness had taken over.

The captain nodded and Tullus continued.

'The business of this tongue-tied rat is torture, not torture for an end, but torture for the love of it! Master of this ship,' he added forcefully, 'I was this viper's victim until by grace Count Thulwin intervened. And, sir, there is no doubt I'm due to be his victim once again.'

The eyes of Tullus and the captain met, but the stocky seaman did not stop the churchmen's guards forcing Tullus back.

'We all believe you, Tullus!' Narco yelled, his rasping laughter full of hatred. The sound repelled the tough, toil-hardened sailors and they turned away, leaving Narco and the churchmen to themselves.

'You fool,' the older churchman hissed. 'You've got the subtlety of an ox. Don't you see he's gained the sympathy of the crew.'

'Whose fault is that?' Narco spat back, his insolence unmistakable.

The hard stares of Narco and the churchman locked, their looks equally poisonous.

Affecting an imperious indifference, the churchman moved away, his eyes searching the horizon over the round head of his squat companion. He was tall, and his thin face, with its leathery skin stretching over a high bone structure, looked strangely bird-like. Best to distance himself from Narco, he thought, for such an association with its attendant rumours could be troublesome. Yet Narco had promised information, and that would aid his reputation for effectiveness. He would wait until the need for Narco passed and then be rid of him.

Tullus lay back on his bed of rags, worse off, it seemed, than when the day began, for now his arms and legs were bound. In the evening, though, when two crewmen brought him supper, his hopefulness returned.

'That peacock priest thinks he's the Patriarch. We liked it when you plucked his feathers,' one chatted on, while loosening the restricting ropes.

'You can feed yourself now, but let them think you're bound,' he added with a wink.

'Good luck. The crew is with you to a man,' the other sailor said and then both left, giving Tullus little time to voice his thanks.

Once more he lay back on his rags. The world had changed again, but he was tired. Anger had played too easily with his strength.

During the night hours he awoke, startled, sensing something close to him. Slowly he turned his head. A few paces away a dark form stood silhouetted against the starry sky. It was Narco. Tullus tensed.

'Don't worry, Tullus,' came the thin whisper. 'I'd be a fool to touch you here, but I can wait. This useless arm can wait. Then vengeance will come sweet, so very sweet.' The whisper ended like a caress, and Tullus shuddered as if something reptilian had rubbed against him.

He did not respond, and Narco moved away. For Tullus, though, the sinister presence lingered. Deliberately he turned his thoughts to Arria but this brought little comfort, knowing that by now news from Thulwin might have reached her. She would be distressed – and the child – it could affect the child. He shifted restlessly until the image of the hermit rose before his mind.

'Surrender all to Christ,' he had counselled him. 'If all is given to the Christ, then what is the remainder?' The innocent laugh of the Hermit rang real and Tullus, breathing deeply, gave his mind to the injunction. Soon he was asleep.

The ship's progress was slow, but once they left the heel of Italy a favourable wind speeded them towards the Peloponnesian coast. After one lengthy stop at Pylos they continued on towards Delos, but it was the final destination of Ephesus that worried Tullus, for it was there that he felt certain Narco would be free to wreak his vengeance.

The ship was now heading north-east, a light breeze just managing to fill the sail. From his confined position he could see the islands grow and then slip past. They were not far from Delos, he judged, remembering the maps that he had studied as a boy.

Suddenly the breeze quickened and there seemed to be a darkness to the south. A brief gust, like a herald, came and went. It had grown cooler, with the darkness more pronounced. A sailor, one who had grown friendly, briefly spoke to him.

'There's a big one coming and I don't fancy our chances with that lot praying for us!'

So a storm was brewing, and a fierce one too, judging by the frantic efforts of the crew to furl the sail. The ship's course changed abruptly to the north, and it was briefly bright again until the wind came lashing from the west.

'It's heading straight for us!' someone shouted.

The ship rocked violently, and Tullus, slipping his bonds, stood up, half bent between the decks. Holding firmly to the side, he eased himself forward, meeting the full fury of the storm. No one noticed him.

There were other ships close by, some much too close, he thought. There was also a grain ship, by the look of it, its sail ripped totally to shreds and flapping horizontal in the gale. One ship, a war galley, was very close, its ramming spur briefly visible. Then he saw another galley, and another. The heaving sea appeared to be alive with ships and then they disappeared behind a wall of spray. It was as dark as night, except for lightning flashes. With all his strength Tullus clung to the wooden strut before him. Up and down they lunged; the well-built ship was holding firm. Suddenly, in the moment of a lightning flash, he distinctly saw a ramming spur, and then above the storm there was a rending crash.

Tullus no longer felt the firmness of the deck beneath his feet and, except for a rushing in his ears, a new, uncanny quietness pervaded. He was overboard. Desperately he pulled towards the surface and its life-sustaining air, and at last he gasped its freshness.

A sudden shaft of sunlight made the furious surface of the sea alive with myriad points of light. There was wood, wood everywhere, both friendly and a hazard, for some large broken sections crashed together with alarming force. Tullus grabbed the nearest piece of wreckage he could reach.

The centre of the storm had moved away. Now all that he could do was hold to his length of splintered wood, and hope.

ooo

# CHAPTER TWELVE

# AFTERMATH

Justinian did not flinch in the face of the storm. He stood grasping the rail before him as if oblivious of wind and spray. At first he was defiant as fear rose to possess him. Then a strange conviction, at first unformulated, grew to certainty. It was not his time. God would not take him yet, for he had work to do. With this acknowledgement came an uncanny peace. Even at the climax of the storm, he was quite calm.

Justinian's bearing did not go unnoticed by the commander and the galley's crew. He was seen now as a man of substance, a leader to be followed and no longer labelled as the wealthy nephew of a guard commander.

The sun was bright again and steam rose from the wet clothes and the drenched deck of the galley. Indeed, a perceptible haze clouded the ship as she heaved in the heavy swell.

The swell made detection of the galley squadron difficult, but the signal to assemble, flying from the mast-top, soon gathered the scattered warships. Justinian was impressed by the routine calm of the operation, not least the towing of a disabled merchantman.

One galley was still circling, the only one with obvious damage. 'Searching for survivors,' the commander explained. Some men overboard – he hoped not many.

'Were there not two merchant ships?' Justinian asked.

The commander looked hard at Justin's nephew.

'Of course! Why did I not think of it? They rammed the merchantman, which explains the splintered bow – for that's not sea damage – not at all. Of course!' he repeated. 'It's obvious – the galley's looking for survivors.'

Eventually the search was abandoned, after which they sailed in ordered convoy to the east, reaching their anchorage at Delos before dusk.

The following morning Justinian watched the dawn rise over the granite island.

He had a strong sense of history and was well aware that Delos, the birthplace of Apollo, had been a major trading centre in ancient times. The island's wealth had been legendary. Now only empty ruins remained. Inevitably, Justinian's thoughts shifted to the Empire and Constantinople.

Great treasure, the city's treasure, needed matching might vested in its guardianship, otherwise the plunderer would come. Justinian had the habit of ordering his thoughts like an orator.

Constantinople was rich, incredibly so, but greater than gold and silver was the wealth of culture. Philosophy, law and all branches of the arts were flourishing. Knowledge abounded. This was the city's treasure; a treasure not for herself alone, but for the world. It grieved Justinian that the Empire in the west was in the hands of cut-throats. If he were Emperor both Gaul and Hispania would once again be Roman. The unity of East and West; the unity of the Church; these were Justinian's cherished dreams, his natural mode of thought. It never once occurred to him that his thinking was in any way pretentious.

Justinian's preoccupation was disturbed by the first arrivals from the sister galleys of the squadron. There was a stream of people, for as well as the captains reporting to their commander, there was the master of the damaged ship brought to the anchorage on tow and the survivors of the rammed merchantman.

After receiving the reports of the galley captains, Justinian and the commander descended to the main body of the galley to interview the other arrivals. First were the survivors of the stricken ship.

The first man presented was a priest, to whom the commander listened with deference. Justinian recognised the churchman as one of the ambitious sycophants that circled round the Patriarch. The priest droned on about his diplomatic mission to the Franks. Then in tones of solemn gravity he lamented the loss of his friend and colleague. Pure theatre, Justinian judged. The vulture had no heart.

Next to the priest was a small, lean man, whose right arm was hanging strangely. The creature bowed and smiled too many times and his eyes, darting bird-like, rarely rested – a spineless wretch.

After the survivors of the stricken ship were questioned, the master of the ship that had been towed stepped forward – a square-built man with a distinctive bushy beard. The commander was suspicious and was forceful with his questions. The master, though, held firmly to his story.

'Don't trouble yourself,' Justinian eventually intervened. 'He's an honest man – and what's your name?'

'Martin, sir.'

'He's my cabin boy, your honour. He wanted to see the big ship,' the bushy-bearded seaman said.

'And so he will,' Justinian responded.

'I've come to find Marcus Tullus, sir,' the boy piped up naively.

A shock of interest brought new life to the survivors, and Justinian's alert perception picked it up immediately.

'You know this man?'

'He was with us,' one replied, and the rest nodded in support; only the priest remained unmoved, though his wretch of a companion smirked.

Narco could not help himself and, uncontrolled, his gloating bubbled out.

'He was bound with rope,' he said, trying to sound regretful. He failed.

'Hold your tongue!' Justinian barked, well aware of the pretence.

'He wasn't bound, sir,' one of the surviving seamen called. 'We untied his ropes.'

For a moment Justinian's full attention rested on the crewman who had spoken. He rarely forgot a face. Then he turned to Martin.

'Come, boy, you and I will view the wonders of this ship.'

Hatred and frustration blazed in Narco, but he kept his eyes downcast. He had learned his lesson, for if he spoke another word he could find himself in chains.

'Is Marcus Tullus dead, sir?' Martin asked as he and Justinian moved forward to the galley's bow.

'Only God knows that. The sea's not cold and if he found some wreckage he could drift onto an island.'

'There's hope, then.'

'Yes, there's hope; but tell me, who is Marcus Tullus?'

Martin told his new friend everything, though Justinian found the story muddled and confusing. There was a hermit, a Gothic general and another soldier named Theudemir. There was also an important message and Tullus's mysterious disappearance. Why had Tullus been bound like a felon? What had that vulture of a churchman been about? The boy had spirit, that was certain, but he was too excited by the wonders of the galley to be coherent.

They climbed up to the bow and looked over the side at the menacing bulk of the ramming spur just visible below the surface of the water. Next they visited the rowing stations. Martin was full of awe.

'It takes men to handle those,' Justinian said, pointing at the oars.

After this they climbed to the upper deck by the tiller. It was growing hot, and the noises of repair work, some close at hand, some distant, sped across the calm water. To Justinian it meant delay, a prospect he did not relish, for the nephew of Justin found idleness intolerable.

'He's not dead,' the boy said suddenly, regaining Justinian's attention.

'Your friend Tullus, you mean – how do you know?'

'I just know,' Martin returned without elaboration.

Justinian made no comment. He liked the boy and he did not scorn the strange, intuitive certainty in his voice. His master's influence, he guessed.

'Tell me about your master,' he asked pensively.

Martin replied in his usual simple way. There was no thinking, no opinion, just simple observation. Justinian was impresssed.

The commander had returned to the upper deck, and it was time that Martin joined the master of the ship from Forum Julii, but he did not want to go. The look was unmistakable. Nevertheless he obeyed without complaint.

Justinian was strangely moved, not least by the boy's obedience. Suddenly he turned to the commander.

'I'll be responsible for him. He needn't go just yet.'

The commander smiled. The nephew of Justin was showing a new side to his nature.

'Captain,' Justinian's voice boomed out. 'Stay a moment,' he added while descending in his measured way to where Martin and the captain waited.

'Captain,' he began, 'the commander intends embarking on a series of short patrol sweeps. Have you any objection to Martin's joining one of the galleys for a day or so? I know you have repairs to do.'

The captain assented willingly, amazed that his permission had been asked. He would wait two weeks, he thought wryly, for the possible patronage of someone like Justinian. It was the opportunity of a lifetime.

Justinian, of course, could have simply taken Martin. After all, he was the nephew of a palace guard commander, but it was not his way. Justinian was accessible and rarely stood aloof. What was more, he knew the sailors liked the common touch and they would talk.

Before midday the two war-galleys moved out from their anchorage towards the west. On the upper deck of the leading warship was the solid form of Justinian, and beside him was the boy.

OOO

The commander's premier galley remained at Delos with the survivors of the shipwreck, including both the priest and Narco. The commander was obliged to feed them; and, what was worse, obliged to entertain the churchman, a man who drew his loathing. The commander had faced death on more than one occasion and when he prayed he meant it, but the so-called prayers of the tall, bird-like priest were cold as a mosaic in winter.

The commander regretted stopping at Delos, for the island was barren and bereft of supplies. As well as that, pagan custom – now a rigid superstition – kept the men from staying overnight upon the island. Even during the day they were reluctant to go ashore. There was one advantage, though – it stopped fighting between the galley crews.

Narco did not go there even though he found the ship a prison. The priest ignored him and the crew survivors shunned him. He ate alone, isolated, fearful and believing that his life would soon be taken. At night he was disturbed by dreams of being thrown overboard. Another dream, recurring too, was Tullus with a red-hot iron in his hand and laughing with abandoned mirth as he approached. More than once he woke up shaking and it was quickly getting to the stage when he was afraid to sleep.

In desperation he determined to escape the ship. His plan was simple and one his fevered mind had endlessly rehearsed. There was a small boat close by the galley and near a dangling ladder. There were no oars but he had stolen a platter from the cook. In any case he had only one good arm, he thought bitterly.

In the dead of night he carried out his plan, and after distancing himself from the galley he relaxed, the vision of the House of Cyprian before him, not least the comfort of the widow's arms.

Next day Narco and the boat were both reported missing. Soon another boat was lowered down to take its place and then the matter was dismissed.

OOO

Within the time allotted, the two galleys returned to Delos. The voyage had been uneventful, but Martin had enjoyed it to the full. Now it was time to join the merchant ship from Forum Julii. This time his reluctance was more obvious and Justinian did not have the heart to let him go.

'Ask permission,' was all that Justinian said. He could easily absorb another servant, he thought, justifying the indulgence.

The boy left, and Justinian sat down on the creaky folding chair positioned for him near the tiller – his favourite place.

'He'll be back,' he joked with Demetri, the captain of the galley. 'The navy's at the call of a boy!'

'It would be better for it,' Demetri quipped, but Justinian did not hear. Already he was lost in thought, and a sense of wasting time fed his growing restlessness. One more sweep to the south, perhaps. Then he would return.

His uncle needed him, for Constantinople never slept. There were always some fools stirring things, men of little consequence.

Justinian could understand ambitious men, but not ambitious mice.

OOO

# CHAPTER THIRTEEN

# PIRACY

Placed on rising ground, the neat, modest building of the small monastic community shimmered white in the hot sun, contrasting strongly with the deep blue of the surrounding sea. On the horizon the deeper blue of an island lined the distance.

Close by, seated at the end of a small promontory, Marcus Tullus watched the lazy movements of the local fishing boats some way out to sea. There were at least a dozen craft, a few quite large, and close together. Tullus looked on them indulgently, for it had been fishermen who had hauled him from the water and brought him safe to land, the island Siphnus.

He watched the swirling water as a shoal of fish swam by. Then his gaze lifted again to the horizon. A sail was visible, approaching from the south-west; probably on the same course that his fated ship had taken just a few days earlier.

He had been very lucky. Indeed, he had thought himself lost when the galley rowed away. Then, just as the sun was dipping, a fishing boat appeared as if from nowhere in the hillocks of the swell.

The approaching thumb-sized sail had grown to a bulky merchant ship. It was closing on the fishing area, where the pattern of the boats kept changing like some slow, deliberate dance.

Turning his head, he narrowed his eyes against the sun-bright whiteness of the monastery. The autumn weather was holding well, but winter was approaching. He could be stranded until the spring if no one called within the next few weeks. Like a Roman from the past, he felt the sea to be a barrier in winter.

Slowly he turned back to view the fishing ground. Something was amiss, for the fishing boats were buzzing round the merchant ship like bees.

'My God, it's piracy!' he said aloud, 'and for all to see!'

The very people who had saved his life were taking life – or did they spare their victims? Ant-like figures were swarming over the merchant ship, with the distant sounds of conflict clearly audible.

The whole nest of ships was drifting closer. They were transferring cargo. Would they plunder all, or take some pirate toll? Hardly the latter.

Harsh poverty, with the resultant lust for plenty, were not parents of moderation.

Suddenly another sound began to dominate: a strong, rhythmic pulse. A war galley had rounded the headland, its oars digging fast and powerfully. There would be slaughter, yet he could not help admiring the sleek beauty of the warship as it raced across the water.

Lost in their activity, the pirates were slow in their reaction. First, as if a whirlwind had descended, the outer ring of fishing boats began to scatter but the larger boats moored to the drifting merchant ship were trapped. Tullus could almost feel the panic and the frantic efforts to push off.

The galley seemed to shoot across the water, the rhythm of the oars relentless until, suddenly, it stopped. Now they would be braking, the oars deep and steady.

With surprising ease the galley changed direction, masking the merchant ship. A crashing sound echoed across the water. The pirates' ships were being crushed between the larger vessels. The momentum of the galley was carrying her onwards past the merchantman until, like a toy boat, the smaller vessel rocked and followed after.

'Grappling hooks!' Tullus muttered through clenched teeth.

The pirate fishermen had lost two, maybe three, of their boats but the others were receding fast and when out of sight they would join the quiet anonymity of their village harbour. No one would betray them there. A warship was powerful, yet a blunt weapon in the face of such a scattered foe.

Tullus stood up – he was sore from sitting long and awkward on the rocks.

The bow of the galley was now pointing towards him, its oars moving at an easy pace; and the merchant ship, separated from the galley, lay listless and alone. She was not deserted, though, for men were busy on her deck.

Tullus soon realised that the warship was heading straight in his direction. Larger and larger it became, until it glided past the promontory to the shallow water of a sandy cove about three hundred paces distant. At once a number of the crew clambered down rope ladders, and when in the shallow water a litter was lowered carefully into their waiting arms. A well-built man, obviously an officer, and a boy followed. Once assembled, the party moved off quickly to the monastery behind him.

Tullus turned his attention back to the merchant ship. Its sail was full; the boat was on its way again. Instinctively he spun round, to find three sailors striding purposefully towards him.

'You're wanted for questioning,' one called officiously.

'Let go – I can walk,' Tullus reacted as they grabbed him roughly. So that was why the men about the monastery had kept well hidden.

On board the galley, Tullus was held under guard close to the steps that led to the upper deck. Another man stood waiting, an islander, and no doubt a pirate. The man turned and their eyes met in recognition. It was the fisherman who had pulled him from the water.

OOO

# CHAPTER FOURTEEN

# MEETING

After returning from the small cluster of monastery buildings, Justinian made for his usual position on the upper deck and sat down carefully on the rickety folding chair. At his side the hierarchy of the ship's command dutifully waited.

'How is the captain, sir?' the first officer asked.

'Thankfully the arrow missed his lung. The monks seem to know what they're doing, so I've decided he should stay within their care. The long sea journey would be too disturbing.' Justinian had made his decision and wanted no debate. 'We'll row out shortly and wait for the other galley,' he continued. 'No doubt they've had an uneventful trip round the eastern side of the island.'

'The boy's not with you, sir,' the first officer interjected. Martin was rarely absent from Justinian's side.

'He's with the monks. He likes the peace, he says – strange boy. We'll collect him before we leave.'

For a time Justinian sat reflective, and the first officer, embarrassed by the silence, searched for something he could say. Relieved, he remembered the two men waiting to be questioned.

'Send them up immediately,' was Justinian's response. 'and, Leo …'

'Yes, sir.'

'You're in charge. It's your right as first officer. You were out of sight amongst the oar stations when the captain was wounded. I took control, but only temporarily. I'll see the prisoners, though.'

'Yes, sir. Thank you, sir.' Leo's awkwardness prevailed, for he found the nephew of Justin a formidable presence.

The pirate was the first to be questioned.

'You're the only one?'

'Yes! The rest are either dead or they escaped. We never surrender,' the pirate answered defiantly.

'You're here!'

'I fell and was unconscious, that's why.' The defiance did not lessen.

'I saw you in action. You were brave and resourceful, and now defiant as a prisoner; but however brave, you are a pirate. What would the ancients have done? Strung you up in your own village. Then decimated the menfolk as a witness to your foolishness. There are men, clever men, who argue that such punishment is valid in a scattered empire.' He paused, staring long and hard at the pirate. 'You are an able man. Why play the fool?'

'The Emperor's agents strip us bare,' came the straight reply. 'Why torture me with words – get it over with!'

'Would you add your widow's weeping to the sum of tears so soon?' There was no sound of sarcasm.

Justinian's stare was unrelenting and never left the island fisherman.

'I'm loth to waste a man like you,' he said eventually. 'A sailor's uniform will be your punishment, but not on board this ship; they'd tear you to shreds.'

'My family ...' the pirate mouthed involuntarily.

'Don't trouble me with details – you've got your life.' There was anger in Justinian's voice as he swung round to the acting captain. 'Have him guarded well.' Justinian did not question his decision, for the crew of the merchantman had not been slaughtered. That one fact had saved the pirate.

He looked up at the other man waiting to be questioned. A well-built man, and certainly not an islander. His ill-fitting clothes looked as if they had been borrowed. There was a natural dignity about the man and, if fearful, he certainly showed no sign of it.

Tullus, he suddenly conjectured. Was the boy right? – it was a long way from the shipwreck.

ooo

Tullus stepped forward to be questioned. The officer before him was impressive and had that ageless look that men of stature have. Clearly he was powerful, but Tullus was not awed.

'Would you prefer to speak in Latin?' the officer asked.

'Yes, I would prefer it,' Tullus answered, his deep, mellow voice matching that of his questioner.

The officer stood up, a wisp of humour playing on his face.

'Welcome, Marcus Tullus,' he said strongly, holding out his hand.

'You know my name – how? ... Of course, the survivors would have told you.' Tullus was puzzled, and why the warmth? Narco and the priest must have perished, otherwise they would have poisoned his reputation.

'You look surprised,' the officer remarked.

'I am.'

'Have patience, you'll understand the mystery soon.' Another flicker

70

of humour played on the round, serious face. 'Look, here the mystery comes!'

Slowly Martin's head appeared above the upper deck as he climbed the steps.

Tullus had been with the boy a few hours only, but they had been desperate hours and Martin's face was clearly etched upon his memory. He recognised him instantly, yet how could he be here? Was he mistaken?

'Marcus Tullus!' the boy shouted as he ran towards him. They embraced.

'Martin, what are you doing here?'

'Looking for you, Marcus Tullus.'

Amazed, Tullus shook his head in apparent disbelief and the officer roared with laughter.

'This is ...' Tullus began but did not finish. 'I'm lost for words ... It's ... It's unbelievable!'

'Tullus, my name is Justinian,' the Officer interjected, his mirth subsiding.

'And his uncle is in charge of the Excubitor Guard,' Martin added excitedly.

The name Justinian meant nothing to Tullus, but Commander of the Excubitors was a powerful office.

'Well remembered.' Justinian smiled broadly at the boy. 'There are four main guard companies in the city, Tullus. The Excubitors are one of them.'

'Four guard companies,' Tullus repeated. 'There must be rivalry!'

'There is, but it keeps them from uniting against the Emperor.'

'A clever system,' Tullus returned.

The arrival of the galley's sister ship closed the conversation. Indeed, her appearance heralded their imminent departure for Delos. At once Justinian decided to pay a final visit to the injured captain at the monastery.

'Come with us, Tullus,' Justinian invited.

'Yes, sir – but may I speak to the pirate captive for a moment?'

Justinian hesitated. It was his habit to be careful of other men's intentions.

'If I know his full name and his village I can ask the monks to tell his family of his fate,' Tullus said in explanation.

'Why trouble yourself, Tullus?'

'He was the man who hauled me from the sea.'

'Sufficient motive,' was the blunt retort.

The tough, sun-blackened face of the pirate was lined with misery.

Tullus guessed that exile from his village and his family would be little more than living death. The pirate's first response was dull and listless, but his face lit up as Tullus outlined his intention.

'Christ be with you, friend,' the pirate said with fierce sincerity.

ooo

The journey back to Delos was leisurely. The sails were up, the oars retracted and the sailors, happy with the day's results, began to sing. Greek songs, though, and unfamiliar to the western ear of Tullus, and of Martin too, yet there he was amongst them.

Justinian and Tullus were seated on the upper deck and the conversation seemed to be unceasing. The nephew of Justin liked to talk, especially in the presence of a mind that he admired. Tullus pleased him and he knew that he could place him on his uncle's staff with ease.

Justinian was not bothered by Tullus's connection with Thulwin and the Goths, for he knew that nothing would be changed until the old King went. For this the world could wait for years, but when Theoderic left the stage, then there would be trouble.

'What do you think of Thulwin?' he asked suddenly.

'He's a man of honour and a good general,' Tullus answered directly.

'Honour will watch men follow fools.'

'Fools follow fools; that's not the fault of honour,' Tullus shot back.

'Then you would have men wise,' Justinian prompted.

'How could honour have it otherwise?'

Both men laughed.

'Tullus, we need you in the capital. The city is bereft of men like you.'

'Sir, my duty is in Rome – my wife – my unborn child -!'

'And Thulwin – you are a Roman and the Empire is your duty.'

'Sir, you strike at my weakest point – yet to be a Roman is to quit oneself as such.'

'Tullus, don't retreat behind the face of honour, for honour must take second seat. The Empire and its cause come first. She and the cultured world are one!'

Tullus sat unmoved.

'You are stubborn, Tullus, but beware, there is no time to waste.'

Again Tullus did not speak. Eventually he lifted his head.

'I cannot break my word,' was all he said.

'If you had answered otherwise I would have deemed my judgement false,' Justinian returned. He had retreated, but it was no matter. Tullus would see his point of view in time.

'Is your wife with family friends?' he asked.

'No, we have no friends in Rome. She is staying at the house of the Senator Symmachus. It was Thulwin's choice.'

'The philosopher Symmachus! Thulwin chooses well.' Justinian was impressed.

'You know Symmachus?'

'Only by reputation – but mark his son-in-law, Boethius. He's the one to watch. I vow he'll be a consul soon.'

The connection of Tullus with the family of Symmachus was a wholly new aspect for Justinian to consider. Tullus could be useful, very useful. He pondered long, only half aware that the wind had dropped and the oars were out again.

Tullus was enjoying the peace, and the slow rhythm of the oar strokes was soothing. To the east the large, hazy bulk of an island was receding. He had been fortunate, incredibly so.

He smiled, thinking of the bird-like priest, now by Justinian's order a passenger on the ship from Forum Julii, his dignity deflated. And Narco, the rat, had fled, but he had a cunning. He would survive.

'How do you plan to get to Rome?' Justinian suddenly asked.

'I don't know.'

'The Egnatian Way is open, but it's long, and prey to robbers.'

'How long?'

'Five hundred miles or so,' Justinian replied.

'All that before a foot is set in Italy?'

'No!' Justinian spoke abruptly. 'Such thinking brings division. The East and West are one.'

Tullus made no response and the passion in Justinian's voice, for the moment prominent, was swallowed by the wind. Once more the slow pace of the oars dominated.

'I've little influence in Ephesus, but I can help you in Constantinople. I propose you journey with me there.' Justinian's words, though a suggestion, were clearly a command.

'And the boy?' Tullus asked.

'Yes, the boy as well.'

OOO

# CHAPTER FIFTEEN

# CONSTANTINOPLE

In many respects Constantinople was a shock to Tullus. The numerous churches with their Eastern richness and their mosaics were one thing, but it was the people that impressed him most. The Christian imagery in their speech; the raw selfishness mixed with generosity, the licence with penance. The city surged with energy: an energy: seemingly at home with both a Christian present and a Roman past.

This was a new nation, Tullus thought, not a Rome reborn.

What was true in general, of course, could vary in particular. Justinian's closest friends were thoughtful men, discreet men, men of learning. Some were pure Hellenist in their philosophy. He had the habit of gathering such men about him, the practice of a leader. Indeed, the more Tullus observed the nephew of Justin, the more he saw the image of a future Emperor.

There was another side to Justinian's activity that Tullus simply labelled as unsavoury. The city's politics were turbulent, if not violent, and Justinian, closely associated with the Blue party and its partisans, was in the midst of it. To control the partisans of either faction, Blue or Green, meant power. It was the way things worked and, whatever were his private thoughts, Justinian did not shrink from this involvement.

Tullus and the boy had only a few days in Constantinople before the time was set to journey westward and, during this brief period Justinian or those in his employ were their constant guides. They were introduced to Justinian's uncle and his homely wife, Euphemia. Indeed, in all respects, both were catered for as honoured guests.

Under Justinian's patronage they saw the races at the Hippodrome. The boy was speechless with excitement. They saw the Emperor in his royal box but they did not meet him – few did. To the ordinary citizen the Emperor Anastasius was more a marvel than a man.

Justinian chose the Imperial post, with its armed guard, as a travelling party for Tullus and the boy. The post, he said, would cover the whole length of the Egnatian Way. They would enjoy protection and, what was more, there was a guarantee of food and shelter. This was important, as winter was approaching.

The leave-taking was brief and Justinian's final words, as was his habit, were pronouncements.

'We will meet again, Tullus – it is written.' And, Martin – you'll be a man in not too many years, but this city's not for you. Somewhere in the west you'll find a simple life in service of the Lord.'

They embraced, and then abruptly Justinian turned away.

To travel on the Egnatian Way was to travel with history. The great road had carried the armies of Julius Caesar in their pursuit of Pompey. Octavian, the young Augustus, and Mark Antony had used the road to march against the legions of Brutus and Cassius, and thus avenge the death of Caesar. The resulting clash at Philippi had decimated the Republican aristocracy.

'That was forty-three years before the birth of Christ,' Tullus explained to Martin as he pointed out the field of battle.

As they journeyed west they found the famous road in disrepair. Bridges were down, which meant delay, but above all, it was cold. Winter had descended and snow was on the hills.

Grey skies and the frequent sight of crumbling neglect weighed heavily on Tullus and, after fourteen days, they were still well short of Pella. The Via Egnatia, that once great artery to the east, was a mere provincial track. Even after a hundred years of chaos, Tullus was reluctant to accept that Rome had fallen.

Eventually they reached Dyrrachum, where the men of the Imperial post took their leave. Now Tullus and the boy were on their own.

Justinian had been generous and Tullus had more than enough to pay for their passage to Brindisium. So when the local seamen judged the weather to be favourable, they found themselves afloat. It was now well into January, the year five hundred and eight.

OOO

# CHAPTER SIXTEEN

# ITALY

The sea wind was bitterly cold and Tullus, with Martin close beside him, sought what cover they could find. By midday the wind had grown to gale force, driving them northward. The predictions of the seamen had been wrong.

The master of the ship cursed the inconvenience. They would miss Brindisium, and Barium as well, he shouted, but he showed no fear, not even when the light began to fail; he merely swore the louder.

In comparison to Tullus and the boy, the crew were poorly clad, yet they braved the elements with indifference. It was a brutish life, and for most a short one, Tullus guessed.

It was a nightmare journey, seemingly without an end, yet they found the lee side of a jutting neck of land just as first light broke. How the master and his crewmen had achieved it was a miracle.

Seeing the firm earth of Italy before him, Tullus did not hesitate, but resolved to leave the ship at once.

'There's nothing here but burnt-out hovels!' the master objected.

'So be it. All I want is solid ground beneath my feet. I've had the sea in plenty.'

Boundless relief filled both Tullus and his young companion when they felt their feet on land. The wind had fallen and a light, misty rain enveloped them. The stillness, after the violence of the storm, was eerie.

'I don't like this place,' Martin complained.

Tullus said nothing. He was used to Martin's sudden statements, but evidence of the boy's subtle sense was soon apparent. Burnt-out houses and the signs of systematic pillage were everywhere. Indeed, they searched for some time before they found the shelter of a lean-to shed. There they rested, sharing out their meagre stock of food. They tried to sleep but managed little, and when the sun came out they soon were on their feet again.

It was Martin who saw the monk, the ravaged settlement's only occupant, it seemed. He was milking his goat and the rhythmic sound alerted Martin's memory. So often had he watched his master do the same. They were already in conversation when Tullus came upon them.

'Why have you chosen this bad place to serve the Christ?' Tullus heard Martin ask.

'Terrible things have happened here,' the monk replied. He stood up but his bent and crippled body only reached to half his natural height. 'The earth is soaked with pain,' he added, looking up at Tullus. 'Prayer is greatly needed, greatly needed.'

A mason would be useful too, Tullus thought cynically, but he held his peace.

'What happened?' he asked quietly.

'The coast was ravaged by the navy of the Emperor to teach the Gothic King Theoderic a lesson.'

'Recently?' Tullus pressed.

'No, some years ago. Theoderic, I'm told, clashed with an Imperial force – somewhere in the east – and won.'

Tullus shook his head. All justified, no doubt. All seen to be the only way.

'How can prayer restore this stricken town?' he asked.

The old monk hesitated. He had not thought to formulate the faith that powered his life.

'My master said that prayer was a communion with the Christ.'

'Yes! yes!' the monk confirmed.

'But how can such prayer help this place?' Tullus pressed.

Again the old man hesitated and again it was Martin who replied.

'A place that's soiled with sin cries out for righteous works – so my master taught.'

'Well said, well said!' the monk acknowledged, while eyeing Tullus quizzically.

'Prayer and solitude remain a mystery to me,' he responded.

'You'll understand in time, you'll understand. Why not join me – there's much to do.'

Tullus made to speak, but Martin answered first.

'We're going to Rome – it's not the time.' The boy's blunt words gave no offence.

'The will of Christ, the will of Christ,' the old monk murmured, holding out his earthenware pot. 'Would you like some milk?'

Martin's eyes sparkled. He was a boy again.

'I have only one bowl,' the monk said. 'We can drink in turn.'

For a while they sat in silence. Tullus closed his eyes and turned his face towards the winter sun.

'Who has lordship of the land about these parts?' he asked eventually.

'The Goths – their lust for wealth is boundless – Christ forgive my bitterness.'

'I thought the rule of Theoderic was just,' Tullus retorted.

'Theoderic is just, but we never see him here. It's his men that rob us of our lands. I know – my family's wealth was plundered!'

'Is there no redress?'

The old man shook his head.

'The law's a snail and the endless accusations that the Goths invent are difficult to fight.'

'Are all the Goths like this?'

'Not all, not all – some are just.'

'What of the Senate – can't they help?'

'The Senate! – Christ purge my anger – they mind their own!'

The old man patted the goat absently then, straining his head, he turned to look at Tullus.

'Every month the monks visit me from Sipontum – it's a little way up the coast. They tell me of the Church and of the world. There are good men in the Senate, they say – Symmachus and his son-in-law. They are only names to me, but honest men speak well of them.'

Here again was confirmation. Arria was in good hands.

'Where can I buy a horse and cart?' Tullus asked.

'You're sure to get your wants at Sipontum. Take my advice – buy mules. They're not so dear to greedy eyes.'

ooo

# CHAPTER SEVENTEEN

# THE NEW MASTER

At Sipontum Tullus bought two mules, a peasant's cart and some provisions – Justinian's silver was lasting well. Once their business was completed they headed for the Via Adriatica, which they planned to use until they met the road that crossed the spine of Italy. Tullus recalled the three-part name, the Tiburtina-Valeria-Claudia. He did not need directions, for as a boy he had learned the roads of Rome by heart.

He had expected Italy to be different from the old provinces of the Empire, but this was not the case. Neglect was just as evident, yet nothing like it was in Britain and in Northern Gaul.

Signs of wealth increased, however, as they travelled north. The road was busy near the towns, but no one questioned them or paid much heed. The mules, the peasant cart, the travel-worn clothes, excited little interest. Twice, a troop of Gothic soldiers passed. Tullus left the road on each occasion, making sure the soldiers had an unimpeded path, but there was no hint of trouble. Even so, Tullus hedged his every move with caution. It was not the age of Trajan.

He had not contacted the authorities, as he was far from sure of his position and the unforeseen delays officialdom might cause. Better to press on himself and be his own efficient messenger. And if things went wrong he could name Count Thulwin as his patron. Hopefully they would believe him.

The mules were not the speediest means of transport but they were steady, and at noon on the fifth day, Tullus turned westward for Rome. Mounting anticipation gave him energy, but he knew that he was tired. The journey had been punishing. Martin, on the other hand, was full of energy. He liked driving the cart and the mules responded to his kindly chiding. He had a way with animals.

It grew colder as they climbed further into the hills and by the second day their extra clothes became essential. The terrain was now dramatic.

On the third day after leaving the coast they heard the sound of shouting from further up the twisting road. Tullus acted instantly.

'Take the track to the right,' he barked. Martin pulled hard and both jumped clear to help the mules in their struggle up the steep incline. Then, after tying them to a tree, Tullus and the boy quickly climbed to where the road was visible as it cut its curved path round the hillside. It was raining, but not heavily.

The sounds grew louder and vicious, and the rhythmic pulse of marching feet meant soldiers.

'They're close,' Tullus whispered to the boy.

First into view came a single horse and rider, a low-ranking Gothic officer, Tullus judged. Flanking him were six foot-soldiers, three on either side, all of whom were shouting their approval at the rider's tricks of horsemanship. Suddenly his hand shot up, bringing the strange troop to a halt. Out came the wine-bags. They were all half drunk. Humorous to watch, but frightening to meet.

A far from humorous spectacle followed, when a line of prisoners, twelve in all, roped neck to neck, shuffled forward, occasional lashes from the soldiers goading them to brief acceleration. The last prisoner, clearly in a state of near collapse, almost fell, his rope jerking sorely at the necks of his fellows.

The soldiers screamed abuse and one, seeing the prisoner's hopeless state, decided to be rid of him. Angrily he cut the rope that joined the prisoner to the line and then he lunged. Instinctively the weak, defenceless man stepped back and in the process stumbled headlong down the steep slope on the south side of the road. The soldier watched his victim tumble hopelessly and then lie still. He laughed, shouting something to the other guards.

'What did he say, Marcus Tullus?' Martin whispered, his expression a mixture of fascination and horror.

'It sounded like "one Roman less",' Tullus answered. During his time with Thulwin he had learned some basic Gothic words.

They waited noiselessly until the soldiers and the line of prisoners passed well out of sight and hearing. Then Tullus, ignoring Martin's questions, descended quickly to the road.

'Come, follow me,' he said sharply, as he slithered down the slope on the far side, with Martin following like a mountain goat.

They found the prisoner unconscious, wedged between two clumps of bush and breathing heavily. Tullus slapped his face gently, then roughly, until his eyes blinked open – haunted, staring eyes. With a sudden fevered energy he sat bolt upright.

'You've taken my petty piece of land, my remaining cattle. You've defiled my daughter. Damn you! Use your sword!' The blaze of passion fell to nothing in an instant and his body crumpled like some half-filled sack.

Tullus slapped his face again with urgency.

'Open your eyes, man,' he said sharply. There was no point in sentimental dithering.

The man responded weakly and Tullus held the nozzle of his wine-bag to the prisoner's lips.

'Drink!'

'Thank you,' the man said weakly, his gaze fastened on Tullus. 'Who are you?'

'Never mind that,' Tullus returned impatiently. 'Any bones broken?'

'No,' came the reply, after he had checked.

'Right! Up!' Tullus barked, pointing at the road above. 'You need warmth and shelter.'

With Martin pulling and Tullus pushing, they reached the level of the road. For a moment they paused. There was no sound other than their heavy breathing and Tullus judged it safe to get the cart. Hastily they bundled the emaciated figure into it, a heavy rug about him. Then they moved off quickly.

Tullus watched the limp, prostrate form shift helplessly with every jerk and bump. He was a tall man who, Tullus guessed, had once been handsome. Tullus had believed the outburst on the hillside, as men who feel their end is close have little motive for deception.

The cloud cover had descended, obscuring all but a few paces in front, and the noise of mules and cart seemed isolated, cocooned by the surrounding mist.

'Run! Run!' the prisoner shouted, shattering the stillness. 'God, it's too late!'

'What's wrong, Marcus Tullus?'

'It's a nightmare. He's reliving the horror!'

Tullus shook the man and he came to, staring wildly.

'It's all right,' Tullus said quietly, lifting him to a sitting position.

Again he put the nozzle of his wine-bag to the man's lips.

'Sir, you will have me merry.' A wan smile lived briefly, but it showed the prisoner to be younger than Tullus had first thought. Not far from his own age, he guessed.

'Eat this,' he said, offering some oil-softened bread.

The food was taken graciously; in fact the man's dignity was impressive, especially in his present plight.

'Is there a religious house near here?' Tullus asked.

'Nothing I dare trust – my enemies have men for ever on the watch.' He spoke with difficulty and took his time to gather energy. 'There's a road that branches to the south' – once more he paused, breathing deeply – 'not far from here ... leads to the remains of Nero's villa ... in a gorge-like valley ...Hermits live in close communion there ... I know them.'

'Is it far?'

'It will take us most of the day,' the man replied, anxiously grabbing the side of the cart. 'Sorry, dizziness,' he explained. Another smile showed briefly.

'What's your name?' Tullus asked abruptly.

'Valerius.'

Tullus was alerted, his thoughts flashing to his ancestor, a Chief Centurion, and a Tribune named Valerius. The story ran that both had been in Galilee at the time of Christ – no doubt a tale made large by too much telling.

What was he thinking? That this Valerius was of similar stock? It was a foolishness, a coincidence too far-fetched to warrant credence. In any case this was not the time to speculate on such obscurities.

They found the road that branched off south just as the mist began to lift, a fortunate occurrence, as the way was treacherous and in serious disrepair.

When they reached the crumbling shell of Nero's villa there was no one to be seen.

'Just wait,' Valerius said, pointing to the steep slope rising high above them. 'They're in their caves – they'll come.'

First one, then two, followed by a further two, descended to the road.

'It's you, my friend,' their leader said directly to Valerius. 'You look ill – what has happened?'

'I was searching for my daughter,' he responded. 'They caught me ... and someone bore false witness ...'

'But why?' another hermit interjected. 'They've taken all you have!'

'Not all – his life and name are his,' the leader of the hermits answered. 'Crime cannot hide completely when its victim's free.'

'A toothless freedom, Father Benedict ... who would dare to speak for me? ... they could be victims next.'

'I'll speak!' Tullus snapped with some impatience. 'But first you must have rest.'

'Have no concern, sir,' the man named Benedict responded quietly. 'We'll take care of him.'

At that, as if from nowhere, a litter was produced. The noble Valerius, they said, could not climb the steep slope to the caves. Witnessing their obvious care, Tullus relaxed. After the troubles of the day, it was strangely peaceful

ooo

Valerius, too, felt peaceful. His pains were less now that the bumping of the cart had stopped. Slowly he felt cognition slip. The voices close to him seemed distant, though he knew that Benedict and his new friend Marcus were conversing. 'Marcus Tullus' – it was the boy's voice, clear and penetrating, and at once he was awake, the family legend circling in his mind. Could it be? No, it was preposterous – not after all the generations; but surely Marcus must have told him who he was before? Why had he not heard?

The sudden burst of energy faded, leaving in its wake a fevered muddle. He moaned, and those at each end of his litter quickened pace.

ooo

From the moment of their arrival Tullus noticed something new in Martin's manner. The boyishness had receded and his energetic questions all but stopped.

The reason for the change was very obvious, for Martin could not keep his eyes off Father Benedict. He had found another master, and Tullus knew that he had chosen well. So it came as no surprise when Martin spoke his mind.

'I want to stay here, Marcus Tullus.'

'With Father Benedict?'

Martin nodded. 'He knows the Christ.'

For a time Tullus said nothing. What could he say? It was Martin's world, not his. Tullus, of course, was not asleep to the qualities of Benedict. There was a serenity about the hermit, a serenity born of service. Nothing was held back, nothing owned in any private sense. This was rare, very rare indeed.

'I will speak to Father Benedict, if that is what you want.'

'It is, Marcus Tullus.' And so the conversation ended, brief, uncomplicated and very much in Martin's mode.

Tullus stayed two days at Sublaqueum, as the place was called, and in that time Valerius recovered sufficiently to talk, yet it was not until the morning of Tullus's departure that the subject of the family legend surfaced. In fact, it was Martin who unwittingly cut the cords of inhibition.

The legend, dear to both, was something to be guarded, but when Martin spelled out Tullus's full name, Valerius could not hold his tongue.

'Marcus Valerius Tullus!' he exclaimed. 'It's not the first time that a Marcus Tullus has aided a Valerius!'

'The legend's true, then!' Tullus reacted. 'This is incredible, like the hand of providence. But it can't be – perhaps it's sheer coincidence.'

'It's not coincidence. It's not a legend – Father read the records – so he told me. Alas, they perished with the villa in 410.'

'Amazing! Quite Amazing! Tell me, what was the name of the sister – the one who married the first Marcus ...?'

'Drusilla,' Valerius interjected. 'My daughter's name,' he added, pain written on his face. 'God help me! – I must find her.'

'What age is she?'

'Eighteen – and she's beautiful – now you know my anguish.'

Tullus looked at the tall aristocrat suffering a father's torment, but it was not the time for sentiment.

'Stay where you are, Valerius. They'll get you if you venture forth. Leave it to me. I've a friend close to the King.'

'Who?'

'The Gothic general, Thulwin'

'Yes – I've heard of him. But, Tullus, this would stir a hornets' nest. They're vindictive. They won't forget.'

'Thulwin is close to the King, and if the King gives you his protection who would dare to touch you or your daughter?'

Valerius hesitated. His terrible sufferings had emphasised an indecisive factor in his nature.

Tullus continued.

'I'm setting out for Rome this morning, bound for the villa of the Senator Symmachus.'

'Symmachus!' Valerius interjected. 'He spoke for me. Tullus, you have friends indeed!'

'We'll find your daughter,' Tullus said forcefully, 'but first I need to know the names of your tormentors.'

Again Valerius hesitated, his tall frame bent in thought.

'If you link your name with mine, you'll bring trouble on yourself. This Thulwin that you know could turn against you.'

'Valerius – I want to sleep in bed at night. How could I do nothing? Now – the names!'

Valerius nodded.

'All right – Opilio was the young Roman advocate who acted for the Goths – they at first were shadowy. One day I was given a specific name and the next day it was changed. They wanted my estate and the figure that they offered was derisory. I appealed to the Senate, and in the wake of this the false accusations started. I lost, of course, and was "graciously" allowed to retain a parcel of land some twenty miles from my old home.' Valerius paused, a feeling of resigned weariness weighing on him.

'For a year my daughter and I were left in peace. Then it started up again, but this time the aggression was overt and physical. I was accused of desecrating an Arian church and was exposed to passionate abuse. My daughter was snatched from my arms, but I was "rescued" by the Gothic soldiery – probably genuine – only to be handed back to my accusers. The chief among them I remember well; Triguilla was his name. He was vicious. Opilio and Triguilla are the only names I know.'

'They'll do!' Tullus answered. 'My advice is this: Stay here until I return. Don't leave. I'll be a month or more, or maybe less, but I'll be back. And keep an eye on Martin. See how he settles in with Father Benedict.'

OOO

CHAPTER EIGHTEEN

# A DAUGHTER

Before he reached the walls of Rome Tullus sold the mules and cart. It was morning, and when he asked directions to the villa of Symmachus, the answer was immediate.

'Go to the centre. Head for the baths of Trajan and ask again.'

Tullus set out briskly but he soon knew that he was lost.

'You're going north,' they told him when he asked. 'Turn left. Keep going until you see the temple on the Capitoline. Then head for that.'

The area he was walking through was very poor, a dilapidated nest of tenements. No one paid him much attention, as his ragged garments blended all too well. The narrow streets were crowded and the smells were foul. Dear God, what would it be like in summer?

Walking on, he found himself within the Jewish quarter. In the main it had an ordered look. Certainly the smells were different. He passed a synagogue, its door daubed crudely with a large, uneven cross.

'Mindless bigots,' he muttered.

The Jewish quarter ended abruptly as he joined the main thoroughfare, and there was the bulk of the Capitoline, with the temple of Jupiter to his right and the temple of Juno Moneta to his left. He was approaching from the north and must have wasted, at the very least, an hour.

Skirting the Capitoline, he headed for the Via Sacra. As a boy he had studied every detail of the city's heart and what had often been a dream was now before him. So it was not surprising that the past was real and present as he stepped below the arch of Septimus Severus. To his right across the Forum, the temple of Divus Julius, and to its right the temple of Castor and Pollux. Although tempted to linger, he walked on quickly past the Basilica Aemilia and the temple of Antoninus and Faustina. Just after the Basilica of Constantine the road swung right up a small incline to the Arch of Titus. There he stopped to look back at the main area of the old Forum. To explain all this away as superstition could only be a nonsense, but the temples, except for those converted to Christian ritual, were sadly neglected.

He turned abruptly, determined to avoid delay, but the huge bulk of

86

the Flavian amphitheatre stopped him in his tracks. Its size was almost brutal. He sighed. There would be time to see it all again.

Awed by his surroundings, he had barely noticed the crowds, but now they pressed about him. It was time to ask directions to the villa of Symmachus.

The man he approached responded immediately with precise instructions. He was apparently close to his destination.

'Have you come far?' the man questioned, his gaze noticing Tullus's rag-like clothes.

'From the east,' Tullus answered briefly.

'I hope you have a pleasant stay in this great city.' The man smiled, moving on in a smooth, fluent way.

Charming, Tullus thought, almost too much so.

OOO

At last the plain, unpretentious villa of Symmachus was before him. Tullus's heart was beating strongly. What would he find? God! Let her be well. He clenched his fists, then resolutely pulled the bell-chain by the heavy courtyard gate.

The pilot door opened.

'My name is Tullus,' he announced, his voice forced, reflecting his anxiety.

'Step inside, sir,' the doorman said with undisguised excitement. 'This way, please.' Another servant raced ahead.

As Tullus mounted the portico steps he heard a brisk but steady footfall from within. It was a man's tread.

'Welcome, Marcus Tullus,' the man exclaimed, his voice deep and generous. 'My name is Boethius.'

'Sir, I am honoured.'

Each grasped the other by the arm.

'Tullus, your coming is most timely, for within the hour, if God so wills, you'll be a father.'

'Is my wife ...?' Tullus stammered.

'Don't worry, sir, your wife's in good hands. Her labour is a little premature, but all is well.'

'Should I see her? – Does she know I'm here?'

'She will be told, and that will be a blessing.'

'She has a nurse, of course?' Tullus questioned in a daze.

'Yes, her nurse is there. My wife and the old family nurse as well – it's a woman's world and all that we can do is worry here! – I've sent for wine – ah! Here it comes.'

Tullus accepted the wine-cup in a dreamlike way. He drank deeply. It was good, even better than the wine he had enjoyed at Justinian's villa.

'Sit down, Tullus,' his host directed amiably.

'I dare not, sir. My clothes are filthy, for I've been travelling like a tramp, and the smell confirms it.'

'I'm sure that wooden bench will accommodate your sensibility,' Boethius returned; 'meantime we'll have the baths prepared. That I'm sure you'd welcome.'

'A longed-for luxury, sir.'

Tullus sat down gratefully. He had been on his feet continually since selling the mules and cart.

'Tell me, where have you been?' Boethius pressed. 'For Rome and all Ravenna, as it were, have searched in vain.'

'The East – Constantinople.'

'Thulwin was right.'

'Thulwin! Where is he?'

'At Fidenae – just outside Rome. I must send word. – He came to see your wife.'

'Thulwin is an ancient Roman with a Gothic name.'

Boethius smiled.

'Yes, he is a man of honour, but he's very much a Goth.'

His host's generous smile alerted Tullus to what he sensed had been there all along – a still, unruffled presence. Not unlike Benedict, he thought, and Justinian had had a touch of it as well.

Boethius was a young man, though that seemed totally irrelevant. This was the man of substance praised by Thulwin, by Justinian and by the old priest in the burnt-out village. Tullus had no doubt that his reputation was well justified.

'A rumour broke several days ago that you were safe,' Boethius continued. 'A rumour, I know, but it helped your wife. Poppe, one of the servant girls, heard the tale at the house of Cyprian.'

'Cyprian!' Tullus reacted. 'That means Narco has returned.'

'You know this Narco?'

'Too well!'

The sound of a door opening, followed by the unmistakable cry of a new-born child, arrested both men's attention. Then a nurse appeared at the doorway of the library where they were sitting.

'Sir, you have a daughter.'

'My wife ...?' Tullus asked involuntarily.

'Your wife is well, sir. She wants to see you, but we suggest she rests a little first.'

The nurse bowed and hurried off.

'Tullus! Let me fill your cup.'

At that the two men held their wine-cups high.

'May the grace of truth walk with your daughter.'

'Amen to that, sir.'

They drank and Tullus felt immensely happy.

'Have you a name for her?'

'Cornelia – a favourite of mine,' Tullus answered without hesitation.

'Ah! The mother of the Gracchi.'

'Yes,' Tullus responded. 'A strange sensation, being a father – a completeness – a broadening out. Well, sir, I feel the need to bath. I cannot see my wife like this.'

'Of course, and fresh clothes. Your good wife had them ready for you soon after she arrived. Well, Tullus, this is indeed a happy day. My father-in-law will be greatly pleased when he returns from the Senate. For him it will be another grandchild. Now the baths. I'll show you their location.'

Tullus glanced sideways at Boethius as they walked towards the bath house. The same unruffled presence was still there. Indeed, it seemed more powerful. Tullus shook his head and looked again. It was the same. What manner of man was this?

OOO

After the luxury of the baths Tullus dressed in the new clothes laid out for him. Then, restless and impatient, he waited for the nurse's summons. It came quickly, though he thought it was an age.

'This way, sir,' the nurse said, walking before him.

At Arria's room he was met by another nurse; Boethius's wife, he concluded quickly.

'Not too long, sir.' The gracious note in the lady's voice gave no offence.

Arria shone with happiness as he entered.

'I thought it was going to be another Marcus Tullus,' she said softly, 'another piece of ancient history.'

'Instead we've got another one of you,' he laughed, pushing her nose lightly with his finger.

'What happened., Marcus? Where have you been?'

'Constantinople, Ephesus,' he answered with mock casualness. 'A little sea air!'

'You missed out Antioch and Alexandria – Marcus, you're joking.'

'Alas, no. But later – we'll talk later, when you've rested. There's much to tell.'

'This evening?'

'Yes, of course. Tell me, where's our daughter?'

'With the nurse next door.'

He looked at her for a long time, his eyes full of affection. Then he kissed her on the forehead. She was very pale.

'Dear Arria,' he said, and kissing her once more he left the room. Next door the nurse beckoned him to a large and ornate cot.

He looked down at the tiny red face so recently released from the confinement of the womb. It was not pretty.

The feelings of fatherhood deserted him. Absently he scanned the panels of the room. He thought of Arria lying weak and helpless, and a surge of affection almost made him weep. Smiling at the nurse, he walked slowly from the room and down the corridor. He looked back. Boethius's wife was quietly entering Arria's room.

'You look concerned,' Boethius observed when they met in the vestibule.

'She's very weak.'

'My wife assures me that the worst is over.'

Tullus brightened.

'I hope so. Dear God, I hope so.'

'Come into the library,' Boethius invited. 'My father-in-law has returned from the Senate and is anxious to meet you.'

As they entered, the rugged features of Symmachus warmed with a smile.

'Marcus Tullus – the man for whom both King and Senate have been searching – welcome.'

'I am deeply grateful, sir, for all the kindness you have shown my wife.'

'A pleasure, Tullus. Your dear wife is one of us, one of the family. Oh, how remiss – congratulations, sir!'

Tullus responded to the friendly conversation as best he could, for he felt confused and tired, and again the pale, pinched face of Arria troubled him.

Servants brought food and wine, but Tullus had little appetite. It was Symmachus who pressed him for his story and in response he outlined the events, keeping the harsh tale of Valerius until the end.

'They broke their word!' Symmachus reacted with agitation.

'Seek the help of Thulwin,' Boethius advised quietly. 'Suggest that Valerius be put under his protection, or better still, the King's.'

This was the confirmation Tullus wanted.

'And his daughter?' he questioned.

'It's a brutal world,' Symmachus said bluntly.

Tullus sighed. The bleak realities were undeniable.

'What was Sublaqueum like?' Boethius asked, changing the subject.

'Raw and basic,' Tullus responded. 'And steady. Their leader is impressive.'

'I sense a new beginning,' Symmachus pronounced.

Tullus nodded.

'That sounds right. It's a different context, I know, but I got the same feel from Clovis and, strangely, Constantinople as well.'

'A new Byzantium!' Boethius interjected.

'Yes,' Tullus agreed, 'Constantinople's full of Roman features, but there's something new and full of energy.'

Tullus felt better. The confusion had lifted, and Arria's state seemed less worrying.

OOO

Both Boethius and his father-in-law had duties in the early afternoon but later, when the three men were again in conversation, a servant entered and handed Symmachus a letter.

'It's Thulwin,' Symmachuus announced. 'He's at Fidenae and will be here to see his friend Tullus in the morning.'

'To see me!' Tullus reacted. 'Should it not be the other way round?'

'Tullus, don't underestimate yourself,' Boethius answered evenly. 'The information you delivered to Thulwin through the boy was vital. It brought him victory. All Ravenna knows this.'

OOO

Arria was brighter, though still weak, when Tullus went to see her later in the evening. They chatted lightly and he told her of his visit to Constantinople and his friend Justinian.

'What do you think of our little one? Isn't she delightful?' she asked happily.

'My dear, I can't say that she's beautiful.'

'Marcus,' she said in a tone of mock reproach.

'More like a wizened orange,' he joked, pretending to shield himself from imminent attack. 'It's all right, my love, in a few weeks she'll be as beautiful as her mother.'

'Flatterer!'

In the morning Arria's condition had further improved. Tullus was relieved, though a residue of worry still remained, but his concerns were brushed aside by Rusticiana.

'Sir, your wife has borne a child. Mother – and father – take a little time to mend.'

Her voice was liquid, her smile full of laughter.

OOO

The Count Thulwin arrived by mid-morning. The same Thulwin, Tullus thought. Straight of speech and upright. His greeting was warm, his usual reserve hardly evident.

'Before we talk, Count,' Tullus began, 'I must tell you the good news. I'm a father; my beloved Arria's had a baby daughter.'

'My friend, I'm truly pleased.' Thulwin's warm response was clearly genuine.

First one and then the other spoke of their experiences. Thulwin was full of gratitude for the information Martin had delivered. It had been vital, he kept saying.

They talked with little thought of time.

'The boy's a living miracle,' Thulwin emphasised. 'His urge to find you was to ordinary mortals an obsession, but to him it was a simple matter – and he found you. Tullus, men do not rule this world.'

Both fell silent for a while and Thulwin, Tullus saw, had grown reflective.

'This Justinian that you met seems powerful.'

'Yes, very,' Tullus confirmed.

'Well, at least he hasn't gained the purple yet!'

'No, not yet.'

Thulwin was alluding to the constant Gothic fear that a powerful and ambitious Emperor could challenge their lordship of Italy, but the subject was not carried further.

Rising from his couch, Thulwin began to pace the floor.

'I'm returning to the area near Arelate within the next two days. Indeed, the army is already mustering on the border. I'm not asking you to join me, but I'm sincerely hoping you'll manage my estates – four of them. The King keeps giving me more land!'

As Tullus began to express his appreciation Thulwin shook his head in casual dismissal. He had more to say.

'You will need a three-man bodyguard.'

'A bodyguard!'

'Yes, a bodyguard!' Thulwin confirmed unsmilingly.

Disbelief flooded Tullus's expression.

'Narco has returned to the house of Cyprian,' Thulwin continued. 'Last week he was seen at the circus with Cyprian's widowed mother.'

'Narco is nothing!' Tullus reacted.

Thulwin raised his hand.

'It's not only Narco. It's the road. A lone rider is an easy prey to banditry, not least drunken soldiery. And, Tullus, many of my race see Romans as a conquered people and a valid prize.'

'Valerius suffered that all right ...'

'Valerius,' Thulwin interjected. 'You know him?'

Tullus nodded.

'A shameful business,' Thulwin continued. 'The trouble was, those who gained were powerful and there were certain alliances. There was a compromise, however.'

'It didn't hold.'

As Tullus recounted the story of Valerius, Thulwin grew furious.

'By my ancestors, I'll take this to the King. And, Tullus, from this moment Valerius is under my protection. There is plenty of accommodation. Two of my villas are practically empty – did Valerius mention names?'

'Yes, an agent named Opilio and a Goth named Triguilla.'

'Opilio! – the wine-drenched brother of Cyprian; and Triguilla – a man consumed by greed. Surely the King will see through this!'

Thulwin began to pace the room again.

'There's much to do before I travel west,' he said directly. 'I have two requests, though: first that I pay respects to your good wife and second that you visit me tomorrow at Fidenae. There are people that you need to meet and documents you need to see before I leave. And, Tullus, you'll have a bodyguard. That's an order!'

OOO

# CHAPTER NINETEEN

# TRAGEDY

Arria's eyes were full of tears when she saw Count Thulwin and he, seeing her emotion, was moved and awkward. Tullus, however, was quick to ease the situation.

'You didn't weep for me!' he jested, and they all laughed.

'Marcus, dear,' she said, holding out her hand towards him. 'You've often repeated that we owe everything to the Count. My tears are an acknowledgement.'

Tullus spoke of the post that Thulwin had offered him and again tears came.

'We'll have a place of our own,' she innocently exclaimed.

'A country villa,' Thulwin added with a smile.

OOO

In the morning Tullus found a three-man mounted escort awaiting his instructions. It was what he had been promised, yet he was amazed. Their leader, Ufilias, spoke Latin in a halting way, but the other two were limited to words of greeting. It was clear to Tullus; he would have to learn the Gothic tongue.

As soon as Arria was awake he went to see her. She looked stronger and Tullus was much heartened.

They talked about his new post in Thulwin's service and joked about his bodyguard, but time was pressing. An early start was necessary for his meeting at Fidenae.

'I'll only be away for a day or so, my dear,' he said, kissing her. He lingered for a while, the fullness of affection forced him to; and then he quickly left.

The presence of three mounted Gothic soldiers had a near-magic effect in clearing the busy streets before them, so the journey to the city walls was swift, and once on the Via Salaria they moved easily.

Thulwin's villa was a low building, laid out in the form of a square with a large inner courtyard; an Equestrian property once, and typical of the country. Nearby, and well disguised by cypress trees, was a large enclosure circled by a ring of open-sided sheds. The villa was on raised ground and, although adjacent to the river, was well beyond the reach of floods.

Thulwin greeted his new agent with enthusiasm and they set to work immediately. They studied ground plans, stock levels and the complicated details of the tenants and their holdings. Then there were the problems centred on the villa staff, the labourers and slaves.

'It's a mess, Tullus,' Thulwin said with some exasperation, 'and honest dealing has been rare. My last agent, I fear, grew rich at my expense. So do what you think best; you have my full authority.'

Thulwin was anxious to be off, but they still had not discussed the properties at Ravenna and Verona. Briefly Thulwin outlined how things were. Both estates had stable agents. What they needed was some drive.

'Well, my friend,' the Count concluded, 'I should have been away three hours ago. My men are waiting.'

'God be with you, sir,' Tullus called out as the tall Goth mounted his horse.

'And with you, Tullus.'

Then Thulwin and his men were off and in a little time they disappeared from view.

Tullus ate alone at noon while sifting through the mountain of documents. There was no order, no systematic method whatsoever. His priorities were obvious, but first there was the villa staff. He would need to meet them all individually. He sat back in his chair and yawned. It was just like Britain! He was managing estates again.

Faintly at first, and then with mounting urgency, the sound of an approaching horseman grew in strength. Tullus walked to the portico to investigate. He recognised the rider instantly. It was one of Symmachus's men. Suddenly he was gripped by fearful premonition.

Without speaking, the rider handed him a message, and as he read the blood drained from his face. He closed his eyes, his head bowed.

'My God! My God!' The explosive cry was full of anguish.

'We are all deeply sorry, sir,' the rider said, embarrassed by the grief he saw before him.

'Yes, thank you, yes …' Tullus answered absently.

Arria was dead. A haemorrhage – one moment she was there, the next – life had simply slipped away. There had been no distress or pain.

Tullus sat down on a low wooden bench beside him.

'Dear God,' was all that he could say.

Slowly, and with undisguised despair, he turned towards the servant who had followed him.

'Ask my bodyguard to present themselves immediately – and see that our friend has some refreshment, please – he's ridden hard.'

Devastated, Tullus took the road to Rome, sitting on his horse like one asleep. His grief was painful, like an iron band about his chest.

Rusticiana embraced him when he arrived. Her eyes were red. Then Boethius greeted him and Tullus played the man as best he could.

'She knew no pain, no unhappiness,' Boethius said. 'Surely that's a blessing. Come,' he added, leading Tullus to the library where wine and cups stood ready.

'Drink this.'

The cup was large and Tullus drank gratefully.

'I saw your wife not many moments before her death. She was very happy.' Boethius watched Tullus closely.

'Did she say anything I should know?'

'She talked of her daughter and the miracle of life.'

The room grew still and when the Senator Symmachus joined them he nodded but made no attempt to speak.

'Can I see my wife?' Tullus asked, his voice controlled.

'Yes, of course. I will come with you,' Boethius answered.

They stood before the body of Arria for a long time. Then Tullus bent and kissed her gently on the forehead. He turned away, his eyes full of tears, but he did not lose himself in noisy grief. The presence of Boethius had helped to give him strength.

That night and in the days that followed he slept little. He managed to control his anguish, yet he longed to be alone, away from everyone, but formal duties had to be obeyed. He had one source of comfort, however: his little daughter. Her tiny fingers, her contented face, the button of her nose – he never seemed to tire of watching her. She had a wet-nurse and Rusticiana had offered to be her guardian. Tullus was full of gratitude.

Somehow he lived through these bitter days. The funeral passed and Arria's body was laid to rest. Now the future lay before him, but it was a grey and lifeless prospect and he felt no will at all for action. Yet reason forced him forward. He had to move, not least for little Cornelia. That was his duty, and the plight of Valerius, of course, needed prompt attention. So next day Tullus and his bodyguard set out for Sublaqueum.

As he rode it seemed that everything reminded him of Arria. In fact, the least flash of recognition was enough to set his mind on fire. He thought of Boethius. How direct the Senator had been, but he had shown enormous sympathy. 'In all adversity of fortune,' he had said, 'the most wretched kind is once to have been happy.' How true, he thought, yet there was no end to the spinning wheel of fortune and misfortune. Each turned upon the other. How could a man draw clear of it?

At Sublaqueum the approaching Gothic horsemen sent a flurry of anxiety through the small community, but when Tullus was recognised the mood transformed.

'I've come for my friend Valerius,' he told one of the monks. 'And where is Martin? Is he behaving himself?'

'He's gone off further down the valley with Father Benedict – they'll be back by nightfall.'

Tullus was not sorry to have missed them, such was his present state.

He found Valerius helping with some building work and they talked a while about the plans proposed. But Tullus was impatient to be off, for standing idle magnified his anguish. Relentless action seemed to be his only solace.

'Can we leave now?' he said bluntly.

'Well, yes, we can,' Valerius responded, though puzzled by the strange abruptness. 'You look strained, my friend,' he added.

'Later, I'll tell you later.' Tullus had no wish to show his grief before the monks.

'Tullus, the men below are Goths,' Valerius said cautiously, looking down the slope.

'They're Thulwin's men. You're under his protection. No one dare touch you!'

'How will I travel?'

'We've brought a horse,' Tullus answered, as he started to descend towards the road

'You've worked wonders,' Valerius called, but Tullus did not seem to hear.

OOO

# CHAPTER TWENTY

# THE WIDOW

The widowed mother of Cyprian had lost heavily at the races. She had been rash and extravagant and she knew it, but then, she liked being rash and extravagant. She lay back languidly on her cushions like some sleek feline creature sleeping off the daylight hours. She was still a woman of some attraction.

Her son would undoubtedly be tiresome, she thought. He always was when she asked for money and this time it would be difficult. If only there was something she could bargain with. What a nuisance. She yawned, and then it came to her. Of course – Cyprian had eyes for one of the girls. Perhaps a little trading would be possible. She would strike a hard bargain, though, and in the meantime she could buy on credit.

Lazily she leaned across her cushions and pulled the bell-cord. It was time to dally with her little one-armed Narco. Why? Something said within her. You loathe the little snake.

'My lady.' It was Narco, full of sugar sweetness. Sheer lust and nothing more.

'I'm heartbroken at my losses, my little Narco. Come and soothe me with your soft caresses.'

Narco's lean body approached with soundless speed, his one good arm outstretched.

'How passionate is this single arm. Oh, my little Narco!' She was playing with an adder, and what fun it was.

Suddenly a loud knocking on the door disturbed them.

'Yes – who is it?' the widow reacted with annoyance, while Narco darted to the corner of the room.

Cyprian burst in, clearly in a rage.

'Mother!' he shouted, 'the news is all round Rome. You've lost a fortune at the circus!'

'A trifle, son. Tomorrow it will rain with gold! Will it not, my Narco?'

Narco's smile was nervous.

'Get out, Narco!' Cyprian barked.

'Stay, my Narco,' the widow softly urged.

'Go!' Cyprian was furious and Narco slipped away, a smile frozen on his face.

'Why do you entertain that grinning viper?'

'I like his sting, my son,' she smiled, patting the cushion beside her. 'How is your little Poppe? Are you tiring of her yet?'

'Mother, don't change the subject.'

'Sit down, my son,' she whispered.

'Your creditors come to me – Mother! – are you listening? If they come to me in future I'll not pay. Live off your own. You have wealth in plenty.'

'You know it's all tied up in property. My son, don't let a little silver come between us.' She looked at him reproachfully. 'Now, you didn't answer me. Does your little Poppe still adore her Cyprian?'

'Mother, she's an innocent. The word may have escaped you..'

'You are tiresome tonight, my son – sit down.' Again she patted the cushions and this time he obeyed.

'How is your darling wife?'

'Mother, what are you trying to say?'

'Don't be so suspicious, Cyprian.' Her voice was velvet soft.

'My wife is in the country and *that's* where I intend she stays.'

'It's my duty – a mother's duty!'

'She's not coming here. Is that clear?!' He rose, full of agitation.

'Of course, my son – sit down, sit down!'

Cyprian remained standing.

'Of course, my son,' he mimicked. 'If you pay my debts, my son – It won't work, Mother!'

'I know I've lost a little at the races, but, Cyprian, I have other debts. My household servants and the kitchen staff – I've spent so much to keep them free of Gothic hands.'

'Mother, your "sweet boy" – my drunken brother Opilio – knows you are an easy prey. He'd tell you any story if he thought you'd pay.'

'That's not true!'

'Mother, when it comes to my "dear" brother you are blind!'

'No! that poor mindless thing that's in the kitchen – he stole her from the Goths!'

'He took your money, Mother. Stop investing him with Christian motives.'

'He had expenses,' she countered defiantly

'Really,' Cyprian said with mock surprise.

'He had to bribe her minders!'

'Oh yes.'

'You like her?'

'Who said I did?'

'My servants are observant.'

'She's special.'

'Well, my son, I saved her from the clutches of the Goth, but you are not a Goth!'

'Mother! Credit with me with some integrity – the girl has lost her memory!'

'When she recovers she could be very grateful,' the widow whispered.

Cyprian shook his head, viewing his mother with a kind of amused admiration.

'You never give up! As a matter of interest, how much?'

'Two thousand.'

Cyprian burst out laughing.

'A mere two thousand,' she repeated. 'To you, my clever son, a trifle. Do some more favours for your Ostrogothic friends. They pay so well. Opilio your "baby" brother has been quite successful.'

'With fraud, Mother.'

'Never!' she exclaimed.

'I must go,' he said impatiently.

'To Poppe – must you, son?'

'Remember, no more debts and, Mother, don't take Narco to the circus. Think of your reputation!'

'I didn't think I had one,' she muttered.

'What was that, Mother?'

'Nothing. I'll be good, I promise.'

That will be the day, he thought as he was leaving. But Cyprian felt uneasy. The dull-eyed creature in his mother's kitchen was high-born. God knows who she was. There could be a scandal, and if there was it would be he who would be blamed! The trouble was, he had appointments that would keep him out of Rome for weeks. Why had he not thought of this before? He knew. It was his mother's kitchen and his mother's girls. He always left such things to her.

As Cyprian closed the door behind him, another door eased open and the grinning face of Narco reappeared.

OOO

# CHAPTER TWENTY ONE

# POPPE

Tullus did the best he could to disguise the greyness that afflicted him. His friend Valerius knew well what he was suffering. The signs were unmistakable. There was the sudden breaking off from conversation – even in mid-sentence – the lack of laughter, the frenzied pace of work and the heavy drinking in the evening.

The early weeks at Thulwin's villa were not easy.

Valerius, too, was grieving. The likely fate of his graceful daughter haunted him. Like Tullus, he found little rest. He made endless enquiries and through the good offices of Symmachus, the Church and all the major towns in Italy had been alerted – but nothing!

Again with the help of Symmachus, Opilio was questioned, though predictably he denied all knowledge of the matter. He was a lawyer, not a jailer. Opilio, Symmachus reported, had been half-drunk, unashamed and brazen. Nonetheless, he left for Southern Italy the day after he was questioned – to serve another Gothic client, it was said.

At Ravenna the Senator Boethius had confronted Triguilla, the Gothic owner of the vast Valerian estate but he, like Opilio, disowned responsibility. His Roman lawyer had handled everything, he said.

The search seemed hopeless.

After a month at Thulwin's villa, Valerius was much stronger and the lines of deprivation left his face. He was a handsome man, academic in both look and inclination, but there was no desire for study while his daughter's fate remained unknown; his lovely, graceful daughter! His anguish seemed to match his growing strength.

Every week Tullus rode to Rome to see his baby daughter and on each occasion Valerius accompanied him with the urgent purpose of pressing his enquiries. On the fourth visit, while waiting for Symmachus, he asked if he might browse within the library – a request quickly granted by Rusticiana, still resident at her father's villa.

For a time Valerius forgot his troubles. This was his world, and time passed easily. After a while he sensed a presence and, turning, found a small, wide-eyed girl watching him.

'My lady asked me to wait upon you, sir. May I bring refreshment?'

'That is kind,' Valerius said gently. 'A little lime water, please.'

She smiled and left the room. What a charming creature, he thought as he resumed his reading. The girl soon reappeared.

'Thank you,' he said, sipping at the drink. 'What is your name, my dear?'

'Poppe,' she answered lightly.

He smiled.

'You are the Lord Valerius?' Her voice was soft.

It was a long time since anyone had called him that.

'Yes, I am Valerius.' Again he smiled. He could not help admiring her. She spoke so well. Involuntarily his eyes returned to focus on the page before him.

'Sir.' The voice was tentative but compelling.

He looked up slowly. 'Yes, Poppe?'

'Sir ...' She hesitated.' Sir, we hear a lot of stories in the servants' quarters.' She swallowed hard.

'I'm sure you do,' he responded quietly.

'Your daughter, sir,' she suddenly burst out. 'I think I know where your daughter is.'

'Where, Poppe?' Valerius was on his feet, his voice eager.

Again she hesitated, her face fearful.

'Where, Poppe?' Valerius repeated urgently.

'The house of Cyprian,' she said quickly. Then she seemed to crumple. 'Oh, sir! You'll not let them be angry with me. I've a friend who's nice and gives me presents and I went there without permission. Please, sir, oh, please, sir, don't let them put me out!' She was on her knees before him, tears streaming down her cheeks.

He held out his hand and raised her to her feet.

'Poppe, Poppe, no one will cast you on the street. Now dry your eyes.'

'Yes, my lord.'

'Now, Poppe, tell me everything about the person you think to be my daughter.'

'She speaks like my lady Rusticiana and she looks like you, sir and, sir, she's – she's special – and her hair is fair, not blonde.'

'How is she? Is she well? What's she doing there?' Valerius had no doubt it was his daughter. 'But why has she not ...?'

'She's lost her memory, sir,' Poppe interjected. 'Doesn't know who she is – shock, they say.'

'Dear God, no wonder. What's she doing?' he repeated.

'She's in the kitchen, sir.'

'Come, Poppe.' Valerius knew that there was more.

'The servants say the Lady Widow saved her from the Goths.'

'Then why has she been silent? – She must have heard! – What's she hiding?'

'The Lord Cyprian is due back today,' Poppe ventured. 'The servants say he's cut his journeys short.'

'They know. They've heard and that's why he's come back. God knows what he'll do to save a scandal, for I'm near to certain that Opilio's mixed up in this!'

Valerius began to pace the library floor.

'There is no time to waste.' He grated. 'Already my ancestors are thundering at the doors of Cyprian – Poppe, don't go to that accursed place again!'

The wide eyes looked back, startled.

'I'm not angry with you, Poppe – on the contrary,' he said quietly, holding her head between his hands.

'Oh, my lord,' she whispered. Tears welled up and then she fled.

Impatiently Valerius began, once more, to pace the floor. 'Hurry, Tullus,' he muttered, but it was hardly any time before the doors swung open.

At once Valerius related all that he had heard from Poppe. Tullus listened keenly, and as he did his grey look ebbed away.

'I'll go,' he said abruptly.

'No, Tullus – it's my duty.'

'I know, but you're much too full of ire to be effective. You're certain Poppe's right?'

'Tullus, doubt comes easily to me, but this time it hasn't surfaced.'

Tullus looked hard at Valerius.

'If I were Cyprian and I found myself in his position I would take her to the country and give her to the Church. In some way I'd get rid of her, for if Opilio and his mother are involved he can't act openly.'

'He could speed her out of Rome this very night,' Valerius emphasised. 'We must act immediately!'

'But how? We can't confront him openly, for heaven knows what he might do. Cyprian's on the ladder of ambition and a scandal that could echo in Ravenna could be disastrous; Thulwin, as you know, has spoken to the King. Valerius, we must move cautiously, but we must move quickly too!' Tullus paused, his head bent in reflection.

'I've got it,' he said sharply. 'Thulwin's estate owes the house of Cyprian quite a lot of money; something forgotten in the general chaos at

Fidenae. So I've the perfect excuse to call and apologise for the oversight. Then I'll casually raise the subject of your daughter while dropping hints of compromise; the age-old art of leaving your opponent room to move.'

'What about Narco? He could be there!'

'He's a crippled flea,' Tullus grunted. 'And if they're wise they'll keep him out of sight. Anyway, I'll take Ufilias, the leader of my bodyguard. I know he frightens me!' A smile began, but did not finish.

OOO

CHAPTER TWENTY TWO

# THE ANICIUS VILLA

Anicius Manlius Severinus Boethius sat alone in the library of his family villa. The room was lofty, its structure decorated in a rich display of ivory and glass, but Boethius, deep in reflection, was oblivious to the luxury.

In his mind the breadth of the old Empire lay before him. Long since the West had crumbled and scholarship was weak. Philosophy, generally ignored, was replaced by passionate beliefs, and the wisdom of the Greeks despised. How could this madness be arrested? How could discipline in debate be reinstated? And Italy, fragile, brittle, full of unchecked lawlessness, was held together in reluctant unity by the force of alien power embodied in a Gothic autocrat. How long would King Theoderic live? Was chaos inevitable? Would the Roman Senate last much longer?

What of the East, the new Byzantium? What was Rome to her, other than a distant relic, and too often troublesome? Again, there was the schism, madness built on madness and maintained by points of dogma – or was it? Would either Pope or Patriarch ever bow the knee in true submission to the other? Was unity a hopeless myth?

Boethius sighed. He had no illusions.

The door opened and the Senator Symmachus entered. Immediately Boethius rose to greet his father-in-law.

'I'm glad you've come early before our friends arrive, for there is much to talk about,' he began. 'I attended a Church council today. I must say I found it hard to bear.'

'That's not surprising,' Symmachus responded as he took his seat.

'To have tried to reason with those madmen would have proved me insane; so I held my tongue.'

Symmachus laughed.

'Did they discuss the schism?'

'What else, Father! They shouted their unbending opposition to Byzantium, hoping that the Pope would hear of it, no doubt – the ladder of promotion ever glitters!'

'Alas, there's much in what you say,' Symmachus returned. 'And all about the Blessed Trinity!'

'Would that it were so,' Boethius retorted, 'for we've reduced the Godhead to a piece of parchment!'

'Boethius, you'll have to write and clarify the subject.'

'And have my writing scorned by fools.'

'Dedicate your work to one of the more enlightened of the Church's hierarchy. Such patronage is useful. Even the ignorant may think it fashionable to take you seriously.' Symmachus smiled knowingly.

Boethius stood up, poured a cup of wine and handed it to his father-in-law.

'What a grace, to grow old quietly,' he said with feeling. 'To surrender the clamour of ignorance we call public life.'

Symmachus was much amused.

'A pleasant sentiment, Boethius,' he said easily. 'Do you expect me to take you seriously? For you of all people know that good men should not rest idle while the state falls into chaos. But I sympathise; the library's peace is golden.'

'Golden indeed when set against the palace intrigues at Ravenna.'

There was now no humour on the face of Symmachus. The court was full of treachery and the greed that circled round the honey-pot of sovereign power was merciless.

'Father,' Boethius said, changing the subject, 'I'm thinking of asking Tullus to join our mid-week meetings.'

Symmachus nodded.

'An obvious candidate. There's also Valerius.'

'I haven't met him yet, but you have, of course.'

'Yes, a number of times. He knows Greek, I'm sure, probably very well. His family had that reputation.'

'Good! We'll invite them both.'

Symmachus sat back in his chair.

'I wonder how many of our fellow Senators are fluent in Greek?' he questioned.

'Few; and how many send their sons to study in the east – I mean Athens.'

'Even fewer; they say the Eastern schools are full of occult superstition,' Symmachus said.

'Who? The superstitious! Did you hear the rumours accusing me of necromancy?'

'What! Who'd believe such rubbish?' Symmachus was indignant.

'A slander oft repeated can gain the force of fact.'

'Damned lies,' Symmachus growled. 'Who would spread such poison?'

'Some purist fanatic, maybe, or a drunkard, or someone full of shy resentment.'

'Of what?'

'The family wealth, to start with.'

Symmachus shook his head.

'That's not the reason – your love of truth's a mirror to their selfishness!'

'Boethius is not blameless, Father: his impatience is intolerant and sharp of tongue.'

'Gross ignorance needs a dagger!'

'Without the venom, though,' Boethius returned.

'You are provoked.'

'I know. Smug churchmen who dismiss Plato and the Greeks are hard to bear...'

'And those who thwart your every move to heal the schism!' Symmachus interjected. 'Is there any hope of unity? Is there a will within the Church to make it so?'

'Father, unity is in Christ, but how we mortals love our dogma.' Boethius shook his head. 'There's no easy answer. Take language: Greek is declining in the West and Latin in the East. This clearly does not help. And can you see the master of the Eastern Empire allowing his Patriarch to submit to a Western Pope? Anyhow, the political pressures faced by the Eastern Church are wholly different from what we experience in the West. Again, there are the simple facts of geography. Rome is at the perimeter of the new Empire. The roads that join us are poor, the stations in disuse, and who knows when the Egnatian Way is cut? There are no Roman legions on the Danube now. Then there are the Goths, our masters; isolated by their Arian belief. Do they want a greater Empire with a triumphant Church determined to extinguish heresy? No, like every powerful ruler, Theoderic sees a thousand years of Gothic rule.'

'What you say is all too true,' Symmachus said flatly.

'There's always hope, Father. A little tolerance and a broader vision would make all the difference. I feel Theoderic would respond; there's something of the noble warrior about him and his word would hold. But he's an Arian, a fact intolerable to many round the Papal chair and in the Empire's capital. It's all so petty, for with a little wisdom all could live at peace.'

Symmachus sighed deeply, his head buried in his hands.

'The Lord God is neither Jew nor Greek nor Gentile, not Orthodox, Arian or Monophysite, not even Roman! It amazes me that no one seems to grasp the fact.'

'Yes, Father, but most minds need a creed – a system, if you like. Don't we follow Christ and Plato?'

'Perhaps we have a subject for this evening's gathering?' Symmachus suggested.

'Perhaps. We'll see what happens when our friends arrive.'

OOO

# CHAPTER TWENTY THREE

# SAD EYES

At the house of Cyprian servants were busy with the lamps. It was early evening and in the Widow's large, luxurious room they rushed about, ever careful of the fickle moods that ruled their mistress.

She sat amongst her cushions, bored and brooding. She had been to see some wrestling and gymnastics – a tame affair. It was her friend Fausta's fault. She had dragged her there. She liked the wrestlers' glistening bodies, but tomorrow it would be the Circus Maximus again. Narco would take her there – or would he? She was tiring of the little man. His beady eyes were sickening.

She moved restlessly on her cushions. Nothing was going right. She was short of money. Her creditors were pressing and Cyprian had left instructions with his agent not to pay, but her son was due back soon. She had received a fussy note from him about the mouse-haired girl, with strict instructions to keep her out of sight. How could she? How could she lock the poor thing in a room? Cyprian was in a panic, thinking that the dull-eyed creature was the daughter of Valerius. How could she be? Surely her boy Opilio would have warned her? Yet she felt uneasy.

Where was Cyprian? It was unfair of him to leave her on her own so long. She punched the cushions with frustration. She did not like her lazy ways disturbed.

Suddenly the door burst open.

'Mother! That girl is in the kitchen, plain for all to see!' Cyprian was back.

'You're back,' the widow reacted mildly.

'Of course I'm back!' he snapped. 'I told you to keep her out of sight!'

'How could I lock the poor thing up?'

'By all the sacred gods!' Cyprian exploded with sheer exasperation.

'There's only one God now, my son.'

'Stop your playacting. We've got the daughter of Valerius in the kitchen and all of Italy is looking for her; and the King is asking questions too!'

'Are you sure it's her?'

'It's her all right. She's her father's image. I saw him recently.'

'I wouldn't know. I haven't seen Valerius for years. But Opilio ...'

'Opilio!' Cyprian barked. 'It's a good thing he's hiding in the south, otherwise I'd wring his neck!'

'You think he knew!'

'Of course he knew. If he'd told you, you would have paid him nothing, but done the decent thing.'

'I don't believe you!' she said defiantly.

'Mother, when will you wake up? Opilio is a drunken, scheming fraud!'

'He is your brother, Cyprian!' she reacted angrily. 'And he saved the poor girl from the Goths.'

'Yes, and put his family in real trouble. Remember Theoderic is asking questions!'

'Well, I'm not convinced. Opilio would have told his mother ...'

'Right,' Cyprian interjected. 'let's have a look at her!' He pulled the bell cord and a servant soon appeared.

'Ask "Sad Eyes" to attend upon us,' Cyprian ordered. 'Tell her to bring some wine.'

'"Sad Eyes"?' Cyprian's mother repeated.

'That's what they call her in the kitchen.'

The girl was quickly present.

'Just leave the wine here, my dear', the widow said sweetly.

'Will that be all, my lady?' the girl asked flatly, like one who had been told exactly what to say.

'Yes, my dear,' the widow answered and, seeing the girl's confusion, showed her to the door.

'My God,' Cyprian said tensely, 'even in her present state she's regal. And her voice, right from the highest levels of society – well, Mother?'

'She's special, my son, but still we can't be sure ...'

'I'm sure, and I certainly won't take the risk. We'll get her out of here immediately.'

'Where to?'

'Somewhere, anywhere, but not here!'

Another servant entered, after knocking loudly.

'Marcus Tullus to see you, sir.'

'Conduct the noble Tullus in immediately. Now, Mother, are you convinced? – This is the bosom friend of Valerius!' he whispered fiercely.

The widow stood up as Tullus entered. This was a man. Above average height, he had a soldier's bearing and he had power. His nose was straight, perhaps a trifle long.

'Tullus, welcome to our villa. First, may I introduce my mother.'

'Madam,' Tullus said quietly.

She acknowledged his greeting, her natural instincts barely disguised.

'We have met before, Tullus,' Cyprian was saying. 'You asked me the way to Symmachus's villa. Then, shall we say, you were wearing your travelling clothes.'

'Yes, of course; that's why your face is so familiar.'

Cyprian had charm, Tullus thought.

'Now, sir,' Cyprian began, 'before you state your business you must have some refreshment.'

Tullus waved his hand in polite dismissal.

'I'll take no refusal, sir,' Cyprian pressed, deliberately pulling the bell cord by his mother's couch; but immediately on doing so he realised his error. He had summoned the girl, for she was still in attendance. He hesitated, his poise forgotten until the widow, seeing his dilemma, rose quickly from her couch.

'I think we need something special,' she said confidently as she swept from the room, but before she shut the door behind her the rich patrician sound of 'Yes, my lady' was clearly audible.

'You have impressed my mother. She rarely leaves the fastness of her cushions!'

Cyprian had recovered well. Even so, the momentary flash of panic and the knowing looks between the widow and her son had not been missed by Tullus. But far more potent was the sound of 'Yes, my lady' coming from the open door. That had been no servant's voice.

On the surface Tullus remained calm and affable; while his mind raced wildly. What should he do? Should he act, or wait? And if he waited, would the chance be lost? He felt he had to come to a decision, yet no clear course was obvious.

'We were deeply sorry to hear of your tragic loss, my friend,' Cyprian said respectfully.

'Thank you, sir,' Tullus responded, and instantly painful memory swamped his mind. He bowed his head, only to straighten up immediately. There was work to do.

'Sir, you may wonder why I've troubled you at this somewhat late hour,' he began.

Cyprian tensed.

'No trouble,' he reacted as casually as he could.

'I simply came to apologise.'

'Whatever for?' Cyprian responded with genuine surprise.

'You may have heard that I am managing Count Thulwin's estates. Well, I've discovered we owe you considerable arrears. This, I assure you, will be settled shortly.'

'A trifle, sir, but I thank you for the courtesy in informing me – I must

111

confess to finding estate matters troublesome,' Cyprian continued in a man-to-man way. 'But you have three estates – how do you cope?'

'Honest and conscientious staff – even so, some details, often important, can get overlooked,' Tullus answered, playing the game of pleasantries.

'Exactly,' Cyprian agreed. 'Indeed, these details are often discovered at the most awkward of times.'

'And what is innocent can be seen as some deliberate deception,' Tullus continued, leading the game another step.

'A little understanding, though, can soon resolve such matters – public scandals are a trouble to both sides.'

Tullus nodded knowingly. The play of words had gone beyond coincidence.

'Your experience as a lawyer, of course, will have made ...'

'Too true,' Cyprian interjected. 'I remember one case, a public one, connected with the Senate, when we simply let the prisoner escape. If we hadn't, the wrangling would still be going on.'

'Very sensible,' Tullus responded.

'Now, where did all this start? – oh yes, estate management – conversations thread about like unconnected dreams. Ah! here come my mother and the faithful Rufus with the wine.'

'This is our best,' the widow said, offering Tullus a brimming cup.

'Excellent,' Tullus responded politely.

Soon she was questioning him about Constantinople. The conversation flowed easily and to Rufus, waiting in attendance, it was a scene of friendly affability. He did not sense the undercurrents.

When the time was ripe Tullus took his leave.

'I liked your story, sir,' he said, looking straight at Cyprian. 'When troubles come, let them all escape!'

Cyprian laughed, his gaze fixed on Tullus.

'Perhaps I'd better follow that advice myself.'

OOO

'Do you think he knows?' the widow asked.

'He knows, and he played his part extremely well. Now it's up to us ...'

'And what about the part I played, my son?'

'Superb, Mother, you saved the hour!'

'And my debts?' She was again amidst her cushions.

'You're impossible!'

She had won, but he could only laugh.

'Where's Rufus?' he asked.

'He's gone to the kitchen with the wine and cups.'

'Good! Now, here's the plan. There's someone I know who is discreet. I've used him in the past. He'll have a cart drawn up within the hour. If unchallenged, he'll take her to a church some way out of Rome. But if Tullus stops the cart, as I believe he will, it's his!'

'What about the driver?'

'I know him well. He's pretty fleet of foot.'

'What if he's trapped?'

'He saw the poor girl walking aimlessly and gave her his protection – there are many likely tales. The man I've hired is good.'

'How did Tullus know, I wonder?' the widow said reflectively.

'The servants must have talked.'

'Your beloved Poppe, I suspect.'

'Well, if Poppe knows, the kitchen knows, and if the kitchen knows, Rome knows – we've acted just in time!'

'Will you punish her?'

'Poppe?! Of course not, Mother. She's the servant of Symmachus. Anyway, she's an innocent.'

'There may be more to Poppe than you think.'

'Maybe, but I'll tell you one thing, Mother. Your poor boy, my dear brother Opilio, needs to be strapped in irons.'

'Well, Cyprian, if your brother hadn't brought the poor girl to us, what would have become of her?'

'I don't know, Mother, but I do know that we must protect our family and its reputation.'

'It's your career that you're protecting,' his mother countered.

'Be thankful that I have one,' Cyprian snapped. 'If I hadn't, who would pay your debts? – Well, I'd better go and see my orders are obeyed, for if I don't there's no one else who will!'

'What's that supposed to mean?' his mother called as he went through the door.

He made no answer.

The widow was alone again but she was no longer restless. Leaning slowly to the side she pulled the bell cord.

'Yes, my lady.' It was Rufus.

'Will you take me to the races tomorrow?'

'Of course, my lady.' The open face revealed an obvious pleasure.

'Oh, darling Rufus, why did I reject your tenderness? Come to the comfort of my arms.'

Rufus approached, embarrassed by his shyness, and the widow smiled encouragement. Narco's hour had passed.

ooo

The villa of Cyprian stood apart from the surrounding buildings. Close by was a small wooded park, to which Tullus returned after making a show of riding off.

Tullus had no doubt that the daughter of Valerius was in Cyprian's villa and he had no doubt that Cyprian knew he knew. Then there was the coded message, as it were, that Tullus felt was Cyprian's plan. He would simply let her go – but how? If only he had Poppe's help. If she could enter Cyprian's villa on the pretext of delivering a present or meeting with a friend, he might discover what was actually happening. Immediately he sent Ufilias with a message to Valerius.

With one of the Gothic guards he settled down to wait. The other guard was watching near the servants' entrance.

Time passed slowly. Why was he playing this silly game? Why had he not simply claimed the girl? He grew self-critical, but soon concluded that his actions had been prudent. Cyprian was ambitious. God knows how he would react if his public face were threatened. It was an age when people simply disappeared.

At last Poppe, Valerius and Ufilias arrived and with the minimum of instruction Poppe slipped away towards the servants' entrance.

'Be careful.' Valerius cautioned.

'Yes, my lord,' was the soft reply.

The servants' door was open and Poppe entered noiselessly. No one was about. Clutching a basket of fruit, the suggested present, she slipped quickly down the corridor. There was still no one to be seen, but in the spacious kitchen she found the girl sitting alone at the large working table.

Poppe set her present down.

'Where is everyone?' she asked.

'Some meeting,' the girl said absently.

'Come, "Sad Eyes"! come,' Poppe called, her heart beating strongly. The girl followed in a dream.

'Quickly, quickly, "Sad Eyes"!' Poppe urged.

Poppe's heart was pounding when she reached the door, but no one challenged her. They were outside.

'Run!' Poppe shouted.

In the shadows opposite, the Gothic guard was watching. First he saw two girls running; the ones he had been told to guard. Then another figure followed, a man of slender build. With a cat's stealth, the Goth crossed the narrow way and came up close behind. The man was grasping a knife. The Goth closed in and, swinging with his short lance, felled him with a single blow. Hearing the sound, the girl stopped, but Poppe urged her on.

The guard used his foot to push his fallen victim over. The blow, it seemed, had caught him on the mouth, but he was still breathing. The Goth grunted. A mean face, he thought. One of the arms was odd and wizened. The guard shrugged, straightened up and walked away to join the others.

OOO

# CHAPTER TWENTY FOUR

# St. Sabina

Life was not easy at Sublaqueum. Sometimes they were short of food, but just as they were getting desperate a gift of produce would arrive. And so they lived, trusting that their needs would be fulfilled. To Martin, the mode of life was similar to his past, for the Hermit of the Rocks had lived that way.

The reputation of his new master had spread far and wide, and tales of the miraculous were common. Some grew fantastic in the minds of simple folk, shading the clear, unsullied power of faith with the gaudy colours of the supernatural; because of this a number called him Antichrist, an enemy of the Church, trading in deception. A local priest, mad with jealousy, had denounced the small community to his Bishop, and he, sceptical of the hermit monks, was asking questions.

It was necessary to answer such enquiries, for Church law required it. In fact, the council of Chalcedon had decreed that all monastic settlements should have a Bishop's care; a sensible precaution to curb the growth of error and corruption. This Martin understood, though he found the acrimony levelled at his master impossible to comprehend. Father Benedict was a good man who worked at all times to promote the good. How could men inform against him?

'Men are hardly men when ruled by bitterness and hate,' an old monk said in answer to his questions, yet Martin remained puzzled.

A reply to the Bishop's questions was ready and required a messenger. For this Brother Maurus was selected, with Martin as companion. A short journey, as the Bishop was at Tibur.

The Bishop was not at Tibur as expected, and the priest there told them he had gone to Rome, though he was unsure of the address.

'Our Abbot asked that we deliver his letter to the Bishop personally; will he be long?' Brother Maurus asked.

'Could be,' the priest answered coldly, while eyeing the monk and his young companion closely. Experience had made him cautious of the monk's habit, as such clothing did not always cover holiness.

'Who is your Abbot?' he asked.

'Father Benedict.'

'Ah, the man who would regulate the solitary life,' the priest returned with urbane cynicism. He was a tall man, too tall for his thin body. 'I hope that he succeeds, for he failed at Vicovarus. They even tried to poison him,' he added carelessly. 'Try the church of Sabina on the Aventine,' he concluded bluntly.

Without delay, Brother Maurus and Martin set out for Rome and after a mile or so they got a lift from a passing farm cart.

The sun was warm and the freshness of the spring exhilarating. Yet Martin was depressed, for what the priest had said had troubled him.

'Why would they try to poison Father Benedict?' he questioned.

'These are difficult times, my son,' Brother Maurus answered quietly. 'The Devil has many servants.'

'But they were monks!'

'Passion ruled them, Martin. True monks put the Christ before all else.'

'I still don't understand.'

'You will, my son,' Brother Maurus said indulgently. He looked at Martin. The wisp of hair growing on his young companion's upper lip was getting longer. The boy was growing up, with all the youthful pressures of his age.

'Stop brooding, Martin,' he said brightly, his smile encouraging and warm. 'Enjoy the Lord's creation.'

'Thank you, Brother Maurus,' the youth responded dutifully, but his sadness still persisted.

OOO

On coming to, Narco struggled to his feet and automatically his good hand sought the throbbing pain on the right side of his face. Warm blood seeped between his fingers as he felt his broken teeth. They had deeply cut his cheek and already he could feel the swelling.

Like any other wounded creature he instinctively sought a refuge and, dazed with shock and pain, he rushed through the servants' entrance, down the corridor and across the kitchen. He charged on, heedless of anything to his left or right. His head held low, he continued on, racing down the colonnade of the inner courtyard to the widow's quarters. Gently he opened the door, but his movements stopped, frozen, as it were, by what he saw before him. Rufus was with his mistress and there was little doubt about their intimacy.

Soundlessly he closed the door, all the while blood dripping from his mouth; but he did not notice, for a bitterness, intense and all-pervading, had possessed him.

White-knuckled, he held his knife in readiness, the passion of his rage a pillar standing firm against his maddening pain.

The door opened. It was Rufus.

Narco leaped, catlike, his knife flashing and Rufus, caught unawares, failed to ward him off. The knife went home.

With headlong haste, Narco fled the scene. Servants in the path were knocked aside. A blind force drove him on and no one thought to stop him. Back through the kitchen, down the long corridor, and then, at last ,the street. Narco had escaped.

OOO

Cyprian sat alone in his library, sipping wine and deep in thought. There was much to think about and much to make him squirm, not least his own stupidity. He had been silly to think that he could keep the whole thing quiet. Indeed, he had been much too clever and instead of earning the gratitude of Valerius and his friends, he had excited their suspicion. He had panicked, though at the time he felt that he had acted prudently. He should have taken "Sad Eyes" to the old boy Symmachus and said his mother had befriended her. Yet the question would have surfaced, 'Where did you find her?' He conjured a direct reply – 'My idiot brother, sir, the one who helped to ruin Valerius, brought her in!'

Perhaps, when all was said, he had been prudent. He had kept his distance. After all, the girl was in his mother's kitchen, and what had he to do with kitchens? He would play it just like that and keep himself apart.

The noise outside was getting louder and his mother's frantic mood was reaching a crescendo. Cyprian suspected she was blotting out a rare emergence of her conscience, for the current trouble was the product of her own desires.

Rufus would survive his jab; he was tougher than an ox and, thank the Lord, there would be no more Narco. He would never dare to show his face again.

Slowly his mind turned to contemplate the weeks to follow. He was a good lawyer, with a reputation for presenting cases well. But Cyprian was impatient and despaired of getting anywhere in Rome while Symmachus and Boethius dominated things. Ravenna was the place. The King was there and real power lay with him.

'Yes,' he said aloud. He would go to Ravenna and, if fortune smiled, place himself within the circle of the King's advisors. He had been wise to learn the Gothic tongue.

There would be women there, he thought. They were always buzzing round the court. And Poppe; he liked the little wide-eyed girl; even so, it was time for change. It never occurred to him that Poppe herself might have tired of her Lord Cyprian.

Without ceremony the door swung open. It was his mother.

'Your little sweet-faced innocent is mixed up in all this,' she burst out.

'Poppe?'

'Yes! Poppe! Her basket was sitting on the kitchen table. One of the servants recognised it. She must be punished!'

'Mother, Poppe is the servant of Symmachus – I've told you that repeatedly.'

'So you're going to sit there and do nothing!' she shouted in exasperation.

'Exactly, Mother,'

She looked at him, her fury boiling.

'Mother, if Poppe helped the girl escape she was doing us a favour.'

'And what of Narco? Does he go free as well?' she retorted angrily.

'Do you want the case made public? Remember, Narco is a rat, and cunning, too!'

'Oh!' she reacted, speechless with frustration.

Suddenly Cyprian noticed that his mother was dressed soberly, as if for church.

'What's all the black lace for?' he asked.

'I'm going to church.'

'What for?'

'To pray for Rufus.'

'Pray! At this time of night!' Cyprian's face showed disbelief. 'Do I detect a troubled conscience?' The beginning of a smile hovered at the corner of his mouth.

'Cyprian, that's enough,' she said sharply.

He shrugged. 'All right, Mother, but it's late. The Lord God may prefer a morning call.'

'That's blasphemy!'

'Think of something original. To breathe in Rome today is blasphemous.'

She stumped indignantly to the door and turned to face her son again.

'I suppose you haven't bothered to visit Rufus!' she blazed.

'Rufus is a Tuscan ox. He'll live to be a hundred. Go to church, Mother,' he returned, affecting weary tolerance.

'You should come with me.'

'Me!' he exploded.

'Please, Cyprian. I don't like going alone.'

'You have the servants.'

'It's not the same,' she said, her voice full of a mother's pleading.

'Oh, all right,' he said with resignation. 'What's this?' he added sharply, as a servant entered with a letter. 'The Senate never sleeps,' he muttered as he broke the seal.

'Damn!' he exclaimed angrily. 'Damn!'

'What is it?'

'Boethius and his stupid law committee. They're going to review the Valerius case.'

'But, son, you told me that the case was documented properly.'

'Boethius is as sharp as a needle. He'll find something, and if he questions that idiot brother of mine, who knows what will happen? Damn! I'll have to stay in Rome while this is on. Damn Boethius and his principles!'

'I'm sure you could come to some compromise,' she suggested quietly.

'Compromise!' Cyprian burst out. 'He doesn't know the meaning of the word. It's truth he follows, like a dog sniffing out a rabbit!'

'It's awkward,then.'

'That's the understatement of the year. Are you still intent on this church business?'

'Yes,' she said firmly.

'Well, Mother, take my advice and pray for Opilio. That "sweet boy", as you call him, can't discriminate fraud from fact.'

OOO

Martin sat cross-legged on the cold stone floor of the church. He was waiting for Brother Maurus, who had gone to seek the Bishop. It was the third time he had tried and it was clear to Martin that the good man's patience was wearing thin.

He sat close to one of the pillars where he could see the altar with the Blessed Presence and the candles fluttering on each side.

It was late and the church was almost empty, yet there always seemed to be some movement. From time to time loud whisperings persisted. Then there were footsteps and the whisperings would fade, but in general Martin's perception was dull, for the sense of sadness and depression that had afflicted him since leaving Tibur still persisted.

Martin did his best to remember the injunctions of the community. It made little difference. Indeed, if anything, it was getting worse. What was happening to him? He had never felt like this before. All, everything he looked upon, was meaningless.

He heard the swish of clothes and turned his head. A rich-looking lady was approaching, darkly dressed and with a veil. Accompanying her was an equally rich-looking young man who smiled a greeting to any who were close. The man was clean-shaven, not unlike those statues he had seen. Servants walked behind, carrying cushions. Martin was fascinated, his depression forgotten.

The servants placed the cushions before the altar and the two rich people kneeled in prayer. Martin watched. The woman's form attracted him. She stood up, her worship completed, and began to walk towards him. Suddenly she threw her veil back. She had a mother's age, but still retained her beauty.

'What an open face,' she exclaimed to her companion, and taking a cushion from one of the servants, she handed it to Martin.

'Here, my son, take this. The floor is cold,' she said softly.

Martin stood up. He was just about her height.

'Thank you, ma'am,' he stammered.

At that moment Brother Maurus blustered in upon the scene, his irritation undisguised. Reluctantly Martin turned towards him.

'He won't see us until the morning and there's no room in the church house – too full of painted women,' he muttered inaudibly. 'The Devil is abroad, my son. Let us go from here!' He nodded briefly at the lady as he turned.

'You could rest at our villa,' the lady said silkily.

'Mother!' her companion reacted with annoyance.

'Oh, forgive me. This is my son,' she said, her gaze fixed on Martin's face. 'You can rest with us, and in the morning you can see your friend.' Her smile washed over Brother Maurus.

The monk hesitated, thinking of the many prohibitions of the solitary life, but the journey to Rome was a special duty. They were in the world.

'God has sent you to us in our need,' he said simply. 'We accept with thanks.'

It was only a short walk to the lady's villa.

'Cyprian, my son, please show our friend to his room. You will find it isolated from the rest of the villa. You'll not be disturbed.' The lady spoke softly. 'Now, if you approve, I should like to show your young friend the bust of an ancient ancestor – the likeness to his fine looks is quite remarkable.'

'Mother,' Cyprian interjected, 'it is not proper that the young man be separated from his superior.' The look Cyprian gave his mother was not complimentary.

'My son, it will only take a moment. The likeness,' she added sweetly to the monk, 'is astonishing.'

Brother Maurus smiled approval. How could he offend such charm?

The mother of Cyprian could not help herself. She had fed desire too long.

'Come, my son,' she said softly, leading Martin to the inner courtyard and talking quietly all the way. Her clothes rustled as she walked and he followed her meekly, mesmerised by her woman's form. With a flowing grace she glided to her rooms, closing the door noiselessly and deftly fastening the bolt.

The lamps shed a soft light and her face shone warmly. She was an angel. He was on fire, and tears came to his eyes.

'What is wrong, my son?' Her voice was a caress.

'You are a lovely lady.'

'Oh, my poor boy.' She meant it.

She drew him gently to her and her warmth and perfume overpowered him. Then his awakening adolescence had its way.

ooo

Brother Maurus tried to repeat the night office, but sleep defeated him. It had been a long, hard day. When he awoke it was close to morning and he was alone, but he had no misgivings. Martin would be in church, for the youth's measure of sleep was small.

As he expected, he found Martin before the altar. Something was wrong, however; even at a distance he could see it. In fact, he found the youth in great distress. Full of concern, the monk knelt down beside his young companion.

'My son,' he said gently.

At once a tear-stained face turned towards him.

'I have sinned terribly, and I still want to go back to her!'

With a shock, Brother Maurus knew exactly what had happened and immediately blamed himself. He should never have accepted the invitation, even though he had received the offer in a church – this very church.

'I am unworthy of Sublaqueum,' Martin said miserably. 'I have stained the community.'

'The spirit is never stained, beloved Martin. Clouds may spread across the sun, but it is always there.'

Martin looked up.

'You should be angry with me, Brother Maurus. I have ...'

'Martin, what are those blotches on your face and arms?' Maurus interjected.

'I threw myself on a bed of stinging nettles to blot out the desire.'

'Our blessed master did the same when he was tempted. This is God's work!'

'Father Benedict did the same?'

'Thorns, it may have been, but that's a detail – my son, the Lord has blessed you with the same resolve.'

'The temptation is still strong.'

'And so are you. Rise, Martin. We'll deliver the letter and then we will be free to tread the road to Sublaqueum – beloved Sublaqueum.'

ooo

# CHAPTER TWENTY FIVE

# INTRUDERS

Valerius was overjoyed to see his daughter running towards him, but his joy soon turned to anguish when she stood stock-still.

'Drusilla, my daughter,' he said, holding out his hands.

She stepped back, almost fearful, grasping Poppe's hand.

'It's all right, "Sad Eyes",' Poppe whispered.

'Don't call her that!' Valerius snapped, but the hurt on Poppe's face prompted his immediate apology.

'It's the only name she knows, my lord,' Poppe said defensively.

'I know, I know.'

Valerius stood before his daughter, hesitant, not knowing what to do, and it was Tullus who broke the spell.

'We need to get away from here,' he muttered tensely.

Once on their way, Poppe was showered with questions. How did she do it? Why had no one stopped her? and so on. Poppe soon told her simple story and, in turn, the Gothic guard who felled the man was questioned by Ufilias, his words relayed to Tullus.

'Narco appears like clipped coinage,' Tullus growled.

The daughter of Valerius walked arm-in-arm with Poppe, and her father followed, his emotions in a violent mix. He was elated at finding Drusilla yet anguished by her state. Her dull, uncomprehending look haunted him. Would she always be like this? Dear God, no! But now, what would they do tonight? Where would they stay? His mind raced, conjuring difficulty. It was his failing.

He was concerned for Poppe also. She had left her basket in Cyprian's villa and just a little thought would link her with his daughter. Would Cyprian be vindictive? Again, he was concerned at implicating Symmachus. He beckoned Tullus.

Tullus listened to his friend's concerns and as he did the greyness sparked by Narco's name began to lift.

'Poppe will have to join us,' he said easily, 'not least because your daughter needs her. And I doubt if Symmachus will be overly concerned by any of the points you've mentioned. In any case we can make the journey to Thulwin's villa tonight. There's a full moon. We have the Gothic guards and we only need a cart.'

Valerius nodded. Why could he not think decisively like that? He had forgotten that his years of awful hardship were still close.

In the event the Senator's response to the evening's news was enthusiastic. He was optimistic that the stunned state of Drusilla would not last, more than happy to release Poppe and to lend his friends a cart and horses.

'I have more servants than I need by far,' he chuckled, 'for my daughter Rusticiana cannot turn a destitute away – my son-in-law has the same problem!'

Before they left, Tullus excused himself, hoping to steal a look at his baby daughter, who would be sleeping, no doubt. So Symmachus and Valerius were left alone.

Both men were tall, but the impressions they gave were wholly different. Symmachus was rugged, like a pioneer of the old Republican days, while Valerius had the studious look of the academic. Yet the two men had a natural affinity.

'Boethius has expressed the hope that you and Tullus might join his translation sessions. I suspect you would like that.'

'I would,' Valerius replied emphatically.

'I also suspect you speak Greek fluently – one of the fading few who were educated in the East.'

Valerius nodded.

'I thought so. Well, come next Thursday if you can. By the way, where's your daughter?'

'She's with Poppe; getting ready for the journey to Fidenae, I expect.'

'Take heart, my friend. I'm sure she will recover. You should have stayed the night and journeyed in the morning.'

'After what happened at Cyprian's villa we felt it might embarrass you.'

'Embarrass me! – It's the house of Cyprian that should feel embarrassment. The question is, how did your daughter get there? Certainly not Cyprian's doing, he's too astute. And his wanton mother, Julia? No – but someone put your daughter in her care. She's known to be kind to the unfortunate. That's her saving grace.'

ooo

Tullus took the reins and Valerius sat beside him. Poppe and Drusilla were behind, leaning on the backrest of their seat, and by the time they reached Fidenae both were practically asleep.

Next morning they went to church at Fidenae to receive the Holy
Sacrament and to offer thanks for Drusilla's deliverance. She was included
in the party but her world continued dull and dreamlike.

As they emerged from the church, the sun was hot. It was a beautiful
morning and the surrounding buildings were etched against a cloudless sky.
The small square before the church was crowded and included many in
religious orders.

Leisurely, Tullus and Valerius escorted Drusilla and Poppe to their
light, two-wheeled cart.

Suddenly Tullus froze.

'What is it?' Valerius questioned.

'Narco! – in the clothes of the cloister. His face twice the size, but I'd
recognise those pig-eyes anywhere.'

'Did he see you?'

'Oh, yes – he saw me. Why's he here? Why isn't the widow bathing his
wounds?'

'Maybe she's kicked him out?'

'Maybe – but why seek sanctuary?'

'We'll have to be cautious,' Valerius warned.

'Of Narco!' Tullus spat the words. 'It's he who needs to watch!'

They rode in silence behind the cart carrying Poppe and Drusilla,
Tullus wrapped in thought and Valerius watching his daughter, her body
swaying listlessly, her head bent forward. God! How long? How long?

The remedy was another shock, so it was said. That might be the
theory, but the practice was another matter. He continued watching, his
gaze including Poppe. Then, as if sensing his attention, Poppe turned
impulsively and smiled. What wide, beautiful eyes, he thought.

At his side Tullus rode engulfed in thought, oblivious to the
surrounding countryside.

'Where are the Romans now? Where are the men who won the
Empire?' he asked suddenly.

'Gone where we will go ere long!' Valerius quipped.

'Seriously, though – when I looked about the town this morning I saw
no one I could call a Roman. We're all pygmies. No wonder Rome was
sacked!'

'Rome died long before 410 when Alaric did his work,' Valerius
recounted. 'I remember grandfather growling how the clergy preached
doctrines of meekness while the invading hordes were plundering the
north. We lost the will to defend ourselves long ago and now we have the
Goths to do it for us.'

They turned off the main road and swung towards the villa.

'This is a new age, Marcus. The age of faith, of the church triumphant, with the monk's cowl its symbol.'

They drew their horses to a halt.

'Be careful, or you'll become a poet,' Tullus joked as he dismounted.

'Well, Horace did enjoy himself at times.'

OOO

Next day Tullus left for Thulwin's large estate near Verona and there he laboured at his usual unrelenting pace – his antidote to painful memory. After three weeks he returned to Fidenae to find things much as he had left them. Drusilla's condition was unchanged and for Valerius it was difficult to disguise his anguish. Even Poppe found it difficult to draw a smile from her Lord Valerius.

As they dined together the atmosphere grew heavy. Tullus was weary from his journey and they all retired early.

Tullus awoke suddenly. He had no idea how long he had been sleeping. All was quiet, yet he sensed that something had disturbed him. He lay listening. There was no sound, yet his heart was beating strongly and he felt uneasy. He rose, put on his tunic and stepped out into the inner courtyard. The first faint light of dawn was in the sky and here and there birds were heralding a new day, their song emphasising the stillness. He stood motionless, his senses alert, the mosaic path cold beneath his feet. Then he heard something unfamiliar, like a person gasping. He moved quickly to its source. The sound was coming from Drusilla's room. Again he stood listening, and again there was the gasping sound, but this time more distinct, and full of fear. Slowly he opened the door. The light was faint and it was difficult to see. He stood a moment, his eyes growing more accustomed to the gloom. He could make out three figures. Two had their backs to him. The third was Drusilla, standing with her back against the right-hand corner of the room. It was she who was making the gasping sound, like someone trying desperately to speak, and the man closest to her had his finger to his mouth, counselling quiet.

Tullus looked quickly to each side, hoping to find some object as a weapon. There was nothing. Noiselessly he approached the figure immediately in front. The figure turned and Tullus sank his fist deep in the intruder's stomach. He gasped and doubled up, exposing his neck to a powerful downward blow. At once he crumpled and lay prone.

The other intruder had a knife and it was pointed at Drusilla.

'Come closer, Marcus Tullus, and she gets it,' he said quietly.

'How do you know my name?' Tullus spat.

'Quiet, quiet!' The knife moved closer to Drusilla's face. 'My friend described you well, Marcus Tullus.'

'Narco!' Tullus reacted bitterly.

'Back, Marcus Tullus, back!' The knife went too close and pricked Drusilla's neck.

'Damn you!' Tullus hissed.

'Quiet.' The word was menacing. 'Come, my lovely, you are rich pickings. My friend was right,' he added, edging Drusilla towards the door.

On the floor his felled companion began to move. He pushed him with his foot.

'Get up!' he snapped. 'Move!'

The man rose painfully to his feet.

'No tricks, Marcus Tullus, or she will have her beauty marred – I mean it! His voice was sinisterly quiet.

Tullus nodded, but his attention was with something the intruder could not see. Drusilla was mouthing 'Marcus Tullus'. It was clearly so, and her head was bowed no longer in dull docility. Suddenly she wrenched herself from the grip of her unsuspecting captor and in an instant Tullus stood before her.

'Valerius! Guards!' he bellowed.

For a moment the intruder hesitated. Then he and his companion fled.

Tullus turned to Drusilla, who was sobbing in near-hysteria. Gently he put his arms about her.

'Calm, my dear, calm.'

Slowly she grew quiet, her tear-stained face looking up at him in the growing light of dawn.

'Marcus Tullus,' she whispered. 'Father told me a story when I was small about a Marcus Tullus.' She was limp in his arms.

'My dear, you really ought to rest.'

Then suddenly everyone, it seemed, was at the door. Valerius, Poppe, the household servants and the Gothic guards.

'Father!' Drusilla exclaimed in excited recognition.

'My darling daughter. Thank God a thousand times.'

OOO

# CASSIODORUS

Cyprian abandoned his immediate plan to visit Ravenna on account of the Senate committee hearing, which involved his brother Opilio. He was angry that his intent had been frustrated; angry, too, at his brother's ineptitude, but above all angry with Boethius for insisting on a public hearing. The whole matter could have been settled out of committee. Indeed, any normal senator would have agreed to such a course – but naturally, not Boethius.

What happened in the high-ceilinged, elaborate committee room was much as he expected. Boethius, as chairman, left the questioning to his panel. His summing-up, however, was masterly, and as an observer on the visitors' benches Cyprian had to admire his skill.

The magistrate who had authorised the confiscation of the last Valerian property was given a lecture listing his numerous infringements of the law. The unfortunate man's career was clearly at an end. Opilio, though, fared much better than Cyprian had dared to expect. Inexperience was no excuse for malpractice, Boethius told him. Of course he should act forcibly for his client, but he must not cover up a basic wrong. That was inexcusable. Opilio answered back and Boethius told him to be quiet, and again his stupid brother got off lightly.

In time the text of the hearing would reach the city's Praetorian Prefect. He, in turn, could suggest a retrial and the case could go before the King. Cyprian doubted it, however. The Praetorian Prefect had more sense.

Just a little bargaining at the start and it could have been settled quietly. Even Triguilla, for all his greed and arrogance, would have compromised, but not Boethius. Oh no, he had to subject everything to the theatre of a public hearing.

It was all right for him, sitting in his palace, supported by the Anician wealth. Boethius could afford his piety. And with all that fortune, why did he bother with these stupid hearings? What did he hope to gain? Plato's paradise? Cyprian did not understand Boethius.

OOO

Boethius and his father-in-law were seated in the library of the same Anicius palace conjured in the mind of Cyprian. It was early evening and sunlight was still dancing on the marble pillars spaced around the library. Symmachus had just arrived.

'Now that you have set me down with a cup of wine,' he said, 'you must tell me what happened at the committee hearing.'

'I've lived a week today. Most of the morning was spent with my kinsman Bishop Ennodius. Then John the Deacon joined me for a meal. Both focused on the same vexed subject; how to reconcile Rome's Pope and the Empire's Patriarch. Alas, it was little more than a wringing of hands. As for the hearing – predictable to a word. It was the meetings beforehand that revealed the most. Do you know, I was approached by four Senators, respected men who ought to have known better, to settle out of committee. The law and its integrity was brushed aside by facile pleas for compromise. '"Don't stir the Gothic pot,"' they said. '"Face reality." Indeed, I was supposed to feel sorry for the jackals who had robbed Valerius.'

'I'm not surprised,' Symmachus responded.

'No one seems to understand that once the law is breached and breached again it soon becomes a tool of tyranny. Anyway, we questioned the magistrate – a wretch in the pay of Triguilla and the so-called agent, young Opilio. He was stupefied with wine and not worth talking to.'

'Will there be a retrial?'

'That depends upon the Prefect, but I doubt it very much. He'll be pressured to settle out of court and there'll be the usual compromise.'

'What about Cyprian?'

'He was careful to distance himself. He's not a fool by any means. Father, to change the subject: I met our friend Cassiodorus on emerging from the hearing. He's here on a mission from Ravenna.'

'I'm told he's helping with the King's correspondence?'

Boethius smiled.

'Yes – making Theoderic sound like Cicero!'

'A laudable deception!'

'His manner is amusing – slow, priest-like and unassertive. Very much the public servant; his family's tradition. While we, sir, are relics of the senatorial past.'

'And toothless, like our Mother Senate!' Symmachus bemoaned.

'The Senate's still a check on tyranny.'

'Ah, Boethius – when the tyrant growls the Senate grovels – I've seen it all too often.'

'It's still a body where the law can be proclaimed. We must not let it go.'

Symmachus nodded.

'Well, Father, I've invited Cassiodorus here this evening. We can let him know the Senate's still alive! I hear noises outside. It sounds like Tullus and Valerius.'

OOO

It was the first time Tullus had visited the Anicius palace. Its scale and elegance impressed him, but as always when he met Boethius, it was the man himself that drew his full attention. Physically Boethius was on the heavy side, but it was his inner stature that impressed.

Unlike Valerius, Tullus enjoyed no instant enthusiasm for the suggested translation work. Yet he agreed to help, for he knew it meant the company of Boethius.

'The informal gathering is in honour of Cassiodorus, the King's Quaestor,' Boethius explained. 'It will be an excellent opportunity for you to meet him and our friends.'

In half an hour or so the gathering was complete, and although it included churchmen and city officials it was not an important one in the accepted sense. However, Tullus was quick to realise that the men about Boethius had a common quality. This was evident in their conversation, with its lack of platitude and self-assertion. Tullus felt at home amongst them.

'Marcus Tullus.'

Tullus turned towards the voice. It was Cassiodorus.

'At last I meet the man whose reputation speeds before him.'

'A generous fiction, sir,' Tullus returned.

'You are the friend of Thulwin. That's no fiction. Be not surprised, sir, if the King himself should honour you.' Cassiodorus spoke firmly, his tall figure bent forward in earnestness. He looked gaunt for a man in his late twenties.

Tullus did not respond to the prediction of royal favour, and the conversation moved to general topics. Cassiodorus was in Rome to check on the condition of the aqueducts, as reports had been received that water was being diverted illegally for private use. Also, special funds, set aside for public works, had been embezzled.

'How can this happen?' Tullus questioned.

'The sin of greed has many in its power.'

'What of Roman law?'

'It's usurped by bribery and intimidation.'

'Does no one stand against this?'

'Fear is potent, sir. But God will punish.'

Tullus resisted a surge of cynicism.

'God will punish' Cassiodorus repeated emphatically. 'There's much more than this life, Tullus.'

'But in this life fraud prospers. It's what the people see.'

Cassiodorus nodded ponderously.

'We forget the Church, Tullus. Few can ignore the withdrawal of the Sacrament!'

What about the Arians, what about corruption in the clergy? Tullus could have pressed his questions, but he held his peace. Cassiodorus, he observed, did not think in the same way as Boethius and Symmachus or his friend Valerius. His was a Christian world, a world of faith, and in some strange way he heralded the future.

'You're from Britain, I'm told,' Cassiodorus said, interrupting Tullus's reverie. 'What do you think of us? What do you see?'

'I've been struck by contrasts,' Tullus began. 'Contrasts in people's lives. A savage licence lives beside a vehement piety – at times in the same person! There is at once a wild indulgence living with an equal drive for penance. For example, the lives of the wealthy bishops contrast dramatically with the hardship of the hermit monk, as I have witnessed, say, at Sublaqueum.'

'Sublaqueum! I've heard of it. What is the name of their leader?'

'Benedict.'

'Yes. I believe he hopes to introduce a moderating rule to curb this very passion that you speak of. Sins are not forgiven in some crude bargain according to the harshness of our penance; yet our sinful souls need purging.'

'We seem to wallow in our sin at times,' Tullus interjected.

'Sir, our sins are black.' Cassiodorus was emphatic.

Both men turned as one to find that Boethius had been listening.

'I do believe, my friend, that Tullus has a point. Some monks love their guilt-soaked misery more than God. Their poor defenceless bodies feel their wrath, while all the time the serpent coils in their mind. Such men are deluded.'

'The body's instincts need to be subdued,' Cassiodorus insisted.

'By mind,' Boethius smiled.

Cassiodorus nodded.

'Men,' Boethius continued, 'who have long been idle in applying their minds, adopt rigid positions. Monks are not immune to this, Yet, on the

132

other hand, Christ is not known through splitting of hairs or great learning. Christ comes to the man he loves.'

'What is this love?' Tullus questioned.

'He who knows this love knows none to be a stranger, for no one is outside his love.'

With this, Boethius passed on to speak to Valerius and his father-in-law.

'He pauses, gives our conversation point and then moves on,' Tullus remarked with humour.

'That's Boethius. He has no equal that I know.'

OOO

# CHAPTER TWENTY SEVEN

# FIDENAE

Tullus and Valerius spoke little on the dim moonlit journey back to Fidenae. They were accompanied by only one of the Gothic bodyguards. The other two had remained at Fidenae as a guard for Poppe and Drusilla.

Even though the dark hours were half spent, Drusilla and Poppe were waiting to greet them.

Drusilla embraced her father and greeted Tullus with shy formality. Poppe did not push herself forward, but Valerius always acknowledged her. He liked Poppe. From the first time he had met her in Symmachus's library he had liked her. Poppe, for her part, adored her Lord Valerius and her wide eyes followed his every move.

Poppe was a servant enjoying unheard-of privileges in the company of people from the highest orders of society, and all because she had guessed that 'Sad Eyes' was the daughter of the Lord Valerius. And in Drusilla's dull and disconnected days Poppe was the one Drusilla knew and trusted. Yet withal, Poppe had a servant's status. But that had never been a barrier to the heart.

After they were served refreshments, Tullus was quick to leave the room.

'Is Marcus Tullus well, Father? He looks grey,' Drusilla commented.

'He mourns his wife, my dear. It's still just weeks ...'

'I know,' she nodded sleepily. 'May I retire, Father?'

'Of course, my daughter.'

Drusilla rose with lissom ease and glided from the room. Grace was in her every movement.

'Your daughter is very beautiful, my lord,' Poppe said softly.

'Yes, little Poppe, and highly intelligent.'

Valerius lay back on his couch and closed his eyes. He felt very tired.

'Beloved Drusilla, marriage will come too soon,' he said almost inaudibly, but Poppe heard.

'No, my lord! Please, not yet!'

'What do you mean, Poppe?'

She shook her head.

'I can't say, my lord,' she replied, her voice hesitant.

Valerius stood up, walked over to Poppe's couch and raised her small chin with his finger.

'What's the matter, Poppe?'

She looked at him, her eyes swimming.

'Oh, my lord!'

Suddenly she fled from the room.

Valerius shook his head. Why was she so upset? Well, it was late and everyone was tired. He yawned and slowly made his way to bed.

Poppe looked her cheerful self next day and all seemed as before. Indeed, the pattern of life changed little in the following months. Tullus continued to immerse himself in work, and once a week both he and Valerius journeyed to Rome, strengthening their connection with Boethius and Symmachus. Tullus, of course, never failed to see his baby daughter.

Thulwin came briefly in the autumn. He was impressed by Tullus's stewardship and said so plainly. The villa no longer looked neglected. Clean within and without, even the driveway from the Via Salaria had been weeded.. The cattle looked well fed, the vines, too, had been husbanded and, above all, the staff looked happy. His trust in Tullus had been more than justified.

He also brought good news. The King was anxious to reward the Roman from the north, and the Master of Offices had been instructed to trace the old Tullus estate in Tuscany. Marcus Tullus could barely believe his ears.

Thulwin had already heard of Arria's death and, when appropriate, he voiced his sympathy fully.

'Your wife,' he said to Tullus, 'will always occupy a special place in my memory. What a brave lady she was. I can still see her holding that rusty sword.'

Tullus nodded. He was much too moved to speak.

Later, when Thulwin was introduced to Valerius, he immediately acknowledged the wrongs that the Roman had suffered.

'Sir, you know the dark side of our race,' he said, while also hinting strongly that there would be compensation.

He was enraged when he learned about the kidnap attempt and, on the instant, promised a further two soldiers. This relieved Tullus considerably, for with only one guard on their weekly visits to Rome, security was merely token.

OOO

Late the following spring, Valerius received a grant of land and monetary compensation.

His first action was to visit Sublaqueum with gifts in recognition of their help and kindness in those days of desperation.

Accompanied by Tullus's original three-man bodyguard, he reached the small community after two days of travel, and was warmly welcomed. His gifts, they said, had come just as the jars of flour and oil were almost empty.

In the evening he dined with the Abbot and his monks. Martin, his boy's voice gone and with the beginnings of a beard, was placed beside him, and the subject of Tullus was prominent. News of Arria's death brought a respectful hush, but they rejoiced when they learned that Drusilla had been found, for they had watched the anguish of Valerius and had felt his pain.

It was the activities of Boethius and his father-in-law that focused the attention of their leader, Benedict. His questions were penetrating and his final comment was interesting.

'The path Boethius has taken is difficult and dangerous.'

Valerius waited for some elaboration, but none came. Strange, he thought, but he let his question rest. It was remarkable how similar Boethius and Benedict were, each displaying that same assurance and quiet authority.

Next day Valerius left at first light. By mutual consent he and Ufilias, the guard leader, decided not to break their journey at Tibur. Instead they continued on, skirting Rome towards the Via Salaria. Rome beyond the walls was not a pleasant place; it was getting dark and Valerius began to regret his decision. Thankfully they reached the Via Salaria without incident, aided by the faint light of a waxing moon.

On the journey's final stage his mind turned to Drusilla. Valerius was uneasy, for something was troubling her, though she would not admit to anything. Always reserved, despite a flashing sense of humour, her ways were stoical. Lately, though, this had hardened into isolation. Was this some long-delayed reaction to her abduction? Perhaps there was a simple explanation – the desire for company, for marriage and for Rome. Yet it did not seem to be the case, for when he had taken her to the city she had shown scant interest in the social life. He was still reflecting on his daughter's state when they reached the turning for the villa.

The guard on the night watch greeted them. No one had expected his return at this late hour and the household had retired, he said. Wearily Valerius dismounted. Then a faint flickering light appeared on the portico and moved towards him.

'My lord.' Poppe's soft voice sounded in the night air.

OOO

The following evening Valerius sat reading. Opposite him Poppe was busy sewing, and in the distance the faint sound of a flute was just audible. Somewhere in the low, rambling villa, Drusilla was practising, and as usual, Tullus was in his office. It was quiet.

'What are you reading, my lord?'

'The trial of Socrates.'

'I remember. You explained it to me. You were very patient.'

'You must have caught me in one of my better moods.'

She flushed perceptibly as he returned to his scroll.

The distant sound of the flute ceased. It grew very still and Valerius found he could not concentrate.

'Where did Drusilla find a flute? I meant to ask her.'

'From my Lady Rusticiana. Marcus Tullus brought it. Your daughter has never met my mistress.'

'I know. The few times we've been in Rome together we've missed her, but Drusilla seems to have little interest in going to the city.' He hesitated a moment before confiding. 'I'm worried about her, Poppe. I fear that her abduction has left its scar. As a little girl she had a strong sense of family and maybe she feels she has dishonoured the Valerii in some way; I don't know; but I do know that she often looks unhappy – and as for marriage, well, she seems hostile to the whole idea.'

'My lord, you do not know?' Poppe looked surprised.

'Know what, Poppe? Men are often blind to what's before them.'

'Your daughter is in love.'

After a moment's pause he ventured, 'It could only be Tullus.'

'Yes, my lord.'

'And he?'

'He is polite, but keeps himself aloof.'

'He still honours his wife's memory. They suffered much hardship and danger together and that is a powerful bonding. A man needs time, and my daughter will know this, but the pressures of nature are hard to bear.' He sighed.

'He is an honourable man.'

'Nothing would please me better, Poppe. Did I ever tell you the story of the first Marcus Tullus?'

'No, my lord.'

'Well then, that will be a tale for tomorrow evening.'

He dropped his gaze, his eyes following the pattern of the rug between their couches. Poppe was watching him. He knew it and he knew that it was time to speak and acknowledge their own growing relationship. Yet he hesitated.

'May I retire, my lord?' Poppe asked formally.

'Yes, Poppe.' His voice grated hatefully.

Glancing up, he saw how sad she looked, almost miserable, as she walked towards the door. He remained immobile. Then, intense and fine, an overwhelming affection rose within him.

'Poppe.'

She turned.

'I need to speak to you.'

She came slowly towards him.

'Give me your hands,' he commanded gently.

She was shaking.

'I'm twice your age, Poppe.'

'That doesn't matter, my lord.'

'It may one day.'

'No! my lord, no!'

'I'm very fond of you, my dear' he said simply.

'My lord, I love you.' She threw her arms about him. 'I love you so very much.'

As he had done once before, he held her head gently with his hands.

'I'm not wholly free yet, Poppe. While you are my daughter's companion and under the same roof ...'

'I know, my lord,' she interjected. 'It wouldn't be right.'

ooo

Three months later, during the summer, the Senator Boethius and his lady called briefly on their journey to Ravenna.

Boethius was interested in the system Tullus had evolved for managing the estate, but most of his time he spent talking to Drusilla on the subject of music. He appeared to enjoy his visit and apologised for the need to travel on so soon. He had little option, he said quietly, for Ravenna and its King were pressing hosts. His knowing smile was eloquent.

As he and Rusticiana were leaving he turned casually to Tullus.

'Your little daughter needs to see her father more than once a week.' He beckoned his wife. 'I'm sure baby Cornelia and her nurse could move to Fidenae.'

Rusticiana nodded her assent and Tullus was delighted. He had wanted to make the suggestion, but uncharacteristically he had hesitated, fearing that once Cornelia left the villa of Symmachus the fine-etched memory of his wife would fade, but now that the decision had been made he desired the move to happen instantly.

Boethius said no more on the subject, for it was inevitable that the beautiful daughter of Valerius would come to be Cornelia's guardian.

Boethius and his wife were well clear of the villa before the Senator spoke.

'My dear, I think you should see those young ladies from time to time.'

'You seem concerned.'

'Strong feelings are running unfulfilled, and likely to be for some time. Tullus will marry her. That's as near to certain as human actions are, but he will be slow to move. Again, Valerius will be restrained while his daughter and Poppe are under the same roof.'

'Poppe's devotion is beautiful,' Rusticiana said wistfully.

'He ought to marry her.'

Rusticiana turned to her husband in surprise.

'Poppe lived in your shadow for five years, my dear. She even speaks like you. She will not diminish him. Anyway, he needs someone to look after him, especially as he's prone to neglect his daily needs.'

'What about the Cyprian affair?'

'Poppe is attractive and a servant, Cyprian charming and high-born. Would you condemn her?'

Rusticiana shook her head and moved closer to her husband on the bench-seat of their cart.

'No detail escapes you, my lord Boethius,' she said affectionately.

OOO

The following year, 510AD, Boethius was made Consul without companion. That the ancient dual consulship had been vested in one person was a signal honour. What was more, it meant that both Theoderic and the Eastern Emperor had supported it, for the practice was to have one Consul each from the East and West.

The sole Consul was a symbol of the hope of East-West unity.

OOO

# CHAPTER TWENTY EIGHT

# CHANGE

Owing to the relentless activity of Tullus, Thulwin's estates were now working with an ordered smoothness. His treatment of staff was direct, for he left them in no doubt as to his attitude. Those who worked were rewarded and those known to be honest and reliable were given responsibility. The fraudulent were rooted out; Tullus wasted little sympathy on them. However, in his drive against corruption he did make bitter enemies. One Gothic sub-agent threatened to revenge himself, but Tullus did not flinch.

As time went on, the estates needed less and less supervision. This was especially so at Fidenae, where Valerius kept a watchful eye on things. In short, Tullus found himself with ample time for leisure. He saw much more of Cornelia, whose bouncing steps and lively ways amused him greatly, though shining in her face he also saw the image of her mother. Sometimes the picture was too vivid and at once loneliness would possess him.

One such experience happened in late autumn. Its effect lasted several days, but something else took place which brought Tullus face to face with feelings he was loth to recognise.

It happened one morning as he approached the open door of his daughter's room. Hearing Drusilla's voice he could not help admiring the soft, rich tone. Involuntarily he paused to listen. She was teaching Cornelia to count.

'Where is Papa?' Cornelia asked suddenly.

'He's busy, my little one.'

'I love my Papa.'

'We all love your Papa very much,' Drusilla said gently. 'Now, young lady, how many blocks have I got?'

Tullus turned quietly to retrace his steps so as not to pass the open door. He stopped. Why was he walking away? he asked himself with irritation. The question was irrelevant, a clumsy self-deception, for he knew the answer. The affection he had felt on hearing Drusilla talking to his daughter had shocked him, for it was the very same affection that arose with the memory of his wife.

Tullus spent that day on horseback inspecting the estate and it was early evening before he returned. At supper he felt drawn to Drusilla. He had always found her physically attractive and had shunned desire. He had held himself aloof and the memory of his wife had been a powerful ally. But now a much more powerful force was assailing his resolve.

Drusilla had a kind of inner maturity. How had he failed to notice this before? Her sensitive face could look cold, even austere, but when she smiled she shone. The light was tangible. And her voice was music, sheer music.

Tullus sat back on his couch, the usual visit to his office forgotten. He felt light and free, like a person rising from a deep, refreshing sleep.

The conversation flowed, unforced and easy and they talked until the hour was late but no one seemed to mind. Eventually Tullus did retire, followed soon after by Drusilla, thus leaving Poppe and Valerius on their own.

With youthful speed and spontaneity Poppe darted from her couch and curled up beside Valerius.

'Dear Poppe,' he said tenderly.

She nuzzled close.

'Something has happened between your daughter and Marcus Tullus,' she said softly.

'Yes! Even I noticed that.'

'He asked her a lot of questions.'

'Yes, and she answered well. Of course she's been studying the manuscripts of Boethius on music. He sent her copies. How are you enjoying your flute lessons?'

'My Lady Drusilla is very patient.'

'The sounds I hear are good, my Lady Poppea.'

She stiffened, her eyes wide and startled. He had never spoken to her like that before. What did he mean?

'Don't you like your new name?'

'My lord, I have no name or family.'

He put his arms gently round her.

'Well, my dear, sweet girl, you will have soon, I hope. There's no need for the past to be a prison – and my name is Lucius.'

She sat close to him, her head buried in his chest.

'I'm sorry, my lord ... it's just ... I don't want anything to change.'

'I know, my dear,' he said quietly.

That night Poppe slept little. She had never expected to be other than the mistress of her lord, and when and where that happened was outside her control. She was a servant. At times the waiting was frustrating, even painful, for she dearly loved her Lord Valerius. Yet she waited as a servant would. Now an unfamiliar world stretched out before her and it made her feel uneasy, if not fearful. Even so, she wanted the dream to come true, the dream of being the lady of her lord.

The next morning an invitation came from Rusticiana hoping that both Drusilla and Poppe might enjoy a visit to the Anicius palace. The same morning a troop of horse arrived from Ravenna carrying the King's order. Tullus was to present himself at court.

Marcus Tullus, with two bodyguards, was the first to leave. Hurriedly he had seen his daughter and Valerius, but Drusilla and Poppe had been dressing.

'I can't wait,' he had muttered impatiently. 'They take ages with their hair.'

Valerius excused his friend's behaviour. It was natural to be edgy at the prospect of an audience with the King. To a large extent this was true. There was another reason, though. Tullus was angry with himself, for the previous evening he had let his feelings play. How easily he had forgotten Arria.

On the road, however, he could think at leisure, and little time elapsed before regret replaced his irritation. Drusilla would be hurt, but it was too late. What had happened had happened.

Drusilla was hurt, though she kept it to herself and, like her father, she excused him. The prospect of meeting with Theoderic must have distracted Marcus. But the waiting was not easy for her. She knew her mind. There was no doubt and, with nature pressing, she found herself quite often at the limit of her self-control. Yet no one would have noticed. She hid her feelings well; a family trait that she had taken to her heart.

The morning was filled with preparations for the stay at the Anicius villa, and soon after midday she and Poppe, escorted by the three remaining guards, left for Rome. Only Valerius was resident at Fidenae. Tullus had suggested that one guard should be stationed at the villa but Valerius, still anxious for his daughter, decided against it. Anyway, there were at least three tough young men amongst the servants. They could act as guard.

Originally Valerius had planned to escort his daughter and Poppe, but the royal summons had changed that. There were special visitors expected, when only he could deputise. So Tullus's agent had journeyed in his place.

It was unusually mild for late autumn and both Drusilla and Poppe enjoyed their journey.

Drusilla never failed to be impressed by the powerful beauty of the ancient city. The aqueducts, the buildings and their scale filled her with wonder. How many of her ancestors had walked these very streets?

Rome was crowded, the clergy numerous, and here and there a nobleman, surrounded by his servants, hurried past. Near the corner of the Temple of Venus and Rome, one wild man was haranguing the unheeding mass. Repent!' he screamed. Few listened.

Suddenly Poppe grabbed Drusilla's arm.

'What is it, Poppe?'

'The Lord Cyprian,' she whispered.

Cyprian walked towards them, smiling affably.

'Welcome to Rome, ladies,' he called brightly.

'My lord,' Poppe said quietly.

'Sir, we have not been introduced.' Drusilla's rich voice was cool, and at once Poppe satisfied the formalities.

'I hope your visit here will be of generous length. The city needs some charm and colour in the winter months.'

'A gracious greeting, sir,' Drusilla returned unsmilingly.

'When beauty deigns to meet you in the street, how could it be otherwise? Indeed, I hope this fortune will with speed repeat itself.' He bowed. There was a wanton edge to his audacity, Drusilla thought.

She smiled briefly.

'You will excuse us, sir.'

Again he bowed. The driver flicked the reins and the cart jerked forward.

Poppe sat rigid, afraid of her emotions. She was still attracted. Her grip on Drusilla's arm grew tighter.

During the brief exchange with Cyprian, Drusilla had been well aware of Poppe's unease; and she knew the reason, for her father had hinted at it. Poppe's friend at the villa of Cyprian had been Cyprian himself.

'You know, my lady,' Poppe said with undisguised dejection.

Drusilla nodded.

'You must despise me.' Poppe's voice had fallen to a whisper.

'Despise you? Of course not! If I did it would be gross ingratitude; who was it that rescued me?'

'But I still have feelings for him.'

'He's likeable, Poppe, and his audacity has its attraction. Even knowing what I know, I could be lured but, my dear companion, when I think of Marcus Tullus, Cyprian disappears!'

Poppe's wide eyes gazed at Drusilla. It was the first time the daughter of Valerius had declared her love openly.

'I hope you find happiness, my lady.'

'Dear Poppe.'

They embraced.

'Poppe, please call me Drusilla.'

'Yes ...' was the hesitant answer. It was another step towards a new, unknown world.

The morning after their arrival at the Anicius palace, Poppe received a letter from Cyprian inviting her to his villa. The letter filled her with aversion, yet there remained an innocent desire not to offend him. After agonies, she showed the letter to Drusilla. Drusilla's reaction was immediate.

'Show it to our hostess, your old mistress.'

'The Lady Rusticiana,' Poppe responded uneasily. Nevertheless, she accepted the advice.

Rusticiana reacted angrily and Poppe took it to herself.

'I'm sorry, my lady.'

'I'm not angry with you, Poppe. It's Cyprian. He knows your circumstances, for in that wanton villa they know everybody's business. Don't be fooled by him. If you are, you'll end up as a joke between him and his shameless mother. It's ruthless. It would destroy you. With your permission, I'll show this letter to my father. He's due here for the midday meal.'

'Yes, my lady,' Poppe blurted out, her voice distorted by her stress.

The Senator Symmachus grunted disdainfully when he read the brief letter.

'Invite him for the afternoon and I'll remain here to receive him.'

'Will he come?' Rusticiana questioned.

'He'll be curious – he'll come. In any case we've made a private matter public and he'll be careful of his reputation.'

OOO

Julia, the mother of Cyprian, turned with her usual easy grace to greet her son.

'How did it go?' she asked, though with an uncharacteristic note of caution.

Cyprian did not answer immediately, for the tired look upon his mother's face had shocked him. She was getting old. The stark reality was plain to see.

'All right, Mother,' he said eventually.

'What do you mean – all right? Did you see the lissom Drusilla?'

'She's an icicle!'

'I'm told it's icebound in the winter north of Thrace, but in the summer months it's hot.'

'The earth is patient, Mother, but Cyprian's not.'

'Sit down, my son.'

He obeyed.

'And Poppe?' she questioned, after he had settled.

'Poppe was well watched, Mother. Rusticiana never left her side.'

'A servant!'

'Not any more.'

'Your Poppe has done well for herself – the ancient house of Valerius – she's not a fool.'

'Poppe's not like that,' Cyprian said sharply.

'Now, Cyprian, don't be stupid. There are plenty more Poppes.'

He made no answer.

'There's always the beautiful daughter of Valerius, and she's still at the Anicius palace,' his mother continued.

'Don't be silly, she's besotted by Tullus. Anyway, I value my career. Did you know that Tullus had been summoned to the Royal presence?'

'Your turn will come, my son.'

'It will, Mother, it will,' he said, his lips pressed tight.

'Tell me, Cyprian, what really went on at the Anicius palace.'

'Very little, Mother, other than a lecture I received from Symmachus.'

'About your perfumed pastimes, I suppose!'

'Symmachus would never mention that; he's much too clever. No, he accused me of spreading mischief.'

'What sort of mischief, son?'

'Oh, saying that he and Boethius were the leaders of the Eastern party in the Senate.'

'Are they?'

'Well ...' he drew the word out. 'let's say they're not against the east.'

'And you are for the Goths.'

'Exactly, Mother.

'Be careful, Cyprian.' Again there was that note of caution. 'Symmachus and his son-in-law are both good men.'

'Mother, what's come over you? Why this sudden rush of virtue?'

'Rufus was telling me ...'

'Rufus,' he interjected, not letting her finish. 'How is your tame ox?'

'He's good to me. We play dice in the evening. We call it Greens and Blues. I take the green and he takes the blue and we play at being serious.'

Cyprian looked sideways at his mother, but said nothing.
'It's company, Cyprian.'
'I know, Mother.'

OOO

# CHAPTER TWENTY NINE

# POPPE'S DREAM

Fidenae was the first of Thulwin's estates to benefit from Tullus's re-stocking programme. Fresh vineyards had been planted and the growing number of cattle was the subject of frequent speculation. Exaggerated stories grew with the telling – and so did envy.

Valerius first noticed a beast missing in the summer, and although there was no visible breach in the fencing, he assumed that the animal had somehow escaped, perhaps to the river or to some adjacent property where stray stock would be accepted quietly.

In early autumn there was a further loss and again the fencing seemed intact. Valerius was suspicious and with Tullus's agreement established a routine of inspection. There were no further losses, and all was well until the day after Tullus had been summoned to Ravenna, and when all the Gothic soldiery were absent. Then three cattle went missing.

The loss was discovered late in the afternoon. On this occasion the breach in the perimeter fence was visible; the particular section being a dry stone wall.

Valerius sat on his horse studying the breach. It was not the work of cattle, he was sure of that, for the pattern of the scattered stones was wrong. Suddenly it came to him; the wall dismantled, cattle stolen and the wall built up again. Of course, it would explain the earlier losses and, if he was right, the present criminals could be close, for the wall was yet to be built up. He knew he was in danger. There was a hiss. Something hit the horse's neck with force. The animal reared and in one frantic leap bolted through the breach.

Nearby, hidden by a clump of trees, three men roared with laughter. The leader was a Goth, the sub-agent Tullus had dismissed. The other two were Romans, Narco in the habit of the cloister and a brutish-looking man, hired simply for his strength.

'I know that horse,' the Goth said, laughing harshly. 'He'll not stop until he's halfway to Ravenna – now, get this wall built up.'

'Why? He knows,' Narco protested.

'Build it up!' the Goth screamed, his anger blazing out of all proportion.

Narco stood his ground and for a moment the two men glared at each other, each gripping his dagger, but as quickly as it flared, the Goth's anger subsided.

'That horse is a bad one, and I mean a *bad one*. I know him from the time I was sub-agent. It could do for Valerius!'

'Why build the wall, then?' Narco pressed.

'Why? Narco, has your brain withered with your arm!'

Narco's good hand tightened on his dagger, but he controlled himself.

'Tell me,' he snapped.

'If that bastard Roman breaks his neck, no one will know what happened. Remember, I cut the barb from the arrow.'

'If we don't get away from here, he'll come back and find us!'

The Goth's anger blazed again. He drew his dagger, his face white with fury.

'Build!' he bellowed, and at once the thick-set, brutish man obeyed, but Narco only watched.

'You've got one hand, Narco – use it!'

Narco made a token effort, but his resentment was at boiling point.

'We'll sell the cattle quickly and then lie low,' the Goth said confidently. Then he laughed again. He had struck another blow at Tullus; a double blow, he hoped, thinking of Valerius.

It began to rain heavily. It soaked his hair and beard and streamed down his face, but he did not seem to care.

ooo

Full of alarm, Poppe sat up in bed. It was dark. She was wide awake yet she could remember her dream vividly, indeed with frightening clarity. A man was lying on his face and trying desperately to move, and she knew it was her Lord Valerius.

'Oh, my lord, my lord,' she moaned.

In an instant she was on her feet.

'Wake up, Drusilla,' she said, shaking her resolutely. This was not the usual Poppe.

'What is it?' Drusilla's voice was sleepy.

'My lord your father is in trouble. I had an awful dream. He was lying on the ground. Oh, Drusilla, please get up!'

'Poppe, Poppe,' Drusilla said gently, 'it's only a dream.'

'No, Drusilla, no! I know it's true. We must leave at once. Please, Drusilla, please believe me.'

Poppe's features were not visible in the faint light coming from the night lamp, but Drusilla could see her small fists clenched and shaking with anxiety. Drusilla rose at once, for Poppe's conviction was persuasive.

It was Poppe who knocked at Rusticiana's door. In ordinary circumstances it would have been unthinkable to disturb her former mistress. Not now, though. Her Lord Valerius was in danger.

Quietly Rusticiana listened to Poppe's frantic plea.

'I must go immediately, my lady, I must!'

'It's the middle of the night, Poppe!'

'Torches, my lady!'

Rusticiana usually referred such matters to her husband or her father, but neither was present. She hesitated, her eyes searching Poppe's anxious face. Torches at night were dangerous, for they made the traveller an easy target. But how could she ignore Poppe's intense conviction? What if she were right?

'Every moment is vital,' Poppe pressed in desperation.

'We'll summon the guards,' Rusticiana said at last.

Impulsively Poppe embraced her.

Poppe, Drusilla and the agent, openly sceptical, reached Fidenae just before dawn, to find the place lit up by torches.

'There is something wrong,' Drusilla whispered.

The burly servant who had last seen Valerius listened to Poppe's words with troubled awe. How did she know? Was it the work of god or devil?

Drusilla's voice cut into this small, fearful world.

'Has the estate been thoroughly searched?' she asked.

'Yes, my lady, and the tenancies nearby,' the servant replied, his eyes still on Poppe. Maybe she was a witch.

'Where were the cattle? Where would my father have been?'

'At the northern part of the estate, my lady.'

'Get the cart, we'll go now!' The sound of command brooked no opposition.

It was Ufilias, the Gothic guard, who noticed the beaten ground where the stone wall had been built anew.

'Was this mended lately?' he asked the burly servant.

The servant shook his head.

'Pull the wall down,' Drusilla ordered, obeying her suspicions. Like her father, she suddenly knew the secret of the missing cattle.

The servant hesitated briefly, but Ufilias had already started.

They searched beyond the wall in a gradually widening arc. Poppe was growing frantic. Then she suddenly shouted, 'It's here, I feel it!'

Ufilias dismounted, studied the undulating ground and began to walk towards a row of cypress trees. Then his hand rose, beckoning the party.

Valerius was alive, but weakened by exposure. His heavy cloak had saved him.

Impulsively Poppe jumped from the cart onto the soft ground and, running to him, fell on her knees, oblivious of the mud.

'Oh, Lucius, my dear lord!' she said softly, her eyes full of tears.

OOO

# CHAPTER THIRTY

# THEODERIC

The reception hall at the palace was crowded. The few wooden benches were hopelessly inadequate and most stood, or sat cross-legged on the cold, uncovered floor.

Tullus watched and listened as he made his way to register. He had witnessed a similar scene in Constantinople when in the company of Justinian. There the dress had been more colourful, but the weary looks were just the same.

'This is the third day that I've been here,' complained the man in front of him. 'Who are you hoping to see?'

'The Master of Offices,' Tullus answered, which was true in part, but he felt it best to keep the King's name out of it.

'You'll be all right, my friend,' the man returned. 'It's the small fish that keep you waiting.'

The official at the desk looked briefly at Tullus's papers before escorting him to another room.

'Wait here, sir.' The voice was deferential.

Tullus was alone.

Almost at once refreshments were offered, and again Tullus noted the respectful manner. He drank sparingly, a sip from time to time, until it was announced the King would see him. A door opened and he found himself within a much more spacious room. Again he waited, his agitation growing. Then the double doors, flanked by Royal guardsmen, opened. Before him was the King.

Tullus stepped forward.

Theoderic's gaze was hard and unrelenting and Tullus felt his stomach tighten. His mouth was dry. He bowed.

'Marcus Tullus,' the King boomed loud in greeting. 'I can see the praise of Thulwin is well placed. It's true, you have a soldier's bearing.' The King's Latin did not flow too well, but it was adequate.

'Your Majesty is generous,' Tullus replied, quickly, feeling his response to be both weak and insubstantial. His mind raced to find apt words but he turned away from that. Such thinking was a fruitless waste. His weekly meetings with Boethius had made that plain. He straightened his shoulders.

151

'We are ever grateful for the warning that you gave our general Thulwin,' the King said slowly and with formal weight.

'My lord King, the opportunity was given; I did little.'

'That little, though, was vital,' Theoderic returned, while beckoning an attendant.

After instructing the official the King seemed more at ease.

'Tullus, it's time for my daily ride within the forest park. You may join me. I find my soldier's mind thinks better on a horse.'

How very like Thulwin, Tullus thought. The same dignity, the same reserve – and no doubt the same sudden anger. But his eyes were special – clear, totally alive and holding an enormous energy. The King was no ordinary man.

OOO

Theoderic sat upright on his powerful horse, an imposing figure in his gold and silver breastplate. His horse walked slowly, at one with his master's mood, and the royal bodyguard, ever watchful, kept a discreet distance. He was silent for some time before he spoke.

'The war with the Franks and the Burgundians continues,' he began, his gaze searching the tunnel of burnt grass and scrub between the trees.

'After the success of 507 – concerning which your information was vital – Thulwin returned the following year and inflicted further punishment. Recently our Duke Mamo crossed the Alps and once more hammered the Burgundians. Next spring and summer we'll complete the matter. Then the siege of Arelate will be lifted and the coastal regions will be ours. The turncoat Clovis and that shifty schemer Gundobad, Lord of the Burgundians, will no doubt try and thwart our plans, but they don't know when or where we'll act; come to think of it, neither do I! I only know we have the will and strength.'

Tullus listened, amazed at the King's frankness. Why was Theoderic telling him all this?

'With the coastal region in our hands,' the King continued, 'we will secure a safe passage to our Visigothic friends south of the Pyrenees. Here, alas, there is a civil war. I will explain; when you met Clovis in 507 he was on his way to confront the Visigoth Alaric.'

'Yes,' Tullus assented.

'As you know, Alaric paid with his life – a rash and unnecessary sacrifice. Anyway, he left his young son Amalaric as heir. A child king cannot wield a sword, so Gesalic, an illegitimate son, was chosen by some of the powerful nobles. This Gesalic has proven as weak and cowardly as his birth is base, but at present he has the support of Thrasamund, King of Carthage.'

The King looked across at Tullus and smiled.

'My sister is married to Thrasamund. We have good relations and I hope to dissuade them from supporting Gesalic. This would allow me to stand as guardian for Amalaric – after all, he is my grandson!'

Tullus looked at the King in amazement.

'Then, Sire, if all goes well, Hispania, Southern Gaul, Italy and parts of Dalmatia will be under your dominion!'

'That's the theory, Tullus, but we're far from matching the old Empire.'

'And the new Empire, my lord King, how will they react?'

'With distrust!' the King growled. 'Even so, we play the game of unity. A war between us would destroy us both.' Without thinking, Theoderic had switched to the Gothic tongue and Tullus, after a fashion, answered in kind.

'Good!' the King responded with enthusiasm. 'I see you know our language.'

'A little, Sire; I've been practising on Count Thulwin's guards.'

The King laughed and their sudden glances met.

'Since I began to tell the detail of our policy your face has been a mirror to your thought,' the King continued. 'Why am I telling you all this? you think. Why is the King revealing his secrets?'

Again the King laughed and Tullus joined in the humour of his royal host. The meeting was going remarkably well, yet Tullus remained cautious. It was prudent not to take the sovereign power for granted.

'Why is the King revealing his secrets?' Theoderic repeated. 'The answer is simple. I've told you none. All I've said is common gossip in the courts of Europe. We know each other's business well. Now the other question: Why am I telling you it all?'

The King reined hard, facing Tullus squarely.

'I'm flooded with information, Tullus. It comes to me from every angle. But it's what the King should hear! What the King would like to hear or what is thought the King would like to hear! – Tomorrow, Tullus, we'll talk about it tomorrow. Now it's time to let our horses stretch their legs. – A fine animal you've got there. What's its name?'

'Claudius, sir.'

'Ah, the ancient Emperor.'

The King slapped his own horse lightly and the powerful steed shot forward. Tullus sat watching.

The figure of Theoderic moved with natural grace in harmony with the rhythm of his horse. There was an unmistakable dignity about the person of the ageing monarch.

Tullus tapped gently with his heels and Claudius followed.

OOO

On his second audience Tullus was questioned thoroughly by the King.

Certain details caught Theoderic's attention, like the old monk in the burnt-out village and the dedicated life at Sublaqueum. Tullus held nothing back, but it was his relationship with Justinian that impressed the most. Then, the questioning over, they headed for the forest park.

The King praised Claudius again and eyed him closely.

'That's an intelligent animal, Tullus. He's got that certain look.'

They moved off at a walking pace, the King quiet and pensive. Suddenly he reined his horse.

'I'm flooded with information, Tullus, yet I suffer from a drought. There is the Army, the Senate, the ministers of the household and our Gothic peers. They all have their particular interests and their highly-prized opinions – and by all that's sacred, I forgot the Church, both Arian and Roman. God preserve us, they're as blind as bats. Tullus, I want the facts, without the colour of opinion. You will be my ears and eyes. Go where you think fit. I want to know the truth.'

Tullus sat immobilised by shock.

'My Lord King ...' was all he managed to say before Theoderic continued.

'The Emperor Anastasius is old and frail. Immediately I hear of any whisper that the Augustus is ill, I will need your presence in Byzantium. What you have said about the nephew of old Justin disturbs me. I shall also want you to journey south from the Pyrenees, but that can wait a while. Otherwise, travel where you will.'

The King leant forward in his saddle and the horse, knowing its master's will, surged forward, leaving Tullus well behind and reeling at the thought of his appointment.

OOO

# CHAPTER THIRTY ONE

# AUTHORITY

When Marcus Tullus rode south from Ravenna he had a mounted escort of eight Gothic soldiers. Six were Royal Guardsmen. The other two, of course, were Thulwin's men.

The King had insisted on adequate security. Tullus also carried documents giving him the Royal sanction. These were for Roman officialdom; and as a mark of authority to impress the Goths, he wore a medallion bearing the King's seal.

Tullus and his escort were an impressive sight, for six were Royal Guardsmen. But as they passed through the ancient town of Fidenae on their way to Thulwin's villa, the townsfolk stood silent in their doorways, even though they knew the agent Tullus to be fair and honest. They had seen too many soldiers march and counter-march, feeding on the people.

'God bless you, Marcus Tullus,' a woman called.

Tullus recognised her. A widow with three children whose rent he had reduced to a token size. He smiled and passed on, but the incident did not go unnoticed, especially by the captain' of the Royal Guardsmen, a man near fluent in the Latin tongue.

Outside the town it began to rain heavily. Tullus fastened his cloak about him, glad that the villa was close. He was tired.

Suddenly the guards in front reined their horses. Two men lay dead ahead of them, their bodies twisted in the desperation of a fatal struggle.

'What shall we do, sir?' the captain of the Royal Guardsmen asked.

Tullus did not answer and, seeing his pensive mood, the guardsman did not press his question.

'Well, Narco,' Tullus mouthed noiselessly, 'so this is the end.' He felt no elation, rather a weariness. There was something inevitable in the pattern of the stiffly set corpses. Narco's killer was the Gothic sub-agent, the one who had threatened revenge. One lifeless hand still gripped at Narco's tunic, while Narco's good hand was frozen rigid to the knife that had struck once, twice or maybe more before death came. Even with the heavy rain, the ground about was red.

Tullus sighed wearily, knowing well that Narco's death could still bring trouble. A Roman had killed a Goth, for which the Goths were not unknown to wreak revenge. That was bad enough, but Narco wore the habit of the cloister, and Roman outrage could easily be excited, especially when Narco's killer was a Goth well known for his vicious rent-collecting methods. Already wild stories could be circulating, for someone must have seen the gruesome sight; the bodies had been there at least a day. The apathy of officialdom was appalling.

'Untie the litter, we'll take them back to town,' he said at last.

Tullus looked at each of his escort slowly and deliberately.

'I knew these men,' he said authoritatively. 'They were both criminals. They lived viciously and they've died viciously.' His tone did not encourage questions.

After reporting to the town Prefect, Tullus returned along the Via Salaria. He sat upright on his horse, his features like a sculpture. He thought of Narco. His little cunning eyes would gleam no more. And brave, beloved Arria, with her witty ways – gone; and one day he himself. The road of life was short and full of trials. For what reason? For what reason? he questioned fiercely.

The rain was soaking through the layers of his clothing.

'Thank God,' he said aloud as they turned towards the villa.

There was only one figure standing in the shelter of the portico. It was Drusilla. Even in the distance her natural grace was evident. And there was little Cornelia clutching at her dress. Affection rose within him.

Tullus dismounted and bent low to match his daughter's height.

'You'll have to wait for your hug. I'm too wet, my dear,' he said quietly. Then he looked up and into the light of Drusilla's smile.

'Father has had an accident,' she said suddenly.

He stood up.

'What happened?' he asked abruptly.

Drusilla quickly described the events following Poppe's premonition.

'Was he badly injured?'

'His leg was fractured and a knee twisted. He's had a fever, but that is past, thanks be to God!'

'You've had the physician, I assume.'

'Yes, the Anician physician has been here three times.'

'Good. Can I see your father?'

'Of course.'

They walked off down the corridor at once with Cornelia skipping between them. Tullus was not unaware of the symbolism.

'You've increased your bodyguard, sir,' Drusilla remarked.

'Yes – the King thinks I'm worth protecting!'

'It was a successful audience, then?'

'Yes, and conducted mostly on horseback. Theoderic gets tired of royal formality.'

Outside her father's room Drusilla excused herself.

'The servants will need instructions,' she ventured lightly.

Tullus found Valerius wan and weak, but ready to make fun.

'I need riding lessons,' he joked. 'But tell me, how did you fare with Theoderic?'

'Very well,' Tullus replied. 'I've much to tell you, but later, when I've shed these rain-soaked clothes.'

Tullus smiled at Poppe, who was sitting near the bed.

'Poppea, your ministering angel, will soon have you restored.' It was Tullus's habit to use Poppe's formal name.

The wide dark eyes looked back at him and he sensed a new strength in their depth.

'Sir, there's someone from the town who wants to see you urgently,' Drusilla called through the doorway.

The man from Fidenae was agitated. The people were rioting, he said, and if no one stopped them they could burn the Arian people in their church.

'They're making Narco a martyr,' Tullus told Drusilla. 'It would make a cat laugh if it wasn't serious. Come, my friend,' he said to the messenger, 'we'll leave immediately.'

'Be careful, sir,' Drusilla called, but in his headlong haste he did not hear.

Fidenae was in turmoil when Tullus and his guard arrived. The small Gothic population had taken refuge in the Arian church and, incited by fanatics, the crowd was screaming wild abuse, while some were hurling torches.

The scene was ugly. The Royal Guardsmen drew their swords. One word from Tullus and a massacre was certain. Suddenly the shouting stopped, leaving in its place a fearful, eerie silence.

'Let the Church leaders present themselves immediately,' Tullus boomed, his voice echoing round the square.

Slowly the Gothic horsemen took their stand in line, facing outward from the Arian church. The crowd moved back. Tullus's heart was pounding, for he knew that one false move could still cause mayhem.

The Arian churchman was the first to show himself. He was full of praise and gratitude, for Tullus and his men, he said, had stopped a holocaust.

Tullus dismounted, not disguising his impatience as he waited for the leading Roman cleric to emerge from his basilica.

At last he came, a Deacon attended by assistant priests. He approached with studied ceremony, stopping well short of Tullus. The arrogance was blatant.

'I'm not accustomed to being ordered in this manner,' he called. The imperious, high-pitched sound goaded Tullus to the limit.

'And I, sir, am not accustomed to being called to quell a riot; nor is your Arian brother accustomed to the threat of being burned alive.' Tullus's rising anger was evident.

'You grossly exaggerate,' the Deacon returned, his voice again imperious.

'Where is your Bishop?' Tullus snapped.

'In Rome – and he will hear of this!'

'You're right, he will!'

'Insolence!' the Deacon snorted.

Tullus, whose initial fury had subsided, saw little point in public squabbling. Extracting the King's papers of authority, he stepped forward, holding them before the Deacon. The round, well-fed face began to pale.

'This is what you will do,' Tullus said quietly. 'You will call your people to the basilica and tell them that their precious Narco was a criminal. The habit of the cloister meant nothing to him. You will forbid further rioting. Is that clear?' Tullus moved closer. 'If you refuse,' he added softly, 'a minor parish awaits you in the south.'

'It will be done,' the Deacon replied, the tone conciliatory.

Tullus stepped back.

'The two men who have so aroused your passions were criminals,' Tullus called out loudly. 'Go home in peace.'

Obediently, if not meekly, the crowd dispersed.

Tullus left his original three-man bodyguard with the Arian priest and once more took the road. He felt exhausted, yet amazed, for the King's authority had given him enormous power; a power, though, that, if wrongly used, could well destroy him.

The light was beginning to fade when Tullus and his troop of soldiers reached the villa roadway. As before, Drusilla and his daughter were waiting on the portico. His heart warmed.

'Did you quell the trouble, sir?' Drusilla asked.

'I sincerely hope so. I "persuaded" the Deacon to preach tolerance.'

'He saw you! – I thought even God made an appointment!'

'He wasn't exactly eager, but after I threatened his purse, his attitude mellowed. I'll tell you over supper. First I must see to the guards. They should feel welcome.'

'You'll find the servants have prepared their quarters. They're basic, but with time ...'

'Drusilla,' he interrupted, 'after what they've had to live with on the road, it's luxury.'

When he had bathed, dressed and paid another visit to Valerius and Poppe, he joined Drusilla for supper.

First he joked about the pompous Deacon at Fidenae and then he talked at length about his meetings with Theoderic. She in turned described her brief stay at the Anicius palace and how she had encountered Cyprian. The conversation rarely lagged, but there was a subtle conversation too, especially in the few awkward silences.

'I'll be leaving soon for the south.' Tullus's words were almost brutal in their suddenness.

'I suppose ... it will be ... months,' she said. More waiting, she moaned inwardly.

'It won't be long,' he answered easily. 'It's prudent to act quickly when the King commands.'

'You're right, I'm sure ... I'm sorry,' she said shyly.

Their relationship was all but in the open. It needed just a word, but Tullus did not speak. Instead he rose, kissed Drusilla lightly on the cheek and took his leave.

Drusilla sat trance-like, her feelings a mixture of misery and elation. He had never been so open with her, but why was he silent? Why was he holding back? For a moment she felt angry – a brief indulgence. The poor man was exhausted, she conceded. He had had a trying day, to say the least. She sighed. It was time for bed, but how could she sleep?

ooo

CHAPTER THIRTY TWO

# NIGHTMARE

After a restless night, Tullus rose early to begin his preparations for the journey south. There was much to do about the estate, and distractions were unwelcome, but Tullus was distracted. Indeed, only a distant glimpse of Drusilla was enough to agitate his mind.

'The sooner I'm away from here the better,' he muttered to himself.

It was mid-morning when the servants reported a troop of Gothic soldiery approaching the villa. Another delay, he reacted irritably. Quickly, though, his thoughts grew cautious. Who were they? What did they want?

The troop halted and their leader, a man of some importance, introduced himself.

'My name is Triguilla.'

'I've heard of you, sir. What is your business?' Tullus asked abruptly.

'We're seeking one who caused two men to die and who disfigured my companion here.' Triguilla pointed to a soldier, his scar visible and ugly.

'Who is it?' Tullus asked coldly, expecting Triguilla to name one of the guards.

'The daughter of Valerius!' The sound was triumphant.

'That's her!' the soldier with the scar called out, pointing to Drusilla. She had heard the approaching horses and had come to investigate.

Tullus spun round. Drusilla's face was horror-struck.

'Oh, Marcus, it's the face in the nightmare!'

'Nightmare!' Tullus repeated.

She had kept the hateful vision to herself. Such was her stoic nature.

He put his arm round her gently and drew her to him. She was shaking wildly. Angrily he turned to Triguilla.

'These slanders will turn upon themselves. The law is not an ass!' he snapped.

'The law is slow, Tullus,' Triguilla smiled. 'Your mighty friend, the new-made consul, is well versed in this.'

'Consul!' Tullus interjected.

'Yes – sole consul – no partner for the great Boethius – I thought that you were well informed, Tullus.'

'Get off this estate!' Tullus's anger exploded.

160

'And who is going to make me, Roman? – you and Thulwin's tame sheep?!' Triguilla laughed loudly, a drunken laugh. Even by mid-morning they all were soaked in wine.

Tullus nodded to a servant.

'Go inside, my dear,' he whispered to Drusilla.

She obeyed at once, withdrawing into the shadows behind the portico, where she waited, her gaze fixed on his silhouette.

Tullus stood square and silent while Triguilla taunted him.

First one, then two and then the full complement of the Royal Guardsmen drew up before the portico.

'I know these men,' Triguilla reacted in amazement. 'They're from the King's bodyguard.'

Tullus stepped forward, his hand holding Theoderic's medallion.

'You recognise this, of course. Now go! Don't ask me to repeat myself.'

Triguilla threw back his head and laughed loudly.

'You win, Roman, you win! Forget I ever came.'

He slapped his horse's neck, pulling one rein hard. The creature slewed round violently and Triguilla twisted backwards in the saddle.

'A Roman wins,' he called defiantly, and then he laughed again.

Angrily Tullus watched them go. The last rider swayed and almost fell. He was a Roman.

Tullus spun round and Drusilla ran to him.

'That awful dream. It's true. I've seen the proof. It's so horrible, so hideous, Marcus. What did I do?'

'Defended yourself, no doubt. What fault is there in that?' His words were gentle.

'I can't stop shaking.'

'Come,' he said, 'we'll get you a warm shawl and something hot to drink.'

At supper Drusilla's distress was more evident. Her face was flushed. She looked feverish and Tullus was concerned that some hidden horror, suppressed by her amnesia, had risen to the surface. The scarred and brutal face had been the instrument.

'You're troubled, Drusilla,' he said directly.

'Yes,' she said, glad to speak, for she knew she needed help. 'The memory of the nightmare is so real – so thick and clinging – an awful depravity. I'm plagued by fears and new ones crowd upon me – am I condemned? Am I possessed? All the superstitions that I scorned before are now so real. What can I do? What can I do, Marcus?'

An overwhelming pity rose in Tullus, but he knew that pity would not help her. He stood up and moved towards her couch.

'You're shivering again,' he said.

'Yes – it comes and goes – oh, Marcus, what am I to do?'

Her distress and vulnerability affected Tullus deeply, for his instinct to protect was strong. He took her hand.

'Promise me, Drusilla, that you won't give way to panic. Do you hear me, Drusilla?'

'Yes, Marcus.'

'What is the pattern of your nightmare?'

'It never changes.' She shuddered. 'I can't, Marcus!'

'You can!' he pressed. 'Now tell me!'

'It's dark,' she began tentatively. 'There's only one lamp and the figures in the room are shadowy. There's laughter, an awful, harsh laughter. I'm struggling with a man – the man with the scar, only he wasn't disfigured then – suddenly there's blood across his cheek. He screams, he swears; I can see his eyes. They're horrible. He puts his hand up to his face and the blood seeps through his fingers. Then he comes – oh, Marcus, I can't!'

'Drusilla, what happens?' Tullus spoke sharply.

'I'm paralysed, I can't move; and then I wake up,' she said limply.

'I see.'

'What has happened, Marcus? The depravity is like a living force.'

'It's not your depravity, Drusilla.'

'But the man with the scar said I killed two people. That's awful, and I can't...'

'Do you think he spoke the truth? He's bestial, and if he did, what fault is there in fighting for your honour? You are a Valerius.'

'Yes, Marcus,' she said defensively, but he knew she still believed her fears.

'Stick to the facts, Drusilla – facts that you remember – the rest is imagination, or the accusations of a drunken brute!'

'But it's so difficult – it's so clinging!'

'Trust, Drusilla, trust in God, trust absolutely, for there is nothing outside a trust that's absolute. God is not the author of all things, but of good only. These are Plato's words. Trust in that good.'

'Yes,' she answered quietly. She was no stranger to the dialogues of Plato.

'Your eyes are almost as wide as Poppea's!'

A smile flickered in response.

He lifted her to her feet and filled their wine cups.

'Let's drink to the demise of nightmares.'

They drank.

'Now, Drusilla dear, it's time you rested.'

Affection welled in him but he embraced her with restraint.

'You must think I'm stupid,' she said shyly.

'On the contrary, Drusilla, very much the contrary.'

Tullus sat a long time on his own. There was much to decide. Drusilla's trouble could easily persist and she needed care, but who could provide it? Her father had weeks of recovery before him, and he himself could not delay his journey. Rusticiana was the obvious choice, even though the wife of the new year's consul would be busy. It had to be her. There was no one else. In the morning he would consult with Valerius and send a messenger. Assuming confirmation of his proposal, he would take Drusilla to the Anicius palace on the way south, when hopefully he would see Boethius.

ooo

Tullus did see Boethius and Symmachus as well. Their meeting was lengthy and Tullus relayed his news about Ravenna and his recent brush with Triguilla.

'Triguilla is a palace jackal hungry for a job and wealth,' Boethius responded. 'I've been close upon his heels of late.'

'Triguilla said one positive thing, sir – the sole consulship – congratulations!'

'An expensive honour, Tullus. My so-called beneficence is expected by the masses and I'll be forever presiding over things – the races, for instance. The tedium is considerable.'

'Don't believe him, Tullus,' Symmachus interjected. 'It excites his historical perspective!'

As the conversation ran on, Tullus was aware that both Senators were treating him as a confidant, an equal. The men before him stood like giants amongst their contemporaries, yet their behaviour was without pretension, ordinary in a way.

'The King has placed great trust in you,' Boethius said firmly.

'Even kings can be mistaken.'

'Nonsense, he has chosen well. And what is more, you have real power. In fact, more power than this new-made toothless consul. All I can do is repair aqueducts and institute enquiries, while you, if you show your seal, can make men rush to serve you.'

'It's the King's power, sir. A prison cell could be my lot with equal ease, for there's little doubt that I'll be watched.'

'Your prudence is far-seeing, Tullus. It will serve you well. Now I must be going. Another church meeting. John the Deacon has invited me, so I feel obliged to go, though I doubt if anything will happen that will herald common sense!'

Suddenly he was gone, leaving Tullus and Symmachus alone.

'How's my friend Valerius?' Symmachus asked.

'His fever's gone and he's eating well. His leg seems to be setting free of complication and of course he has Poppea to care for him.' Tullus shot the Senator a knowing look.

'I hear you use her proper name – commendable, Tullus. He's going to marry her. I've just given my permission.'

'I'm glad, but it comes as no surprise.'

'The ancient house of Valerius and an orphan servant – amazing,' Symmachus mused. 'There'll be gossip, that's inevitable, and the matrons of the city will be cruel, but that won't trouble Valerius. His family were patricians long before us all. Amazing, though in the old days it never would have been allowed. We were much more rigid then.'

'It was allowed,' Tullus interrupted.

'You're right ... there was a legend ... a Valerius married a freedwoman with the permission of the Emperor. Yes, by all the gods, you're right!'

Symmachus stood up and scanned the ornate library ceiling.

'Tullus.'

'Yes, sir.'

'If it's possible, try to discover what really happened to Drusilla. There may be someone near the old Valerian villa who knows. If there is a simple way to ease her mind it may as well be used.' Symmachus looked stern as he regarded Tullus, but he said no more.

OOO

# CHAPTER THIRTY THREE

# TRIGUILLA

Triguilla sat awkwardly in Cyprian's library, his blunt, bearded face contrasting with the lean, well-shaven features of his host.

Triguilla was listening carefully, for even though Cyprian was a Roman he respected his advice, and that advice he had requested.

Boethius had uncovered awkward facts and the King could well ask questions. Triguilla was concerned, for the damned Valerius case could easily get out of hand. And Valerius himself, that lanky reed, was friendly with the north-man Tullus, who in turn was Thulwin's confidant and now this Tullus had the King's ear also. But Triguilla kept his recent visit to Fidenae quiet. That prank had ended in a disaster the news of which could echo in Ravenna.

'Retreat, be obscure, encase your words with elaborate politeness and delay your answers – delay is your ally,' Cyprian was saying. 'And increase your favour with the King, for, in the end, it's only he can punish you.'

Cyprian paced the floor, turning occasionally to emphasise a point.

'Should you find some glory on the field of battle – anywhere – now *that* would help,' he said forcefully. 'The King respects a warrior and he would be more inclined to overlook your private indiscretions.'

Triguilla nodded. Cyprian's advice appealed to him. He grinned, his red face growing redder.

'You reason well, Cyprian,' he said, draining his wine cup. Four times Cyprian had filled the ornate vessel to capacity.

Cyprian continued to elaborate, but Triguilla had stopped listening, as a plan was growing in his mind. He would present his father's old shield to the King. It would be a rich and noble gift, for his father had fought beside his Lord Theoderic. Triguilla was pleased. The plan felt good and, when before the King, he would request some posting – honest employment for a restless sword.

He emerged from his deliberations when Cyprian introduced the subject of Opilio.

'Triguilla, Opilio is drinking too much. His mind's as sluggish as an ox-drawn cart. My mother is most concerned.'

Triguilla burst out laughing.

'No! no! he doesn't drink too much. His problem is, he can't drink! You Romans have no capacity. As it happens, I'm leaving for Ravenna and your brother won't be joining me. So you can dry him out.'

Triguilla stood up. He had no wish to speak about Opilio.

'You have advised me well,' he commended loudly.

He had needed good advice and he had got it. Even so, he had little use for Romans, and Cyprian was typical of the soft and useless breed. To Triguilla, people were expendable outside the circle of his Gothic tribe, and Romans were no exception. Their culture meant nothing to him. They were a conquered people and any thought of partnership in the governing of the towns had no place in his thinking.

Triguilla left abruptly and Cyprian went straight to his mother's rooms to report the news about Opilio. Instead, he found himself engulfed by the ageing woman's fury.

'Rufus has some slut in the kitchen as a mistress! I've just discovered it!'

'You have kindly informants. Who is she?'

'The youngest one!'

'She's a child. Rufus wouldn't touch her!'

'They say he has!'

'Mother, the kitchen's full of jealous cats. Rufus hasn't touched her. She's a child, for heaven's sake!'

'There are no innocents in Rome!' Julia insisted stubbornly.

'Not when you get near them. When I think of that boy from Sublaqueum ...'

'Cyprian,' she flared, 'that's enough.'

'So you're getting rid of Rufus,' he goaded.

'No! He stays. I need him. Anyway, when I've finished with his little slut...'

'Mother, if you so much as touch her, I'll forbid Rufus to see you. I'm deadly serious!'

'You can't do that!' she exploded.

'Can I not, Mother – now listen for once! If you touch this innocent, Rufus will never forgive you. Your Tuscan is built like an elephant and you know their reputation – they don't forget. Come to your senses, Mother, for once at least. Rufus has probably smiled at the little girl and someone's jealousy has done the rest. He's a simple, honest Tuscan. You're lucky that he shows you kindness.'

'You like him,' Julia said quietly, her rage abating.

'I trust him, and that's more than I can say about my stupid brother! I've just been speaking to that bull Triguilla and he told me he was leaving

166

for Ravenna, and without Opilio. So you'll have your "dear boy" to yourself. Dry him out, Mother. If not, he'll be in the family vault within the year.'

'Yes, yes. Now, Cyprian, how are you? I've heard of a new interest in your life, and as usual I'm the last to know.'

'Can you think of nothing else?'

'Cyprian!'

'Let's say Rusticiana picks her servants well.'

'Audacious,' she responded, her eyes gleaming. 'Which villa – Symmachus's or Boethius's?'

'Neither, Mother, but she used to be at the Anicius palace. Sometimes I think half the house servants in Rome have worked there or at the villa of Symmachus. You know Rusticiana's reputation – no tear-stained wanton is ever turned away.'

'Now, where is your little flower blossoming?'

'At the villa of Albinus.'

'Albinus! A worthy senator.'

'Perhaps,' Cyprian said dryly.

'Your pretty thing will have friends at her old place of work, of course.'

'Of course.'

'So discreet,' she purred. 'I'm told the daughter of Valerius is there, and alone. Well, Cyprian?' Her eyebrows lifted in mild enquiry.

'Don't be stupid, Mother. Any indiscretion would go straight to the Gothic overlord himself.'

'Well, at least you have another Poppe.'

'No, I haven't – and I'm tired of this endless obsession with dalliance.'

'We are angry, Cyprian!' The widow shifted her position amongst her cushions, but her gaze did not leave his face.

'And so were you, not long ago.'

'All right, all right.'

He had taken his little Poppe for granted, and now she was beyond his reach; indeed, everything at the Anicius palace was beyond his reach. Damn Boethius and his precious integrity! It did not occur to Cyprian that his foe was not Boethius but his own indiscipline. From his youth he had satisfied his whims with little caution, and the legacy of his licence had been utter selfishness. He was his mother's son.

'It's only wounded pride, Cyprian.' Instinctively Julia knew what her son was thinking. 'If you had Poppe back again you would soon be bored, as you were before.'

'Save your moralising for Rufus!' he snapped.

'Don't be nasty, Cyprian!'

'Well, don't provoke me.'

Feeling ruffled, she deliberately changed the subject.

'Will the sole consulship of Boethius help or hinder you?'

'Neither, Mother, the real power is in Ravenna.'

'Are you sure, Cyprian? The office of consul is as old as Rome.'

'What is a consul or an ex-consul when Theoderic can ignore them? The real power is where the sovereign is, and that's Ravenna.'

'But the office of consul is respected both here and in Constantinople.'

'It's politic for Theoderic and the Emperor to treat the consuls with some deference, but in real matters of policy they ignore them.'

'Why is Boethius the sole consul? Why not the usual two?'

'He's sympathetic to the Eastern problems and often makes conciliatory speeches in Church councils. In acknowledgement of that, I suppose, the East have not nominated their own man.'

'So that's why you alluded to a pro-Eastern group in the Senate, my clever son.'

'It's good opposition politics, Mother – nothing more.'

'Is that all, Cyprian? Why do you oppose Boethius? Why not join with him?'

'I'd lose all my friends! And my clients too! For when it comes to law he never compromises. Every stupid law the Senate ever made ... He makes things so damned awkward. If, like most of us, he turned a blind eye now and then, all would be well, but no! not he! It's principles, always principles. Damn his principles!'

'Principles, not men, Cyprian.'

'Mother, what's wrong with you? Don't tell me you support Boethius!'

'Well, my son ...'

'Mother, I distrust paragons of virtue.'

'Maybe he's a mirror to your fault and you resent it.'

'Don't be too clever, Mother!'

'Rufus says that Boethius is ...'

'What's Rufus got to do with it? What's he know?'

'Maybe more than ...'

'Mother, really!'

Suddenly Cyprian turned towards the door.

'By all the gods, the prodigal has returned! You smell like a wine-press, Opilio.'

'You are so witty, brother,' Opilio returned sarcastically. He was squat and broad, not at all like Cyprian.

'My dear boy – you look ill,' the widow reacted, rising from her couch. 'And you smell – you need the baths.' She pulled the bell-cord.

'So your drinking friend Triguilla has deserted you. Tell me, brother, did you ever meet his family?'

Opilio shook his head.

'As I thought. I'll wager that even Marcus Tullus hasn't met the wife and family of his great friend Thulwin. What am I trying to say, Opilio?'

'How should I know, wise one?' Opilio sneered.

'I'll talk to you when you're sober!' Cyprian spat.

There was a knock and Rufus entered and, after a few quick words from Julia, Opilio meekly followed the servant to the baths.

'The smell, Cyprian,' the widow said, reflecting her distaste.

'He's been living like a hog for weeks!'

'What were you trying to tell him?' Julia asked as she settled once more amongst her cushions.

'Simple, Mother. If you think you know the Goths, then think again!' He stood up.

'You're leaving so soon,' she pouted.

'A supper party with some friends. And, Mother – leave the little girl you railed about alone!'

'Cyprian, you said you trusted Rufus. That's good enough for me.'

'Mother, what's wrong with you? Your "moderation" worries me – remember, no tricks. I mean it!'

'Yes, yes, my son.'

OOO

169

# CHAPTER THIRTY FOUR

# THE STATUES OF THE GRACCHI

It was winter and the shortest day was not far distant. The worst time to travel, many said to Tullus. Even so, he was determined to respond promptly to the King's command. He was well provisioned, though; the laden pack-horses were evidence of that.

The first stage of his journey, from Rome to Tibur, was full of past associations that sparked his memory of Arria, but her image no longer jarred against his growing affection for the daughter of Valerius. Indeed, in some strange way they seemed to be as one.

Arria would have approved, he thought. She was supremely practical. And of course there was Cornelia. His little daughter adored Drusilla. That was plain to see.

Tullus was well aware that Drusilla's troubled state could be protracted, but was encouraged by the optimistic comments of Boethius. She had 'ample inner strength,' he said. Even so, Tullus knew she would not find it easy. Thank God the servants did not know. Their whispers, with their fearful looks, would have made things ten times worse.

They were approaching Tibur, the once fashionable retreat from the city's summer heat. Then, he guessed, the busy Post House would have catered for all tastes; now it was the Church that often served the traveller. There a man's possessions were considered safe, as the terror of damnation kept the thief at bay.

Tullus stopped at the Arian church, for he knew that it would please the royal guardsmen. The Arian fellowship was much in the minority and, in the manner of minorities, welcomed their fellow Arians with warmth. With Tullus they were generous to a fault. They appreciated his tolerance, for they knew he was a member of the Roman Church. Above all, they knew the gold medallion of their Lord Theoderic hung about his neck.

It was a chill winter morning when they set out for Sublaqueum, but the sun was shining and their pace was brisk.

Tullus's main reason for visiting the small community was the quest for information. The views of Father Benedict, he felt certain, would be simple and direct – and penetrating too. Tullus also hoped to find some clue that might unlock the secrets of Drusilla's nightmare. The estate that Valerius had last occupied was fairly close, and some detail, hitherto considered unimportant, might well be known to the monks. Then there was Martin. There was always Martin when he visited the community. How could he forget him?

After the horses had been fed and watered Tullus and Theodis, the leader of the escort, were invited to the Abbot's table. Martin, who was present, was quick to greet his friend.

'You look well, Marcus Tullus.'

'And you, Martin.'

'God keeps bringing us together,'

'It must be your doing,' Tullus quipped. 'Theodis, this is Brother Martin, the one who, as a boy, relayed the word that was to save Count Thulwin's army.'

Theodis was impressed.

The conversation continued lightly for a time, until Tullus felt it right to introduce the subject of his mission.

'What do people think? That is the question of a wise monarch,' was Benedict's response.

Tullus nodded, but he made it plain that he expected more.

'Look to the land, Tullus. See how it is used and how it is abused. The earth is given; it is the Lord's. We are but sons tilling the Father's fields. Job said, "Out of the earth comes bread." "The earth is full of thy riches," so the Psalmist says, but the sin of greed robs many of their due.'

Tullus was aware that all eyes were upon him and that a response was expected, but it was the Abbot who continued.

'I would expect you to be a student of history,' he said, looking directly at his guest. 'You will recall how the citizen soldiers, returning from the campaigns of the later Republic, found their land had been stolen by the powerful.'

'Yes – I do! That was the greed the Gracchi fought. Thank you, Father. You have given me a clear direction.'

Tullus bowed his head for a moment before proceeding.

'There is another matter concerning the daughter of our friend Valerius which presses strongly and I'm hoping you can help. The lady is greatly troubled by certain statements concerning her abduction.' He spoke slowly, choosing his words carefully. 'The small estate that Valerius last occupied is not far from here, and I wondered if any information, however vague, had chanced your way.'

Benedict's answer was immediate.

'Nothing, I'm afraid. We know Valerius well, and any news would have alerted us.'

'Well, it was an arrow in the dark, but worth a try.'

The conversation continued, and the more Tullus listened and watched the Abbot Benedict the more he was impressed. There was a quiet peace about his person that naturally made him the focus of attention. At one time when he smiled, Tullus actually felt it was a blessing. Not in any sentimental sense – no, not at all, yet a blessing deeply felt. Martin had chosen well.

The meal was drawing to a close when Brother James, an elderly monk, tentatively broke his silence.

'There was one occurrence, sir,' he began, 'but I hesitated to mention it because there appeared to be no connection with the situation you've described, other than the timing.'

'Any clue would help,' Tullus prompted.

The elderly monk turned to his Abbot.

'You will remember, Father – about three weeks before our noble guest arrived with his injured companion and Brother Martin – a broad-shouldered man, his back badly deformed, just managed to stagger here before he died. He had been terribly wounded and was so weak he couldn't even speak his name.'

'Yes, I remember,' the Abbot answered evenly.

'He was an ugly man, sir,' Brother James continued, now addressing Tullus, 'even grotesque, but he had strong arms. "Don't leave me, Father" was all he managed to whisper. He knew he was dying and he said no more. So I held this poor, misshapen creature. I know not how he had received his wounds, but it crossed my mind he was a brigand. Then I looked at him again and what I saw astonished me: a beauty glowing – like a light. The low cave where we were was filled with bliss. Even the memory of that hour still carries awe. Who was he? What way of life, what deed allowed such grace at death? He's buried here amongst us.'

The monk stopped suddenly, overcome by his own words. Then the Abbot quietly gave his benediction. The meal was over.

Martin was given dispensation to be with Tullus until he and the Gothic guards departed. So the friends walked together in the winter sun.

Martin had not grown much taller, but he had filled out both in face and body. His beard, still wispy, betrayed his youth but his voice had grown steady and mature.

'Where will you go from here?' he asked with his old directness.

'To Valerius's last estate near Aletrium. But how to get there is the problem.'

'Ask Brother Maurus – one of us could act as guide – but our mules are slow.'

'I'm well used to mules – you should know that!'

Impulsively Tullus stopped and faced Martin squarely.

'This is the life you want,' he said in the manner of a statement.

'Yes, Marcus Tullus.' The certainty in his voice was simple and direct.

OOO

All the enquiries that Tullus made at the town of Aletrium proved fruitless.

The former Valerius estate had changed hands twice since his friend was driven from his property. No servants remained who had known Valerius and his daughter. So the townsfolk said, but Tullus sensed a barrier of fear which was impenetrable.

The onward journey from Aletrium to Frusino was miserable. An icy wind cut at their faces. Tullus rode hunched against the cold, his thoughts depressed, for he had expected to find some clues about Drusilla's abduction. He continued his enquiries over the next two days in the towns of the Via Latina till, tired and defeated, he turned south. The King's work could be delayed no longer.

They did not stop until they reached Beneventum, the great cross-roads of southern Italy. Bent low against the driving sleet, they rode into the ancient town poised above the rivers far below. But Tullus and his men were much too weary to appreciate the grandeur of the setting or the marble splendour of Trajan's triumphal arch. Even the toughest of the guards craved a blazing fire and food.

There was a sizeable Arian community in the town and Tullus chose their church to seek accommodation. He was not disappointed. As at Tibur, the hospitality was unstinted.

They stayed two weeks and celebrated the festival of Christ's birth. Tullus met the town's officials and the Roman clergy but they told him nothing.

It was predictable that people would be cautious when they faced Theoderic's agent. Of course, some clamoured for redress. Tedious men with petty grievances, but Tullus felt that few came forward with complaints of any substance.

So this was what the King complained about, this same frustration – though no doubt for the monarch it was even more impossible.

Tullus tried the taverns but gave up in disgust. They were little more than dens of vice and, of course, he was a stranger.

Unexpectedly, his first lead came from an old, grey-haired priest at the Roman Basilica.

'Here am I – turned seventy – my pleasures are few and pain is frequent,' the priest said plainly. 'Why should I stay silent? I have no ambition, and death I often think of as a friend.'

Tullus urged him to continue.

'When the Goths came,' the old man responded, 'everyone expected the usual acts of pillage, but that did not happen. Theoderic's army was disciplined, even in their leisure hours. Some of their leaders, though, were greed personified and cheated many of their property.'

Tullus listened intently. This was drawing near the mark. He asked for names and got them, but there was little he could do other than inquire and warn. For as a Roman it was prudent for him to be deferential to the Gothic lords. Theoderic's seal and the presence of the royal guardsmen, however, proved a powerful influence. Indeed, by this they knew the northman Tullus had ready access to the King.

With Roman officialdom Tullus was direct. He was particularly angered by one agent, the servant of a pious Roman senator: a senator who had given two sons to the solitude of the monastic life. His donations to the Church were large but the grey-haired priest was bitter when he spoke of it.

'He forgets the misery of his tenants and his slaves. He comes briefly in the summer and for the rest his agent rules. God save us, his agent is a devil. Every last mite is extracted. Clap him in irons, Tullus!' the old priest said with venom.

Tullus smiled at the demonstration of priestly anger, for his grey-haired friend was anything but harsh.

He shook his head.

'I cannot touch him, father, but I can "advise"!'

The agent's visits to the church were regular and Tullus found it easy to confront him.

'There is no corruption on my lord's estates!' he reacted indignantly.

'Agreed,' Tullus snapped. 'Just starvation.'

'They accept the rent levels!' The agent was defiant.

'And if they don't?' Tullus pressed.

The agent blustered.

'May I give you some advice, sir,' Tullus said quietly, as doubt began to flood the agent's face. 'When questioned in the Senate your pious master will be shocked and there's little doubt that he will blame his well-dressed, wealthy agent for the whole affair. "Over-zealous," he will say. "I have replaced him." – Do you take my meaning, sir?'

The man paled.

'I think you do. I will expect some changes when I return this way. So far the matter remains between us.'

Next day Tullus and his bodyguard headed southward on the Via Appia. At Venusia they turned due south towards the toe of Italy where, close to Squillae, near the family estate of Cassiodorus, they halted. Then they moved north along the coast until they reached Tarentum. There they joined the Via Appia on its last short stretch to the great port of Brindisium. After Brindisium they came to Barium. It was over four months since they had left Rome. The longing to return was strong and, for Tullus, thoughts of his daughter and concern for Drusilla were never far away.

At Barium he rested for two days. Although weary, they had been fortunate in escaping serious illness. Tullus was careful with his men.

Throughout his journey Tullus found things much the same as in Beneventum. There were Gothic lords extending their estates by harassment, while others of their race conducted their affairs with Thulwin-like nobility.

Religious tolerance was official and Gothic arms were there to make it so, but beneath the surface calm there was hostility: the caged hostility of the dominant church towards the Arian heresy in their midst.

Tullus had avoided trouble with the Roman Church, except for one occasion when they failed to intervene to stop a witch-hunt. Tullus lost his temper, shouting that the ruling churchman's faith was little more than superstitious magic. The outburst did not help his standing with the clergy, but it much amused his escort.

Brigandage had been rife in certain parts, but Tullus and the guardsmen escort were a dangerous target for the criminal. Yet Theodis and his men were always careful, especially at potential ambush sites.

While in Barium Tullus's thoughts turned to the ravaged village where he and Martin had landed just two years before; and wondering if the old, bent monk was still alive, he decided on a visit. He found the old man huddled in the shack that was his home, but he was dead; not long, though. Tullus was greatly saddened. If only he had come a few days earlier.

They buried him in a round grave, for Tullus had refused to break his body. After repeating the few words of the burial service he remembered, Tullus walked alone to the dilapidated pier where he and Martin had first set foot in Italy. He felt something brush against his leg and, looking down, saw it was the old man's she-goat.

'Poor creature,' he muttered, bending down and patting the animal gently. 'Are you in need of milking?' He looked and shook his head.

Suddenly he started back towards the guard.

His escort was waiting in a semi-circle with their horses in readiness for departure. He was just about to mount when he saw the goat. She was standing like a dog, gazing up at him. Then the laughter of his guard exploded. They knew the goat would win.

They headed up the coast to Sipontum, where Tullus reported the monk's death. On the way the goat invariably led the column. A hardy creature, Tullus thought. At Sipontum he remembered how the old monk had complained of Gothic greed, and how his family's wealth had suffered. So he made enquiries and quickly learned the Gothic lord in question had died six months before – a hunting accident. Some suggested that a desperate tenant might have helped him on his way. His son, however, most maintained, acted like a saint, helping all the needy, whether Goth or Roman. Meanwhile, Tullus thought, an old, bent monk had died, uncared for and alone.

From Sipontum Tullus returned to Beneventum by way of Luceria and Accae. They were all exhausted and sick of endless travel; even so they rested one night only. The pull of Rome was strong.

Tullus checked on the behaviour of the 'pious' agent he had threatened and soon learned of his transformation.

'He has discovered compassion,' he grunted to his old friend, the grey-haired priest. 'I'd better tell him that his master will expect some rent!'

OOO

With most creatures, human or not, the way home is travelled quickly. Tullus and his escort were no exception, but the goat began to lag.

'Damned goat,' Tullus grumbled. Why had he brought her? And what was he going to do with her?

At the next town he bought a cheap farm cart and harnessed it to a pack-horse. From then on the goat rode like a monarch.

When at last they reached the old site of the Valerius villa, Tullus asked the guard to wait while he went on alone. The very substance of history, he thought as he scanned the crumbling structure. Some of the walls were still standing, but most of the brick had been plundered. He approached slowly, even reverently. Then he saw something move in the direction of the garden. He continued his slow approach. The garden was well tended. Strange, he thought, a square of order in the midst of such decay.

From behind the cypress trees a bent figure emerged, busily at work.

'Preparing for the spring, master?' Tullus called, his voice echoing in the morning air.

'You startled me, sir. I didn't hear you.'

'But this is not an old man's work. Have you help?'

'No. God took my boy.' The stooped posture grew more pronounced. 'This is for him.' Sad eyes turned towards the garden. 'And for my master.'

Tullus stood stock-still.

'Who is your master?' he asked gently.

'They robbed him and they dragged him off – and his lovely daughter – I have no master now.'

Tullus took the servant's arm and led him to a low wall where they both sat down.

'And your boy, did they take him too?'

'No! They never would have taken him.' A note of pride strengthened the old man's voice. 'He went to save my master's daughter. He had a lion's strength, but he had no joy in life.'

Tullus sat without a movement. It was still, very still indeed.

'His poor misshapen body,' the old servant continued. 'They laughed at him, mocked him, called him devil, but my master and his daughter never laughed. They were always kind and he loved them for it.'

Still Tullus sat unmoving. Then quietly he spoke.

'Your master is alive. The Lord Valerius is alive. Drusilla is alive ...'

The old man's eyes were wide. He was too surprised to speak and he did not think to question what the stranger had revealed. There was no elated burst of feeling, just a whisper, barely audible.

'God protected them.'

As Tullus told his story the servant of Valerius did not interrupt, but when Tullus started to relate the tale of Brother James tears fell freely from a father's eyes.

'God's love was with him,' he said eventually.

Tullus nodded. There was nothing more to say.

The old servant suddenly stiffened. Two of the Gothic guards were approaching, their breastplates glinting in the sun.

'We were worried, sir,' Theodis said. 'You've been gone for some time.'

'Sorry, my friend here...' Tullus hesitated.

'Aulus, sir.'

'My friend Aulus and I have been talking.'

Theodis smiled; he was used to the ways of his Roman master.

Tullus helped the old servant to his feet.

'Aulus,' he said softly, 'within the next two days I hope to return with Drusilla. I want her to see how you've kept the garden. Then we will take you to your master. Have you food?'

Aulus nodded.

'And warm shelter?'

'Yes, sir.'

'Here, take my wine-bag,' Tullus said impulsively.

'May I know your name, sir?'

'Marcus Tullus.'

The old man repeated the name to himself, a puzzled look on his face as he watched Tullus and his guards recede.

'I've heard that name before – I know I have,' he muttered, but he could not remember.

He sat down on the low wall again. What he had heard about his boy and about his master he believed. It was a blessing, a great blessing.

ooo

The stables of the Anicius palace were well able to accommodate the horses of Tullus and his escort, and their sudden evening arrival was serviced with the minimum of fuss.

Tullus saw Drusilla waiting by the colonnade, and even at a distance it was very clear that she was not herself. Her face was far too eager and her natural poise was absent.

He went to her at once and she bravely tried to act her natural self, but the trouble in her mind was too immediate. Tullus, all the while, was gentle and considerate.

'Where is Cornelia?'

'With her nurse, Anna.'

'All is well, I hope.'

'Very much so. If Cornelia knew that you were here, nothing would keep her from her Papa.'

'Drusilla,' he said, taking her hand, 'I have much to tell you, much of which may help. Come, let's sit.' He guided her to a bench inside the colonnade. 'I have good news, amazing news. I met Aulus, your father's servant.'

'Aulus!' she repeated, her face alight. 'Where, Marcus?'

'At your old villa.'

'And his son?'

'That is a sad, but beautiful story.'

'Tell me, Marcus,' she pressed, her misery forgotten.

Slowly and quietly he told her all that he had heard from Aulus and from Brother James. Drusilla was slow to weep, but now her tears fell freely.

'Can you remember, Drusilla? Can you remember young Aulus coming to your rescue?'

'No, Marcus, I can't.'

Suddenly she stiffened.

'What is it, Drusilla?'

'Oh, Marcus.' Her despair was obvious.

'Tell me, Drusilla.'

'It's just thoughts. I know it's just thoughts, but somehow they're believed. I can't remember, so I can't be sure and the clinging depravity remains. It's so dark and ...'

'You say you can't be sure. Drusilla, only God is sure!'

'That's what Boethius keeps telling me. Oh, Marcus, why am I so weak?'

'Don't say you're weak. It only feeds your doubt. So, the busy Consul has been seeing you.'

'Yes, Marcus – every day he's here.'

'You've been fortunate.'

'Yes – and Rusticiana – she's been very kind. She keeps me occupied and she jokes a lot, no doubt to make me cheerful. It's getting better, Marcus. When I saw you I wanted to be normal, to be free of heart for you, but the more I wanted, the more the other rose in opposition.'

'Most need to get beyond that pendulum,' he responded, as two servants passed discreetly. Close by, another was busy with the lamps.

'This bench is rather public,' he said, rising to his feet. 'I badly need the baths and then I'll see Cornelia. After that we'll talk about tomorrow's plans, for old Aulus is expecting the daughter of his master. – Will the Consul be in this evening?' he asked as they walked off down the corridor.

'No, he's out of Rome at present, but he's due back soon.'

After supper and when they had discussed the next day's plans, Drusilla thought it best to have an early night. She felt much better, and hopeful that the worst was past. Yet she could not quite forget the finger pointing at her on that awful day when Triguilla called. Then she had accepted guilt, for it mirrored what the nightmare seemed to say. Somehow, she had been to blame.

She was entering her room when a sudden shaft of thought caught her unawares. If she gave up Tullus, her nightmare fears would have no hold, for they rose in strength with her desire. She was horrified, but she could not countenance the devilish deal.

It was an anguished, sleepless night until at last she drifted off, and then the nightmare came again.

OOO

The outer courtyard of the Anicius palace was alive with activity. It was dawn and servants were busy extinguishing the night torches.

In the centre of the paved area a fast two-wheeled cart was drawn up with its canopy extended. The two horses harnessed to it, and those of the Gothic guard, were restless, their grooms kept busy holding them in check. Close by, Theodis and his men stood formally. They were in the Consul's courtyard, and such behaviour was incumbent on a royal guardsman.

Suddenly they came to attention as Tullus and Drusilla appeared in the archway leading from the inner courtyard. Tullus acknowledged their respect, while helping Drusilla into the cart, and then he gave the order to proceed. The journey to the old Valerius villa had begun.

Once settled in the cart, it was soon apparent that Drusilla's state had changed. She looked radiant and he told her so.

'Marcus, I remembered. The nightmare came again last night and I saw what happened and, thank God, it now no longer has a hold. It was young Aulus who saved me, and it was he who fought my captors until another soldier came and led me off. It was so clear, but why did the scar-faced Goth tell lies? Why did he accuse me?'

'You were the cause of his disfigurement. It was you young Aulus defended. He wanted to strike back … to revenge himself …'

'But to come specially to the villa …'

'Some drunken urge. They were sodden when they came, but they went too far. That Triguilla must have understood, for I'm told he went to Cyprian for advice and not long afterwards joined the army at his own request in Southern Gaul.'

'How did you learn all this?'

'Theodis – one night in Rome's enough to learn the gossip of his race.'

Suddenly the low-cast rays of the morning sun penetrated the interior of the canopy. It was dazzling till they changed direction and then the light became diffused again.

'It's going to be warm,' Tullus said. 'We'll roll up the sides of the canopy when we're clear of the city. You're pensive, Drusilla,' he added, concerned that her darker thoughts might have returned.

She smiled, and he knew at once his fears were groundless.

'I was thinking how many of my ancestors must have travelled this same road.'

'Even the first Drusilla!'

She blushed. She knew the ancient story well, and here she was, Drusilla too, and at her side another Marcus Tullus. Surely they were fated to be one.

'Things were better when the first Drusilla lived,' she said lightly, making the subject general.

'Yes, a mighty empire ruled, yet there was harshness in its army-like precision.'

'And squalor too, no doubt, just like today. Didn't Cicero say something about the obligations of the rich?'

'Yes, that wealth should correspond to duty – that's the essence of it,' Tullus answered.

'And Boethius shows us the example.'

'Yes, a tireless service.'

When well clear of the city, Tullus rolled up the side drapes of the canopy.

'That's better,' he said, taking his seat. He glanced sideways at Drusilla. 'Now we can talk of love,' he added with pretended innocence.

'Marcus, you rogue! – you haven't told me anything about your journey to the south. That's a much better subject – and tell me, where on earth did you get that goat?'

And so the conversation continued, on a light and humorous note, as the fast two-wheeled cart swung and jolted on the worn paving of the Via Appia.

Tullus was thinking. It had been her troubled state that had ignored formality, and the barrier of hesitation, that frozen shyness, was no longer there. There was no need for any special move except perhaps to say the actual words. When? When would he propose? For there were no reservations now. Drusilla was a heaven-sent companion. As soon as they got back. Yes, at Fidenae, after he had spoken to Valerius.

ooo

They arrived at the site of the old villa just after midday. At once they headed for the ruins, their sandals crunching on the gravel as they walked.

'This is a strangely arid area, Drusilla.'

'Years ago, I believe, it was a large open space for carts,' she responded.

Suddenly she stopped, her look pained.

'It's been plundered terribly, even the wing that Father had restored. But the garden's as it always was. Aulus has kept it beautifully.'

'Aulus isn't here. I'm surprised.'

'He'll be in his hut. It's just beyond the rise.' She pointed. 'Unless you knew, you'd never find it. I used to play there when I was little.'

Slowly they walked around the garden.

'The garden's wonderful, but ... oh, Marcus, the rest is so neglected.. And that awful man, Triguilla, owns it. Dear God!' Again there was the look of pain.

They stopped before two age-worn statues that stood in front of what had been the portico. Time had rendered them almost featureless.

'Two of your noble Valerii ancestors,' he said lightly.

'No, Marcus, they are the Gracchi.'

'The Gracchi!' he repeated in a whisper, and for a time it seemed the weathered stone was fired with life. Tiberius and Gaius. They had been his boyhood heroes.

This was the moment. He could not let it pass.

'Come close to me, Drusilla.'

Gently he put his arm round her shoulders.

'When I return to Fidenae, my first act will be to ask a father's permission to marry his beautiful and graceful daughter.'

Impulsively she embraced him.

'Marcus, Marcus, dear Marcus.' Her voice spoke softly.

'I take it you approve.'

'You are a rogue,' she reacted happily. 'Marcus, ever since that morning when I heard your name, there's been no other.'

'I'm sorry – I've been slow and stubborn.'

'No, Marcus, you've been honourable – you loved your wife.'

'Yes,' he answered simply.

They parted their embrace. Her eyes were full of love.

'When, Marcus?'

'When I return from reporting to the King. One thing only I will ask my Royal patron – that this old site, this plot of land, be restored to the Valerii.'

She looked at him. Her joy was full.

The sound of approaching footsteps caught their attention.

'It's Aulus!' Drusilla cried, running to the old man and embracing him. 'Beloved Aulus!'

'My dear Drusilla. You've grown to be a lovely lady.'

Tears streamed down the old man's cheeks.

ooo

Gratefully Tullus watched the heavy doors of the Anicius palace swing open as the sun began to set. He was tired of travel and had little thought of anything but the baths. Drusilla, on the other hand, was buoyant. For two long years she had waited, disguising her feelings. Now at last her dreams were firm reality. Tullus had proposed and the restless uncertainty of her youth had ended.

Tullus saw little of Drusilla that evening, as most of his time was spent with Boethius who, contrary to the image of a busy Consul, looked totally at ease, with time in plenty for his guest.

'My dear wife Rusticiana will be pleased,' he immediately responded when Tullus told him of his marriage plans. 'She's been impatient for this day. I can almost hear her say – "At last!"'

Both men laughed and the conversation moved to Tullus's journey south. Boethius listened fully, as he always did, but was particularly interested in Sublaqueum and its Abbot.

'From your description, Tullus, I sense a measured life, free of excess and guided by a man of natural dignity. – Fertile ground: I belive he holds the writings of John Cassian in high regard' Boethius added, but he said no more.

When Tullus told the story of old Aulus and his son, Boethius smiled, the same smile as Benedict, the same inner tranquillity. Tullus was surprised – but why? Tranquillity was universal and ever there for those who would embrace it.

'You'll be reporting to the King, of course,' Boethius was saying.

'Within the next two weeks – when I may find the royal favour brief.'

Boethius shook his head.

'Your position is secure. The King will not forget the vital warning that you gave to Thulwin, for our Lord Theoderic is a warrior at heart.'

'Yes, my first audience was on horseback! He tires of palace life, he told me.'

'No wonder, knowing the jackals that surround him. There's another factor in your favour. You are from Britain, a man from the north. We may forget this, but I doubt if Theoderic has. He feels a certain kinship, or maybe sees you as a man apart, as neither Goth nor Roman.'

'I'm more Roman than the Romans,' Tullus protested. 'I'd have Trajan back tomorrow if I could!'

'Don't tell him that!' Boethius cautioned with a laugh.

'Theoderic's rule is remarkably stable, sir. We are fortunate, are we not?' Tullus continued.

'Yes, he plays the tolerant monarch with no little wisdom, but there are many uncertainties. To begin with, he has no male heir, though there are moves to marry his daughter to some worthy Goth. Then there is the ageing Emperor Anastasius. What will happen when he goes? What will the new Augustus do? How will he view the Arian Goths? Sometimes I feel the Empire underestimates them. As it is, the current schism suits Theoderic well, for while the Pope and Emperor view each other with suspicion, if not worse, the heresy of the Arian Goths is secondary; but Anastasius is old and of course the Pope won't live for ever. Say, for instance, a future Emperor were Orthodox and, unlike Anastasius, leaned towards the Roman way, and say he had a vision of a greater Empire as of old ...'

'That would isolate the Goths,' Tullus reacted, 'and with tolerance gone it could mean war.' He thought of his friend Justinian and the picture fitted much too well. 'An awful war,' he added, 'for if the Empire tried to oust the Goths, it would tear this land apart.'

'Well, thankfully it's only speculation. In any case, no one who had any sense would attack Theoderic.'

'Why, sir?'

'He's an institution!'

'God save the King.'

'Indeed.'

'You have been supporting Church unity, sir,' Tullus said respectfully, aware that such support could be interpreted as anti-Gothic, particularly by those who wanted to find fault or worse.

'Yes, I've been supporting unity. One hopes to find some common ground and at the same time not inflame the Goths or seed intolerance against the Arian population in the Eastern capital. But Constantinople is volatile in such matters, and passions flare with ease.'

'Why is tolerance shunned?' Tullus asked, more in protest than enquiry.

'Lack of reason,' Boethius said tersely. 'The middle way is not a common fashion,' he continued. 'I, of course, am accused of being pro-Eastern. Indeed, I've even been accused of being pro-Goth – hopefully the King heard that.' Boethius smiled knowingly

'Cyprion has attacked you as pro-Eastern.'

'It suits him. It's a way to foster favour with the Goths and, as he sees it, further his career. He even may believe it!'

'He ought to know better,' Tullus grunted.

'You may have struck his epitaph, for he's astute; he has depth, yet he dances on the surface.'

The door opened and Rusticiana's personal servant entered with a note. Boethius quickly scanned the words and mouthed a 'yes'.

'Stay, Tullus. The ladies are coming. I'm sure the noble Valerius will forgive us if we celebrate before the hour of his official blessing.'

ooo

It was a slow four-wheeled cart that stood in the courtyard the following morning. The two horses harnessed to its shaft were listless and the goat, tied to the cart, strained stubbornly on its cord.

Amongst the Gothic guard there was a festive air, for a week's rest lay before them. Suddenly Theodis drew them to attention. The travelling party had arrived.

One by one Tullus helped them into the cart. First Anna, Cornelia's nurse, then Cornelia, who giggled gleefully as he held her high. After that it was Drusilla's turn.

'I dare you to lift me as high as that,' she joked.

'I thought I was supposed to be the rogue,' he smiled affectionately. Then he took his place beside old Aulus on the driver's seat.

Before setting off Tullus glanced behind to check that the womenfolk were comfortable. It was a brief look, but long enough to notice the nurse Anna, preoccupied, her gaze fixed somewhere to the front, but Tullus could see nothing other than Theodis, busy with his restless horse and with Claudius on tow.

'All right, Anna?' he called.

'Yes, sir,' she instantly replied.

They were outside Rome when Tullus gave the reins to Aulus. Casually he beckoned one of the guards who was riding close.

'Cut the cord holding our lady.'

The humorous note in Tullus's voice was supported by the laughter of the mounted guards.

'What was that about, sir?' Aulus questioned.

'The goat.' Tullus winked. 'Just wait, she'll soon be out in front.'

'And there she is, sir!'

'Yes, she likes to lead the column.'

OOO

CHAPTER THIRTY FIVE

# WEDDINGS

The marriage of Valerius and Poppe was simple and private, yet intensely moving, for the joy of Poppe and the patrician dignity of Valerius left few, if any, unaffected.

Rusticiana and Drusilla looked tearful and Anna the nurse wept openly, while the Senator Symmachus, his strong chin jutting forward, stood defying his feelings. Tullus too, though he played the stoic, felt strong emotion rise.

The ceremony took place in the private chapel of Symmachus's villa. It had been the Senator's suggestion, for he and Valerius had become close friends.

'His Greek is brilliant,' the Senator said afterwards to Tullus, 'and he has the happy flair of extracting the essential principle. Boethius respects his ability greatly.'

'The Consul was called to Ravenna, I hear,' Tullus said.

'Yes. Alas, he couldn't avoid it, as Ravenna was responding to his plea to halt taxation on a famine-ridden province.'

'Will his plea succeed?'

'I think so. Even the palace officials will see the reason of his case, but it's a thankless labour and he incurs much enmity. Well, Tullus, this is a marriage feast, not a Senate committee. I must go and congratulate my friend and his Lady Poppea.'

After an overnight stay in Rome Valerius and Poppe returned to Fidenae, while Drusilla took up residence at the Anicius palace to prepare for her own marriage.

Tullus set out immediately for Ravenna. Like Valerius, he had planned for a quiet pre-Easter wedding, but after meeting with the King these hopes were dashed.

'Thulwin will be here within the month,' the King said strongly. 'You must invite him!'

Tullus was amazed by his popularity with the monarch. Three days running they rode in the forest park, and each day Theoderic roared with laughter at the stories Tullus told him. Tullus expected the King's mood to change, but no, this did not happen and he concluded that his own

186

presence was incidental. Theoderic was a warrior, a man of the open air, and he liked escaping from the palace court. Yet when he met the King's Quaestor, Cassiodorus, the story was different.

'The King enjoys your company, Tullus,' the Quaestor began. 'You speak plainly, he says, and what's more, he maintains you're one of the very few who aren't angling for something.'

'I asked him for the old Valerius villa site.'

'That he called a spadeful,' Cassiodorus returned. 'Take it from me, you're well favoured.'

On his journey to Rome Tullus pondered long on his meetings with the King and also on the words of Cassiodorus. Certainly there was no doubt about his favoured position. Even so, he felt uneasy. The King's will was sovereign in the state. He had the power that raised men's fortunes high, but that same power could ruin them.

Abruptly Tullus cut his thinking short: such unease and doubt showed gross ingratitude to a generous patron. Indeed, the King had further commissioned him. He was to visit Hispania in the autumn. Again, there was the restoration of the old Tullus estate in Tuscany. For this his gratitude was unbounded; and, of course, there was his imminent marriage to Drusilla. Few men could boast of such a bride.

Tullus had been fortunate and no one knew it better than himself. The outcast who had fled from Southern Britain had reached the heights of Roman society. Because of this, Tullus was obliged to have a much more public marriage than either he or Drusilla would have wished. Yet compared with the usual society affairs, the marriage of Marcus Tullus was quiet.

The ceremony took place in the private chapel of the Anicius palace.

The chief guests were the Count Thulwin, the Quaestor Cassiodorus representing the King and, of course, the Consul with his wife and children. The Senator Symmachus was also present, and taking first place were Valerius and Poppe, along with Cornelia and her nurse.

The wedding of Marcus Tullus and Drusilla was impressive. Impressive because of the solid strength of Tullus, and again impressive because of Drusilla's striking grace and beauty.

'Cast in the heroic mould,' Symmachus whispered to his son-in-law.

Boethius smiled but did not answer.

'I hope they'll not be over-tested,' Symmachus added with unusual gentleness.

ooo

# CHAPTER THIRTY SIX

# FAESULAE

After a few days at Rome and Fidenae, Marcus Tullus and his wife set out for the old Tullus villa in Tuscany. The journey along the Via Cassia was leisurely, and letters of introduction from both Boethius and Symmachus gave welcome access to comfortable accommodation.

Tullus had always meant to visit Faesulae; indeed, long before the King had granted him the villa and estate. It had been his aim when destitute in Gaul. Though that had been a dream to keep him going. Now it was reality and only days away.

Tullus was accompanied by his six-man Gothic guard. In fact, the travelling party was substantial. Three baggage carts trundled behind the four-wheeled covered cart of Tullus and his wife. Furniture was amongst the pile of baggage, for Tullus did not know how he would find the fortress villa. He had been told that it was sound and solid, but that was all.

Five servants were included in the party. Two were Drusilla's attendants, released to her by Rusticiana. There were a gardener, a cook and an elderly employee from Fidenae who had impressed Tullus with his honesty and common sense – his future agent. The rest of his labour requirement he hoped to hire locally.

Tullus had only one regret: Cornelia and her nurse were still at Thulwin's villa. Perhaps he had been over-cautious. Yet, on the other hand, he did not know what state the villa would be in. But they could follow soon when things were settled.

Many in Rome scorned the actions of Tullus as plebeian. Cyprian, for one, was quick to mock.

'A farmer taking his wife to tend his vines,' he jibed to his mother.

Tullus, however, took scant interest in the fashionable round. He had no political designs and therefore no contacts to cultivate, and further, he scorned the usual indulgent dalliance of the newly wed. Such behaviour was the enemy of marriage.

On the fifth day out of Rome, they crossed the Arnus at Florentia.

'It's behind those hills,' Tullus said, pointing to the north in the direction of Faesulae. 'Do you see the ruins on the hill?'

Drusilla nodded.

'There used to be a temple to Bacchus somewhere on the site,' he explained. 'Grandfather told me all about the place, for his father knew the town well. There's a theatre there, apparently, but I doubt if it's in use today.'

'Are we passing that way?' she asked.

'No, dear, our road is to the west between the hills. Then we turn east and climb into the high ground behind Faesulae. The villa's like a fortress. It was built in the time of the four Caesars in 69, but I'm sure that it's been changed and changed again since then.'

'There seem to be numerous villas in this area – that is, judging by the rows of cypress trees,' Drusilla remarked.

'Yes, but if you look, many of the villas are in ruins, for the valley of the Arnus is an easy prey to marching armies.'

'But your villa wasn't sacked,' Drusilla pressed.

'Too distant a diversion, perhaps.'

'Father's new estate is near the Arnus, is it not?'

'It's all right, Drusilla; the peace of Theoderic is secure.'

The journey through the Tuscan countryside was pleasant. The sun was hot without the baking glare of summer, and a slight breeze added freshness. Tullus rested the horses frequently as they climbed. Then suddenly there it was, the Villa Tullus.

It was as his grandfather had described it, yet Tullus was surprised by its blatant fortress nature. The stones used in its construction were massive and the squat, sturdy watch-tower looked aggressive. A portico, plain in style, had been added later, no doubt to soften the austerity of the building, but the door had since been bricked up.

A generous row of cypress trees flanked the villa to the north and, for all its military pretension, age had given it a mellowness.

'The Tullus wives were well protected! I like it, Marcus,' she added. 'It's like…'

'The Emperor Vespasian,' he interjected. 'Plain and blunt!'

As they approached the heads and shoulders of two Gothic soldiers appeared above the villa wall, their restricted movements suggesting a walkway. Their presence came as no surprise, for the King had told him that his property would be guarded by the garrison at Florentia.

Except for one damaged mosaic floor, the rooms were in good condition. There had been extensive repairs and the heavy inner courtyard door was new. Theoderic had been generous to the point of fatherly indulgence.

Outside the villa to the rear was the dome of the boiler. It appeared to be in working order, and to Tullus's amazement the wood store was completely full. A large enclosure ringed with a string of varied buildings was adjacent to the villa. There were stables, but these were in poor repair.

Behind the villa the ground rose to the rounded summit of a hill a few hundred paces above. There were areas of scrub and thick tree cover, but mostly the scene was of neglected vine and olive terraces. There was also extensive property in the valley below.

There was much to do, and hiring staff was a priority. With this in mind Tullus went to Faesulae the following morning. The old Roman hill town was in decline. The baths were closed, the theatre unused and the nearby temple roofless. Work in the community was scarce and he had little difficulty in securing labour. Tullus hired three sturdy-looking men. Enough, he thought, until there were proper quarters.

Just as he was leaving, a bustling, pompous man approached with two slaves he hoped to sell.

'Next time,' Tullus said briskly, but as he turned away his eyes met those of the tired, ageing slave standing bent beside his self-important master.

'Can you write?' Tullus asked bluntly. A strange, impulsive question, as if some other one had said it.

'Yes, sir.' Hope transformed his face.

Tullus nodded and the owner quickly named his price. Excitement moved him like a puppet.

'Try again,' Tullus said evenly.

Twice the price was lowered and then a deal was struck.

That evening the elderly slave was the first subject that Drusilla raised at supper.

'He says you're a saint, Marcus.'

'Well, you know differently, my dear.'

'I think you have potential – why did you hire him, Marcus?'

'The look in his eyes – a look of naked misery.'

'You're a good man, Marcus Tullus.'

'No! Just a human being, Drusilla. Any man with feelings would have done the same. An old man, tired and weak, yet bound to unrelenting toil and viewed by his unfeeling master as a growing liability.'

'What's he going to do?'

'He can help our agent Quintus with the records.'

'What's his name?'

'Philippus. Now tell me of your day, Drusilla.'

'Busy but enjoyable. It will be primitive for a while until we've settled.'

'I've only one regret,' Tullus admitted. 'We should have brought Cornelia. I mentioned this to Theodis and he immediately volunteered to go to Rome and fetch her.'

'I'm not surprised.'

'Why, Drusilla?'

'He likes Anna – hadn't you noticed?'

'No,' he replied, shaking his head. 'And what of her?'

'Her gaze follows him everywhere.'

'Oh dear, this could be awkward.'

'Religion, you mean?'

'Alas, yes. Roman orthodoxy and Arianism don't mix. But it's too late, for I've said yes. In fact, he's ridden off to Florentia to ask the garrison commander for an escort. So that's why another journey didn't seem to worry him. Well, it's happened. The dice are cast and, knowing Theodis, he's already on his way.'

'He's an honourable man, Marcus.'

'That's the trouble, dear: he'll want to marry her. If his faith were Roman I'd rejoice, but he's an Arian Goth and a Royal Guardsman bound by oath. Only Theoderic could release him.'

'Would he?'

'I fear the answer will be no.'

Within two weeks Cornelia and her nurse were at the Villa Tullus. Cornelia bubbled with joy and Anna looked radiant. The journey had been most enjoyable, she said.

For Tullus, now alerted to the situation, the relationship between Theodis and the nurse was obvious. They were clearly fond of each other, yet restrained in their behaviour, and only met together in the evening when they would go for walks. Even so, they looked relaxed and happy.

Tullus said nothing to Theodis. Part of him concluded that it was none of his business, while the other knew it was. Theodis, too, said nothing. Like himself, Tullus guessed, he knew the summer would be short, and the journey to the west would mean a lengthy separation.

Autumn came too quickly, but before the journey west could start, and before he met the King, Tullus had to take his family to Fidenae, where the care of Valerius and the protection of Ufilias, with Count Thulwin's guard, were both assured. This done, he travelled to Ravenna to receive the King's final instructions.

Theoderic was blunt. His mission would be difficult and dangerous.

'Go to Narbonensis. Seek out Count Ibbas. He knows about your mission and will give you extra men. You'll need them! Avoid warring armies and do as you did in southern Italy. It will not be easy, Tullus, for I fear it's little less than anarchy in that area. Even so, your reports will be a useful guide and will help, when you return in two years' time, to judge the progress of our rule.'

The reference to a further visit did not fail to register, but Tullus held his tongue.

The King stood up, heralding the end of the formal audience.

'The horses are ready, Tullus. It's time for the forest park.'

Theoderic assumed compliance and strode towards the door.

They had been riding for some time when the King reined his horse.

'Your friend the Consul has been with us for the past few days. You've just missed him.'

Tullus expressed his disappointment and the King nudged his horse to a walking pace.

'Boethius is a great lover of the Senate and its laws. Yet he serves our person well.'

Tullus nodded. What did Theoderic mean? Even casual words on the lips of the sovereign could never be ignored.

ooo

After leaving Ravenna Tullus cut across the hills towards Florentia and his villa, where they spent their second night. The next night was at Pisae and on the following morning they joined the Via Aurelia, the same Aurelia that Arria had travelled. Indeed, the journey to the west was full of memories – the playful charm of his late wife; Martin; the Hermit of the Rocks; and Thulwin, standing tall amidst the pattern of the time.

When they reached Arelate they rested a full day. The city, only lately released from a Frankish siege, bore the marks of hardship. Tullus called upon his friend the Bishop and was shocked to find him much weakened. Apparently the good man had refused all privileges, preferring to suffer the same hardships as his people.

At Arelate Tullus learned that Ibbas was at Narbo Martius, and there he headed. Within two days he stood before the Ostrogothic general.

Ibbas was square and solid and very much a Goth. A soldier of plain principle, was the general's self-description.

'Twenty men at least,' was his uncompromising assessment when Tullus asked about his bodyguard. Yet it was beyond his soldier's comprehension to see why Tullus had been sent; but if his King had willed it so, that was law for him.

Tullus liked the general's rough honesty, though conversation with the powerful Goth was difficult. Ibbas, he felt, had no wish to discuss his strategy with a Roman, no matter how well favoured. In any case, the general's Latin was limited and Tullus's attempts to speak the Gothic tongue made the busy Count impatient.

During Tullus's first night at Narbo Martius, trouble broke out between his six-man royal guard and the soldiery of Ibbas. The escort had reacted to taunts about their Roman commander and although there were no serious injuries, the incident proved embarrassing. So a prompt departure was prudent, and the next day Tullus and his guard, now swollen to twenty, headed south.

The smell of the sea was discernible as they rode, and a slight breeze blew the dust cloud of their progress inland. The autumn weather was temperate and pleasant. Lazily he watched the riders: twenty of them, bobbing on their horses, sometimes with a rhythm and sometimes not. A growing sense of unreality seemed to rise above him like a mist.

'What am I doing here?' he muttered.

'Sir,' Theodis called, cutting across his thought, 'there's a troop of horse approaching. There, sir.' His finger pointed. 'They look like our men, sir.'

Theodis barked an order and the escort tightened their formation but his searching gaze did not leave the approaching horsemen.

'It's Triguilla, sir!' he burst out.

'Act normally, Theodis,' Tullus reacted.

Triguilla shouted something to Theodis in their native tongue before he noticed Tullus. Then he laughed.

'Ah, the noble Tullus, our Roman hero. Have you assumed the purple yet?' Triguilla roared with laughter. He was drunk.

Tullus bowed and smiled, careful to convey an air of calm. Only Theodis could understand Triguilla's Latin.

Triguilla's men were caked in dust and looked like men who had recently seen action. It was Theodis who voiced his thoughts.

'Is there trouble up ahead?' he asked.

'Trouble!' Again Triguilla exploded with laughter. 'No, not trouble – only glory for a Roman hero!' he added with pretended deference. Then his heels kicked hard and, startled, his horse shot forward, leaving his troop to follow in disorder.

Tullus turned and watched them go.

'Nothing changes, Theodis,' he said flatly.

ooo

# CHAPTER THIRTY SEVEN

# GREENS AND BLUES

Boethius did not like being carried in a boxed-in litter, yet he found its anonymity useful. As usual, he had hired the litter at the Senate steps, and his bearers were proceeding through the crowd with practised ease. The scene as viewed behind the side drapes was one of fleeting pictures, just like life, Boethius thought. Suddenly before him was a group of youths flaunting the colours of the Greens and hoping, no doubt, to meet an unsuspecting Blue supporter. Such idiocy was as old as time. They quickly passed, and next before his view were traders loudly haggling. Then, unexpectedly, he saw the upright figure of his father-in-law and not a servant or a bodyguard in sight. It was typical.

'Stop!' he shouted, immediately stepping from the litter. 'Father – you're back from the country, I see.'

'Ah, Boethius – what a happy chance. Yes, I returned this morning – my unfinished manuscripts were beckoning!'

They embraced.

'Come, Father, join me at the villa. We can walk across the bridge together.'

Symmachus assented and so they proceeded, the Consul's guard clearing a pathway through the crowded streets.

'Well, what was the Senate like today?' Symmachus asked.

'Full of anger at the rising tide of crime. Old Metellus was the worst. Execute them all, he ranted. Herd them to the archery field. I told him he should send his rent-collecting agents too, for they were little more than vultures. He didn't like it, but his ranting stopped.'

'That's another friend you've made, Boethius! You would have pleased Petillius, of course!'

'The other extreme. He spreads milk and honey over everyone. With him you'd think the victims were at fault – and we heard it all again today. Dear God, the patience that is needed. Well, sir, just a few more months before I put an "ex" before the Consulship. Then peace at last!'

'I doubt it,' Symmachus returned. 'I know when I gave up the Consulship I was just as busy!'

'Well, I'm determined to keep public life at bay.'

'That's what I thought too. Boethius, men will come to you for help. It is inevitable.'

When they arrived at the Anicius palace they went straight to the library.

'Where is Rusticiana?' Symmachus asked.

'Still in the country – the boys love it there.'

Both men fell silent, for after the noise and bustle of the streets the quiet of the library was tangible.

'I received a letter from Constantinople today,' Symmachus said suddenly. 'It was sent by way of Ravenna with the Imperial despatches.'

'What was it – another thesis on the Trinity?!'

'No, the sender was Priscian, the Latin grammarian. I met him when I was over there some years ago and gave him a donation. So he's sent me a copy of his work which he has dedicated to me and which he ends by praising the linguistic arts of the Greeks and Romans as above all other races – not the most diplomatic message if seen by Gothic eyes.'

'Was the seal broken?' Boethius asked.

'No. Anyway, the words were fairly general.'

'To us,' Boethius interrupted. 'But our Gothic overlords are sensitive to such matters and correspondence from the East to Roman Senators is viewed with some suspicion. Even with all our efforts to give the Goths due honour, Theoderic is still not satisfied. Indeed, I feel he sees the Roman Senate as a rival.'

'He's tolerant, though, this we must acknowledge.'

'Yes, he's tolerant all right, and preserves the forms of unity with the East. Yet ...' Boethius paused and rubbed his forehead. 'It's the same old story we have covered many times. Theoderic feels secure while religious chaos rules the Eastern capital and while the Emperor is sympathetic to the Monophysites, for that divides the East and West and keeps attention off the Arians, both here and in Byzantium. So, thus unthreatened, Theoderic feels at ease and so his reign continues tolerant. This is a golden time. A time for work. Hence my impatience for this Consulship to end.'

'How long will this golden period last?'

'About ten years, perhaps. So much depends upon our Lord Theoderic.'

'An uncertain picture, Boethius.'

'Yes, and it highlights the importance of this free and open time. Our studies must proceed.'

The afternoon sun had found some mirror surface in the courtyard and was reflecting on the glass and ivory decoration. For a while the effect was magical and both men watched in silence.

'Has Tullus put his head in the lion's mouth?' Symmachus suddenly asked.

'The Gothic Lion? No, I don't think so. I had my fears, but what I learned when in Ravenna last made it obvious that the King likes Tullus and treats him as a father treats a son. Tullus has no political ambitions and doesn't care too much about a man's religion – a rare gift these days. Apparently he told the King he was only interested in the words of Christ and Plato. That amused Theoderic greatly. His man from the north, the King calls him. Again, there was the vital word he got to Thulwin. Theoderic will never forget that. My dear father-in-law, Tullus is more secure than either you or I, for as I've said, the King still views the Senate as a rival to his sovereignty – and we are Senators!'

'He must have more faith in the Senate than I have!' Symmachus reacted bluntly. 'Our squabbling keeps us impotent.'

'Yes, the King's own comment on the circus factions suits us well; we're hardly a "conference of Catos",' Boethius returned.

'Our Lord Theoderic has a sense of humour.'

'Yes, and I will need one soon as well, for tomorrow the Consul Boethius presides at that same circus.'

'Just think, Boethius, Consuls have done the same for close upon a thousand years!'

Boethius laughed.

'A playful exaggeration, sir, but it makes the point.'

OOO

The Circus Maximus was full, and buzzing with eagerness. Julia, the mother of Cyprian, had just sent Rufus with her wager and was watching from her usual box, her eyes glistening with excitement. Soon the initial parade of chariots would begin, when the charioteers, the heroes of Rome, would receive the thunderous cheers of their supporters.

At first the widow did not see her son Opilio take his seat beside her.

'My boy, you look worried,' she reacted when she noticed him. 'You've gambled heavily. I can feel it. You should keep your wagers light.'

'Like you, Mother!' he snapped.

'Now, now, my son.' She patted his arm. 'I'm an old lady amusing her fading years, while you have still to make your way.'

The squat, square features of Opilio tightened with annoyance, but he said nothing.

Suddenly a shout echoed round the banked rows of supporters

bordering the finger-shaped circus.

'What is it, Opilio?' the widow asked. Her sight was deteriorating.

'Boethius has entered the Imperial box.'

'Ah, the sole Consul. They say his donations to the people are generous.'

'He can afford it,' Opilio grunted, as the buzz of anticipation grew.

'Where is your brother?' the widow asked above the noise.

'Licking the sandals of the Prefect. His ambition knows no limit.'

'Your brother's not a fool, Opilio – you should study his example. You need to settle, son.'

Again Opilio frowned. When would his mother stop her endless lecturing?

The sudden explosive roar of the crowd drowned everything. The chariots were emerging.

First came the entrance of the Whites and the Reds, but no one expected them to win. The main contestants were the Blues and Greens and when they came the crowd erupted. The noise was deafening. Julia cheered with the rest. This was the day that all had waited for, The two best charioteers in Rome were matched, competing for the Consul's prize.

'*Green for the verdant spring,*' Julia shouted at her son.

'Mother, not again,' he protested, 'not that silly rhyme.'

'*Blue for cloudy winter,*' she continued, undeterred, '*red for flaming summer and white for frosty autumn* – and it's not a silly rhyme!'

Once the chariots had completed their parade they retired behind the Ostia. There they waited in their separate stalls, grooms holding desperately to excited horses. They stepped free, a clear sign that the race was imminent. All waited on the Consul's sign.

Boethius stood up, his right arm high. It fell and the roar of the crowd was like a thunderclap.

The race to get the inside position was crucial and dangerous. The crowd knew this well, for many a fine charioteer had crashed into the circuit's central spine. Julia stood transfixed. She had wagered on the Greens and their powerful horses had just gained the advantage. To some the race was over, for the Greens' charioteer was skilled enough to hold to his advantage. Yet races had been won from behind. Nothing was certain.

Boethius sat, intent on the scene before him. It was a magnificent spectacle, he thought, and the skill of the charioteers amazing. To what end, though? Perhaps it did not matter. What mattered was the skill, the fearlessness and the beauty of the spectacle, as all these qualities played before the people. Boethius leaned across towards his father-in-law.

'I suppose you've wagered heavily, sir,' he said with humour.

'My villa for the Blues,' Symmachus returned, both men's laughter swallowed by the frenzied roar.

The Greens' charioteer maintained his advantage throughout, winning by a horse's length and in due course he was presented to the Consul.

'What is the secret of a good charioteer?' the Consul asked.

'Strong hands and sure feet,' was the prompt answer.

Boethius smiled. It was a good reply.

OOO

While Boethius was receiving the circus officials, Julia was slowly making her way to the exit, accompanied by the sturdy and reliable Rufus. Opilio, who had gambled well, had left his seat during the circuit of triumph to seek out his tavern cronies. He had quickly met Basilius, one of his drinking friends, and now together they raced down the stone steps to the area where the litters and carts were parked.

'Let's decorate your mother's litter,' Basilius said aggressively, handing Opilio a handful of green ribbon. As they busied themselves the servants stood back. It was not their place the stop the son of their mistress, but Basilius and Opilio soon tired of their prank and hurried off.

The ostentatious display of green antagonised the Blue supporters and fighting soon broke out among the servants waiting in the carts and litters.

Julia stopped on the steps leading from the circus to watch the turmoil below.

'After the races I didn't expect another spectacle.'

'It's ugly, my lady,' Rufus cautioned, but Julia ignored him.

Suddenly the piercing sound of trumpets filled the air, and just as suddenly the fighting stopped, the crowd's attention caught by the ceremony of the Consul's departure.

Miraculously, Julia's litter had escaped damage. Even the green ribbons were still in place.

'What fool tied these on?' Rufus asked the servants.

'It was Opi ...'

'Leave the pretty ribbons be,' Julia interrupted as he began hurriedly to untie them.

'But, my lady, it could cause trouble in the streets.'

'No, Rufus, leave it. The colour green has served your mistress well today.'

Julia took her seat, and Rufus, still worried, kept removing the ribbons away from her view. He was not quick enough, for suddenly, as if by order, the litter was engulfed by Blue supporters.

'Get the witch!' someone yelled.

A man's hand thrust inside the litter, snatching at Julia's sash and exposing her shoulder in the process. Then his two hands grabbed, brutally hauled her from the litter and, maddened by the passion of the mob, his lust aflame, he dragged her to the labyrinth of adjacent alleys.

Almost as quickly as the Blue supporters had emerged they vanished, leaving Rufus battered, bleeding and alone, the wreckage of the litter at his feet.

The servants and the porters had fled, but where was his mistress? He had to find her; so, dazed and badly mauled, the Tuscan staggered to the nearest alleyway to look.

He found her quickly, lying huddled tight against a nearby wall. He covered her as best he could and lifted her gently into his arms. Behind every shutter eyes were watching.

OOO

A full public hearing was launched the following day by the Consul Boethius, and without delay Cyprian was given leave to speak.

'My mother was defiled. Today she lies shocked and motionless, speaking little to anyone other than her faithful servant Rufus. How long this state will last the men of medicine cannot tell, and all the while the authors of this crime roam free – the Blues roam free! Am I, her son, to let this be? There must be punishment! The patrons of the Blues must purge their ranks!'

The hearing was restless, for both factions were well represented and many resented Cyprian's partisan attack, though they were careful to express their sympathy. They abhorred the crime against the noble lady, but none spoke out until Albinius, a Senator of some standing, said what most were thinking.

'I have heard,' he began gently, 'that the gracious lady's litter was decked with green. If this is true then, with due respect, I feel the passion of the Blue supporters was provoked.'

The nods of many present made it clear that Albinius had support. Cyprian was furious.

'Does a little colour justify so gross a crime?' he snapped.

'Colour cannot justify so gross a crime,' Albinius replied calmly. 'I do agree, for it's the very point I want to make. Clearly the criminal must be found and punished, but whether he is Blue or Green is not the question.'

'He was a Blue, amidst a mob of Blue supporters,' Cyprian reacted defiantly.

A number shook their heads vigorously.

Watching from the Consul's chair, Boethius could see that tempers were rising. Cyprian was being unusually foolish and the allowance that most were making for a son's distress was wearing thin. It was time to speak.

'We are all at one in our abhorrence of this crime,' he began, 'to which I add the united voice of the Senate, and as Consul I convey their sympathy.' He paused, his head bowed in reflection. All eyes were upon him.

His head rose. The timing was perfect.

'It would be a logical nonsense to label all supporters of the Blues as criminal because of one supporter's crime. The crime committed against the mother of our noble friend is as old as fallen human kind and the criminal must be sought vigorously. A reward should be posted in public places and the sum should be substantial.'

The nods of approval were unanimous.

'However, we cannot deny the connection with mob violence. After all, the litter of the noble lady was destroyed. In fact, for some time I've been appalled by the violent behaviour of the after-circus mob, and an enquiry into this curse is long overdue. Clearly the supporters of both colours are equally at fault, and to censure one alone would be unjust.'

The Consul took his seat, after which prominent patrons of both circus factions echoed his sentiments

'That's what I should have said,' Cyprian muttered bitterly to himself. 'Damn you, Boethius!'

OOO

# CHAPTER THIRTY EIGHT

# OSCA

After his encounter with Triguilla, Tullus grew uneasy. There had been something fixed and fearful in the looks of the bedraggled troop that Triguilla's drunken bluster had not covered. They had looked like men who had been mauled in action, yet there were no wounded. Still uneasy, he ordered three riders forward as a scouting party. It was midday and little time elapsed before they galloped back.

'There's a village on fire in the hills to the west.' This was the message that Theodis translated.

It was mid-afternoon when they arrived. The fire had raged much earlier but the smouldering remains were still producing smoke. Some of the dead had been hacked down in the streets, their wounds appalling, and there was perversion in the mutilation of the women. Not even the children had escaped. The scene was sickening.

Alone amongst the burnt-out buildings, the small church at the centre of the village was intact. Its high walls had kept the flames at bay. At once Tullus entered the dim interior, only to find more bodies strewn on the earthen floor. Sanctuary had been violated.

It was dark inside, with two small windows high in the wall behind the altar letting in twin shafts of light. As his eyes became accustomed to the gloom he noticed the motionless figure of a priest kneeling before the altar rail. The priest made no response as he approached and for a moment he believed the man was dead, but he knew a corpse could not sustain itself like that.

'Father,' he called.

The priest turned round as if controlled by puppet strings, his face blackened with grime and smoke.

'Who did this?' Tullus asked bluntly.

'The Devil's work,' the priest replied, his voice locked in an unresponsive monotone.

'You were spared – how did you escape?'

'The priest's cloth – they fear to touch it.' Again there was the monotone.

'They fear damnation, yet they do not fear the wrath of God for this!'

201

Tullus exploded, his voice echoing round the church.

The priest looked at him apathetically.

'They came this morning,' he said flatly. 'It did not take long, for we are a small village.'

'But why? For what reason?'

'I don't know. Our Visigothic lord turned against Gesalic – it may be some reprisal.'

'Surely Gesalic's in the south.'

'He has allies hereabouts.' The priest sighed deeply. 'I don't know – it could be the feud, of course.'

'What feud?'

'The village on the next hill to the south,' the priest answered wearily. 'Hatred has simmered for years and there have been killings. Only last week two of our men were murdered. Then there was a vengeance raid.'

'Is there no law?' Tullus asked forcefully.

'Crime is law, might is law – the brigand rules.' For the first time a note of passion disturbed the monotone, but it was short-lived.

With an air of exhaustion the priest sat down on the altar steps.

'The leader of the band of butchers, the ones who fired your village – did he have an unkempt bushy beard and little beady eyes?' Tullus had described Triguilla.

'The man you speak of came soon afterwards. I asked if he would help, but he only grunted. Then some of them found wine and started drinking.'

'That's Triguilla,' Tullus muttered inaudibly.

Suddenly Theodis burst into the church.

'There's some mounted men approaching – they're a ragged lot. Brigands, I suppose.'

'After loot,' Tullus snapped. 'How many?'

'About ten, sir.'

'You've called the men?'

'Yes, sir.'

Immediately Tullus went out into the sunlit square, the priest following behind.

There were ten riders, as Theodis had estimated, standing in a line before him. Their leader smiled, a broad knowing smile, before speaking rapidly. Tullus found his accent impossibly thick.

'What's he saying?' he asked the priest.

'He's telling you to leave.'

'Ask him how many men he has.'

'Ten,' was the sharp answer.

Casually Tullus pointed to his own men, now assembled.

The brigand turned to see the Royal Guardsmen and the soldiers of Ibbas.

'We will leave,' he said, his Latin just intelligible. He smiled again.

Tullus shook his head.

'In a while, perhaps. My men are digging graves and would appreciate some help.' Tullus grinned, reflecting the brigand's manner. 'Meanwhile you can leave your swords and daggers in a pile before me.'

The brigands looked at each other uneasily. They were outnumbered two to one and the guardsmen were like giants. Once more their leader smiled. Then slowly he unbuckled his sword-belt.

They worked steadily, for no one wanted to stop until the nauseating task was ended. Some of the men retched openly as they watched the mutilated forms jelly together in the mass graves. All the while the priest stood impassive, calmly taking note of what had been his congregation, and the graves in which they had been placed. Shock had robbed him of emotion.

The autumn sun was low when they gathered in the square before the church. Without instruction they had assembled in the same manner as before – the line of unkempt brigands surrounded by the Gothic soldiery. The weapons still lay where they had been left.

Theodis stood by his Roman master's side. What would Marcus Tullus do? For in Italy such men were either sold as slaves or executed. These were the simple Gothic rules, but the brigands had worked well.

A question from Tullus cut his speculation.

'Theodis, where's the priest? I need his help with this man's dialect.'

'He's in the church, sir. Observing the Sacrament, I think.'

'Yes – I see,' Tullus responded impatiently, for he could not wait. A decision had to be made quickly.

He looked at each of the motley band in turn. They had co-operated well, and without resentment. He stepped forward and looked again. Who lived behind those rags? he wondered. Then his gaze fixed on their leader. Still he did not speak, and the silence grew oppressive.

Again he stepped forward, this time stretching out his hand and the lean, unkempt man responded, his familiar smile both wide and generous.

'Have – you – food – wine?' Tullus spoke each word slowly.

The man shook his head and Tullus nodded to Theodis, who sent two men off to the pack-horses.

'Are – you – going – to – Barcino?' the outlaw asked, matching the slow speech of Tullus.

'In time.'

At that the man shook his head vigorously.

'No – the Lords – of Gesalic – are there – you are too small a force. I would not trust them.'

'And Tarraco?'

'The same,' the outlaw leader said emphatically.

This was wholly different from the information received from Count Ibbas.

'What of Caesaraugusta?'

'Yes,' the man nodded. 'The Lords faithful to young Athalaric are there. They would welcome your Ostrogoths.'

Tullus was finding it easier to hear the words behind the man's thick accent.

'How do we get there?'

'Over the hills – I'll take you.'

Tullus looked hard at the bearded face before him.

'Who – are – you?' he asked fiercely. 'You – know too much – to be – a common thief!'

The outlaw's smile beamed.

'You think that we – are – brigands but – we are – soldiers. We serve the needy for a fee but fees are few!'

Tullus continued to stare.

'Yes, fees are scarce!' he repeated, a smile playing on his lips.

Once more he viewed the leader closely.

'You and your men can be our vanguard,' Tullus said sharply. He had forgotten to speak slowly but he had been understood. 'Your name?' he added bluntly.

'Osca, sir.'

At that Tullus turned on his heel and strode into the church to find the priest.

When Tullus and the priest emerged Theodis had the guard already mounted, with the new ten-man vanguard out in front. A pack-horse, its load transferred, had been prepared for the priest, as Tullus was determined not to leave him in the village.

Soon they were off, with Tullus and his guard captain riding together.

'What have you arranged, Theodis?'

'Our new-made vanguard leader says he knows a place where we can stop. A deserted villa, he says, about two miles away. Sir, is it wise to trust these outlaws?'

'Tell me this, Theodis; in a state of anarchy, how do you define an outlaw?'

Theodis ignored the question; instead he pressed his warnings home. 'They could be luring us into a trap.'

'Yes, or out of one! We didn't know that Gesalic's men were masters of Barcino.'

'You're assuming that it's true.'

'Yes, it's an assumption. We do not know for sure.'

They rode on in silence and beside them the priest rode trance-like on his horse. He needed the quiet of the cloister, Tullus thought, and the sooner the better.

On a distant hill in front of them they could see the dust-cloud of the vanguard stop, close to a substantial building etched against the evening sun.

'Rest at last, Theodis,' Tullus called across.

'We'll have to be careful, sir. The dogs who fired the village may be close.'

'We have thirty men, Theodis.'

'I hope so, sir.'

'You still have doubts about the outlaw vanguard?'

'Yes, sir.'

The building, when they reached it, was no more than a shell, but the roof and walls were sound. It was better than the open air.

OOO

The journey to Caesaraugusta proceeded over tortuous terrain and consequently the progress of Tullus and his guard was slow. In this, the caution of the vanguard leader was a major cause, for no bend was rounded before the forward scouts had signalled. Again, he had chosen trackways far from the normal thoroughfare. Both Tullus and Theodis were impressed by the army-like approach. Even so, Theodis remained suspicious.

'Why cross these icy, arid hills for the few coins we have offered?' he questioned.

'Food. Theodis! The last village we passed was famine-ridden. Our vanguard leader, Osca, tells me that marauders steal the sheep and goats and carry off the winter stocks. We'll have to be careful, for our reserves are dwindling quickly.'

'It's not surprising, sir. The outlaw vanguard eat like wolves.'

'When you have been short for months you eat when chance presents itself,' Tullus responded forcefully. He knew the feeling all too well; his flight through Gaul had taught him that. 'Anyway,' he added, 'Osca has pinned his faith on the rich plains surrounding Ilerda. There's a church establishment there, he tells me.'

They came upon Ilerda within three days, but they were exhausted and much in need of fresh supplies. Theodis, knowing that dusk was fast approaching, wanted to proceed immediately, for warm food and shelter were essential. Osca, however, spoke forcibly in opposition.

'We must send scouts,' he kept repeating.

Tullus agreed and Theodis tried vainly to conceal his agitation, sensing that another night without real shelter would push the soldiery of Ibbas to breaking point.

Osca's scouts returned sooner than any had expected, but their news was disturbing. A brigand leader, posing as the friend of Gesalic, was holding Ilerda in a grip of terror. Two of the elders were hanging from gibbets in the square, and the priests, the people grumbled, had said nothing. There were sixty brigands in all, ill-disciplined and only answering to one man, their leader.

'We need supplies,' Theodis said flatly. 'And it's at least four days to Caesaraugusta.'

Tullus was silent. He had no wish to sacrifice the guard in what could be a doubtful undertaking.

'We must help,' Osca said with force. 'We can't ride past!'

Tullus stared hard at the vanguard leader, his features lit by the dancing light of a torch. These were not the sentiments of an outlaw.

'Who in God's name are you, Osca?' he growled.

The vanguard leader made no answer, and for a time the three men stood together without speaking. A decisive course of action was needed and Tullus knew the final word would have to come from him – and he had to speak at once, for further silence would be seen as indecision. But what to say?

Somehow words came.

'This brigand leader; I see him as a large and boastful man who holds the reins himself with little time for deputies. Am I right?'

'You are!' Osca replied forcefully. 'He's big and he's a braggart, as you say.'

Tullus paced slowly up and down.

'Tonight his cut-throats will be drunk, because they always are; while he will dally with his woman.'

'Yes, yes! You're right again!'

'He's a one-man cohort, jealous of his power and very careful not to foster rivals. His men will be a spineless lot.'

'You're absolutely right. How did you know?'

'Such men are predictable, Osca. Puncture him and the bubble of his power will burst.'

'An archer well concealed,' Theodis suggested.

'No! that could send his rabble company mad about the town – there must be another way,' Tullus muttered, his head bent in thought. He looked up. 'I suppose there's nothing for it but a dawn raid with you, Osca, helping from the inside. It could be costly, though.'

The tall figure of Theodis grew agitated.

'Can I have a word, sir?'

The two men stepped aside.

'If Osca's men are inside before we arrive, and if they join their fellow outlaws, we could be massacred,' Theodis said passionately.

'If that were so, Theodis, why did Osca's scouts tell us of the brigands' presence? Why throw the element of surprise away?'

Theodis had no answer, and Tullus beckoned Osca.

'I'm loth to risk men's lives on this adventure,' Tullus mused aloud.

'We need supplies, sir!' Theodis pressed. 'There is no other option.'

'Damn! – there must be!' Tullus grated. 'If only we could capture this bombast and use him as a hostage – but that's a dream.'

'We could try,' Osca responded unexpectedly. 'I know the town. The walls are as low as sheep-pens in places.'

'Try it!' Tullus ordered.

At that, Osca took four men and left immediately, while Tullus and Theodis settled down to wait. They dozed fitfully.

It was almost dawn when they were jolted into wakefulness. Osca had returned and with him was a huge, broad-shouldered man, half naked, his white body contrasting with the darkness of his bearded face. Osca grinned widely.

'He was with his woman – you were right!'

'Brilliant, Osca – audacity at its best!'

The barrier of language between Tullus and the vanguard leader had almost disappeared.

Once the gag was taken from the brigand's mouth he bellowed endlessly with rage.

'He's noisy,' Tullus said casually, taking Osca aside. 'He'll soon wear himself out, and when he does, could you fill him full of wine. I want him drunk – really drunk,' he emphasised. 'Theodis is preparing a guard,' he added. 'We're going in at dawn, but we'll need someone inside to deal with the brigand lookouts.'

'I'll arrange that,' Osca offered confidently.

'Good – there's no point in smuggling the guard inside. A blind mule would know that they were soldiers.'

The brigand leader, hands tied behind his back, drank all that was held for him, and when he shook his head as finished they taunted him until, loud-mouthed and boastful, he swallowed more.

They sat him on a pack-horse back to front; Tullus had remembered a similar scene from a childhood story. The once ruthless tyrant was now an object of ridicule.

The sun was up and rain was threatening. Tullus scanned the town walls, such as they were, but there was no one in sight. Osca's men had done their work.

'Tell them to open the gates,' Osca shouted in the brigand's ear. Instinctively the man refused. He sat up, fighting his drunken stupor, the nightmare of his peril suddenly before him. He swore loudly, but a knife pressing at his throat soon stopped his protest.

'Tell them to open,' Osca's voice repeated, menace in its sharpness.

The brigand bellowed and the gates began to swing apart.

The unquestioning obedience of the brigand's gate-men had laid them open to attack. They stood a moment, paralysed by indecision, then they tried to flee, but the Royal Guardsmen cut them down with casual ease.

Like a formal progress they proceeded, Osca's knife in readiness. The brigand's men, their leader powerless and without a plan, stood helpless until instinct prompted they escape, but then, just then, the people turned on their oppressors.

In the square it was the same. A knife flashed through the air and struck the brigand's chest beside his heart. He slumped, lifeless. To him it was a blessing, for they dragged him from his horse and strung him to the gibbet from where, just moments earlier, the chief elder had been hanging.

Tullus sat impassive on his horse, his guard about him. Slowly the leaders of the town approached.

For two days he and his men rested. Then in the morning of the third day they left for Caesaraugusta.

The reputation of Marcus Tullus had gone before him, and at Caesaraugusta he was hailed as a hero. Repeatedly he gave the laurel of success to Osca, but it made no difference.

Tullus paid homage to the young grandson of Theoderic and met the mighty Lords faithful to his cause. He was not impressed, for each lord felt himself a petty kingdom. A strong unifying hand was clearly necessary, but who would fill that need was quite another matter.

After six days Tullus and his guard began their return journey.

OOO

# CHAPTER THIRTY NINE

# THE SENATOR

The low, rambling villa at Fidenae was dim in the fading light of dusk. It had grown cold and the wind was bitter; even so, Poppea stood waiting on the portico steps as her husband and his guard approached.

It was a familiar sight, for twice a month at least Valerius visited the Senator Symmachus. Yet Poppea always felt a thrill of joy to see her lord approach.

A lesser man might have tired of her devotion, but this was not the case with Valerius. To him the gentle Poppea was a continuing delight. He loved her unassuming ways.

Valerius dismounted, and without delay a servant led his horse away. Then, as he always did, he hurried to embrace his wife.

'Did you have a good meeting with the Senator?' she asked.

'Yes, the noble Symmachus was his usual self, but I also met the Bishop Ennodius, the Senator Faustus and the Consul himself. It was quite a day, my dear. Ennodius and Faustus were just back from Constantinople, so there was a feast of news. I'll tell you all about it over supper – and how is Drusilla?'

'Like her father! She reads and reads! She had a letter from Marcus this morning, so her spirits are high. It was despatched from Arelate.'

'Just at the start of his journey; by now he's probably on his way back.'

At supper Valerius recounted the news he had heard about Byzantium to his wife and to his daughter. The Emperor Anastasius, the travellers had said, had a mildness not unlike the great Nerva who followed the Flavians, but his heretical opinions sullied his reputation. On this the churchman Ennodius was particularly critical. Yet for a man of over seventy, Anastasius was still quite energetic. His age, however, made the issue of succession prominent, and because of this, political undercurrents were strong. Both had met Justinian, the forceful nephew of Justin, Count of the Excubitors, and both agreed he was a man to watch.

'Marcus's friend,' Drusilla interjected.

'Yes, my dear. Apparently he has gathered men about him of considerable power and quality. He's also a patron of the Blue faction and uses their partisans to further his interests. This is the muddier pool of

Byzantine life. Yet all the arts were flourishing, they said. It was an exciting, vibrant city.'

'What did Boethius say to all this, Father?' Drusilla questioned.

'Very little, my dear, except to caution Ennodius to keep his enthusiasms private.'

'The Goths,' Drusilla suggested.

Her father nodded.

The conversation lapsed, and Valerius lay back on his couch, his eyes closed. At his side Poppea was sewing. Drusilla picked up a manuscript and began to read, but after a few moments she stopped.

'He's changed,' she said

'Who? Boethius?'

'Yes.'

'How do you mean?'

'When you took me to see Rusticiana a few weeks ago I met the Consul. I sensed something different about him. It's difficult to say, but he seemed more open and patient in a way.'

Valerius smiled.

'You've noticed too, Father?'

'No! Not really,' he said mildly. 'But, my dear, you would expect a seeker of truth to modify his ways.'

'Is that a hint?'

'No, no! How could perfection be but perfect?'

Drusilla laughed, lay back on her couch and yawned.

'It's time for bed, but first I must check that Cornelia is asleep – late night bursts of glee are not unknown.'

'Drusilla seems to suffer the absence of Marcus well,' Valerius said quietly when she had gone.

'Oh, no, Lucius. She is often wretched, though she keeps her misery private. She doesn't want to be a drag on Marcus.'

'She's right. It's as it should be.'

For some time they sat close together as they often did, content and silent.

'They want me to join the Senate,' he said suddenly.

Startled, Poppea sat upright.

'It would mean moving to Rome,' he added, watching her face closely, for there her doubts were etched. She knew the life of a senator's wife would be wholly different from the quiet idyll of Fidenae.

'Don't worry, Poppe. The role of a senator's wife may seem daunting but, my dear, you have the perfect model – your old mistress Rusticiana.

You know well how she conducts herself.'

'Yes,' she said tentatively. She turned to face him. 'The Senator Valerius,' she whispered.

'I'm still to be approved, my lady Poppea. It's not at all certain, for my property holdings are marginal.'

'It's your right! Who has more patrician blood than you?'

Valerius laughed. His wife was not tall, and the sight of her small figure sitting upright and indignant amused him greatly.

'Well, at least I've one supporter,' he said, smiling widely. Then his mood changed.

'There'll be cruel jibes about your origin. Such pettiness is inevitable,' he said quietly, but she did not seem to hear.

'Everything will change,' she said sadly. She pressed close to him. 'But I'm glad – so very glad they've asked you. Who asked you, Lucius?'

'Symmachus. Boethius and he are anxious for support.'

'Are you glad?'

'Part of me is flattered but the greater part says "No!"'

'Will you accept?'

'How can I refuse?'

'Will Marcus be asked?' she questioned, her head leaning against his chest.

'No, Boethius opposed it. He feared it might upset the King.'

'I don't understand.'

'Don't try, my dear. It is a spider's web.'

ooo

# CHAPTER FORTY

# ANGER

It was January, and an evening mist shrouded Thulwin's villa at Fidenae. Tullus and his escort of six Royal Guardsmen turned into the familiar entrance. Already the night torches framed the portico.

Tullus and Theodis rode in front, the eyes of both searching, one for Drusilla and Cornelia, the other for Cornelia's nurse.

Drusilla was there. Cornelia was there. Valerius and Poppea were there, but the nurse was not amongst them.

Tullus glanced sideways at Theodis, whose face was set rock-hard.

Cornelia ran to her father and embraced him. He held her high.

'Welcome home, Papa,' she said happily. Tullus laughed. They were Drusilla's words.

He embraced his wife, holding her close without speaking, after which he turned to greet Valerius and Poppea.

'Where's the nurse?'

'Oh, Marcus.' It was Drusilla who answered. 'Her lovely hair, they sheared it off.'

'Who?' Tullus exploded.

'The fanatics connected with the Church. We've just found out, for she was ashamed to tell us and kept her head covered for the past few days.'

'Theodis,' Tullus barked.

'Yes, sir.'

'Go and comfort the lady.'

Immediately the tall Goth disappeared into the villa.

'They sent her hair this morning, in a parcel marked "for a heretic",' Drusilla added.

'By the gods,' Tullus hissed through clenched teeth. 'Someone bring me that parcel.'

At once Drusilla rushed into the villa. It was the first time she had seen her husband really angry. When she returned with the parcel he was already mounted and anxious to be off.

'Be careful, Marcus,' she called.

ooo

It was dark when Tullus reached Fidenae. On the way, a low half-moon and the fading glow of dusk had been the only light.

He went straight to the basilica and asked to see the Deacon. A priest hurried off and Tullus waited, his anger simmering.

'The Deacon hopes the honourable Tullus will tolerate a slight delay,' the priest said apologetically on his return.

Tullus forced a smile and continued to wait. Time passed slowly and his rage began to boil. The priest watched anxiously.

'Is this a slight delay?' Tullus snapped, his anger over-spilling. 'What's he doing?'

'He's with some Papal staff from Rome.' A nervous tremor agitated the priest's voice.

'Are they drinking?'

'Yes,' was the hesitant answer.

'Take me to them,' Tullus growled.

'But, sir, they're not to be …'

'Don't ask me to repeat myself.'

Overwhelmed, the priest turned and meekly led the way.

A door swung open, and before him Tullus saw a well-lit, ornate room, its ceiling low. Four men were seated round a heavy wooden table, each with a large wine-cup before him.

'I told you we were not to be disturbed. That's twice you've disobeyed,' the Deacon snapped, not sensing Tullus's presence.

'Leave the good man alone. Address your words to me,' Tullus barked.

'Ah! the noble Tullus,' the Deacon reacted, covering his surprise with a patronising smoothness. He started to get up.

'Sit,' Tullus spat.

The Deacon was jolted and spilled his wine, while his three companions sat transfixed.

With deliberate steps Tullus approached the table, clutching the parcel of hair.

'I returned from the west this evening,' he began in slow, measured tones.

'How interesting – from where?' one of the Deacon's guests reacted nervously.

Tullus glared at him and the man appeared to shrink.

'When I arrived at the villa I was greeted by the news that my daughter's nurse had been seized and, in the process, had her hair hacked off by fanatics connected with this church. The parcel I hold "for a heretic" – I want an inquiry, Deacon.'

'An inquiry! Into what?' The Deacon's high-pitched voice was shrill. 'The whole town knows her shame. What can I do if the people demonstrate their anger?'

'You can stop inciting hatred from the altar steps. Your so-called preaching is well known to me.'

'This is blasphemy!' the Deacon screamed.

Tullus opened the parcel he was clasping and held it close to the indignant churchman's face.

'Deacon – *this* is blasphemy!'

He lifted one of the locks of hair and dropped it on the table. No one moved.

'"Blessed are the merciful; for they shall obtain mercy."' The words were powerful.

Another lock of hair fell on the table.

'"Blessed are the pure in heart, for they shall see God."'

Once more Tullus dipped into the parcel.

'"Blessed are the peacemakers; for they shall be called the children of God."'

For a moment the figures in the room remained like statues. Then the priest made to leave.

'Stop, father,' Tullus said quietly. 'I want you as a witness.'

Again the room seemed fixed in frozen immobility.

'Deacon – on the sabbath you will preach against this monstrous act. Remember, it's the second time we've crossed – a third time won't be in your interest.'

With that Tullus turned suddenly and left the room.

Surrounded by his escort he rode slowly back to the villa. Anger had drained him of his energy. He felt no elation, for little had been achieved. Theodis was an Arian Goth and his daughter's nurse a member of the Roman Church. There was no bridge, no middle path. The gulf between the two traditions made the Tiber look a narrow stream.

'The shackles of belief,' he muttered to himself.

When they reached the entrance to the villa Claudius turned in unbidden. In the distance Tullus could see the white stone of the portico glowing in the light of the torches.

A lone figure stood waiting. It was Drusilla.

'Rest and peace at last,' he sighed

OOO

214

# CHAPTER FORTY ONE

# THE COUNT

Seven days after Tullus's return two despatches arrived from Ravenna; one from the King, the other from Count Thulwin. Both were generous in their praise. To relieve the town of Ilerda without loss of Gothic life was a feat worthy of an ancient triumph. They were the King's sentiments, but the words were those of the Quaestor Cassiodorus. The tall Roman was well versed in the fashion of elaborate language.

The King, of course, wished to see his envoy. Tullus's reports from Hispania had been comprehensive, but it was the spoken word that mattered to Theoderic. The royal command was couched in casual terms, but Tullus had no doubt a prompt response was necessary.

'The road again,' he grumbled to Drusilla, yet he left the following morning.

The meetings were conducted in the usual way. Indeed, for four days running they rode together in the forest park. The King questioned Tullus exhaustively, ending with a growl that Gesalic would be purged by Ibbas in the spring.

On the last day, when the forest ride was almost over, the monarch suddenly reined his horse.

'Tullus, there's something I don't like.'

Tullus felt his stomach tighten but he said nothing

'Theodis and your daughter's nurse. These mixtures are a source of trouble. They never work.'

'Theodis is a man of honour, sir,' Tullus responded evenly.

'I know that!' Theoderic barked.

Tullus swallowed and continued.

'The nurse is beautiful and he is tall and manly. Circumstance brought them together. My Lord King, it's hard to stand against the force of nature.'

Tullus waited, expecting a rebuke.

'He's one of our best young men. I don't like it!'

Theoderic nudged his horse forward: a signal Tullus had learned to interpret. The subject was closed.

'I've sent an angry letter to the Pope,' the King said almost casually. 'Knowing the Church, they'll probably promote your friend the Deacon, especially as you've clashed with him a second time.'

The King missed nothing, Tullus thought.

Theoderic glanced sideways, humour playing with his features. Suddenly his horse leapt forward and he reined it hard. He looked back over his shoulder.

'I'm making you a Count,' he shouted.

Then his horse, as if propelled by some siege catapult, galloped off, leaving Tullus in a daze of unbelief, until he noticed Claudius had followed, and exactly at the speed his master would have wished.

OOO

Tullus's visit to Ravenna coincided with that of the Senator Boethius – now ex-Consul. Reluctantly, the Senator's ability was drawing him closer to the centre of the King's administration. Indeed, his eventual rise to the office of Chief Minister was thought inevitable, but the relationship between Boethius and Theoderic did not have the simple informality that Tullus enjoyed. Boethius was a Senator, an ex-Consul, a man of unusual quality and he was a Roman. He could do no other than represent the Roman people: a political fact that the Gothic King could not ignore.

All this Tullus learned from the confidential asides of the Quaestor Cassiodorus. He also learned that Cyprian was a rising star amongst the up-and-coming at the Palace. He had the admirable quality, the Quaestor said, of presenting his case in succinct terms, and he was charming.

The word 'succinct' sounded incongruous on the lips of Cassiodorus, for even his asides were often prosy. Tullus smiled. He found the Quaestor a man of contrasts. He was forceful, if not rigid, in matters of religion, yet definitely flexible in the world of politics. A survivor, Tullus thought, a student of the palace corridors.

OOO

When Tullus learned that Boethius was in Ravenna he quickly sought him out and by mutual agreement they arranged to travel together. In doing this, Tullus sacrificed a visit to his villa, but the opportunity for conversation with Boethius was too good to miss.

Boethius and his bodyguard, with Tullus and his escort, assembled the following morning for the journey south. Tullus took his seat beside Boethius in the Senator's two-wheeled cart. Claudius, he thought, could have a well-earned rest. In the general bustle, though, Tullus had forgotten to give the animal over to the escort's care and they, so used to Claudius roaming free, did not notice. So when they started up, Claudius, his reins hanging loosely on his neck, quietly eased forward so that he could walk beside his master. Tullus leaned across and patted him.

'An amazing creature,' he enthused to Boethius. 'The King likes him, and greets him in the park as if he were a human!'

The pace grew brisk, for the horses seemed to relish the sharpness of the morning.

'What a grand, important pair we are,' Boethius joked. 'The great ex-Consul and the mighty Count!'

'Count of what, I wonder?!'

'It's a rare honour, Tullus. A Gothic honour from a grateful monarch. Your exploits are the talk of all Ravenna.'

'My exploits! It all happened to me. The most I did was trust one man,' Tullus said, thinking of Osca.

'Even so, it was your decision.'

They fell silent, and Tullus became aware of the all too familiar sounds of travel.

'Sometimes I feel I've seen more roads than any man,' he said emphatically. 'look at those paving-stones; on and on they go. There is no end to them. They come, they are, they go and still they come!'

Boethius laughed heartily.

'Not unlike Counts and Consuls,' he responded.

'What is the meaning of it all?'

'Perhaps there is no meaning!' Boethius answered with a note of studied innocence.

Tullus sat up, suddenly alert.

'Perhaps we ought to follow Plato and say that God is eternal and the world perpetual,' Boethius continued.

'That's a subject that could keep us going right until we see the gates of Rome,' Tullus returned. 'The changeless and the ever-changing. The constant and the ...'

Without warning the cart lurched violently, making both men grab the hand-rails.

'Tullus, your paving-stones have taken some offence. Maybe we ought to praise their smoothness.'

'Flattery might make them undulate.'

'A rhythmic journey, then.'

They laughed and the conversation continued, still centred on Plato's statement.

ooo

217

CHAPTER FORTY TWO

# THE KING'S PEACE

In the year 511 Clovis died. His Frankish kingdom, the labour of a ruthless will, was split and shared between his sons. At the same time the Count Ibbas drove Gesalic from Hispania. This Theoderic had predicted. So with the diffusion of Frankish power and the defeat of Gesalic, the will of the Ostrogothic king was now unchallenged in the west.

In the east, religious riots troubled Constantinople. The Emperor, despairing of maintaining peace between the extreme parties, had sided with his Monophysite friends and dismissed the Patriarch. The result was chaos. Christ was one divine nature, the Monophysites said. No, cried the Orthodox: Christ's nature was both human and divine. Tullus pictured the opposing mobs screaming slogans at each other, but leaving the followers of Arius, the Arian minority, untroubled and free to nurture their belief that Christ, though he was begotten before time, and though through him all things were made, was not co-eternal with the Father. The Father was supreme. How could the people on the streets begin to understand the finer points? Beliefs and more beliefs. There was no end to them. The whole debate left Tullus cold.

With religious controversy raging in the east, Tullus feared the King might send him there, but no such order came. So after reviewing the progress of Thulwin's estates, he gladly set out for his villa at Faesulae.

He arrived before Easter and immediately busied himself with the building. New quarters were constructed for visitors and their servants. He also built an aqueduct, his special pride, which carried water from a spring close by. As well as this, the fortress villa walls were strengthened where there were some hints of disrepair.

During the summer the newly-elevated Senator Valerius and his Lady Poppea were guests. And to everyone's delight, Boethius called on three occasions while travelling to and from Ravenna. It was a happy, carefree time for all excepting Anna, Cornelia's nurse; for Theodis had been ordered by Theoderic to serve within the palace guard.

With still no royal summons and with autumn approaching, Tullus was beginning to hope for a year free of travel. But this was not to be, for at the end of September the Praetorian Prefect, complete in his knee-length purple, arrived with orders from Ravenna. Tullus was to investigate reports of famine in Southern Italy.

To receive a personal visit from the Prefect was, on the face of it, a signal honour. Even so, Tullus wondered who was curious. Was it the Prefect or the King himself? How did the new-made Count conduct himself at Faesulae? Was that the monarch's question?

'He caught you working in the fields,' Drusilla said after the visitor had left. 'The King will like the picture of honest industry.'

Tullus laughed but he knew his wife was right.

As quickly as possible Tullus left for the south and Drusilla once more spent the winter at Fidenae. Tullus's mission was difficult and his reports to Ravenna frequent and urgent. In this way Theoderic cut through the ponderous efforts of officialdom.

The summer of 512 again found Tullus at Faesulae. News of religious riots at the Eastern capital continued and, as before, he braced himself to face the long journey to the east. It was either that or Hispania, he thought. In fact it was neither of these options, for yet again he was sent to Southern Italy.

It was in the following year, 513, that Tullus returned to Hispania. He found Theoderic's rule now well established, though the Lords were much too mighty, the islands of their power bolstered by ostentatious bodyguards. He was pleased to find Osca a respected citizen of Ilerda, where the town's elders, mindful of his prowess, had made him master of their guard.

At Barcino he was introduced to Eutharic, the young Ostrogoth confidently proclaimed as the future husband of the King's daughter Amalasuentha. Tullus liked the young Goth's forthright manner and had little doubt that Theoderic would give his final word when Eutharic eventually came in person to Ravenna.

Eutharic, a man of famous lineage, had lived amongst his Visigothic neighbours in relative obscurity. Now he was treated with all the deference accorded to a future king.

The meeting between Tullus and the young Goth was brief, but sufficient to establish a mutual respect. Eutharic had heard of Tullus and his projected visit from the King, and had also heard about the now legendary relief of Ilerda. Of course, from Tullus's viewpoint there was a clear advantage in meeting Eutharic before he reached Theoderic's busy court.

Tullus returned in late March and went straight to Ravenna. It was not necessary, the King had told him, to await a formal summons.

The meeting with the King was, with the certainty of ritual, on horseback. It was friendly, remarkably so, yet Tullus was never quite relaxed. The King was always the King.

Once dismissed, he quickly made for the south and Fidenae, but without Theodis. He stayed to join the Palace guard as he had done for the past two years. Such was the King's will.

For Marcus Tullus the whole affair of Anna and Theodis was a mess, and the King's directives, being neither harsh nor lenient, left things unresolved.

'He'll find someone of his own race in Ravenna,' the King said confidently, but this had not happened – mistresses, perhaps, but not a wife. Yet there was no royal anger and no forced marriage. It was strange, for like the great Augustus, Theoderic was keen to see his best men wed, but then, the King was never quite predictable.

OOO

The year that Tullus returned from Hispania the Pope died. The accession of the new Pope Homisdas brought, of course, the usual speculation. How would he deal with the schism dividing East and West? Would there be some form of compromise? Would the Henotikon, the Eastern hope of unifying Monophysite and Orthodox factions and the cause of the schism with the West, be in some way accommodated?

The moderate might hope, but the forceful majority saw no need to compromise. Not a word, not a comma, they shouted. Tullus had expected little else.

The following year, 515, the Pope sent two emissaries to the Patriarch at Constantinople with an uncompromising profession of faith. He insisted that the Orthodox conclusions fixed by the Council of Chalcedon be accepted, a number of heretics, mostly Monophysite, condemned, and the Pope's supremacy as the guardian of orthodoxy and successor of Peter acknowledged.

This was defiance and Anastasius, so long the champion of the Henotikon and compromise, refused. The schism was still an unbridgeable gulf.

OOO

At Ravenna the troubles of the Roman and Eastern churches seemed distant, for the Gothic people were rejoicing, happy that the daughter of their King had found a husband worthy of her lineage.

The marriage celebrations of Eutharic and Amalasuentha lasted a week. Gothic noblemen and Roman dignitaries both gathered to pay respect and homage. There were feasts and entertainments, with feats of horsemanship being a popular attraction for the Goths. One Gothic nobleman, famed for his prowess, performed an acrobatic act of riding and was loudly cheered. The Romans applauded politely, but in their hearts they saw a legate behaving like a legionary.

In the palace, counts and senators strained and jostled. It was an opportunity to meet old acquaintances, and because of this Tullus saw little of his friends Count Thulwin and the Senators Boethius and Symmachus. The busy gathering was not a situation Tullus relished but, much as he might wish, he could not leave for Faesulae until due homage had been paid to both the King and the newly-wedded royal couple.

He was called much earlier than expected and at once he went to fetch Drusilla, who was staying with Rusticiana. Without delay they presented themselves.

As they bowed, their full names sounded on the lips of Cassiodorus.

'Ah, Tullus, an acquaintance well renewed, and your graceful lady,' Eutharic nodded with a smile.

All eyes were on Drusilla, as Tullus replied with appropriate deference.

Again Eutharic smiled.

'My royal father-in-law tells me that your husband is a Briton, a man from the north,' he said, addressing Drusilla.

The King laughed loudly, and straightway all were laughing.

'The Count often dreams of southern Britain, especially when the Tuscan hills are baking in the summer heat,' Drusilla's rich voice quietly responded.

The conversation continued on a humorous note for some time, but the bride Amalasuentha remained silent. She looked very young, Tullus thought.

When it was time to take their leave the King stood up. Tullus was amazed. It was a great honour.

'Count, your gracious lady has charmed us all,' Theoderic said firmly. His words were rarely idle.

Tullus and Drusilla bowed low. The audience was over.

Tullus felt proud of his wife, for her grace and intelligence had been evident to all. His praise was generous, but even with the elation of a successful audience he felt no urge to linger in the city. Tullus had no love for formal ceremony.

'I saw Theodis,' Drusilla said as they travelled home together in their two-wheeled cart.

'So did I, but he gave nothing away. No doubt one of the guards is carrying a letter for Anna.' He sighed. 'It's a hopeless situation. It amazes me that it's still going on. For they only see each other once or twice a year, and very briefly.'

'The attachment must be deep. It's tragic, Marcus – just think of us being held apart.'

'At least there's no child to compound the problem,' Tullus responded.

Suddenly the presence by his side seemed to disappear.

'What's the matter, Drusilla?'

'Oh, it's ...'

'I know – our childless state,' he interrupted, drawing her close.

'Providence is just a little tardy, dear.'


ooo


Julia sat on her favourite seat in the inner courtyard of the villa on the Aventine. Dusk was approaching, but it was warm; even so, Rufus had given her a rug. He was very kind, she thought, closing her eyes. Sleep was close. Then she heard the sound of footsteps. She looked up.

'You're back, my son,' she said quietly. 'Where were you? I've for ...'

'Ravenna,' Cyprian returned impatiently. Surely she remembered that. 'I saw the new and mighty Count, Mother,' he added with mock grandeur.

'Did you, son? What count?'

'Tullus, Mother!'

'Oh, I didn't know he was a count,' she answered mildly.

'I told you at least ...' He stopped himself. There was no point in giving way to irritation, for his mother's memory was fading fast.

Julia had never recovered from the brutal violation that she had suffered. She was vague, easily confused and, in contrast with her previous nature, mild. Her speech could be repetitive and undirected, yet at times her comments cut with disconcerting accuracy.

Cyprian continued to talk because he could think of nothing else to do.

'And, Mother,' he said, injecting enthusiasm, 'the Countess, the lissom daughter of Valerius, was there. Age has improved the perfect.'

She smiled wanly.

'The Senator Valerius was not in evidence, though, but then, he's just the lap-dog of Symmachus!' His last words were bitter and sarcastic.

'And little Poppe?' she asked quietly.

'They keep her well away,' he replied hurriedly.

'Who keeps her?'

'It's all right, Mother, it's all right,' he said soothingly. He had no wish to pursue the subject.

'You liked her,' she continued innocently.

'That was years ago,' he snapped, forgetting himself.

'It takes years to forget.' Her voice was a whisper.

Cyprian looked at his mother with exasperation. She seemed to know his thoughts – and so damned accurate.

They sat together without a word between them, and he knew that if he did not speak she could sit for ages staring vacantly in front of her.

'The mighty Boethius was there, of course; nursing his patrician dignity and the Anicius wealth, with sycophants hanging on his every word.'

'Why are you so set against Boethius, my son?' Again her tone was mild.

'Why?' His voice swelled with passion. 'Why? At every turn he's there asking awkward questions. Sometimes I do believe he thinks he's God! You ask me why! When we found the criminal who attacked you, he stopped the case. Insufficient evidence, he said. He called the witnesses paid informers and the Prefect believed him. Anyway, the Prefect's in his pocket. You ask me why: Mother, the list is long.'

She made an effort to turn and look at him.

'That's not the reason, Cyprian.'

'What do you mean, Mother?' he asked with some annoyance. She was playing her stupid prophetic game again.

'Your soul is more important than your job,' she replied gently.

'What's my soul got to do with it?' Cyprian asked impatiently.

'Don't tangle with Boethius,' she returned without assertion. Then, almost in the same breath, she asked for Rufus, and Cyprian pulled the bell-cord.

'Rufus,' she said quietly when the Tuscan appeared. 'It's time for church.'

'Yes, my lady.'

'Not again, Mother.' Cyprian's annoyance was obvious.

'Would you like to come?' she responded mildly.

He shook his head as he watched Rufus help her to her feet. She had acquired a stoop and, with difficulty, looked up at him.

'Are you sure, Cyprian?'

'Quite sure, Mother,' he affirmed.

She walked off, leaning heavily on Rufus. His once witty and vivacious mother was frail and sinking fast.

ooo

In the year that Eutharic married Amalasuentha, Marcus Tullus received no commission to travel and at last he celebrated Christ's birth with his family at Fidenae, but not Faesulae as he would have liked. Rome itself was not the draw, nor indeed Fidenae; it was the nearby meetings at the Anicius palace which followed a regular pattern in the winter months. The knowledge and the wisdom shared was much too good to miss.

Early in 516 he paid a visit to Sublaqueum. He had acted on impulse; a sudden desire to see Martin. When he arrived at the community, he found it had acquired a more established look. Building had progressed. They had planted vines and olive trees and there were patches here and there for corn. There were, certainly, no idle hands.

Martin, of course, was Martin, an adult Martin and, judging by his questions, he still retained his old intuitive mode of thinking. Marcus Tullus spent two nights at the community, so the friends had ample time to talk. Mostly the conversation centred on the care of vines, the planting of olives and husbandry in general. Tullus was pleased that they enjoyed a new and practical interest, as perpetual reminiscing soon grew tedious.

As an honoured guest he dined with the Abbot Benedict, who, as ever, was impressive. Not because of any overt power of erudition, but due to the simplicity and aptness of his comments. This, and the deep peace about the man, made his company a blessing. Yet Tullus knew, as he had always known, that the way of Sublaqueum was not his way. In this there was no disrespect, for he admired the work of Father Benedict and his brethren. It was simply that the teaching of Boethius was closer to his heart.

When he returned from Sublaqueum he was greeted by Drusilla, and he sensed at once that something was wrong.

'It's Anna, Marcus. Cornelia, in her childish honesty, alerted us – her eyesight is deteriorating.'

'How bad?' he asked wearily. A full day on the road had taken its toll.

'Father sent for an expert and he came at once. She may only have a year.'

'Dear God,' Tullus exhaled. 'Does she know?'

'Yes.'

For a moment they stood unmoving on the portico, the red haze of dusk settling slowly into darkness.

'Anna asked when we were going to Faesulae,' Drusilla said in a whisper. 'Poor Anna – she and Theodis liked it there.'

Tullus did not respond immediately. Then he drew his wife towards him.

'Boethius is off to Ravenna soon, and Thulwin's estates manage themselves. There's nothing to keep us here, Drusilla. We can leave as soon as you are ready.'

She turned and embraced him.

'Oh, Marcus,' she said quietly, 'I like Faesulae as well.'

They walked arm in arm into the villa.

'Drusilla, do you think the expert *was* an expert?'

'I sensed he was an honest man. As he said, he gave us "his best opinion".'

OOO

They had been settled at Faesulae for several days before Drusilla sensed her husband's growing restlessness. It was unusual, for normally Marcus was quite happy with his building projects and overseeing the estate. Eventually she felt compelled to speak and, knowing how he kept his worries private, she questioned tactfully.

'You seem unsettled, Marcus. Last night your sleep was restless. Is there something on your mind?'

'It's Anna. I can see no resolution, no hope of marriage, for Theodis is bound by oath and while Theoderic lives he cannot change.'

'The King could release him.'

'There's little chance of that, and even if there were, is it right that a man should change his faith simply as a matter of convenience?'

Drusilla had no answer.

'And Anna!' Tullus continued. 'For her to change would be tantamount to … a denial of the Christ. It could destroy her and the marriage.' He sighed deeply. 'I'm not exactly blameless, for I did nothing to prevent it.'

'Marcus, it was well established before you even knew. Anyway, you're like Father. Religious dogmas and beliefs are not your first concern.'

Tullus stood up and began to pace the room.

'But even if they cannot marry – is it right to do nothing? She may only have a year to see the colours of this world. If this is so, am I to let it pass without Theodis knowing? Yet logic says just let it be, for they cannot marry; and Theodis, if he knew, could well be trapped by pity.'

'That's his decision, Marcus. In any case he'll know in time. There's nothing surer.'

'You're right, of course. So what am I to do? Go and see the King and court the royal anger? He'll not like it, but at least I shall have tried, for something deep within me says that truth should rule, and not division fired by men's beliefs. It may be stupid and naïve, even sentimental, but tomorrow I will set out for Ravenna.'

Drusilla jumped from her couch and embraced him.

'I love you, Marcus Tullus!' she exclaimed.

OOO

# CHAPTER FORTY THREE

# THE ROYAL DREAM

The guard duty of Theodis varied. Sometimes he was within the palace, sometimes without, but he was happiest when his duties took him to the forest park. Such was his role as he sat mounted, waiting for the King. There were five others in attendance. They sat upright as soldiers do, in immaculate uniforms, but as they waited, rigid with formality, banter shot between them untiringly.

'Whether wine or women, you used to lead the field – but now we have to push. You're fading fast, Theodis!' one said, his face impassive, his eyes fixed straight ahead.

'You're a shadow of your former self,' another jibed.

'And someone saw you reading!'

Theodis sat impassive, waiting for his turn to counter. Suddenly they froze. Their Lord Theoderic had emerged. They remained like statues as he passed, and then another horseman came. Theodis held his breath. It was Marcus Tullus.

Theodis was full of speculation. Was it Byzantium? That was the probability, as he knew the Count had been expecting such an order.

Turning from their initial gallop, the King and Tullus began to walk their horses slowly, with the Royal Guardsmen following discreetly. Then the monarch stopped and his speech, borne on a slight breeze, began to be discernible.

'Tullus, I'm running a kingdom, not a nursery.' Theoderic was obviously annoyed.

Tullus had his back to the guardsmen, so his reply was inaudible.

'I know we're human beings,' the King snapped.

There was another exchange, but out of hearing. Theodis sat tense and immobile. This was not the usual easy meeting between the Lord Theoderic and his Roman Count.

'Tullus!' The King's bark made Theodis start. 'I'm not the Deacon of Fidenae!'

Theoderic's horse began to move. Then, suddenly, the monarch roared with laughter. The horses stopped again.

'Count, be content; you've made your plea.'

Again the horses moved and the sound of conversation faded.

OOO

That evening Tullus kept to his quarters, his feelings mixed. He had traded on his favoured relationship with the King; he had asked for compassion, some concession. The King, though annoyed, had listened and had asked him to wait until the morning.

Tullus, though, was ill at ease, and angry with himself for being restless. Had he acted rightly, or had he been a sentimental fool? Was it right to have troubled the busy King with such a matter? Yet when he thought of Anna his perspective changed.

'This is no way to behave,' he grumbled to himself.

In the morning he awoke early and after a brisk walk returned to his rooms to wait. The early bustle had not started, and he could only hear faint, distant sounds that emphasised the stillness. Then he heard footsteps approaching, measured footsteps, followed by a slow, deliberate knocking at the door. It was Cassiodorus.

Tullus did not expect him to come to the point quickly.

The King, he said, had pondered long. He had asked advice but his royal master had not mentioned names, and as Cassiodorus continued it became obvious that Theoderic had not wavered. So eventually when he gave the King's decision Tullus was already well prepared.

His official business over, Cassiodorus grew confidential. The King had been annoyed, but not angry. He was not a nursemaid, he had grumbled. Yet his conclusion had been studied. Mercy would simply add faggots to the fire.

Tullus nodded wearily. That point of view was all too valid.

'You said something about the Deacon of Fidenae that amused him greatly?' Cassiodorus's tone was questioning.

'Yes, after he barked at me, I told him his prediction had been proved correct, for the Deacon had been elevated to the dignity of the papal staff.'

'Yes, I remember drafting a letter of complaint about him. Yes, yes! – Well, I must be going,' he added in his ponderous way. Yet his passing through the doorway was deft and speedy.

Cassiodorus was a Senator and an ex-Consul from the year 514, but Tullus never thought of him as such. He was a court official who could hear a palace whisper through a wall. Nonetheless, Tullus felt he had a friend.

Only Drusilla had known of his mission, so when he returned to Faesulae disappointment was confined.

ooo

The King knew all his palace guard by name. They were the elite whose honour and loyalty were beyond question. In the course of their duty it was

227

natural for the monarch to see his men positioned at their various posts. Theodis, of course, was no exception.

Theoderic was King, and involvement in every tragic circumstance was impossible. With Theodis he had no second thoughts; he had made his decision and that was that. Yet he found himself idly conjuring the image of a blind girl in the Tuscan hills. It was a passing thought that did not trouble. But each time he saw Theodis the image was quietly represented, unobtrusive, hidden, as it were.

Five days after Tullus left, the King was awakened by the dream. Blind girls, pleading with their sightless eyes, assailed him, and among them was his daughter.

Theoderic was disturbed, as portents and omens were the commerce of the time and of his race. That day Theodis seemed to stand in every doorway. Angrily, he barred him from the palace.

At night the dream recurred and Theoderic felt compelled to act. Urgently he sought the advice of the Arian Bishop, but he was cautious and unwilling to commit himself. Someone suggested sorcery and was driven from the palace.

'The man who thinks that Tullus deals in magic is a fool,' the King growled at Cassiodorus. 'What do you think, my noble friend? We can't ignore this warning.'

'Perhaps the great Lord calls for mercy, my lord King.'

OOO

The evening stillness was all-pervading and the shadows cast by the sinking sun were long. Above the Tullus villa a small outcrop of rock jutted horizontal from the hillside. There Tullus had placed a wooden seat large enough for three. Sometimes Cornelia joined them, but on this occasion Tullus and Drusilla were alone.

Below them was the square bulk of the villa, its inner courtyard wholly in the shadow, and on the distant hill in front of them was Faesulae. To the east a mud and stone road followed the contours of the hill, and all about were rows of newly-planted vines.

'It's very peaceful this evening, Marcus.' Drusilla's voice was little more than a whisper.

His arm around her shoulder tightened in response.

Below and to the left, towards the east, in the open space beyond the out-buildings they could see Cornelia walking hand in hand with Anna. They halted and Cornelia pointed vigorously towards the road.

Drusilla turned to look.

'Marcus, there's a rider coming.'

'Probably one of the guards exercising his horse,' Tullus said easily.

Drusilla kept looking.

'It's not, Marcus – Marcus, I think it's Theodis!'

At once Tullus was on his feet.

'It is Theodis – no one else rides as tall as that.'

It seemed from their vantage point that the whole drama was unfolding just as at the theatre.

As Theodis approached, his horse broke into a trot and stopped when level with Anna and Cornelia. Theodis jumped down and clasped the outstretched hand of Anna, while at the same time bending low to hug Cornelia. Then, to Cornelia's obvious delight, he lifted her, laughing, onto his horse. To Tullus and Drusilla she looked ridiculously small.

'What has happened, Marcus?'

'I don't know, Drusilla, other than one thing – it's official. Theodis would never disobey the King.'

'So Theoderic must have had a change of heart.'

'Yes, it seems so – anyway, we'll soon know the facts.'

The sun had dipped below the hills and the light was fading as, arm in arm, they started to descend towards the villa. They were halfway down when they saw Theodis and Anna coming up to meet them, but Anna's movements were tentative. The poor light made it difficult.

'Theodis is staying for the week,' she called out happily.

'That's all the cook could cope with, sir,' Theodis added, echoing Tullus's mode of humour; the result of long months together on the road. 'Count, we're very grateful for what you did.'

'I only threw a pebble in the pool, Theodis; but tell me what made our Lord Theoderic change his mind.'

Theodis explained.

Even the royal dream was sovereign, Tullus thought, but he did not speak.

Sensing that the men would want to talk, Drusilla tactfully escorted Anna and Cornelia back to the villa. Tullus and his escort leader followed slowly.

'What happens after a week, Theodis?'

'The palace again.'

'A week's a short time.'

'Yes, sir.'

The dusk was closing quickly and the stars were already prominent in the darkening sky.

'She cannot change her faith – you understand that, Theodis?'

'Yes, sir – I think I do.'

'She would think herself condemned; no marriage would survive it.'

'And I am bound by oath.'

The dark bulk of the villa was before them. Theodis stopped.

'What is the truth, sir?'

The question seemed to hang in the night air.

OOO

Theodis returned in September, but only briefly, before continuing on a mission to Hispania. Anna's eyesight had got a little worse, but not at the rate predicted. In fact, during the winter months it seemed to stabilise. The experts were divided in their diagnosis, while Tullus felt the cause was purely physical; he had witnessed something similar in Britain. Drusilla, on the other hand, stuck firmly to the view that the visits of Theodis held the answer.

Letters arrived from Narbo Martius and Barcino. These Anna treasured; but Tullus doubted the relationship would last. It had gone too long without fulfilment. Indeed, he was amazed when Drusilla told him that no physical consummation had occurred.

'He'll meet someone else. Nature will win,' he predicted.

'There may be slaves and mistresses, Marcus, but a companion is another matter. He loves her, my dear husband, and tells her all that's happened when they meet. Men are careful whom they speak to in this way.'

OOO

# CHAPTER FORTY FOUR

# RIOT

Tullus and his family spent the winter at Fidenae and once again the meetings at the Anicius palace were resumed: a pattern that continued until he was summoned urgently to Ravenna in early March.

Tullus found the city in chaos. The King was absent in the north and Eutharic was trying desperately to calm an ugly spate of rioting against the Jews. He was pacing up and down and clearly agitated when Tullus entered the audience chamber.

'It's deliberate, Tullus, and no matter what the Bishop says, it's organised – well organised. I've sent Triguilla to inform the King.'

Tullus reacted cynically at the evidence of Triguilla's growing respectability.

'The congregation of the Romans have gone mad,' Eutharic continued, 'and neither their bishop nor I can do anything to calm them. They've burnt one synagogue already – there could be a massacre!'

'What's the cause of it?'

'The Jews are accused of making sport of baptism by throwing each other into the river, and they're supposed to have mocked the Lord's supper.'

'Some fanatic's imagination,' Tullus retorted.

'Maybe, but it's been planned, Tullus, and they've waited until my father-in-law's away, for the numbers of the guard are low. What's more, I do believe they've been deliberately provoking us.'

'That could well be, sir,' Tullus responded grimly.

'What's on your mind, Tullus?'

'Well, sir, once the anger of the mob is raging ...'

'I take your meaning, Tullus. We Arians could be next, but our numbers are quite large. They could provoke a blood bath!'

'And get the Empire to react! I hope I'm wrong, but, sir, don't give them an excuse! Keep the guard well disciplined and hurry reinforcements in.'

'That's what your friend Theodis said.'

'He's back from Hispania?'

'Two days ago – and into this. He's trying to defend a synagogue at present and trying to be patient. Hopefully reinforcements will be with us soon.'

'And when they come the men who fired the mob will melt away. We should mark them while they're prominent and make them build what they have burnt.'

'I like that, Tullus, but imagine the outcry – Eutharic is set against the Church!'

'They'll say that anyway, sir.'

'I suppose they will,' Eutharic sighed with resignation. 'Meantime there is little I can do until the army comes except plead with the Bishop to restrain his flock. It's the Jews, of course,' he added absently. 'They crucified the Christ. They'll always attract trouble.'

Eutharic had repeated the common prejudice. Tullus felt like saying that the Jews of Ravenna were hardly guilty, but he held his peace; yet he could not let the matter pass without some comment.

'Well, sir, the Jewish people were the cradle in which the Christ was born.'

'Good! That's something I can hit the Bishop with.'

Theodis lost the struggle to save the synagogue. He had restrained his sword, and the mob, sensing their advantage, had broken through. He and his men had been hissed at, spat upon and assaulted with a vicious stream of bricks and stones. Then, as if to crown it all, they were accused of wanton brutality and unprovoked attacks against the Church's faithful.

The accusation was brought before Eutharic during an audience given to the Church leaders. Tullus was also present, at Eutharic's request, but most of the senior Roman officials were with the King.

The attack on Theodis came at the end of the meeting when a young priest, articulate and plausible, described how the innocent had been beaten down with clubs.

Tullus could contain himself no longer.

'And what were these "innocents" doing at the synagogue?' he bellowed. 'Were they deep in prayer? Perhaps they were contemplating the divine proportions of the brick! Sir, the synagogue was burnt!'

There were angry mutterings but no one answered.

The next day reinforcements began to pour into the city and an uneasy calm prevailed. The Jews, their synagogues in ashes, had appealed to Theoderic, and all awaited his return.

With the situation stable, Tullus was released and, thankfully, he headed south for Fidenae. With him was Theodis. A grateful Eutharic had been generous with his leave.

'How long have you?' Tullus asked.

'Three weeks, sir.'

'It's like old times, Theodis,' Tullus called above the thudding of the horses' hooves.

Theodis nodded.

'When will we be off on our journeys again?' he asked.

'That, Theodis, depends on the King, but I feel it will be soon. Byzantium is in the air.'

OOO

## CHAPTER FORTY FIVE

# BYZANTIUM

At Fidenae, in late March 518, Tullus received instructions from Theoderic. This time it was Byzantium.

The leave-taking was not easy. Drusilla clung to her husband, for she knew it could be six months, or even more, before he would return. She watched him mount his horse. It seemed so inevitable, so unstoppable. At her side Cornelia stood, unusually subdued. He waved, then briskly turned towards the road. Half way along the arc of the approach road he waved again and just before he disappeared from sight he waved once more.

For Anna there was no parting. Theodis was at Ravenna and would join the Count when he arrived. In some ways Anna had grown to accept her loneliness, though at times her hurt was deep. Theodis had continued to visit her, but his calls were brief and had an air of duty, an emptiness reflecting their hopeless situation. Theodis was a Royal Guardsman, a man of honour – too much honour, Anna thought bitterly. It was not within his nature to take the nurse of his commander's daughter as a mistress, yet they still were friendly. She knew, of course, about the slave-girls at Ravenna, but she could bear that while he did not marry.

ooo

At Ravenna, Tullus had his customary meeting with the King. Theoderic's instructions were simple.

'The Emperor is fading. Stay until his successor is crowned and give our loyal greetings to the Empire's new Augustus. God knows what the long nights of intrigue will hatch. Glean all you can.'

As well as his audience with the King, Tullus was fortunate in meeting Boethius. He, too, was brief with his advice.

'Constantinople is a treasure house,' he told him. 'Seek out the men of philosophy, the artists, the arbiters of music and the men who frame the law.'

'I'll be busy, sir,' Tullus joked.

'I wish I could come with you, but my pro-Eastern reputation is overstated as it is.' He smiled wryly.

234

'Or your anti-Gothic reputation, as your enemies would have it.'

'Oh, yes,' Boethius nodded. 'Anything to score a point. The rub is, one day Theoderic may believe them.'

OOO

In the early morning Tullus left with his six-man escort, Theodis as their leader. They rode north to Aquileia and then down the Dalmatian coast to Dyrrachium, where they joined the Via Egnatia. Tullus was now on familiar ground.

The journey was relentless, but the spring weather kept their spirits high. To pass the long hours, Tullus taught Theodis Greek. He also told him all the history he knew about the great Egnatia and the dramas that it had outlived. Theodis listened with fascination, for to many Goths the old Empire was an object of much wonder. Indeed, there were a number who, like Theodis, seemed more Roman than the Romans.

Without the encumbrance of carts they had made good time, though Tullus was careful not to overstretch the horses. So with this restraint it took four weeks or more before they reached the walls of Philippi. There they rested a full day before they set out again; but at the measured pace that Tullus set, it would take a further week before they saw the Eastern capital.

So far the journey had been trouble-free and the Empire's officials respectful. After Philippi, however, the road grew busy. Slow-moving farm carts, impatient officials, merchants full of purpose and the ostentatious with their numerous attendants. It was not unlike the roads approaching Rome and Ravenna, though Tullus sensed a much more vibrant energy. Certainly the dress was more colourful.

The closer they approached to the capital, the more intense the cultivation of the land became. There were no vacant plots, it seemed, either in decay or out of use. So much so that Theodis pressed Tullus for an explanation.

'It's some form of land-tax, I believe, that does it. If the land you hold is taxed, you use it. That would be the nub of it.'

The Gothic escort drew attention. Three times they were stopped by soldiers on the open road from Philippi, but the official papers Tullus carried soon allowed them to proceed.

At last the massive walls of the Eastern capital appeared in the shimmering haze.

'The walls of Constantine.' Theodis spoke with reverence.

'No, they're half a mile or so further to the east. These are the walls of Theodosius II, built in the Emperor's minority by the Prefect Anthemius.

There's been further work on them, of course.'

'They're unassailable, sir.'

'Yes,' Tullus answered. 'Built to last a thousand years.'

The city guards checked the papers of the Western travellers thoroughly. Then, with ceremonial correctness, they were escorted through the marble archways of the Golden Gate. Tullus was an ambassador, the emissary of Theoderic, the Western Imperial Viceroy. Two official guides were at once assigned to them and, thus honoured, they proceeded towards the city centre.

They passed close to part of the old walls of Constantine, then on to the Forum of Arcadius and the Forum Bovis. The bustling population was now in evidence. Tullus could not help recalling how Martin and he had wandered through these very streets. That was ten years ago, with a few months added. He shook his head. The ten years had been full.

'I didn't think the city was like this, sir – I mean large and hilly,' Theodis called above the noise.

'Yes, it's some way under four miles from the wall to the Hippodrome, and the same distance along the wall. I always think of Constantinople as a blunt triangle jutting into the sea.'

'The Hippodrome's at the point, sir?'

'Yes, Theodis – and that is where the heart is.'

'And the palace?'

'It adjoins the Hippodrome. In a way the palace of the people and the Palace of the sovereign lie side by side. I'm told this is very evident when a new Emperor is chosen.'

Steadily the guides led them forward through the Forum Tauri and that of Constantine. The crowds were dense, but they took scant notice of Tullus and his guard. They were used to visiting delegations. However, there was one exception: a conspicuous group of men dressed in loose, balloon-like clothes, who stared belligerently.

'Who are they?'

'Partisans of the Blue faction, and men to be avoided. Offend them and half the city is your enemy.'

'We'll have to keep the men in check.'

'Closely, Theodis!'

Gradually the dominating bulk of the Hippodrome appeared before them. Then without warning the guides stopped before two massive metal-studded doors. The doors swung open, and at once the party was engulfed by servants pleased to cater for their needs. The Imperial hospitality was unstinted.

The large building where they found themselves also housed a troop of the Imperial Guard. They were called Scholarians. Tullus remembered their distinctive uniform from his previous visit.

'They're a different corps of guard from those who escorted us from the outer wall,' Theodis observed.

'Yes, there are four main troops, I believe, with different patrons, and all serving the one Emperor. Their rivalry keeps them from uniting to unseat their august sovereign!'

Theodis shook his head. He understood, of course, but such thinking was foreign to Theoderic's guardsmen.

Both men were promptly escorted to their separate quarters and Tullus quickly bathed and changed. He had just settled when a servant told him that he had a visitor. It was Justinian.

Ten years seemed to disappear, for there before him was the same round, serious face, the same ageless expression, with the same restless energy.

'Welcome, Tullus – the Count Tullus. We know all about you, about your exploits in Hispania. Tullus, the trusted friend of the Arian King and his son-in-law Eutharic and, what is more, the friend of the world's first Roman.'

'You mean Boethius?'

'Who else but the Sole Consul of 510? We would all wish him as our neighbour, but you sit at his feet! Tell me, what of the boy?'

'Martin's now a monk.'

'Inevitable,' Justinian responded. Then, pausing, he looked straight at Tullus.

'The Emperor is ill,' he said abruptly. 'You may have to wait some time for your audience, but who could be idle in the city of Constantine? You'll dine with me tonight?'

Tullus assented with thanks and Justinian, after a few brief pleasantries, took his leave. He was a man in a hurry, a man with much on his mind.

This was evident when Tullus arrived at Justinian's villa, for the place buzzed with activity and the comings and goings seemed to be continuous. The presence of some Blue partisans was not lost on Tullus, but they were in the ante-rooms and not within the private chambers where he was escorted. Here he met Justinian's close associates and friends: among them lawyers, churchmen, architects and town officials.

Tullus was introduced as the friend of Boethius and Symmachus, which of course impressed.

'They should be here,' Justinian pronounced, 'for the city of Constantine is the new Rome.'

'Boethius says the need is in the West. The East has got the Empire.'

'What of the West?' Justinian prompted.

'Learning is in decline, especially outside Italy. The benign rule of Theoderic has provided a breathing-space for the Italian cities, but standards are still falling.'

'It's the damned Goths. Rome should be ruled by Romans!' Justinian said bluntly. Then he laughed. 'Don't worry, Tullus. It's frustration I have voiced, not fact, for most agree the Gothic King rules well.'

'He's been good to me,' Tullus responded, feeling it necessary to make a stand, 'and his rule is tolerant and just. Indeed, his common sense would rival any Roman from the early times.'

'He's an Arian, Tullus. That's where the trouble lies. Why, even that Frankish savage, Clovis, had the sense to change.'

'A conversion of convenience would never be Theoderic's way,' Tullus returned.

'That's a pity,' Justinian said playfully.

'Moderate Arians say the Son is like unto the Father, as the scriptures declare. That seems free of dogmatic error,' Tullus responded, a glint of mischief in his eyes.

'No wonder, Tullus! It says nothing. Just think what would happen: a hundred interpretations and a hundred Churches. Philosophers may debate, but bishops need certitude, for their flocks demand it.'

'And certitude brings unity?' Tullus prompted.

'Yes, and keeps violence off the streets, Justinian responded knowingly. He shook his head. 'Would that such unity were possible. I doubt it, though, for quibbling about the creed is the common passion of both senator and slave. Everyone's an expert.'

The unflagging conversation was steered deftly to the subject of philosophy by Justinian's friend Tribunian. Tullus liked him, even though he felt Tribunian was testing him. He was a quiet man by nature and one Justinian trusted: a fact made obvious as the evening proceeded. Certainly he knew his Plato and his grasp of the Hellenist tradition was profound: an odd facility in a city mad with Christian controversy.

'There's someone here most evenings,' Justinian said as Tullus made to leave. 'Join us, you'll be welcome.'

He found Theodis and two of the guard waiting to escort him to his quarters.

'There was some trouble tonight, sir, but the men didn't react.'

'What happened?'

'Just cat-calling. Anti-Arian slogans.'

'We're new arrivals, Theodis. They'll get used to us, for I've a feeling we'll be here some time.'

The next day Tullus was told that the Emperor would grant an audience the following morning, but at the last moment it was cancelled. No one, of course, would officially admit the Emperor was dying, even though it was a source of constant speculation in the street.

The Emperor had three nephews, men of average ability, who were unambitious and unlikely to be nominated as successors. Few, however, spoke openly on the subject. It was a time of whispers in secret inner rooms. Tullus noted that Justinian consistently refused to discuss the matter, but there were significant asides. 'Amantius, the High Chamberlain,' he said, 'has a faithful hound he wants to dress in purple.'

Apologetic officials continued to assure Tullus that his audience with the Emperor was imminent. It was a temporary indisposition, they kept saying. He got the feeling, though, that the Emperor's Monophysite friends were desperately hoping for their master's recovery, for they knew too well that the next Emperor could be Orthodox. Because of this there was much relief in Monophysite circles when the Emperor suddenly rallied towards the end of May. In fact, to many he appeared to be his old self.

In due course Tullus was summoned to the palace and, flanked by two eunuchs, with another leading, he passed through an endless grandeur of corridors. At every doorway guards stood rigid, their silver armour glinting. They were the Excubitors, the great rivals of the Scholarians. Tullus was very well aware that Justin, Justinian's uncle, was Count of the Excubitors.

At last he found himself in the audience chamber. The throne was huge, whether of bronze or wood he did not know. Approaching respectfully, he prostrated himself three times as custom required. Officially, of course, Tullus was not the envoy of a foreign power, but the representative of the Emperor's own viceroy, Theoderic, Lord of the Goths.

His obeisance completed, he raised his head and looked at the Emperor. Anastasius was frail. He was eighty; indeed, many thought him to be ninety, but neither age nor frailty detracted from his tall, dignified appearance.

'Count,' the Emperor began. The voice, though weak, was rich. 'We are told you are a native of the ancient province of Britain.'

'The August Caesar is correct.'

'Well, Count, you are welcome to the city of Constantine, for, as you know, our noble founder was raised to the purple in your land.'

The conversation proceeded easily, with Tullus relaying the good wishes of Theoderic and the proposal of a consulship for Eutharic who, being a Goth, needed the Emperor's special permission. Anastasius gave this instantly. It was clear he had no wish to dwell on state matters.

Tullus liked the mild and moderate ruler, but he could see that the old man was painfully weary. However, it was Anastasius who kept the conversation running.

'We believe you are friendly with the nephew of the Senator Justin, Count of the Excubitors.'

Briefly Tullus outlined the circumstances of his first meeting with Justinian. The Emperor was fascinated, and pressed Tullus to elaborate the detail of his story.

'What happened to the boy?' he asked.

'He became a monk, sir.'

The Emperor withdrew within himself, and for a moment Tullus thought that sleep had closed an old man's eyes. He waited, his head bowed respectfully. The attendants flanking the throne remained passive, indicating that the audience was still in progress.

'Mystical Count.' The voice of the Autocrator Caesar Anastasius was thin and distant. 'You are one of the blessed.' The words hung in the air, independent of the frail body in which they sounded.

A cleansing humility cleared the mind of Tullus. He was indeed blest: his beloved wife, his daughter, the teaching of Boethius, his friendships – all given.

'Convey our blessings to the noble Theoderic,' the Emperor continued. 'We've had our differences, but that is past. May he have a long life and a peaceful old age.'

The audience was over.

Accompanied by the same eunuchs, Tullus retraced his way through the corridors and out into the heat of the courtyard, where Theodis and the guard were waiting.

'Was the audience satisfactory, sir?' Theodis asked tentatively, aware of Tullus's air of preoccupation.

'The Emperor was gracious,' Tullus replied quietly. The look in the old man's eyes was still strong in his memory and a sadness clung heavy about him. He had just met the most powerful man in the known world, but he had also met an old man whose human distress was silenced by little other than dignity. Man's life, he thought, was at best a short adventure.

'To what purpose?' he said intensely.

'Were you speaking, sir?'

'No, Theodis – it's nothing.'

OOO

His official business over, Tullus was quick to accept the hospitality of Justinian's villa. He saw little of his host during the day, but late in the evening there was the usual gathering of friends. A regular visitor was Tribunian the lawyer. Tullus grew to know him well. Another regular visitor was Anthemius, an architect, a gifted man, but lacking patrons.

By mid-June, when the summer sun was making the city like an over-heated kitchen, Tullus learned that Anastasius was sinking. At once the memory of his audience was recalled and he hoped, with all sincerity, that the old man would go peacefully.

Speculation, new-fired, was barely kept within the bounds of decency. Justinian, however, appeared neither to say nor do anything. He waited and, as the days went on, the whole city seemed to join the waiting. The evening gatherings at Justinian's villa continued, but the usual ease of conversation had now acquired an awkwardness. Few could be indifferent to the prospect of a new man at the palace.

During this time Tullus was not idle. He had frequent callers – men hoping to relay greetings to their western friends and those with documents and manuscripts seeking a reliable carrier. To many, of course, the news from Rome was fascinating. Every trivial detail held attention. There was one group, known to the lawyer Tribunian, whose enquiries were anything but trivial and centred mostly on the teaching of Boethius. Tullus enjoyed their company but, as he freely admitted, their questions quickly exposed the limits of his learning.

Such meetings as those with Tribunian and his friends provided topics for his letters to Drusilla. Another favourite subject was the rich ceremony of the Byzantine Church. He also wrote in respectful terms about his meeting with the Emperor, but in all cases he avoided political issues. He knew it would be foolish to expect his letters to be private.

The days passed into July and the city, temporarily forsaken by the sea breezes, grew stifling. There was no improvement in the Emperor's state and all believed the end was near. Yet Anastasius had not nominated his preferred successor. Tullus was puzzled, and approached Tribunian for an explanation.

Tribunian smiled in his quiet way.

'The Emperor,' he explained, 'blatantly sided with the Monophysites some time ago, and any nominee would not be trusted by the Orthodox majority. Suppose his favourite was presented in the Hippodrome, who would support him? The Greens, perhaps, and the Scholarian Guards to spite the Excubitors, though that is doubtful. Such an unfortunate would be howled down by the masses and, what is more, his life could be in danger if the next Emperor decided to eliminate potential rivals – for his predecessor's candidate could not be viewed as casual. Of course, all this speculation could be wrong, as the old man may still feel that he has years to go. Again, his wishes may have been suppressed, but that's unlikely.'

'How is that?' Tullus interjected.

'Too many people would need to agree. The Palace system is full of checks and balances.'

'Gold,' Tullus suggested.

'Gold would buy many, but not all.'

Tullus nodded thoughtfully.

'If Anastasius fails to nominate a successor, how is a future Emperor selected?' he questioned. 'I've had partial answers, but never one I've understood!'

'I'm not surprised. The city's politics is an endless labyrinth. Shall we say, "It all depends", for even if the Emperor picked his favourite, and even if the candidate had an established power base, he would still have to court the approval of the Senate, the Guards and the factions Blue and Green. With a powerful candidate this might be a formality. However, if the Emperor's nominee were not a certain winner, he would have to subject himself to the whole mad business of election in the Hippodrome.'

'Elections are chaotic, Tullus, with the proceedings bordering on riot. Nominations can come from the Blues, the Greens, the Scholarians or the Excubitors, and so on. If the Hippodrome crowd approves one of these candidates, there is little the Senate can do; so consequently, behind the ivory door of the Palace, the Senate must act very quickly and, what is vital, canvass support from the Factions and the Guards – and where possible manipulate the crowd. In this situation, the partisans of the Blues and Greens become key figures; hence their blatant arrogance.

'Ideally, the Senate should nominate someone, a known moderate, and one who would appease the losing factions. Again, he should have the support of two major participants and the possible support of a third – say the Greens, the Scholarians and the Candidati Guard – or the Domestici, for that matter. With such support, and provided he behaved with dignity, the crowd would generally approve – especially after a long day at the Hippodrome!'

Tribunian smiled knowingly.

'So it's a kind of organised madhouse,' Tullus responded.

'Indeed.'

ooo

# CHAPTER FORTY SIX

# ELECTION

The Emperor Anastasius died on the 8th of July, and the next morning the people gathered in the Hippodrome. Tullus, escorted by Tribunian, took his seat in the visitors' box just above the podium. As he watched, the crowd began to chant.

'Long live the Senate,' they cried. No doubt there were men well placed to prompt their memory.

'Senate of the Romans – be victorious!'

'We demand our Emperor, given by God, for the Army!'

The election proceedings had begun and the noise of the crowd rose and fell with every tremor of excitement. Tullus could see the Ivory Gate that communicated to the palace. There the Senators, the high officials and the Patriarch were assembled in the Great Hall, where, no doubt, work had started early.

The first to proclaim a candidate were the Excubitor guards. He was John the Tribune, a friend of their commander Justin, but the Blues would not have him. They threw stones and the Excubitors reacted with a charge. There had to be casualties. Tullus grimaced. Then it was the turn of the Scholarians, who raised their candidate on a shield, only to be scorned by the Excubitors. A clash between the two main corps of the Guard seemed all too probable, until suddenly the figure of Justinian, surrounded by the white-robed Candidati Guard, moved between the two opposing forces. Quickly and efficiently he escorted the Scholarian candidate to safety and immediately the Excubitors clamoured to proclaim Justinian, but he refused.

Tullus turned to Tribunian and spoke close to his ear. The noise of the crowd drowned normal conversation.

'I don't understand the logic of it all. Why would the Blues, who are friends of Justinian, stone the Excubitors, whose commander is Justinian's uncle?'

Tribunian nodded, his face intent and serious.

'A diversion, Tullus,' was all he said.

'But that diversion may have cost life!'

Again Tribunian nodded.

'That, alas, is probable. Take my word for it, John the Tribune was never meant to succeed.'

'Justinian refused?!' Tullus pressed.

'Another diversion. He's not the candidate!'

'Then it's his uncle!'

Tribunian did not contradict him.

'Tell me,' Tullus continued, 'why did Justinian trouble to rescue the Scholarian candidate?'

'It's in no one's interest to have a brawl,' Tribunian returned quickly.

Another candidate was proclaimed and, as with John the Tribune and the Scholarian nominee, knocked at the Ivory Gate, calling with ceremony for the Imperial robes. The Chamberlains refused. They only acted when the issue was beyond all doubt.

Suddenly there was a hush. A figure stood alone in the Imperial box. It was Justin, Senator and Count of the Excubitors. The Senate had made their choice. His own guard roared their approval, followed by the Blues and the white-robed Candidati, but it was the general roar of the people that silenced all opposition. Even the Greens and the Scholarians, seeing their position to be hopeless, ceased their protests.

At last the Chamberlains released the Imperial robes and all eyes turned towards the Kathisma – the royal box – to witness the arrival of the Patriarch. The roar of the crowd thundered to a new peak, as they knew the coronation would immediately begin.

Tullus regarded the scene before him in a detached, disbelieving way – a strange play acting out its plot. The sense of unreality was strong. His friend's uncle was Emperor; plain, ponderous Justin. Only two days ago he had been in his company. He was a man of sixty-six years, old and moderate, but Tullus knew the real ruler of the Empire would be Justinian.

The coronation proceeded, and with due ceremony the Emperor Justin was presented, wearing the Imperial robes and holding the ceremonial lance and shield. For many in the long finger of the Hippodrome the figure in the royal box was little more than thumb-nail size, yet they cheered just the same.

Suddenly a great excitement stirred the Guard troops on the circus track.

Tullus turned to Tribunian.

'The Scholarians are not turning vindictive, I hope,' he said, leaning towards his companion.

'Oh, no. They've been told the Emperor's donative. A wise move at this stage. It keeps the guards happy and placates the losing faction. It's

THE LAST ROMANS

customary. They would expect it. Well, Tullus, we need stay no longer.'

'You expected the result?' Tullus asked as they walked from the visitors' box.

Tribunian's nod was just perceptible.

ooo

Despite staying at Justinian's villa, Tullus was unable to make a firm appointment to see the new Emperor.

'After the funeral of Anastasius,' Justinian indicated, as he rushed to the palace and his uncle's side. So again there was delay.

While he waited, Tullus received a letter from Drusilla. It had been two months in transit and its news, though joyful, was disturbing. Drusilla was with child.

Although the thought of fatherhood elated him, Tullus could not help being anxious. Understandably, painful memories were prominent. Please God, let all be well, he said intensely to himself. Trust, he told himself, but dark thoughts kept arising. Had he not been in the East when Arria was with child? He wanted to return to Italy at once. The desire was strong and pressing, but he had to wait. In fact, it took days before an audience was arranged.

'It comes of being too friendly with the family,' Justinian said by way of apology; the note of humour hardly altered the round, serious face. 'You could have seen my uncle privately, of course, but custom demands a formal audience for the envoy of the Royal Theoderic. To be truthful, we thought you would be the least likely to take offence – hence the delay.' This time Justinian's smile was more expansive.

It had been expected, and was generally acknowledged, that the new Emperor had begun his reign in a moderate and conciliatory way. There was no widespread purge of his opponents and the relations of the late Emperor were left in peace. Two men, however, the High Chamberlain Amantius and his candidate Theocritus, were not so fortunate. They were quickly put to death, and three others, Tullus heard, were either exiled or executed. There were official reasons, of course, but unofficially, rumour spread, especially about Amantius. It was alleged that he had given Justin gold to bribe the Excubitors, and Justin had withheld the payment, thus nullifying the High Chamberlain's designs. If the tale was true it was pitiless, but few blamed the Emperor. These were the cruel unwritten rules, and the Chamberlain had lost.

The gatherings at Justinian's villa continued, though with a different

245

note, for all knew the nephew of the Emperor was now a powerful man. One guest was much elated, the architect Anthemius. Patronage at last was possible. There was also the darker side that no one mentioned at the gatherings: the Blue partisans and their shadowy activities. They were always hovering about Justinian's villa.

The evening before Tullus was due to meet the Emperor, Justinian escorted him to some old haunts. A few Candidati guards were in attendance, for the nephew of the Emperor no longer had the luxury of privacy.

The sun was setting and torches began to blaze about the great buildings when, as if by impulse, Justinian suddenly turned into a deep archway. The double doors were open and beyond the entrance was a well-lit courtyard. They stopped, invisible in the shadows. 'She's in,' he whispered. Then he pointed to a woman who was spinning wool.

'That's the one,' he added, before retreating backwards to the street. 'I plan to marry her!'

They were in the street again.

'Does she know?' Tullus asked.

'I haven't said as much, but women have an instinct. She's not young, but she's intelligent and resourceful; she must be, knowing what she's suffered.'

Tullus's look was questioning.

'She was abandoned and was befriended by holy men. Because of this she has a great respect for men of faith.'

'She looks bright and most attractive,' Tullus offered, but the questions that arose he left unspoken.

'Yes,' Justinian responded quietly, 'but there'll be trouble, for she has a "past". I fear my aunt the Empress will certainly object.'

What past? Tullus asked himself, but, as before, he held his peace.

They walked on, passing through alleyways and streets unknown to Tullus: the native city that the visitor rarely saw. His friend, he felt, was paying final homage to a youthful past.

Suddenly Justinian stopped.

'Yes, my aunt will set herself against the match, but in time my uncle will agree.' Clearly he had been pondering on the subject and had come to a conclusion.

'What's her name?' Tullus questioned.

'Theodora.'

OOO

The next day Tullus presented himself to the Emperor Justin, traversing the same corridors and making the same obeisance as he had done with Anastasius. This time, however, a wholly different atmosphere suffused the Imperial throne room. The confidence and energy were obvious.

His request regarding Eutharic's consulship was immediately confirmed, with the added dignity that the Emperor himself would share the ancient honour with the royal Ostrogoth. Tullus was gratified, knowing that the news would greatly please Theoderic.

Justinian stood close by his uncle, the suspicion of a smile just discernible. The pomp of the throne room was a strange contrast to the memory of the previous evening. Nevertheless, the dignity of the occasion was carefully observed.

The audience over, Justinian escorted Tullus through the corridors to the ceremonial entrance, a further honour to the envoy of Theoderic.

At last Tullus was free to return to Italy and to Drusilla.

OOO

# CHAPTER FORTY SEVEN

# RETURN

A number of the Gothic guard showed a marked reluctance to leave Constantinople, and Tullus guessed their leisure hours amongst the city's Arian community had been full. Only Theodis remained constantly on duty, even accompanying his Roman commander to church.

Tullus knew that his impressive escort captain was unsettled. His faith no longer lay unchallenged and his questions had become a daily custom: a custom that found ample time to play on the long journey home.

'The Monophysites?'

'Yes, Theodis?'

'They have a large following.'

Tullus nodded in rhythm with his horse's stride.

'Larger than my faith, sir.'

'Could be, Theodis.' Tullus was reluctant to be drawn.

The sun was hot and the pace necessarily slow. The horses, their heads low, walked like creatures drugged, and Tullus knew that it was time to stop. Wearily his eyes scanned the arid land for shade.

'They divide the Empire,' Theodis said suddenly.

'Who?'

'The different faiths, sir.'

Tullus looked at him in disbelief.

'Theodis,' he barked, 'are you a Roman or a Goth? I sometimes wonder!'

'They do divide,' Theodis pressed. He was used to his commander's blunt retorts.

Tullus thought of Justinian, forever preaching the unity of the state.

'Yes, they're a potent force for division,' he eventually responded. 'But why are you troubling yourself with this?'

'Well, sir, while I was waiting for you at Justinian's villa I often had discussions with the staff.'

'Not the partisans, I hope!'

'No, sir, the villa staff.'

'And they spoke Latin?'

'Some did. They were Orthodox, sir, but usually one took the

248

Monophysite view to stimulate an argument. They asked me to defend the Arian position, but I quickly lost.'

'The Byzantine mind, Theodis!'

'There was no anger, sir – no passion like that about the streets.'

'There was nothing at stake, Theodis!'

'Tell me, sir, if you'd been in my place, how would you have defended the Arian position?'

'If the Father and the Son are co-eternal, as the Orthodox maintain, how then is the Son begotten of the Father? That's one shaft, Theodis.'

'I never thought of it.'

'If you had they would have countered quickly. The words of Christ, "I and my Father are One" would have been an obvious response. So much depends on the point of view. Anyway, it's too hot to ...'

'But, sir, how can that which is begotten be co-eternal?' Theodis pressed. 'It seems to be a valid question, regardless of the point of view.'

'Theodis, you seem to be oblivious of the heat! All right! I'll ask you a question: In a state of unity, how would you define begotten?'

Theodis made no answer.

'We must find some shade,' Tullus emphasised. 'Poor old Claudius is ...'

'There, sir.' Theodis pointed.

They rested while the midday heat subsided and Tullus, propped against a tree, alternated between sleep and concern for Theodis, as the tall Goth's open-minded questioning and his pro-Roman sentiments did not mix with the family nature of his race.

When the sun's heat had lessened, Theodis assembled the escort and soon they were on the road again. Even so, it was still hot. In fact, since leaving Constantinople the sun had baked them mercilessly. In such conditions night travel was the obvious option, but the moon was young and the darkness treacherous. Necessarily they progressed slowly.

Four days passed without change in the weather; routine days which Tullus found quite soporific. Theodis did not raise his religious questions and Tullus was content to let the matter rest, hoping that the agitation of Byzantium was on the wane.

Theodis, however, had not forgotten, and the next day he shocked Tullus into wakefulness.

'Surely, sir, the great God cannot have a point of view.'

'That seems reasonable,' Tullus managed to respond. 'But be careful,' he warned strongly. 'When we get to Ravenna, remember that it's not Byzantium!'

Theodis nodded. He knew exactly what was meant.

'It's still true, sir. God is neither Arian nor Orthodox. Such points of view are not his doing.'

Tullus looked hard at his guard captain.

'Clearly so, Theodis; but a man's mode of worship is to him a precious thing. If he thinks, however wrongly, that his faith is under threat, he will be your enemy.'

There the subject rested, though not for long, for during the journey to Ravenna Theodis continued to ply his questions.

OOO

It was almost mid-September when they rode into Theoderic's capital. Tullus was granted an immediate audience with the King, and for three days they had their customary meetings. As usual, Theoderic was quick to isolate the key issues, one of which focused on Justinian.

'Justin will play his nephew's game, but what exactly is that game? Should the Gothic nation fear the rise of this young man?'

Tullus did not answer directly.

'Well, Tullus?' Theoderic prompted.

'Sir, his aim, indeed his mission, is the restoration of the Empire,' Tullus said, deciding, as he often did, to speak openly. 'The Empire's unity is his passion; the same passion I saw in him ten years ago.'

'Count, you haven't answered my question. Should we fear him?'

The meeting was, as usual, in the forest park. Tullus sat upright, his mind searching for appropriate words, but none would come. Still bereft of speech, he viewed the military bearing of the King and then, unbidden, the words were on his lips.

'The lord King's stable rule upholds the law. There is nothing to fear.'

'A prudent answer, Tullus, which contains a warning.'

The King clearly expected a response and Tullus felt his tensions grow.

'Yes, sir, the warning is implied.'

'You're right: instability would invite the Empire's intervention, and in the event my people would suffer sorely.' Theoderic looked squarely at his Roman Count. 'No one can predict the day the great Lord calls. Tullus, I am getting old.'

Tullus swallowed. The King was being very frank.

'My hope and trust lie with Eutharic and my grandson,' Theoderic continued.

'My lord, you have a grandson?'

'Yes – the blessing came when you were in Byzantium – did no one tell you?'

'All thought I knew, no doubt.'

The King smiled.

'I'm told the Tullus household is about to grow. My blessing to your gracious lady.'

A sudden surge of emotion caught Tullus by surprise.

'Thank you, sir.' His sincerity was obvious and for a moment he felt close to his Gothic master.

OOO

On leaving Ravenna, Tullus made no detour to Faesulae. Instead, he went straight to Fidenae, accompanied by his six-man escort which, of course, included Theodis. In fact, since the riots against the Jews, when Theodis had distinguished himself, attitudes towards him had relaxed. Whether this was due to Eutharic or the King, Tullus did not know, though he suspected that Theoderic had accepted Eutharic's initial ruling and, knowing the reported restraint of his guardsmen, had let the matter rest.

At last they sighted the longed-for entrance to the villa, and the horses, knowing they were close to home, quickened pace. They were halfway round the arc of the approach road when the lone figure of Poppea stepped onto the portico.

Fears and forebodings suddenly crowded Tullus's mind. Was Drusilla too ill to greet him? Where was Cornelia? His fears stabbed viciously, but when he saw Poppea's smile they disappeared. Poppea was transparent. If the news was bad it would be plain to see.

'They're all at the Anicius palace,' she said as Tullus dismounted.

Immediately he was anxious.

'Are they concerned for my wife?'

'Oh no, sir,' Poppea said emphatically. 'Don't worry, your dear lady is in the care of my old mistress.'

'I see,' he said reflectively.

His eyes rested on Poppea for a moment.

'And how are you, my dear?' he asked, gently embracing her.

'Well and happy.' Her face beamed in confirmation.

'And your noble husband?'

'He's very busy with the Senate and his translation work.'

'I thought you stayed in Rome.'

'We do, but we stay here when we can. The Senator will be back this evening, but he does get very tired.'

'None of us are getting any younger, my Lady Poppea,' he smiled. 'Except you!'

Deftly he drew her aside and out of Theodis's hearing.

'How is Anna's eyesight?'

'Not good, but stable. She seems to think it's slightly better.'

'I see – and my lively daughter?'

'Playing the boy with all and sundry.'

'I can imagine!' Tullus smiled. Then he turned abruptly to face his waiting guard.

'It's Rome, Theodis, but we don't need all the guard.'

'Three, sir.'

Tullus nodded.

OOO

# CHAPTER FORTY EIGHT

# RUFUS

Drusilla was delivered of a baby daughter in early November. The birth was some twenty days premature, but both mother and daughter grew in strength as time went on. For Marcus Tullus the relief was enormous.

'I think my knees have worn holes in your palace chapel, sir,' he joked with Boethius afterwards. Then his face grew serious. 'It's not easy to await God's will with equanimity.'

'No, Tullus, it's not easy. Yet, for the reasonable, there is no other way.'

The babe was christened Valeria Drusilla. Valeria in honour of her grandfather and Drusilla at Tullus's insistence. Even so, from the beginning all called her by the single name Valeria.

The Tullus family stayed at the Anicius palace until the first week of the new year, after which they moved to Fidenae. There they stayed until late March when, much to the delight of the womenfolk, they journeyed to Faesulae.

Theodis had to enquire about his position before being summoned to Ravenna. Even then his tour of duty was brief, and by the time the Tullus family had arrived at Faesulae he received instructions to rejoin his Roman commander. Theodis did not know why attitudes had changed towards him, other than that the spur had been the anti-Jewish riots. The long stays with the Count had grown to be customary and it was a custom best left undisturbed.

Theodis, of course, continued to meet and talk with Anna. He was dutiful, if not brotherly towards her, but he kept their meetings short. The affection he felt for the gentle, dark-haired nurse and the pity that her failing sight had prompted could too easily flare, so he gave such emotions no encouragement. The discipline of the Royal guardsman ruled.

Anna, for her part, lived for his brief visits. She adored the tall, taciturn Goth, yet for fear of losing him she kept her feelings private. Such were the unspoken rules of their relationship. When Theodis was present at the villa she was happy and when he was away she simply waited. One day, she hoped, one longed-for day, God would, at last, allow their union.

Anna's great source of comfort was Cornelia. She loved the Count's lively daughter and was rewarded by the little girl's affection. At the age of eleven she was full of pranks, her boundless energy tending to excess, but Anna's gentle ways restrained her; a fact well known to Tullus and Drusilla. With Anna's partial sight, however, coping with the added responsibility of Valeria had proved too much, so an assistant nurse was hired; a sturdy young woman, rich in common sense, from Faesulae, named Maria.

Anna's assistant was not the only addition to the villa staff in the summer of 519, for late in July a strong, well-built Tuscan presented himself to the agent Quintus and asked to see the Count. Tullus recognised the man immediately. It was Rufus, the servant of Julia, mother of Cyprian.

'My mistress is dead,' he said simply, 'and I seek honest employment.'

Tullus hired him at once and within days it seemed that he had always been a member of the household.

Rufus spoke only to Tullus about his mistress. Julia had collapsed in church, he said. There had been no struggle, no pain.

'Was her memory as bad as rumour had it?' Tullus questioned.

Rufus confirmed that it had been so, but described how she had shown sudden flashes of insight, appearing at times to know what people were actually thinking. He related how she often spoke of Boethius. Indeed, she seemed almost obsessed by the scholar Senator and often warned her son not to oppose him.

'Cyprian never listened, sir. He called her a witch, but no one else did.' The greying Tuscan spoke bitterly.

'The privilege of a son, Rufus,' Tullus responded lightly.

'No, sir, he meant it.'

It was very evident that Rufus hated Cyprian.

In August Theodis returned from a second spell of duty at Ravenna, and the villa seemed complete. They were contented days for Marcus Tullus and his wife. Drusilla loved the evenings when they walked to their table of rock above the villa, to sit on the weathered bench that Marcus had positioned there the year they married.

Sometimes they were silent and sometimes not, but mostly it was silence, for Marcus was no friend of idle chatter and he never seemed to know the local gossip. Indeed, he could be distant. It was one of his 'things', as she named his habits, but she never criticised. That had been the rule right from the beginning: a practice fostered by her father. Criticism was a poison, he had told her; never let it grow.

'I wonder why he came?' she mused one evening.

'Rufus, d'you mean?'

'He can't be a spy.'

'A spy! If he is he could revive the theatre at Faesulae, and that would be something. No, it's not in his nature, my dear. He's a Tuscan returning to his homeland. There's one thing, though – he's caught the habit of Theodis!'

'What's that, Marcus?'

'Asking awkward questions. As I told you, Julia became prophetic, and he can't forget her strange insight.'

'And Theodis?'

'Just the same, still questioning.'

'You should start a discussion group for these frustrated thinkers – I'm serious!'

'Drusilla – this is a farm, not an academy!'

She laughed and they fell silent.

Sounds from the villa and the countryside were faint and emphasised the stillness. The smell of burning wood drifting from the boiler was just discernible.

'Do you think Theodis will change his faith?' Drusilla asked reflectively.

'He's bound by the Royal oath – that's his dogma!'

Once more the silence of the evening lived about them. In the distance the silhouette of Faesulae was dark against the sky. They rose and began to descend towards the villa. Half way down Rufus met them with a roll despatch which had just arrived by way of Florentia. It did not have the Royal seal.

'What is it, Marcus?' Drusilla's voice was hesitant.

'It's Cassiodorus – one of his bulletins. The churches of Byzantium and Rome are making sounds of unity and the King is supportive.'

'You're worried, Marcus,' she responded, hearing the tension in his voice.

'It's a nest of adders. In truth, the ending of the East-West schism is not in Theoderic's interest, for it isolates the Arians. I suppose the King hopes that tolerance will beget tolerance. It's the act of a statesman – the question is, can Byzantium respond?'

'You're doubtful?'

'I don't know, Drusilla – I just don't know.'

He put his arm round her shoulders as they walked into the villa. Inside he continued to read the bulletin.

'There's a threat of plague in Rome,' he said, looking up, 'but that's all it says.'

They looked at each other, for such news was always disturbing.

'Thank God Father's at his new villa ... and Boethius?'

'In the country as well. But where Symmachus may be is another matter. Anyway, let's hope it's only a threat.'

OOO

# CHAPTER FORTY NINE

# A LULL

The outbreak of disease in Rome was brief in cycle and the pestilence soon receded. Nevertheless, the threat had disrupted official business. Senators and dignitaries, secure in their country villas, were reluctant to return. The Pope kept court in his country palace and all, regardless of their station, blamed the trouble on the poor condition of the sewers and aqueducts.

The Senator Symmachus did not leave the city, but remained deep in the cool of his villa. It needed more than a whiff of plague, Boethius joked, to shift his father-in-law.

Symmachus, however, had been busy with matters other than his histories, particularly the problem of the drains and aqueducts; and at last, with the threat of plague his ally, the Prefect had agreed to fund repairs. His sense of satisfaction was marred, though, for on the very day that work commenced, his villa walls were daubed with accusations of necromancy. Symmachus, more saddened than annoyed, had become resigned to such lunacy, yet he wondered at the dark suspicions that prompted the attack.

All this he wrote to his friend Valerius. The Goths, he added, had fled the city and he advised Valerius to remain in the valley of the Arnus, where he hoped the noble Senator and the sweet Poppea were enjoying the Tuscan air.

Ten days later Valerius broke the seal of the Senator's letter. Sitting down on the portico steps he began to read, and as he did he laughed.

'What is it, Lucius?' Poppea asked.

'It's the Senator, my dear,' he said, turning towards her. There was no need for further explanation. She knew he meant her former master Symmachus.

'What does he say?' she asked, sitting down beside her husband.

'Oh, he's angry about the tenements, for as you know, they're a breeding ground for plague. At least the crisis has got work started on the aqueducts and drains. The Great Drain's all right, but the tributaries have been neglected for generations. Anyway, it seems the outbreak has been more of a scare than a reality.'

'So the Senator's not in danger?'

'There's a risk; there always is. Listen to this,' he added, his eyes twinkling with humour. "'Think of Rome free of Senators and the mighty of the Church – imagine the tranquillity! No bickering about dogma; no fanatics firing the people. Even the Jews are left in peace – and not a Goth in sight. No doubt they hanker for their northern forests and their uncontaminated streams.'"

'Speaking of Goths, Lucius, we've had more trouble from our neighbours.'

'Have they been shifting the boundary marks again?'

She nodded.

Valerius sighed with resignation.

'That's how it all started before. It's the tribal mentality. They would never do it to their own, not within the circle of their tribe, but outside that circle what they gain by stealth and war is seen as fair advantage. We're outside their boundary. I feel it's as simple as that.'

They sat together looking eastwards towards Florentia, but it was too hazy to discern the outline of the walls. On a clear day, though, visibility could be very good, as the villa was perched on high ground well above the Arnus flood plain.

'We are used to Thulwin and the Gothic friends of Marcus,' he continued, 'Theodis and the like – the few who stand outside the tribal ring.'

'You could ask Theodis to speak to our Gothic neighbours,' Poppea ventured quietly.

'My dear, what a good idea. We'll do that. In fact, I've just received an invitation from Drusilla, so we can ask him, or leave a message for him when we get to Faesulae. I've a mind to ask old Aulus to travel with us to the Villa Tullus. He'd like to see our granddaughter, I suspect.'

'Did you say *old*? He's getting younger by the day.'

'Yes, the garden keeps him fresh.'

'What's he going to do with the statues you brought from the old villa?'

'The Gracchi? I've left that to him.'

OOO

Apart from the winter months spent at Fidenae, the following year – 520 – found both Valerius and his son-in-law resident in their Tuscan villas. It was a happy and relaxed period and one in which Tullus received no Royal commission.

In the summer the Senators Boethius, Symmachus and Valerius were guests at the Villa Tullus. The capacity of the fortress residence was stretched to its limit, but no one seemed to mind, least of all Tullus. In any case, the conversation more than recompensed for any inconvenience.

There was nothing static or habitual in their discussions. Even within six months Boethius had moved forward, as it were, his understanding more precise, more penetrating and thus more simple. Tullus was particularly impressed by his father-in-law, Valerius. Clearly his close association with Symmachus and latterly with Boethius, had had its effect.

Boethius's stay was limited, however, as the King required his presence. The morning that he left, Tullus escorted him along the Ravenna road until midday, when they parted warmly.

Tullus was reflective as he journeyed home. The Senator's company had been stilling, a fact that seemed more evident than before; even so, he felt uneasy, owing to what Boethius had implied about his dealings with the King. Certainly he had not said so directly, yet it was obvious that the Senator had encouraged Theoderic in his tolerant attitude towards the healing of the schism, and no doubt in his forthright way he had pledged his reputation. The political dangers were real, very real, Tullus thought bitterly.

OOO

# CHAPTER FIFTY

# THE SECOND JOURNEY

Several days after the remaining summer guests had left his villa, Tullus received orders from Theoderic requiring him to proceed to Byzantium immediately. The peremptory note of the directive was unsettling and not Theoderic's usual style. Nevertheless, Tullus said nothing of his fears to Drusilla. Those she could conjecture well enough herself.

Leaving his wife and daughters was not easy but he resolutely turned his face towards Ravenna and confronted his uncertainty. It was the nature of human affairs to be fraught with anxiety, he thought, recalling a conversation he had had with Boethius. Life never prospers perfectly and never remains constant. It was very true, and his life, Marcus Tullus knew, was no exception. One frown from Theoderic and the whole idyll of Faesulae could disappear. So far the King had been a constant and generous patron, but the monarch of the Goths was growing old, and old age, pressured by the awesome troubles of the sovereign power, could crack

Tullus sat upright on his horse and shook himself, as if discarding pessimism. There was little he could do other than act truthfully and trust.

It was late evening when he reached Ravenna, but the next morning he was granted an immediate audience. As usual he found himself in the forest park. This time, however, the King did not urge his horse into a gallop. It was a detail, yet to Tullus, significant. The monarch was weary.

'We did not expect you so promptly, Count,' the King began.

'You said "immediately", my lord.'

'Damned officialdom, but not the King.'

Tullus smiled, an outward token of his relief.

'Your friend Justinian is the force behind the Emperor,' Theoderic continued in a serious tone. 'Tell him that both the Senate and the Roman people live at peace with our Gothic nation. Tell him that where Theoderic rules the Empire rules – a Praetorian Prefect has just been established in the area around Arelate – that is a Roman office. Tell him we have supported the healing of the schism and tell him we are angered by the voices of intolerance that issue from the city!'

If Tullus had thought about his reply, he never would have spoken.

'My lord King, you are my benefactor, my friend. I trust your word.

Justinian has also befriended me. I was a guest at his villa during my last visit. All this you know. I have honoured your person in all my dealings in the Eastern capital. Indeed, I told the forceful nephew of the Emperor that the truth was followed and not led, but Justinian is no ordinary man. Willingly I will do your bidding. I will press for tolerance and co-operation, but, sir, my position of dual friendship could be attacked by malicious tongues.'

'Tullus, are you questioning my grace?' the King growled

'My Lord King, I'm merely stating my position' Again the words came without thought.

'Count, you will never suffer my wrath. You have the word of Theoderic!'

ooo

Tullus and his full escort arrived in Constantinople during the first days of November, and at once he found himself amidst the buzz of Byzantine activity. He was treated with elaborate respect, but whether this was due to his role of ambassador or to his friendship with the Emperor's nephew was another question.

Almost immediately he was taken to see the Emperor and, as before, he found Justinian's uncle straightforward and dignified. What impressed him most was the unmistakable atmosphere of confidence. The tired days of Anastasius were past.

The formal audience was a required necessity and the least omission was an insult, so Tullus was careful to obey the rules. A story of the palace went that if the eunuchs smiled the formalities were correct. A rare event, Tullus thought, judging by their stony features.

Tullus, however, expected little from the public audience. To him, his meetings with Justinian held the key. In these he was direct.

Orthodox belligerence was rampant, he said forcefully, and wrongs against the Arian people present in the city went unpunished. The King was angry. Voices, high-ranking voices advocating Eastern intervention in the west, had reached Theoderic's ears. Such talk was gross stupidity and acted as a gift to Gothic separatism. The King should be given reassurances.

Justinian waved Tullus's protests aside as if they were trivial, while hastening to outline his building plans for the city. Tullus reacted impatiently.

'Petrus,' he interjected, 'don't undersetimate the Goths, and remember, the old King has ruled wisely for many years. He has kept within the Empire, even though many of his lords would have it otherwise. Sometimes I think he stands alone. Don't push him, lest he loses patience. Beware his Gothic anger.'

'Tell the old heretic to change his faith,' Justinian responded lightly. 'Don't worry, Marcus,' he added. 'Theoderic's an institution. To attack him would be madness – that is, while he's sound of mind.'

'That's the very point. He's getting old. Don't enrage him, for God knows what would happen if he cracked. Petrus, he's honourable and just – he needs support.'

'He's an Arian, Marcus. The Goths are Arians. They frustrate the unity of the Empire.'

'You can't make all men Orthodox. What of the Monophysites?'

'We can try – we must try! All right, Marcus, you have made your point – now let's talk of serious matters,' Justinian quickly said, reverting to his city building plans.

Tullus did not push the Gothic question. To have done so would have dulled its edge.

Marcus Tullus remained in Byzantium until the beginning of January. There he renewed his acquaintance with Tribunian the lawyer and the architect Anthemius. This time there was another frequent visitor to the villa. It was Theodora. Her dark eyes, her witty ways and her considerable intelligence had captivated the serious-minded Justinian. Marriage, though, would have to wait, for Justinian's aunt, the Empress, was set against the match. She wanted more for her nephew than one she called 'a dancer with a doubtful past'.

ooo

When it was time to leave, Justinian, with a troop of the Candidati guard, accompanied Tullus and his escort to the city walls. There, grasping each other's arm, they parted. Their eyes met unflinchingly and to Tullus the future was already written. Strong, solid, serious and determined, Justinian would be Emperor and his Empress would be Theodora. No man would stop him.

After the warmth of Justinian's villa, the Via Egnatia was bleak. The northern winds were icy, cutting at their faces without mercy. The days were long and hard and many of their night stops afforded little more than shelter. Fortunately they were well clad.

At the end of February they reached Ravenna, exhausted by the unrelenting cold and illness that had dogged the journey. Rotten food disguised with spice had caused the trouble. Theodis lost a tooth. The pain had been a torment and the tooth's extraction brutal.

Tullus saw the King without delay. His report was blunt. The Empire, he relayed, was powerful and they knew it. In their puffed-up confidence they seemed heedless of advice. Even so, he had pressed the King's case strongly.

'We know,' Theoderic returned.

Tullus did not mask his amazement.

'We have our common agents, Count. They send reports, and this report outstripped you by a day.' Theoderic pointed at a roll despatch half-opened on a desk nearby. 'You look weary,' he added.

Tullus did not respond immediately. He should have known, for the King had agents everywhere. He scanned the tall, timbered chamber in the evening light. Oil lamps flickered round the walls. The King had dismissed his staff and thus formality. He breathed deeply and then he told the monarch of his troubled journey.

'Well, Count, all your men returned. It's a wonder to us how you've never lost a man.'

Wine had been served and they both drank deeply. Tullus held his wine-cup out admiringly. The workmanship was delicate and beautiful.

'Our Gothic craftsmen, Tullus,' the King murmured.

Theoderic and his Roman subject sat in silence for a time, and Tullus saw a monarch weary of it all, yet imprisoned by his sovereign power and therefore bound to act. It was disturbing, for a lack of will and energy could cloud the King's perception. Theoderic's greatness lay in his breadth of vision. He had stepped outside the narrow circle of his race, but if he once returned the trammelled working of the tribal mind could cause a havoc.

'It never stops.' The King said, rising to his feet. His voice conveyed all that Tullus had been thinking. 'Thank God we have Eutharic,' he added.

Tullus rose, following the King's example. They had been sitting informally beside the dais. Slowly Theoderic mounted the two carpeted steps to his throne and pulled the silken cord. At once the royal servants flooded in.

'Count, give the King's good wishes to your gracious lady.'

Tullus bowed low. The audience was over.

The twin doors opened and, as he walked through to the ante-room, he met the smiling face of Cyprian – no doubt next to see the King.

Cyprian was, as ever, charming and the usual pleasantries were exchanged, after which Tullus proceeded through the now familiar rooms and out into the night air. He felt frustrated, even angry. The King was meeting the wrong man at the wrong time. Cyprian was out for himself. He would tell the tired monarch what he wished to hear but not what he should know.

Two of his escort were dutifully waiting with torches. He nodded in acknowledgement and walked off, leading the way.

Over the years Tullus had learned to speak the Gothic tongue in a fairly fluent way and when he reached his quarters he invited his faithful guards to have some wine. Weeks of shared hardship had left few barriers. Indeed, the two men had accompanied him to Byzantium on both occasions. Tullus called them the 'twins', at first because they looked alike. Their nickname, though, was strangely apt, for they both were in their twenties, both spoke slowly, both had lost their parents at an early age and both had sought the army as a guardian. Now they were devoted to their Roman commander.

They had not finished their first cup of wine before a messenger arrived from Cassiodorus. The tall official was entertaining some friends and hoped the Count could join them. It was the last thing Marcus Tullus wanted, but nonetheless he donned his cloak once more.

The villa of Cassiodorus was close. The Twins escorted him and were prepared to wait, but he sent them to their quarters. Like him, they were exhausted.

The one-time Quaestor's house was full and Tullus struggled through an hour of tedium before speaking with his host. Cassiodorus was, as usual, secretive.

'I've a piece of information, Tullus,' he said in his customary confidential manner. 'Cyprian has been made Referendarius, the reporter at the King's court of appeal. It's a demanding role, reporting the pleas to the King and drawing up the documents of judgement.'

'He's able enough,' Tullus answered sharply. 'Too able!' This was indiscreet, but he was too tired to care.

'He's a man of unusual parts and the King likes him.'

'Yes, I know,' Tullus responded flatly.

Cassiodorus looked at Tullus gravely and moved closer.

'Keep out of trouble, Count.'

The two men viewed each other without speaking and Tullus nodded. The advice had been given in good faith.

They continued to talk until suddenly Cassiodorus threw up his hands in elaborate exasperation.

'My noble sir, I'd almost forgotten. Here's a letter from your good lady. It arrived some weeks ago.'

Tullus looked anxiously at his friend. Then, excusing himself, he broke the seal and read. At once he sighed with relief.

'The Countess is at Faesulae. She wanted to save me journeying to Rome. Thank God that's all.'

Cassiodorus moved his hand as if in benediction.

'In this uncertain world few break a letter's seal with equanimity.'

OOO

On the way to Faesulae it rained heavily and the roads were treacherous. Reluctantly Tullus broke his journey. There were four in the party, Theodis, the Twins and himself. The inn he knew was small and primitive, yet it afforded shelter and the fire was blazing; their steaming clothes evidence of its heat. The guards stretched themselves on wooden benches and Tullus used the high-backed chair, but they slept little and all were glad to see the dawn.

It was still raining when they started out again but it failed to dull their spirit of anticipation. The Villa Tullus was no more than a morning's ride away.

They arrived at midday and at once Drusilla was alarmed. She had never seen her husband look so haggard. With equal priority baths and dry clothes were made available to the travellers.

At last Tullus felt himself in a fit state to greet his wife. He held her close for a long time.

'Would to God I never had the need to leave this place again,' he said quietly.

'Marcus, my dear lord,' she spoke softly. 'I have bad news.'

He broke their embrace anxiously.

'I had a miscarriage and the physician says I cannot have another child.'

Tears filled her eyes. Her reserve could not hold and silently she began to weep as his arms gently closed around her.

OOO

At the opposite side of the villa Anna was looking intently at Cornelia. She could see, but her vision had a narrow focus.

'Your hair will do, and your dress, young lady.' Anna bent forward and made a slight adjustment. 'Good! Now, off you go and see your papa, and don't forget to take little Valeria with you. Hurry, now. your papa will be waiting.'

Cornelia skipped off, but stopped abruptly at the door.

'Nurse, the Captain's here,' she called over her shoulder.

'Theodis, don't lift her up. I've spent ages on her hair.'

The tall Goth's laughter echoed in the room.

'Your favourite chair is waiting,' Anna said, her face alive with happiness.

He sat down, relishing the comfort.

'The thought of this has kept me going for the past two weeks!'

He looked across at her. She was wearing his favourite gown and in his weariness he allowed the old appeal that he had fought against and almost conquered to rise once more. God, she was attractive. Her narrow waist, the way she held herself, her dark hair, her soft oval face, her eyes, her very vulnerability, all were a drawing force. He longed to take her in his arms, but instead he talked.

'What age is Cornelia now?' he asked.

'Fourteen.'

'She's going to be quite a lady.'

'She's very like her mother.'

'You knew her?'

'Yes – I was eighteen then,' she said wistfully.

'I thought a Roman lady never revealed her age.'

'Theodis!' she reacted with pretended indignation. 'Now, tell me about Byzantium.'

'It's an exciting city,' he responded, describing the buildings, the churches, the crowded streets and the market full of wares not dreamed of in the west. He had been to the races at the Hippodrome. That was a madhouse – worse than the circus at Rome.

Anna listened and laughed at his jokes. It was like the early days before they had drawn apart.

'I met a number of Monophysites. I even met a Latin-speaking Nestorian. But they were hopeless. I knew more about their dogma than they did ...'

'Theodis,' she interjected, 'you shouldn't trouble your mind too much.' The subject of religion made her uneasy.

'How did the Count manage the long hours of travel?' she asked, to change the subject.

'He's exhausted.'

'He's almost fifty, Theodis. I know the mistress gets very worried about his long journeys.'

'She would, Anna. Have you ever watched them? They're like lovebirds.'

'Yes, and her father's marriage is just the same. Dear Poppe is devoted to him. I remember well when it all happened – marriage to a mere servant. Now even the matrons of Rome have grown to accept her.'

'Never, Anna. Time has accepted her, but not the matrons. You're weaving a woman's dream.'

'I'm not,' she reacted, matching his banter. 'You're getting like the Count. That's what he would say.'

'The Count would also say that happy marriage happens once or twice a decade!'

'Well, if that's so,' she responded firmly, 'the house of Valerius has managed it twice.'

'Maybe we can make it ...' He stopped, shocked at what he had almost said. The 'thrice' had been on his lips, and Anna knew it. He stood up, reflecting his confusion.

'The horses – it's time I looked at them; they've had a punishing time.'

Anna was hurt. It was unmistakable, and a surge of pity rose within him. He turned back at the door.

'I have to visit the Senator Valerius soon to check that his Gothic neighbours are behaving themselves. Would you like to come? We could take one of the carts.'

'Oh, Theodis!' Her face betrayed her joy. Then she remembered her position. 'I shall have to ask permission. The mistress expects me to ...'

'I'll speak to the Count,' Theodis said gruffly, and at that he walked off, angry with himself. He had raised the old false hopes and that was stupid. Then he recalled the happiness on her face, and his pace relaxed.

OOO

# CHAPTER FIFTY ONE

# AD 522
# GREATLY HONOURED

The large inner hall of the Palace was growing dim in the fading autumn light. Servants with tapers ran from lamp to lamp as if some punishment had been threatened for delay. A constant buzz of conversation rose from a scattering of men grouped here and there between the marble pillars. Occasionally, a busy official strode across the floor, before suddenly disappearing to another room, leaving in his wake the lingering memory of his hurried footfall.

Close to the entrance to the Royal chambers two guards stood erect and motionless. Only their eyes moved; otherwise their statue-like appearance was complete. Theodis was one of them, back for another spell of duty. He missed little, yet he often noticed that he himself went unobserved for, standing as he did, many passed him by as if he were inanimate.

Slowly the figures of Cyprian and Triguilla moved towards him. Cyprian was obviously heading for the Royal chambers. His mood was calm, whereas Triguilla was full of passionate intent. They moved closer, near enough for Theodis to hear their conversation.

'A stallion, Cyprian, a stallion that no Goth worthy of his race would lose, is yours, my noble Referendarius.' Triguilla pressed his harsh whispers close to Cyprian's ear.

'Such a noble beast for such a trivial request. Do I hear aright, my noble Chamberlain?' Cyprian responded coolly.

'Not trivial, my friend. He does not want to lose the Royal grace, and just a word from you could ease the issue.'

'A word! A word can change the world. A word can make a man a heretic! Who's taken up the case against him?'

'The Senate,' Triguilla answered.

'The Senate! You mean Boethius!'

Triguilla nodded.

'A horse for that! I'd need a royal four!' Cyprian's face remained expressionless.

'Four horses you will have!'

'What's in this for you, my long-time friend?' Cyprian retorted cynically.

'Oh, just a little oil to ease the wheels, my noble Cyprian. This is how it works. A mistake is made, a little help is given, the question is resolved and all are happy.'

'What will happen to your cosy dream when Manlius Boethius is Master of Offices? The rumour's strong that he's been greatly honoured.'

Triguilla bent closer to Cyprian's ear.

'If he disturbs our simple ways we'll have to stop him.'

'Take care he doesn't stop you first!'

'Ah!' Triguilla waved his finger. 'He's not a Goth.' Then, realising what he had just said, he placed his hand on Cyprian's shoulder. 'No offence to you, my friend,' he said quietly.

'Of course.' Cyprian's voice was cold. 'I'll see what can be done, but first you'll have to tell me more about the case,' he added, moving closer to the tall door of the Royal chambers and out of Theodis's hearing.

Fools, Theodis thought. They had stood within a pace of him and had not marked his presence. Even Triguilla, for all his pig-eyed cunning, had not noticed. He felt like laughing, but the impassive image of the guard remained.

Theodis was not surprised by the conversation he had heard. Corruption was never far from the Palace corridor, and no one expected a Referendarius to be poor. Yet he felt the rise of anger. How dare they tarnish the great King's justice! He felt the need to speak to someone, but who? Whom could he trust? The Count Thulwin was in the north and out of reach. The Senator Boethius was in Rome. There was Cassiodorus, of course. Theodis found him strange; more like a priest than a court official, yet Count Tullus trusted him and that was good enough for Theodis.

Immediately his guard duty had ended Theodis went straight to the ex-Quaestor's villa. He was graciously received.

'Ah, Captain – welcome. Any friend of the Count is welcome.'

Cassiodorus, his robes hanging loosely from stooped shoulders, listened intently as Theodis told his story.

'Those of your race will help their own. It's understandable, noble sir,' he responded.

'Help is one thing; corruption is another!' Theodis barked.

'Spoken like the Count, sir – the long hours in his company have left their mark.'

'It's corruption!' Theodis pressed.

'That I can't deny – but hear me, Captain. For many years I've trod the Palace corridors. Seek what can be done, not some ideal. The Palace is the Palace.'

'Triguilla is a criminal!' Theodis returned defiantly.

'Be careful, sir.' Cassiodorus dropped his voice to match the note of caution. 'The Grand Chamberlain Triguilla is well-connected. You know this – you're a Goth.'

'Does that make him any less a criminal?' Theodis retorted.

'Captain, you have a soldier's honesty. But remember, black and white are opposites. The Lord created many shades between.' Cassiodorus raised his hand as if in blessing. 'leave all this to me. I will ask questions and alert the Senate's delegate. The trouble is, we have no names.'

'Not everyone could trade four horses, sir.'

'That's true – leave it to me, Captain – leave it to me.'

Theodis bowed in acknowledgement. The matter was closed and after a few general pleasantries he took his leave.

Outside the bustling noises of the town engulfed him. It was growing dark, and children playing in the street bumped into him, yet he strode on, oblivious of it all. The King's justice, he thought bitterly, was a mess of compromise.

At his cramped soldier's quarters he found a king's messenger awaiting his arrival, and instantly his mind filled with irrational fears, but the Goth in the Royal livery brought no fearful summons. Instead, he was ordered to deliver a roll-despatch to the Count Tullus and to remain with him according to his pleasure. The order carried the seal of the Lord Eutharic.

Theodis left well before first light the next morning. It was mild autumn weather, progress was good and he soon reached the hills. The Triguilla incident, so pertinent the day before, became remote. It was Anna who now occupied his thoughts.

Once more their relationship had become awkward. It had started on the evening of his return from Byzantium when exhaustion had lowered his defences. The old attraction was as strong as ever.

He had purposely distanced himself at Ravenna, for no one had summoned him. But now he was returning to the Villa Tullus by order.

ooo

Darkness fell before he reached the villa, and for the last few miles Theodis led his horse. When the torches about the fortress villa became visible his pace quickened and when close to the perimeter he shouted out his name. At once the Gothic guards responded and familiar voices bade him welcome.

He was admitted to the Count's well-lit rooms without delay.

'Theodis, this is an unexpected pleasure.'

'Orders, sir. I was told to deliver this,' he said, handing over the roll despatch.

'I hope it's not Byzantium again – the Countess will take it badly if it is,' Tullus muttered tersely.

As he broke the seal, Theodis made to excuse himself.

'Stay, Theodis, there may be something here that you should know.'

Theodis obeyed, his gaze fixed on his commander.

'Boethius has been greatly honoured,' Tullus said quietly.

Theodis listened expectantly.

'His two sons are to be joint Consuls. It's a rare honour. There must be few, if any, precedents.'

'But his sons are still young, sir.'

'I know; Boethius is the real Consul.'

'What has prompted this, sir?'

'It must be connected to his work in furthering the reconciliation of the Byzantine and Roman Churches.'

'I wonder who proposed it.'

'Ah! – that's a question. It may have been initiated by Constantinople, or it may have been the King, with Cassiodorus whispering in his ear. Again, the Pope may have been instrumental. Pope Hormisdas is trusted by the Lord Theoderic, and he could have suggested honouring Boethius – a man held in high esteem by the East – as an act of good will on behalf of the Arian people. The Emperor would have to agree, of course, being required to resign his nominee.'

'So Boethius could be a kind of peace-offering, sir.'

'You've put your finger on it there. Theodis, let's not push our analysis too far. It's time for celebration – you will come to supper?'

'Thank you, sir.'

'The Senator Valerius and his lady are with us. It will be quite a gathering, and Cornelia will be pleased to see her favourite Captain of the Guard!'

ooo

The main hall of the villa had been newly decorated and the fresh, warm-coloured panels reflected perfectly in the still water of the sunken marble cistern. Above this central pool Theodis could see the stars through the open rain catch. The Count had told him how he had tried to preserve the

271

old style. He looked at the large-patterned mosaic floor. His ancestors
would have stood amazed at such luxury, yet here he was, like the Romans,
taking it for granted.

Apart from a formal toast to Boethius, the supper was a casual family
affair. Theodis talked at length to the Senator Valerius and his daughter, but
most of his time was spent with Anna. The long journey from Ravenna,
however, had taken its toll, so when Anna retired he excused himself. Soon
afterwards Drusilla, Poppea and Cornelia retired as well, thus leaving Tullus
and Valerius alone.

'Cornelia has grown quickly, Marcus.'

'Too quickly – daughters are a heartbreak, sir.'

'You married one.'

Tullus laughed.

'I married a blessing, father-in-law.'

Valerius looked knowingly at Tullus.

'Marcus, you cannot plan your daughter's happiness. That's the Lord's
work.'

'Yes, but I can try and prevent misery. I'm certainly not taking her to
one of those social gatherings in Rome where the matrons seek fat dowries
for their useless sons – that's a lottery!'

'I don't blame you for avoiding that. But Cornelia is fast growing to the
restless age.'

'Yes – when she's caught by the first adolescent who smiles at her.
Nature's powerful.'

'Marcus, why don't you write to Boethius? He has gathered many fine
young men about him.'

'I'll do that,' Tullus said briefly. Impulsively he stood up. 'It's all so
damned practical,' he grumbled.

Valerius did not respond. Instead, he changed the subject.

'This dual consulship elevating the sons of Boethius is a rare honour.
What do you think? Is the King being pushed or is he pushing?'

'The former mostly, I would say. Even so, he has chosen tolerance as
his policy, hoping, no doubt, that the Empire will respond, for all agree the
ending of the schism isolates the Arian Goths,' Tullus replied.

'Yes, and some say this honour to Boethius isolates them further.'

'My fears are sharper, sir,' Tullus returned. 'I fear the honour isolates
Boethius, for if the Empire grows intolerant of the Arians he could find
himself a hostage to their fortune.'

'A vulnerable position, to say the least. Nonetheless an influential one,
for we're close to Plato's ideal. A philosopher at the helm of state affairs. '

'Can it hold, though? That's the question,' Tullus sighed. 'So much depends upon the King, but the signs are still good. I didn't tell you, but he has asked me to write informally to Justinian applauding the present good will uniting Byzantium and Ravenna.'

'Well, Marcus, from his point of view it makes good sense, for either separatism or confrontation would sharpen division in Italy and isolate the Arians in the East. Tolerance is practical.'

'Pray God no one provokes him,' Tullus said intensely.

'That does beg prayer, for the ending of the schism has made men mad and anything but tolerant!'

'What about this new unity? Is schism dead?'

'Ah, Marcus, bickering over dogma has been practised much too long,' Valerius responded wearily. He tried to stand, but a stab of pain kept him seated.

'What's wrong, sir?' Tullus asked anxiously.

'Oh, a twinge I get from time to time – it's passed.'

'Be careful, sir, I only have one father-in-law!'

ooo

The Tullus family spent the winter at Fidenae and in the new year they joined the solemn procession of Boethius and his sons from the Anicius palace to the Forum. There the two young Consuls were inaugurated with the blessing of the Church. The applause of the people and the Senate was tumultuous and the joyful father, the real Consul of the Roman world, pronounced an oration in praise of his Royal benefactor, Theoderic. It was a memorable day.

At the preceding games a triumphal largesse was distributed. This was the second time in twelve years that Boethius had withstood the financial shock of the Consulship. Few were capable of sustaining such a burden.

Marcus Tullus remained at Fidenae for over six weeks after the inauguration. During this time both he and Valerius had access to Boethius, but meetings were irregular. It was obvious that the consulship of his sons, the demands of Ravenna and the ever-simmering troubles in the Senate and the Church were eroding his time for study.

Just before Easter, when Boethius and his sons left Rome for Ravenna, Tullus headed north for Faesulae. Travelling with the Tullus family was a young man named Petrus Quinctilius Atticus. A senator's son, he served as secretary to the ex-consul Albinius and was a close follower of Boethius, whose pupil he had been from an early age.

On the face of it, Atticus had come to learn estate management. But there was another purpose, a purpose not without success, for already Cornelia had grown shy and awkward in the young man's company. Nature was playing her inevitable game.

'He's a handsome devil,' Tullus growled as he sat beside Drusilla in their jolting cart. 'Not unlike your father.'

'But not as tall,' Drusilla responded. 'Don't fret, Marcus. There's nothing we can do.'

'It's all right for ...' He stopped short, appalled at what he had almost voiced. Unuttered, the words remained. The whole unthinking sentence made him shudder. – 'It's all right for you, she's not your daughter.' How serpent-cruel could a human be?

Impulsively he kissed her.

'Whence this sudden burst of passion, sir?' The beauty of her voice was full of mock surprise.

'It's the spring, my lady,' he returned flippantly.

'Look, Marcus.' Drusilla pointed suddenly. 'Those men – what's wrong with them?'

'They've been branded. Caught stealing, who knows?'

'It's horrible, Marcus,' she reacted.

'It's a harsh and brutal world for many,' he answered tersely, and as the cart passed by the men held up their hands in supplication. Tullus was generous in the coins that he threw in their direction.

'Such awful misery,' Drusilla whispered, while thinking of her father and what he must have suffered.

Guessing her thoughts, Tullus drew her close and she leant against him affectionately.

'It's good to be going back to Faesulae,' she murmured.

ooo

# CHAPTER FIFTY TWO

# CLAUDIUS

During the summer Tullus spent much of his time in the company of the 25-year-old Atticus. They journeyed together to Thulwin's large estate near Verona, where Atticus could see in practice how such a property was run.

Because of the common connection with Boethius, philosophy was often a subject of conversation and so was politics. Atticus was a keen advocate of the Empire and was looking forward to an autumn visit to the Eastern capital in the company of his master, the ex-consul Albinus. To this the reaction of Tullus was vehement.

'Atticus,' he began, 'take this advice to heart. Say nothing, either in private or in public, against the King of the Goths – certainly not in writing. The King has eyes everywhere. Don't take him for granted!'

Atticus nodded in agreement but Tullus, not yet satisfied, still pressed his point.

'In the church at Faesulae they talk as if there were no Goths. Time and time again I've cautioned them. I tell them that they speak the way they do only by the grace of Royal tolerance. For if, by God, the King withdrew his grace, they would quickly know the Goths were present. Do I make myself quite clear?'

'Yes, Count!'

'Good,' Tullus returned. He wanted his message to take root, for when he looked at the young nobleman he saw his future son-in-law.

At first Atticus did not seem to notice Cornelia. His greetings were formal, and she responded in a tongue-tied, nervous way. But all this changed one day when, casually, he asked her about the old horse her father fed each morning.

'That's Claudius; the most travelled horse in the Roman world. He's been to Byzantium and back,' she answered. The question had released her from her shyness and she smiled radiantly.

'Father talks to him for ages,' she continued. 'Sometimes you would think Claudius was hearing his confession!'

Atticus laughed heartily and looked at her anew, his eyes full of amusement.

'Come, Cornelia, and introduce me to this wise old animal.'

Quickly she led the way to the outer quadrangle.

'Claudius,' she called gently.

Immediately, but stiffly, the old horse came to her.

From that time the relationship between Cornelia and Atticus flourished, and by the end of the summer their betrothal was announced. Tullus, though, would not hear of marriage until his daughter was sixteen.

OOO

Anna knew that Cornelia's betrothal heralded inevitable change. Almost certainly she would follow the Count's daughter to her new home. It was the custom.

She loved Cornelia, but she also loved her life at Faesulae; the Count was honourable and the Countess was a lady. Above all she feared the loss of Theodis. Would he visit her in her new position? Her future home could be in Rome. It could be anywhere. He must visit her, she thought with desperation. She dared not think it could be otherwise.

OOO

Theodis was not at Faesulae. He had been recalled for special duties in connection with the Lord Eutharic, a privileged posting, for the King always selected his best men to guard his son-in-law. Theodis sensed a permanence about his new posting. It was obviously promotion, with further advances possible; Eutharic had not forgotten the part he had played during the anti-Jewish riots.

His career looked bright and he had every reason to be elated. Yet this was not the case. Anna, the Count and the draw of Faesulae were powerful reservations. But Theodis was a Royal guardsman and orders were orders. There was no other way, but the resulting conflict between desire and duty made him restless.

Theodis made a brief visit to Faesulae in early September with the news that Boethius had been made Master of Offices: a development that both Tullus and his wife distrusted. Too much rested on the shoulders of Anicius Boethius. Too easily he could be blamed for every ill.

Almost immediately Theodis returned to Ravenna and the staff of Eutharic. Months passed, but in the following year the shocking news was suddenly released; Eutharic was dead. The special duties of Theodis were at an end.

OOO

# CHAPTER FIFTY THREE

# 'THE LORD HAS TAKEN AWAY'

'Naked came I out of my mother's womb, and naked shall I return thither: the Lord gave, and the Lord has taken away; blessed be the name of the Lord.'

Tullus listened as the Arian Bishop intoned the stark words of Job, and the lifeless day that he had stood before his first wife's bier came vividly to mind. Then the same prophetic words had been repeated.

About him the central hall of the Palace was lit by a myriad of flickering lamps and Tullus allowed his gaze to circle its perimeter. The hall was filled to capacity. He looked ahead at the guardsmen flanking the bier on which the body of Eutharic rested, and there was Theodis, tall and erect, his armour draped with a broad black sash.

Absently he scanned the Roman guests. There were present the Prefects of Rome and Ravenna, Boethius, the new Master of Offices, with his sons and a number of his senior staff and, of course, the tall, stooped figure of Cassiodorus. To his right sat Symmachus, now the father of the Senate. With them were other Senators, including Valerius. To his left the Referendarius Cyprian was seated beside Triguilla and a Gothic official named Cunigast – a man who resorted to fraud for the meanest advantage. It was strange how the able mind of Cyprian consorted with such company. The Roman churchmen were few, a fact reflected by their attitude, for since the time of the anti-Jewish riots Eutharic had been labelled 'an enemy of their Church'. A similar myopic view was nurtured by the Gothic community, in the rumour that the Lord Eutharic had been poisoned by agents of the Roman clergy. Fortunately the grieving King dismissed such tales.

Tullus's roving thoughts were arrested as Cassiodorus – Senator, ex-Consul and ex-Quaestor – rose to deliver the official eulogy.

Vainly he attempted to straighten his tall, stooped figure, and then the panegyric began, in slow, solemn tones. Tullus groaned inwardly. The predictable tedium seemed endless, yet when he looked about him, all eyes were on the speaker. Thulwin, too, who sat beside him, was wholly intent. He, of course, would have to concentrate to follow the Latin. Tullus tried to listen, but the wordy elaborations smothered his effort. It was the current manner of speech. Bishop Ennodius, he recalled, had a similar delivery. Boethius, though, was free of this. In fact, there was a light about his words that set the Senator apart. His ability was widely appreciated, yet many of his class resented his pre-eminence.

Tullus looked ahead to where Boethius sat. The Senator's head was bent forward in an attitude of deep attention. It was a salutary lesson, and Tullus turned his mind once more to Cassiodorus, only to stray again when the upright figure of the King came into view.

The death of Eutharic had been a cruel blow to Theoderic. Politically it was disastrous, for where there had been certainty there was now uncertainty. Plainly a three-year-old grandson would impress neither his own Gothic Lords nor the Emperor Justin in Constantinople. Indeed, the Empire's noisy advocates of intervention had received the perfect gift.

Tullus continued to watch the ageing monarch as the rounded tones of the eulogy continued. Sorrow rose unbidden, for with all the King's forbearance, his Roman subjects saw him as a heretic. They had a Trajan in their midst but only saw an Arian.

Slowly it became apparent that the ex-Quaestor's words were drawing to a close, and with the last solemn flourish past, Cassiodorus bowed to the King and took his seat.

There was an odd, anonymous air about Cassiodorus. He had been a Consul a few years back but no one seemed to remember. Strange, Tullus mused. Perhaps it was the long-practised mode of the public servant – a subdued and pliant mode. Such behaviour could be practical, of course. Cassiodorus was a survivor.

For Tullus the ceremony was over, but this was not the case for his companion, Thulwin. He was required, as was the rest of the Gothic nobility, to witness the burial.

OOO

After the funeral the King's time was crowded by visiting ambassadors. Ostensibly they carried messages of condolence, but all knew that their eyes and ears were open to any sign of weakness in the Gothic capital. It was a time of enormous strain for the ageing monarch.

Tullus had been told to await the King's summons. During this time he saw Boethius only briefly, when they joked about young Atticus and Cornelia. Clearly the Senator was pleased about the match.

The short time with Boethius contrasted with the lengthy conversations he had with Thulwin. But when he told his Gothic friend of

Cornelia's betrothal the Count was shocked.

'Where have the years gone?' he muttered.

'It's fifteen years since we first met,' Tullus said, and then they talked about old times.

Thulwin, as ever, impressed him with his nobility, but he witnessed, as he often did, the Count's strong love of Gothic tradition. Thulwin's treatment of the Roman people was always just; even so, he had few Roman friends. In truth he distrusted the soft habits of the body of the native population and saw them as a threat to the martial vigour of his race. Yet like the King, he firmly believed in the need for co-operation. For all this, Thulwin was a solitary man who kept his own counsel. Even among the Goths his confidants were few, but those he trusted he trusted fully.

Tullus enjoyed this trust and was grateful. He knew, of course, that Thulwin did not view him wholly as a Roman. In the manner of his Royal master he saw him as a man from the north.

Thulwin, like Tullus, was waiting for an audience. The many uncertainties arising from Eutharic's death concerned them both, and continually the conversation was drawn to this subject.

Tullus was certain that another journey to Byzantium awaited him.

'The King will want to test opinion. I warned the Countess, but she ...' He shook his head. 'The trouble is, some indiscreet fool told her of brigandage on the Via Egnatia.'

'I assume you will travel directly from here,' Thulwin suggested.

Tullus nodded.

Thulwin then explained that he was due at Pisae and could easily call and reassure the Countess.

'Sir, that is friendship,' Tullus responded warmly. 'And a blessing,' he added, 'for my wife will heed your words. She thinks I underplay all danger.'

'Perhaps you do,' Thulwin returned knowingly.

OOO

# CHAPTER FIFTY FOUR

# FATHER AND SON

The winter sun shed a soft light on the hilly terrain. It was pleasantly warm for the time of the year and Thulwin's troop of twenty horse were very much at ease.

Thulwin rode upright at the head of his men, his son beside him mirroring his father's posture.

'Remember, you must speak Latin to the Countess,' Thulwin said forcefully.

'Yes, Father,' the youth responded, but his look was puzzled.

'Is the Countess a heretic?'

Thulwin's anger exploded.

'Who put such nonsense in your head! God sees no heretics. Remember that!'

'Yes, Father.'

Thulwin's son had seen his father lose his temper twice before, so he knew to keep his peace, but his puzzlement remained.

Thulwin's anger quickly passed and soon he fell to pondering the problems of his spring campaign against King Sigismund, Lord of the Burgundians. It would not be easy, for there could be no treaty with the man who had murdered his own son; the grandson of his Lord Theoderic.

'No treaty!' he muttered audibly.

'You spoke, Father?'

'Oh, nothing, son. I was thinking about the spring march.'

'You promised to take me, sir.'

'Yes, yes I did. It will be good experience – but no combat for you, my boy.'

'I'm fourteen!'

'In two months' time,' Thulwin corrected. He smiled. He liked his son's enthusiasm.

'Father, is it true that Sigismund was an Arian, like us, before he joined the Roman Church?'

'It's true, and no doubt when he changed his faith he saw all Arians as heretics. Now do you see why I was angry?'

The youth nodded.

'Look!' his father called, pointing to the neat rows of vines ahead of them. 'We're now within the Count's estate.'

Thulwin looked at the sun's position and judged it to be midday.

'I'm hungry, Father.'

Thulwin laughed.

'You're always hungry. Don't worry, we'll be at the Villa Tullus soon. Then, I promise you, you'll have your fill, but remember, you're not a wolf!'

'Yes, Father.'

The horses plodded on, their heads low. In the wake of their progress a mist of dust rose from the stone and earthen road and a slight breeze carried it to their left. The road was flat, but wrapped round the side of a large and gently rising hill. Suddenly the villa was before them in the distance.

'It's like a fortress, Father.'

'It *is* a fortress.'

They rode on, the details of the villa becoming more discernible.

'Look at the tables, Father – they're laden,' the boy enthused as they approached.

'I sent word that we were coming … That's for the men. Now don't touch, even if you're starving,' Thulwin said with humour. 'look,' he added, 'there come the Countess and her daughters.'

Thulwin and his son quickly dismounted and at once the villa servants took their horses, leaving father and son free to walk forward.

Thulwin's son was mesmerised by the grace of the Countess, and when she spoke to them he stammered in reply.

'He's not usually so quiet, my lady,' he heard his father say. He blushed. A dog nuzzled up to him and he looked down, glad of the distraction.

'He likes you,' little Valeria said, her wide eyes looking up at him.

He looked at her, dazed for a moment, but remembered to smile. Then he glanced at the Countess and Cornelia and they were smiling too. Suddenly he felt happy.

Without haste they walked towards the villa entrance. Thulwin relayed the good wishes of Tullus and proceeded to reassure Drusilla of her husband's safety. Six men were quite adequate protection. They were fully armed and all Royal guardsmen, men formidable in their own right. No self-respecting brigand would risk attacking them.

The conversation during the midday meal was light and humorous. Thulwin joked about his son's appetite. The boy coloured and Drusilla took his part. Afterwards the Count walked with Cornelia. He talked fondly of the old days, the early years when he had first met her father and mother.

'Your mother was very brave,' he said, patting her arm, 'and remember, my dear, if ever you or your future husband are in danger, use my name.'

The young girl was moved. Impulsively she rose on tiptoe and kissed him on the cheek.

Eventually, when Thulwin and Cornelia returned to the main hall, they found Drusilla alone.

'Has my son run off as usual? He needs a halter to restrain him,' Thulwin joked.

'Not so, my lord. Your son has been the perfect guest. It was my daughter who led him off. 'Come and see Papa's library,' she said, and straightway took his hand.' Drusilla shook her head. 'Why the library? Whence this strange impulse? Sir, the ways of children can be fascinating.'

The Count Thulwin had to leave mid-afternoon to keep a planned engagement at Florentia. He had enjoyed his brief visit and had been especially pleased to see Cornelia. There was little doubt about his son. He had been clearly happy and had shown a marked reluctance to depart.

OOO

Father and son rode off together, their escort following behind.

'My Latin is very poor, Father.'

'At last you've noticed! Some time I'll ask Count Tullus to take you with him on one of his journeys. That might help.'

His son did not seem to hear.

'She's very nice.'

'Who? – the Countess?'

The boy nodded.

'The cream of Roman nobility, my son. But don't forget that you're a Goth. You too are noble.'

Thulwin sat impassively on his horse and his son looked at him quizzically. At the villa he had forgotten that there were Goths and Romans.

OOO

# MASTER OF OFFICES

Drusilla received a letter from her husband in the latter days of March. Written in Constantinople, it had taken almost six weeks to arrive. The weather was mild, he wrote, and the hospitality was, as ever, generous. He had seen quite a lot of Atticus. They had gone to church together, where the singing had been wonderful. His description of the service was detailed, but as usual there was not a word on politics.

Drusilla read and re-read the letter.

'Dear Marcus,' she murmured. She was so much part of him.

On the second day of May she received another letter. Tullus was at Ravenna. Two days later he was home.

'I've never had such an easy journey. Not too hot and not too cold; but it's wonderful to be back,' Tullus whispered as he held his wife closely.

Releasing their embrace, they sat together.

'Why did they send you? To calm fears, I suppose.' Drusilla spoke, answering herself.

'Yes, and to emphasise that Boethius was Master of Offices. What better proof of the King's goodwill than that? The foremost Roman was his best man. I feel our Royal Lord is rather like a general who's thrown in his last reserve.'

'Is Boethius popular?'

'Only with good men. The rats are running for cover.'

'What do you mean, Marcus?'

'When Boethius sees corruption, he attacks.'

'You're worried. I can see it in your eyes.'

'The men Boethius opposes have a cunning. They will group and face their scourge.'

'And Cyprian?'

'He doesn't like a rival in the Palace. Boethius thwarts his plans and no doubt hidden payments come less often. My dear, I do not wish to trouble you with this.'

'Marcus, I am your wife, your dear, dear friend.' She moved closer to him. 'What of the King? How does he view the Senator?'

'That's what worries me the most. I do believe he sees him as a threat.

It's such a tragedy, but I fear it's true. Theoderic is getting old. His thinking is ...' He stopped, searching for an apt word. 'I don't know, Drusilla. He seems more subject to his Gothic past.'

'Is there a public rift?'

'Oh, no, the King supports his minister. In fact, without Theoderic's favour Boethius could not operate. Dear God, I hope my fears are groundless, for if Boethius and the King would work as one, a miracle could be wrought. If not, I see disaster.'

Their conversation was interrupted as Valeria burst in upon them.

'Papa, Papa!' she called, racing into his arms.

Cornelia came behind almost shyly.

'My darling Cornelia.' Tullus embraced his daughter warmly. 'How well you look! My rival Atticus sends his love. We saw each other in Byzantium.'

'I know, Father – a letter came a few days ago. He hopes to be home soon.'

Impulsively he again embraced his daughters.

'Now your dusty father must to the baths and then to supper. My dear,' he added, turning to his wife, 'we'd better ask the Captain and Anna – it's traditional.'

Drusilla looked questioningly at her husband, but did not speak. However, after supper, when they were alone, she voiced her thoughts.

'I'm worried about Anna. Did you notice?'

'I did. Her sight seemed poor, and she's very thin.'

'She's so unhappy, Marcus. Theodis should never have taken her to Father's villa.'

'That was two years ago, my dear.'

'I know, but that's when it all began again. She tasted happiness.'

'So we're back to the old situation.'

'Yes, Marcus – only worse.'

'And there's nothing we can do. Nothing!'

They sat together, her head leaning against his shoulder, and for a long time they said nothing.

'He will never compromise the truth,' Drusilla said, breaking the silence.

'What's that, Drusilla?' Tullus was close to sleep.

'Boethius – he's bound to live by Socrates' rule. He'll not assent to falsehood or conceal the truth. Has he any allies?'

'He has supporters, Drusilla, but even they would have him turn his gaze aside and leave the trickery at the Palace undisturbed. Such advice is termed prudent by many, but not by Boethius. In any case, how can he remain silent when Paulinus the ex-Consul is being savaged by the greed of Cunigast and his like?'

'He can't – the house of Valerius knows that well.'

OOO

During the time Tullus had been absent in the East the weather had turned bitterly cold. At this time Aulus, the old servant of Valerius, died. His passing was soon followed by that of Quintus, the frail and elderly agent of Tullus. No one was surprised when Rufus was appointed to the vacant post, for to all it was the natural choice. Tullus liked him. He was reliable, a man of few words, and he got the job done. Yet it was a strange appointment.

'Who would have guessed,' Tullus said to his wife, 'that the servant of Julia would come to be our chief man? Certainly not Marcus Tullus!'

Following Rufus's appointment, Atticus arrived. Unlike his prospective father-in-law, he had caught unsettled weather; but he made light of the hardship and his nimble wit brought ready laughter. Tullus could see that his daughter was captivated and reluctantly he turned his mind to the subject of her marriage – when and where – and to the pressing question – what to do with Anna?

A week after Atticus arrived, Tullus went to see the nurse. She rose abruptly, startled by the unusual occurrence.

'Please be seated, my dear Anna,' he said kindly.

'You've been with Cornelia from her birth,' he began. 'You knew her beloved mother.'

Anna stiffened, guessing what he was about to say.

'I know my daughter loves you dearly, but you must know that she'll be leaving soon. Indeed, I've just agreed to her marriage being in July.'

He paused, but Anna made no comment. He could see that she was very tense.

'The Countess and I have discussed the matter.'

Again he paused. He felt awkward. This was Drusilla's job. She could do it so easily. Never mind, he had agreed to speak.

'It would be customary for you to travel with Cornelia but, my dear, your eyesight is not good. Atticus's villa in Umbria would be strange to you and you wouldn't see your friend the Captain quite so often.' Damn, he thought. He almost swore aloud. He had not meant to mention Theodis.

Tears rose in Anna's eyes.

'If you are giving me a choice, my lord, I have no answer. I don't know what to do.'

He took her hands in his.

'Both the Countess and I think you should stay here. Maria can go with Cornelia. In any case, Umbria's not far distant. You can go there as a guest from time to time.'

Her face brightened and Tullus knew that he had made the right decision.

ooo

Cornelia was married in Rome, in the private chapel of the Anicius palace. Boethius, as usual, had been generous.

Soon after the bride and bridegroom left for Umbria, Tullus and his family, along with Valerius and Poppea, headed north on the Via Cassia for Florentia.

Tullus's feelings were a mixture of relief and sadness. Relief that Cornelia had a worthy husband and the sadness of a father when a daughter leaves the family. However, there was one consolation as far as Tullus was concerned: the whole fuss and formality of the wedding was over; that was a blessing.

He felt peaceful as the carts trundled northwards, yet one concern kept troubling him, and Valerius too. The Pope, Homisdas, was ill and rumour said it was grave. Indeed, in Rome there was much speculation as to a successor.

Even though Homisdas was strictly Orthodox, he was trusted by the King and any severance of a bond uniting King and Pope was serious. If the worst were true, much depended on the Pope's successor. Here gossip favoured John the Deacon, a man believed to be pro-Eastern, and a factor to arouse Theoderic's suspicions. The whole sorry business meant more trouble for Boethius.

ooo

At first, life at Faesulae seemed strange without Cornelia, but soon her absence was accepted. Only Valeria kept asking questions.

'Nurse, why is Cornelia not coming back?'

'Your sister is married, Valeria. The noble Atticus and she are a new family,' Anna explained.

'Will she come to see us?'

'Yes, Valeria – often, I hope.'

It was at the beginning of August that Atticus and Cornelia first visited

Faesulae as man and wife. Cornelia was radiant and the reunion of the family joyous. Subsequently it was the turn of Tullus and Drusilla to visit Umbria. There they were treated royally, though it was clearly obvious that their relationships had changed. Cornelia was a wife and the mistress of her house. It was she who gave the orders to her servants; her parents were the guests. After a few days the Count and Countess returned to Faesulae. They were well pleased, for Cornelia was very happy and their son-in-law was manifestly a sensible and intelligent young man.

Ten days after their return news came that the Pope had died, and by late August word arrived of his successor. As had been expected, it was John the Deacon. Tullus could only hope that his rule would not antagonise the King.

Being busy with the estate, Tullus began to lose his unease. The days passed into September and for a time both Rome and Ravenna seemed remote. Then suddenly he received the King's summons to present himself without delay at the port of Genua. The Count Thulwin had achieved a great victory, without loss of life, and Tullus was requested to join the welcoming party. He set off immediately with the Twins as guard. Theodis was still on palace duty at Ravenna.

OOO

# CHAPTER FIFTY SIX

# DELIVERENCE

The port of Genua was crowded with Ostrogothic nobles accompanying the King. Their mood was clearly one of celebration, but not many had the dignity of the man that they had come to honour. Heavy drinking was the boast and problem, with petty squabbles the inevitable result. The King did not seem to mind the rough carousing of his peers, but he would not tolerate indignity within his presence.

Thulwin was overdue, yet no one was concerned, for a ship out of Massilia would hug the coast and never be too far from shelter.

Tullus waited with the rest, but felt isolated and apart. Indeed, of the few Romans present, the only one he knew was Cyprian, and though the Referendarius was pleasant, with a ready wit, Tullus regarded him as dangerous. The instant smile, he judged, concealed a ruthless will.

There were the Goths, of course, and Tullus spoke with many of their number, but the barrier of language made the conversation stilted. Triguilla passed him, smiling honey sweetness, his pig-small eyes glowing with the relish of a torturer. Tullus could not stand him. There was Ibbas, of course, but the General was, as usual, terse and brief, and looking more than ever like the blunt-faced Emperor Vespasian. In fact, the only one that Tullus would have called a friend was Theoderic himself.

It was from Theoderic that Tullus learned the details of Count Thulwin's triumph. The Count had marched against the Burgundians in the spring, only to find that the sons of Clovis had already done his work. Sigismund was dead, and the new king, already at war with the Franks, was desperate to avoid a second conflict. Because of this he was forced to trade the southern part of his kingdom as the price of peace. Thus the murdered grandson of Theoderic was avenged and honour satisfied. Tullus, however, knew there was more to the King's elation than the acquisition of a strip of land. Theoderic had struck back, however remotely, at the Roman Church's rising power.

Three days after Tullus's arrival, the weather grew overcast and windy. Just after midday the darkness in the western sky turned black and menacing. A lone ship was sighted, racing with full sail before the storm. It looked tiny, yet was plainly visible against the blackness of the sky. The King was told, and suddenly everyone was at the harbour. The ship, speeded by the storm-force wind, was fast approaching. They could see the pennants. Undoubtedly it was Thulwin.

The storm-clouds swirled towards them, spreading overhead and making it like dusk. Then the rain began, lashing with ferocity. Tullus stood, water streaming down his face. His greying hair was soaked and his oilskin cape whipped violently, but it kept his shoulders dry. Tullus, though, was only half aware of this, for his full attention was focused on the boat.

'Please God, let him come to land!' he cried urgently, his voice swallowed by the storm.

Battered relentlessly by the gale, the ship drew closer. The crew had failed to furl the sail and it had ripped to shreds. Tullus could see that they had lost control and had no hope of reaching harbour. Suddenly the mast snapped and, only half severed, it hung heavily to one side, causing the ship to list and take water. In no time she would be gone.

About him men were shouting. They could see Thulwin's tall figure, so very near, yet so very far. Desperately Thulwin and his son were pushing at a heavy rowing-boat and, against all odds, they launched it overboard where it bobbed like a wooden wine-stopper. It needed only one chance wave to smash it into kindling wood against the stricken vessel's side. They were lucky, and with the aid of a rope ladder the boy jumped. Then came Thulwin. He dared not jump, for his weight could smash the boat. Miraculously, for a moment a wave pushed the boat high against the ship's side and Thulwin scrambled aboard. It was a sturdy, substantial craft, like those used for inshore fishing. Frantically Thulwin cut the ropes that held the oars secure. Then he began to row.

Tullus felt he was watching a miracle, while knowing all too well how fortune's wheel could turn. Still the rowing boat survived. Frequently it dipped behind a wave, but there it was again. Thulwin's strength seemed superhuman. Then, oddly, in the midst of all the roaring frenzy, Tullus felt himself fall still. Quickly he moved from the harbour vantage-point to a nearby patch of shingle where Thulwin would be forced to beach, and there he stood, continually drenched by spray. Behind, the King was being forcibly restrained from moving forward.

The boat was close and Tullus edged towards the waves. Again he waited, until a violent surge propelled the boat ashore.

'Get my son,' Thulwin yelled. 'My strength has gone!'

Tullus grabbed the youth at once and hauled him from the boat, but another wave was bearing down on them. There was no time to run. Instantly he fell, shielding the boy, while grabbing desperately at the sand

and shingle. The wave broke over them. Tenaciously he clawed the beach against the powerful suction of the water as it drained away. Then strong hands were helping them to safety. He looked back. The boat was gone, but mercifully Thulwin had been helped ashore.

Thulwin hugged his son before turning to the King. The slanting rain drenched all, yet Tullus could have sworn that Theoderic's eyes were full of tears.

'Search for survivors,' he heard the monarch order, for the white ship, as they called it, had disappeared.

'Well done, Count!'

Tullus turned towards the voice. It was Ibbas.

'I never knew before why the King made you a Count, but now I do! We watched you act alone like rabbits in a trance.'

Tullus laughed.

He viewed the heavy stick that Ibbas leaned upon. A war wound, he had heard. He smiled and the large, square-faced general smiled back. All the while the rain streamed down their faces.

The search for survivors proved fruitless and Thulwin sadly accepted that his closest aides were lost.

'Swept overboard,' he said to Tullus. 'One moment they were there, the next ...'

He shook his head. 'The crew thought I was mad to try the small boat. I probably was. It was God's work, Tullus, not mine.'

That evening at supper the King placed Tullus between Thulwin and his son. Tullus's efforts on the beach were loudly praised by the monarch. He was clearly in high spirits – too high, Tullus thought. The King was nearing seventy and the drama of the day had been demanding.

Halfway through the banquet a despatch was handed to Theoderic. It was from his sister Amalafrida, the recently widowed wife of Thrasamund, King of the Vandals at Carthage.

The King gave the despatch to Thulwin. His eyes were not good, he said. Tullus could not help hearing Thulwin's voice, and even though the quickly-spoken Gothic tongue was hard to follow, he caught the gist.

Thrasamund had been succeeded by his cousin Hilderic, who was of the Roman faith. This Hilderic had ignored his pledge to the dying Thrasamund and was busy persecuting the Arians. Thrasamund's widow, the sister of Theoderic, had rebelled and was now in prison. Her letter begged for help.

'The Roman Church is marching everywhere,' the King growled in exasperation, his elation forgotten. 'We must do something.'

'They have a navy, sir. Our ships would be destroyed,' Thulwin cautioned.

'Then we must have one as well – damn!' he shouted, hammering the table before him. 'But for that stupid strip of water we would have that cursed Carthage razed as did the Roman ancients!' Impulsively he stood up, and at once all were on their feet. Then he stormed from the hall.

Thulwin followed the King, but his son remained with Marcus Tullus.

Next morning Theoderic headed north – his destination Mediolanum. Much to his surprise Tullus was ordered to join the King's train, but no reason was given. Thulwin, on the other hand, remained at Genua to await the arrival of his army. It was at Genua where the majority would disperse. After that he hoped to travel west to Ravenna.

'We will be calling at Florentia again,' he told Tullus. 'Any message for the Countess we will willingly deliver.'

Tullus was quick to accept the offer and hurriedly wrote a letter to his wife.

'Young Thulwin will be pleased,' the father responded when Tullus handed him the roll. 'He liked your villa. He was awed by the Countess and he loved the food!' A smile wavered on the face that mostly showed the picture of reserve.

OOO

# CHAPTER FIFTY SEVEN

# THE CONSISTORY

The King did not linger on the road. The pace was brisk. However, most of the day's journey was covered in the morning, for in the afternoon he stopped early. Then some unsuspecting town, with little more than three hours' grace, played host. Yet this was not wholly true, for most knew that the King was in their region. It took four days to reach Mediolanum. First they stopped at Dertona. Then they swung east and crossed the river Padus at Placentia. Next day they turned west to Ticinum and at last they entered Mediolanum, where they were joined by Boethius and a number of the Palace secretariat. A group of prominent Senators was also present. Cyprian, of course, had travelled with the King from Genua.

Theodoric held court for seven days, and Tullus did little other than to listen and observe. Two things impressed him. One, the brilliance of Cyprian, the other the workload of the King, but the strain about his face was plainly visible. No one knew his age for certain and no one dared to ask, though most believed it to be seventy. One thing was clear, however, all too clear. Theodoric's years were telling.

Tullus saw Boethius most evenings, and most evenings the Senator's frustration was in evidence, yet he readily saw the humorous side. It was all so predictable, he said. Even men of honest stock were slow to speak against corruption. They did not like their easy ways disturbed. To Boethius the court was a travelling circus that kept him from his studies. It was also dangerous, for Tullus saw the greed, the hate, the naked fear, raw beneath the bows and smiles, but it was on Theodoric that he focused his concern.

'He looks withdrawn, sir,' he told Boethius.

'He's failing, Tullus, and the circle of his tolerance is contracting in proportion. It has happened quickly, for just a year ago his whole desire was fixed on partnership between the Goth and Roman. Now suspicion rules. Why, even yesterday he raged against the Senate as if it were an enemy.'

'The news from Carthage may have maddened him,' Tullus interjected.

'It hasn't helped.'

'And there's Byzantium,' Tullus added. 'Their will for co-existence with the Arian Goths is like a surface dressing, and the King is losing patience.'

'Yes,' Boethius agreed, the word drawn out almost prophetically.

Next day Theoderic left Mediolanum for Verona. Tullus still remained with the Royal party. He had expected to be told of his release but a stilted audience with the King cut short his hopes.

'We may need you, Count,' the King had said, without an explanation.

What Tullus noted from a distance was very evident face to face. The King was unresponsive and preoccupied, as if his mind was in some distant place. He needed rest. Urgently he needed it, but Tullus knew that there was little hope of that.

On the journey Theoderic mostly rode on horseback.

'Carts are for Romans,' Tullus heard him growl. And as he rode he summoned his officials each in turn. Tullus was close enough to observe their comings and their goings. Cyprian was called more than most, and it was very clear to Tullus that the King respected him. Tullus was not called. Indeed, he was totally ignored. For the first time he sensed a coldness in his benefactor and it troubled him.

After five days they reached Verona, and once again Tullus hoped to be dismissed, but nothing happened. He was beginning to loathe the court and all its undercurrents. So when he judged it prudent, he escaped into the town. He liked Verona with its many churches and its amphitheatre – the largest outside Rome, the townsfolk said.

As Tullus moved through the busy streets, the Twins, his guards, drew closer. At one of the many stalls he bought a roll of silk for Drusilla, and then he made for the outer wall. There, on the high, broad structure, he breathed deeply. The air was fresh. To the north he could see the hills that led to the mountains beyond.

The break from the tedium of the court was sweet, but his absence had been noted.

'We searched everywhere, Count,' said a troubled official. 'The King wants you to attend the consistory.'

'The consistory,' Tullus repeated stiffly. It was the court that dealt with treason.

'What time?' he barked, disguising his unease.

'At once, Count. The Senators Albinus and Cassiodorus have arrived and the King has called the court forward.'

'Is Albinus accompanied by his secretary?'

'Yes, sir, the noble Atticus is here,' the official answered with appropriate deference, for he knew that Atticus was the Count's son-in-law.

Tullus wanted to ask why he was being summoned, but he held his peace. To display fear was in itself a statement, so he walked on resolutely to the Palace – the one-time property of a Roman Senator and now the seat of Gothic power. Unobtrusively he took his place at the back. The proceedings were just beginning.

The King glowered fixedly before him – a now familiar sight. Boethius and Cyprian were in conversation but Tullus could see that Boethius was angry. Close by, Cassiodorus sat with his head bowed looking, as usual, older than his years. Tullus scanned the hall looking for his son-in-law, to find him two rows in front and directly behind the ex-Consul Albinus.

The first man before the court was a pitiful creature who shook and cringed before Cyprian and the King. The monarch's reaction was worthy of his reputation.

'This man is incapable of treason. Confine him at our pleasure.'

At once the accused fell before the King in gratitude. His life had been spared. Theoderic gestured impatiently and guards dragged the prostrate Roman to his feet.

After he was led away Cyprian mounted the dais and spoke at length with the King. No one thought much of this, as it was the duty of the Referendarius to explain the details of the next case.

Tullus was alert and watchful.

Slowly Cyprian descended from the dais. Then he held a roll of papers high with a theatrical flourish. Boethius was furious, but Cyprian took his time, his gaze circling the court with studied ease.

'Here in this hand are letters written by the friends of the Patrician Albinus. They are all addressed to the Emperor. Shall I read them?' His voice was mild.

Cyprian waited until the whispering died down. Then he began to read.

The Emperor was lauded as the pious and august protector of the one true Church and of the Senate. Tullus winced. That alone was sufficient to enrage the King. He looked across at the dais to judge his reaction, but Theoderic's stone expression gave no hint.

Anxiously Tullus listened as Cyprian continued. He could see his son-in-law bent forward in earnest conversation with Albinus. Was the young man implicated? Tullus was fearful.

Cyprian exploited every damning implication to the full. Such phrases as 'the liberty of Rome' and 'the Senate's ancient rights' were natural to the Roman ear, but to the Goth they conjured insurrection. There were complaints about the rapacity of the strangers, and worst of all, pointed reference to Theoderic's failing health. All true, Tullus thought bitterly, but not subjects to be put in writing. It was gross stupidity and Albinus was hopelessly compromised. There was one grace, however. The name of Atticus had not been mentioned.

Cyprian turned dramatically to face the King.

'The writers have one thing in common – one patron – one oft referred to in their letters. He is the Senator, the ex-Consul, the ex-Praetorian Prefect Albinus.'

Again Cyprian held the letters high. Then he spun to face Albinus.

'Answer to our Lord the King!'

Albinus stood up. He was shaken yet his movements were measured and dignified. He was a devout man who had laboured tirelessly for Church unity. Slowly he made his way to the dais and bowed low.

'My Lord King, I am no traitor. I seek the good of both our peoples.'

'Honeyed words, Senator,' Cyprian interjected. 'Look at these letters and beg that your end be easy.'

'But they're the work of scribes!' Albinus reacted.

'And the signatures as well,' Cyprian responded with mock innocence. 'Yours in support.' Then he raised his voice in pitch. 'Treachery and treason,' he trumpeted.

Cyprian was prosecutor. Everyone expected rhetoric, but Tullus sensed vindictiveness.

Troubled and exasperated, Albinus turned to the King.

'My Royal lord, we mean no treason. Our words have been corrupted by a false suspicion.'

'False suspicion,' Cyprian exploded. 'These letters are the proof. And do you think you were not watched when you were in Byzantium? Every move, my noble sir. Remember, I was there!' Cyprian squeezed the last words out with obvious relish.

'This is a monstrous slur!' Albinus reacted, and once more he faced the King.

'My lord, I challenge anyone who would maintain that I dishonoured you,' he appealed, but his words failed before the cold and unresponsive stare of Theoderic.

The look of dismay on Albinus's face was obvious. What had happened to the King's good sense?

Tullus watched anxiously, his eyes scanning the court. Cassiodorus still sat doubled up. Boethius, though, sat upright and was clearly poised to act. Again Tullus turned his attention to the King, but the ageing figure on the throne was not the man he knew. Something mean and set possessed him.

Theoderic nodded and Cyprian mounted the dais to consult.

The King raised his hand, the signal for pronouncing judgement.

'Guilty,' he said bluntly in the Gothic tongue.

Immediately Boethius was on his feet. He bowed.

'My Lord King, the law requires a trial,' he said with deference before turning upon the prosecutor.

'You have ill-advised our Royal Lord. Your behaviour is indefensible!' he thundered.

Involuntarily Cyprian stepped back; then, recovering quickly, he smiled.

'Most learned and honoured sir, I do not question our Lord the King.'

The look of cunning in Cyprian's eyes was all too plain, and Boethius turned away with clear disdain. Facing the King once more, he bowed low.

'I respectfully move that this case be tried according to our laws – a privilege your Grace has always granted.'

There was a moment's silence before Theoderic spoke: a moment when the whole hall seemed to hold its breath.

'Master of Offices, we have given sentence!' The King spoke harshly.

Boethius bowed once more.

'My Lord King, you have been wrongly advised. The Patrician Albinus and his friends were acting as Senators. If they are guilty, then the whole Senate, including myself, is responsible. There can be no action against Albinus as an individual, but he must answer to the Senate.'

'Wonderfully obscure, learned sir,' Cyprian muttered cynically.

Boethius ignored the interjection.

'My noble Lord, you have ever been the guardian of our laws. We appeal to you!'

Theoderic stared straight ahead, his expression blank. Tullus was fearful, not only for his son-in-law, but for Boethius too. Indeed, in his selfless defence of Albinus he had isolated himself, a fact not lost on Cyprian.

'Most noble Master of Offices,' he began with mock deference, 'you have stated that the whole Senate is responsible for the guilt of Albinus.'

Boethius made no comment.

'Well, whether you respond or not, that is what you said, my honoured sir.'

Boethius remained silent, and with a dramatic gesture of his arm Cyprian indicated the circle of the consistory.

'How many noble Senators here are willing to stand with the Master of Offices? How many agree they share the guilt of Albinus?'

'Referendarius!' The power of Boethius once more made Cyprian step back. 'That is a cheap trap to set for men of righteous impulse.'

'Cheap trap,' Cyprian reacted angrily. 'It is criminal to withhold evidence in order to obscure the treason of your friends. If you had received these' – he held the letters high and pointed at Albinus – 'the traitor would be walking free!'

'You know what is withheld, sir. Yet once again I will remind you – the foolishness of the simple-minded – the jibes of clever mischief – the poison of the paid informer and the lies of jackals panting for the wealth of honest men.'

'That is your opinion,' Cyprian muttered.

'My gracious Lord, please forgive this ...'

'Enough!' Theoderic shouted. Suddenly he stood up and, full of rage, strode from the hall.

There was a moment of shocked silence before the court broke up in loud confusion. Everyone was on his feet and talking to his neighbour. Tullus stood alone; the sense of tragedy he felt was overpowering. Then, as if rising from the floor, the tall, stooped figure of Cassiodorus was before him.

'Count, take your son-in-law away from here.' The whispered advice was full of urgency.

'How can I, sir? I cannot leave without the King's consent.'

'I will see to that.'

'But, sir, what of Boethius?'

'You cannot help Boethius. No one can. The King is set against him.'

'But why?'

'Theoderic sees the Senate as an enemy, and Boethius is the focus of that rage.' Cassiodorus moved closer. 'A devil has possessed him,' he whispered. 'That's the cause.'

'The devil has allies, though,' Tullus returned.

'Indeed. Boethius, of course, does not make it easy for himself, and his constant stand for truth has made him many enemies. As you know, he doesn't suffer fools too readily.'

'I must try and speak for him. The King has always given me a hearing.'

'Tullus, the lion is enraged and dangerous.'

'I must try. How can I walk away from here without a word, for the fall of Boethius is an unthinkable tragedy. I must do something!'

'Be careful, Tullus, be very careful. I fear the daemon speaking from the body of the King.'

Cassiodorus quickly left, making for the door the King had used. Tullus watched him go, noting how carefully he had avoided contact with Albinus. In fact, apart from Atticus, Albinus was isolated like a carrier of plague. At once Tullus stepped over the benches towards them.

'Ah! Count,' Albinus responded, 'it's a brave man who speaks to me. See how my colleagues stand apart. Take my advice, sir; leave this devil's playground and take your son-in-law.'

'That's exactly what I hope to do!' Tullus said, his gaze fixed steadily on Albinus. Neither spoke. The shadow of the treason law was long.

Albinus shook his head in disbelief. Clearly the charges had taken him by surprise.

'Thank God for Boethius,' he said eventually. 'But for him I'd be ...' He shrugged his shoulders with a sigh. 'I fear, though, that the respite will be brief.'

Tullus nodded in a curt, agitated way. He had resolved to see the King and the resultant turmoil of anticipation had him in its grip.

'I'm going to seek an audience,' he said bluntly.

'But, sir!' Atticus began, his voice full of alarm. 'You'll be ...'

'Wait for me,' he said fiercely, turning resolutely towards the Royal quarters.

OOO

To his astonishment Tullus was ushered into the King's presence immediately. Theoderic was seated with his Gothic advisers standing about him in an informal circle. His rage had gone and in its wake he looked old and haggard.

Tullus bowed and the King nodded perfunctorily. Quickly Tullus scanned the ring of Gothic nobles. He knew them all by sight, and a few he knew too well, like Triguilla, whose pig-eyes watched him from a florid face, and the brutal Cunigast. He was relieved to see the square face of the Count Ibbas. It was Ibbas who broke the silence.

'The King commands the Count Thulwin to his presence – and feels that you would be the most efficient – messenger – after which you may return to your villa.' Ibbas spoke in his usual halting way, occasionally searching for an unfamiliar word.

Tullus bowed to show assent. Suddenly tension gripped him. He had to speak. It was now or never. He straightened up.

'Count.' Again it was the voice of Ibbas. 'Can you explain to an old soldier what the Master of Offices meant by the whole Senate being responsible?'

Tullus sighed with relief. The dangerous subject had arisen without his initiation.

'I repeat – it's a threat,' Cunigast reacted.

'Yes,' Triguilla supported, 'and one to be rooted out..'

Both men had spoken in the Gothic tongue and Tullus pretended not to understand. Obviously they had been debating the subject.

'Sir,' Tullus began. He spoke slowly. 'The Senator Boethius was stating an old principle, the principle of collective responsibility. For example, if a soldier kills someone in battle he is judged as a soldier, not as a private individual, for it is the army which is responsible.'

Ibbas nodded. 'Of course – yes – I see.'

'Well, I don't see – all I see is Roman trickery, with Boethius as chief exponent!' Triguilla said, spitting out the words with relish.

'That is not so,' Tullus answered with a force that quite surprised him. 'Boethius is a man of truth.'

'Silence,' the King growled, glancing up at Tullus wearily. 'Count, we need Thulwin urgently.'

Tullus bowed respectfully and left. No one had asked him why he had sought an audience, but it did not matter.

When he emerged from the King's quarters Albinus and Atticus were still in conversation. Otherwise the hall was almost empty.

'The battle is not lost,' Tullus said without explanation, before rushing off to seek Boethius.

He found the Master of Offices seemingly unmoved. Tullus described his brief audience in detail, but Boethius was cautious.

'Do not build upon the King's apparent change of mood. Age has returned him to his tribal ways. His wider vision has deserted him and in its place suspicion rules. Cyprian exploited the situation shamelessly.'

'But the hatred in Cyprian's voice, why?'

'Oh, yes!' Boethius said with resignation. 'I've thwarted him too often and his clever mind is set against me!'

'It has all happened so quickly,' Tullus interjected.

Boethius did not respond.

'Have you any messages you would like delivered to your family?' Tullus asked after a brief silence.

'Have you need to visit Rome?'

'I have need, sir – yours!'

Boethius paused awhile before responding.

'Should you visit Rome, I would be grateful if you called upon my father-in-law. Tell him the full facts, but do not distress my beloved wife. She, of course, is in Ravenna.'

'And your sons?'

'Hopefully on the way to Constantinople.'

For a moment the look in Boethius's eyes was distant.

ooo

299

# CHAPTER FIFTY EIGHT

# ISOLATED

When Tullus arrived in Ravenna with Atticus and the Twins he learned that Thulwin had gone to visit Rome and was staying at Fidenae. Immediately he sent messages to the King at Verona and to Drusilla. He called on Rusticiana but she was out with friends. Tullus felt relieved, feeling that in his presence she could well discern unspoken fears and grow distressed. So after a brief word with Theodis at the Royal Guard headquarters he, Atticus, and the Twins as guard, set out for Rome.

On the third night they rested at Atticus's villa in Umbria, but there was little time for either husband or father to spend with Cornelia. The sooner Thulwin was at the King's side the better.

At last they passed through the familiar entrance to the villa at Fidenae. The first servant to recognise the well-known figure of Tullus alerted the rest, and soon it seemed that all the staff were on the portico.

'You're popular, sir,' Atticus observed.

'We're old friends, Atticus.'

After greeting the servants Tullus learned that Thulwin was in Rome but was expected back that evening. He also learned that Valerius and Poppea had left for Florentia a few days earlier. It was late afternoon, so there was little they could do but await the Count's arrival.

Tullus was tired, yet he found it difficult to rest. Too many worries were racing in his mind, and in the circumstances it was prudent to occupy himself. He could inspect the estate, he thought, and Atticus could join him.

'The cattle are doing well,' Tullus commented as they rode by the perimeter wall. 'That's the Senator Valerius, of course. He keeps an expert eye on things.'

'But he's not the agent.'

'Oh no, it's his way of repaying Thulwin, for the Count will accept no formal rent.'

They rode on unspeaking. Tullus noted everything.

'That land needs draining,' he observed, pointing towards the river. For a while the troubles of the court had been forgotten.

As the light began to fail they turned their horses back towards the villa.

'I must remember to send some flour and oil to Sublaqueum. Remind me tomorrow, Atticus.'

'Yes, sir.' Atticus made no further comment. The story of Martin was well known to all connected with the Tullus household.

For Tullus, thoughts of Martin quickly linked with Justinian and in an instant the crisis at Theoderic's court was circling yet again.

'Atticus,' Tullus said, drawing the young man's attention, 'your master Albinus is an ex-Consul and an ex-Praetorian Prefect – in fact, a famous Senator.'

Atticus nodded.

'He's also a well-known friend of Byzantium. Do you agree?'

'Yes, that's so.'

'Now, Atticus, if you were the Emperor and you heard that Albinus had been held or put to death for reasons well displayed at court, what would you do?'

'I should be very angry.'

'Yes, but what would you do?' Tullus pressed.

The two men drew their horses to a halt, their faces dark and featureless in the fading light.

'I would take revenge on the Arian community in Constantinople, and I'd take hostages against future good behaviour ...' Atticus stopped short.

'I know what you're thinking, Atticus – the reverse could happen. Albinus could become a hostage against Orthodox belligerence. No. I don't believe the Goths would think like that – certainly not the King in his present state.'

'There's a cunning in the eyes of Triguilla; and, sir, someone else might do their thinking for them.'

'Like Cyprian,' Tullus grunted.

The horses shook their heads restlessly but their riders paid scant attention.

'Sir, may I ask a question?'

'Of course.'

'If you were king and you were angered by Orthodox aggression, who – who would you choose to be the most effective hostage?'

'Don't even think it, Atticus!'

'I know, sir, but many, including myself, have noticed how the King has turned against his Master of Offices.'

'Dear God!' Tullus exhaled loudly. 'let's forget we had this conversation.'

He nudged his horse and the two men headed for the villa.

When they arrived they were met by the tall, dignified figure of

Thulwin. Tullus did not mention the purpose of his visit until they were inside and seated. Even then he was reluctant to break the easy mode of conversation.

Thulwin had taken his son to Rome and was recounting his many questions. Tullus waited and then the moment came.

'Count, we are here as messengers,' he began.

Immediately Thulwin's look changed to his customary reserve, and without further delay Tullus relayed the King's command. Then he gave the full detail of the crisis.

'I'm not surprised,' Thulwin eventually responded, shaking his head. 'The belligerence of Byzantium and the arrogance of the Roman Church have borne their bitter fruit. The case against Albinus is but a straw to tip the scale. The trouble is, once the King says "guilty" he never alters. His word's like rock.'

'Even if he's ill-advised?' Atticus pressed.

Thulwin nodded.

'Even then he's loth to change. I'll speak plainly,' he continued, getting to his feet and facing Tullus. 'To many of my peers you Romans are a conquered race. Why, even now they think that plunder is their right. Indeed, to punish them for such an act is past their understanding. Like a city wall, the King has stood against their savage greed, but if his ageing years allow his guard to drop...' He paused, looking at the low ceiling. 'God help both our nations, Tullus.'

'All Goths are not as Cunigast.'

'Tullus, it's easy to tell men to take more. It makes instant friends. Many would be quick to follow Cunigast.'

Again Thulwin paused, looking at Tullus and Atticus in turn.

'You can imagine how the militant arrogance of Byzantium and the Roman Church angers me, for such stupidity is the ally of men like Cunigast.'

Wine arrived and cups were refilled before conversation resumed. This time Thulwin confined himself to matters of organisation.

'I will leave by first light in the morning, but my son is somewhere east of Rome by now. He's gone hunting with family friends. Could you collect him, Tullus?'

Tullus willingly assented and the details of Thulwin's plans continued.

At supper the conversation moved to estate matters, and even though the crisis at the court was present like some hateful apparition, it was not mentioned. For Thulwin it was much too close and painful; his lord the King was failing.

It was in the morning, when Thulwin was about to leave, that Tullus made his brief appeal.

'Count, speak for Boethius!'

'Tullus, my friend, I will do what I can.'

'God be with you.'

'And with you, Tullus.'

Thulwin swung into the saddle, and soon he and his troop of well-nigh twenty men were lost in the faint morning light.

Shortly afterwards Tullus and his son-in-law left for Rome

OOO

The usually alert features of Atticus looked drawn and tense. He had slept little during the night, for the thought of meeting the family of Albinus haunted him. The cold morning air made him shiver and the sound of horses' hooves rang harsh. Their number had been swollen by a further six. They were Thulwin's men, an escort for his son.

Atticus was glad to have the company of his father-in-law but he could not bring himself to speak. His weakness was too raw. He glanced quickly at the upright figure of Tullus riding beside him, his eyes straight ahead, like some heroic centurion from the past.

Atticus pulled his cloak about himself. He desperately wanted the support of Tullus at the villa, yet he rode on, tight-lipped.

It was Tullus who first spoke. The need of his silent and shivering son-in-law was obvious. Briefly he voiced the outline of his plans. They would go to the villa of Albinus together. That would be their first call. Atticus was at once relieved.

OOO

The reception hall in the villa of Albinus was large and opulent. Round the walls statues of family ancestors gave evidence of continuity. Before each statue rugs were laid, but the circular mosaic in the centre of the floor was bare.

The curly-haired, youthful Atticus and his father-in-law stood silently awaiting the presence of Albinus's wife. It was very quiet.

Faintly at first, they heard approaching footsteps and their heads turned towards the sound. In a moment the wife of Albinus and her two teenage daughters stood before them. Behind them three elderly manservants waited at a respectful distance.

'Welcome, Count Tullus; welcome, Atticus. We are honoured.'

The wife of Albinus was a stoutish lady, and appeared to Tullus very much the Roman matron.

The two men bowed.

'You have word of my lord?' she asked, the note of strain betraying apprehension.

'My lady, the news is not good,' Tullus said evenly.

The daughters drew close to their mother, and Tullus nodded to Atticus, who detailed the awful happenings at Verona. The daughters began to weep but their mother, though clearly shaken, held her poise.

'This is martyrdom,' she cried, her fervour covering her distress. 'We must seek an audience with the Holy Father.'

'Madam, seek the protection of the Church for your family,' Tullus said forcefully. He turned aside to his son-in-law.

'Go with the ladies to the Pope. Get them out of here: for who knows when the Goths may come to vent their lusts? Make sure it's only property they find.'

Atticus had been immobilised by the piteous scene before him; but now he knew exactly what to do.

'I must go,' Tullus continued. 'I'll leave the Twins, but billet them at the villa of Symmachus. It will be at least two days before I return with Thulwin's son.' He paused and looked sharply at his son-in-law. 'Stay with Symmachus – not here!'

Tullus was about to leave when Albinus's wife caught his arm, her eyes frantic with confusion.

'Who spoke for my lord, other than Boethius?'

'No one, madam.'

'Only Manlius Boethius – and he was a man my lord Albinus often opposed.'

'For what reason?' Tullus heard himself ask.

'My husband felt that he was over-influenced by philosophers who had not known the Christ.'

Tullus blinked. He had not expected such thinking in the home of a Patrician.

At that, he bowed and quickly left.

The short journey to the villa of Symmachus took little time. Tullus spent two hours with the father of the Senate. Symmachus was shocked and concerned; not least because Rusticiana was in Ravenna. Notwithstanding, his rugged features remained rock-like.

'Boethius is fearless, but without the King's support he is dangerously isolated. Countless times he has stood against the fraudulent plunder of the Goths. They hate him, and amongst the Romans he also has his bitter enemies. There are the ignorant, of course, who see his various studies as dark, un-Christian practices. Above all, though, there are the envious. Tullus, the friends of truth are few.' Symmachus spoke the last words gruffly.

'Sir, he must have friends in the Senate. His excellence is obvious.'

'Friends! They'd denounce him tomorrow to preserve their useless skins!'

OOO

Since Tullus's departure for Genua, Drusilla had received letters from Mediolanum, Verona, Ravenna and now Rome. There was no political news – her husband never committed such matters to paper – but she strongly sensed that something was amiss.

Two days after the letter arrived from Rome her fears were tragically confirmed. Boethius had been arrested and imprisoned at Ticinum. The news came by special messenger from Cassiodorus, the new Master of Offices.

Drusilla was stunned and wandered in a daze from room to room, then out into the chill November air. Instinctively she made for the rock platform above the villa. The wind had a biting edge and it was not long before she saw the figure of Rufus hurrying towards her

'My lady, your cloak,' he said breathlessly.

The squarely-built Tuscan looked anxiously at the Countess. He had noted her strange behaviour and feared that some misfortune had visited the Count.

'The Lord Boethius is imprisoned at Ticinum. He is accused of treason,' she said, the wind whipping at her voice, making it difficult to hear.

'Boethius in prison!' Rufus repeated in shocked tones.

Drusilla nodded.

'Dear God, I wish it were not so.'

'Cyprian is behind it!' Rufus said sharply. 'My late mistress told him time and time again not to tangle with Boethius. She knew. She told him it would blacken his soul.'

'Rufus, we don't know if it's Cyprian.'

'It is, my lady. I know it!' He spoke emphatically.

'It's cold, Rufus,' she said, drawing her cloak about her.

305

Slowly they walked down the hill without speaking. At the bottom, where the ground levelled out, they halted. Rufus watched her closely. Her troubled state was eloquent.

'Rufus, I'm worried for the Count,' she said, her control barely holding.

'It's all right, my lady – you said yourself that the Count was escorting Thulwin's son and had six extra guards. With such a charge, who would challenge him?'

'Yes, you're right,' she answered slowly, yet her anxiety remained.

'The Count will be here within the next three days at the most,' he said encouragingly, but there was little response. The Countess was not herself. For an instant the image of the frail and ageing Julia flashed before his mind and pity rose in response.

Tentatively he took her arm, for normally it would have been a gross impertinence.

'Come, my lady, the dusk is falling and it's getting cold.'

Gently he led her towards the villa.

'The anguish Rusticiana must be feeling,' she moaned. 'I cannot bear to think about it.'

After leaving the Countess in the warm comfort of her own rooms, Rufus quickly went to see the nurse. Hastily he explained the situation, suggesting that their mistress needed company. His suggestion had the peremptory note of an order, but Anna was too shocked to notice.

'Valeria,' she called. The little girl came running.

'Lead me to your mother, dear – the corridors are dark. The Countess has nightmare memories,' she added, turning to Rufus. 'We'll have to watch lest they ...' She left the sentence incomplete, but followed Valeria's tugging hand.

Rufus watched them go. He could not help thinking of his old mistress and her strange obsession with Boethius. What had she known? he wondered. He remembered how she would pray – for hours, it seemed. Most thought she was asleep, or in some forgetful dream, but he never thought so.

He made his way to his quarters and sat down heavily on his chair behind the agent's table. What action would the Count expect? The question was practical and it sounded right.

If there was any danger to the Countess and her daughter, he began to reason, then his duty was defence. Florentia still sent two guards, but they could switch to being enemies by order of their officers. He would have to watch them closely. However, there were more than Ostrogoths to guard the villa, for it was plainly evident that the young Tuscans working on the estate were strong and tough. Marcus Tullus was no man's fool, he thought. And there was the secret stock of arrows known only to himself and to the aged Philippus.

The broad, honest face of Rufus lit with a smile. The fortress villa was indeed a fortress.

OOO

# CHAPTER FIFTY NINE

# YOUNG THULWIN

In the space of two days Tullus returned to Rome with Thulwin's son and after collecting Atticus and the Twins he headed for the Via Flamina. The passage through Rome, however, was continually delayed by young Thulwin's passion for the ancient sites. Time and time again he asked to stop. Tullus was indulgent – in fact, he was amazed at how much the young Goth knew.

Once outside the centre they progressed quickly, largely due to the Gothic guards. Their presence was enough to discipline the crowds.

At first Thulwin's son rode beside Atticus, but Atticus was too preoccupied and troubled to converse. Slowly the young Goth edged his horse forward and alongside Tullus, for the questions in his mind were pressing.

'Sir, what made the Roman army invincible?' he asked suddenly.

Tullus turned, not disguising his surprise.

'Well, if you're asking about the armies of Augustus and Trajan, one word repeats, and that is discipline. Their drilling was conducted with unremitting rigour, and each legion had a fierce pride in its record. Honour was a strong ingredient and their determination was relentless, but they were not invincible.'

Young Thulwin was unfamiliar with some of the Latin words but Tullus was patient in his tutoring. The youth listened intently, repeating the difficult words to aid his memory.

'They were not defeated, sir,' he pressed. His voice had just broken and the tone fluctuated between boy and man.

'I agree, not when Rome was Rome – not the mass of legions. Even so, they suffered heavy losses, in fact whole legions. In AD9 there were twenty-eight legions ...'

'Twenty-five, sir,' the youth interrupted, too eager to restrain himself.

'You know?!'

'Yes, sir. General Varus lost three legions in Germania.'

Tullus was astonished. This was uncommon knowledge, even for a Roman.

'You have a good tutor,' he prompted.

'No, sir, not my tutor; he knows no history,' he said disdainfully. 'It was my father's Latin scribe. He died three months ago. I was sorry, for I liked him. He left me his notes on history, but my Latin is very poor.'

'What does your father think of this?'

'I've heard him say to others that too much learning weakens a soldier's spirit. What do you think, sir?'

Tullus smiled.

'It depends on the learning, young man.'

Thulwin's son smiled back and they both laughed.

The conversation continued intermittently, with Tullus answering the frequent questions of his young companion. Indeed, Thulwin's son appeared to have an endless thirst for knowledge, and he had a rational way of thinking. He should be sitting at the feet of Boethius, Tullus thought, but there was little hope of that.

They made one overnight stop before reaching the Umbrian villa of Atticus. There it was arranged that Atticus and Cornelia would follow in a day or so. Tullus left the Twins as escort, for the Royal guardsmen, still not recalled, were devoted to Tullus and wholly reliable.

Tullus, Thulwin's son and his father's six-man guard left the next day to make the short journey to Arretium. Stopping overnight, they were poised to make the final journey to the fortress villa, with one diversion, the home of Tullus's friend and father-in-law, Valerius.

Tullus left the guard on the flat ground below the Valerius villa. Then, with Thulwin's son beside him, he climbed the steep path past the statues of the Gracchi to the modest portico where Poppea was waiting.

'Dear Marcus, I am pleased to see you,' she said, embracing Tullus warmly but with a kind of urgency.

'This tall young man looks familiar.' She smiled in greeting.

'Thulwin, son of Thulwin,' Tullus said.

'And so like your father,' Poppea responded; then, unable to contain herself, she turned to Tullus. 'Oh, Marcus, have you heard the awful news? The Lord Boethius has been arrested.'

Tullus suddenly felt old and tired.

'Dear God,' he whispered.

'My lord is so distressed.'

'Where is my friend?'

'Inside. He can't have heard you. His hearing is ...' The sentence trailed.

'But the Senator is a philosopher,' young Thulwin interjected with indignation.

309

Both Tullus and Poppea reacted in amazement, but at that moment the tall figure of Valerius appeared on the portico.

'Ah, Tullus, my friend. And it must be – yes! – the son of the noble Thulwin.'

The youth bowed respectfully.

'Sir,' he said, straightening himself, 'may I ask a question?'

'Of course.'

'The statues in the garden, sir – whom do they represent?'

'The Gracchi.'

'The Gracchi!' the youth repeated, his eyes wide with wonder.

For a moment the tensions working in the adults eased. Valerius displayed his obvious surprise and Tullus responded knowingly.

'This young man,' he said emphatically, 'knows more Roman history than most Romans.'

Excusing themselves, Valerius and Tullus went inside, leaving Poppea alone with the son of the high-born Goth.

Poppea felt awkward and the conversation remained stilted until the youth asked to have a closer look at the statues. He had only had a passing glimpse, he said. Poppea was pleased to oblige.

'They're very worn.' His voice was full of reverence.

'Yes, they've been standing for hundreds of years,' Poppea responded.

'They would have known the great days' he said, giving life to the ancient stone.

She smiled and looked up at him. He was going to be tall like his father.

'Thank you, my lady. Shall we go in now?'

How well-mannered, and so young. His behaviour ran counter to all the brutish stories she had heard of Gothic youth.

Inside the villa, Valerius and Tullus had just emerged from the library. Both were grim-faced, reflecting the conclusions of their conversation. Tullus had taken a strongly pessimistic view, especially in the case of Valerius's safety.

'You're a Senator,' he had emphasised, 'closely associated with both Boethius and Symmachus. God knows what will happen if those jackals at the court are free to act. Remember what they did before.'

The two men stood silently. They could hear Poppea and young Thulwin approaching.

'My dear,' Valerius said quietly as his wife entered the atrium, 'we're leaving for Faesulae tomorrow.'

She nodded in response as if it were a routine matter. There was no indication of her feelings, even though she knew the reason for the move.

Almost at once, Tullus and his young companion left. They had been at the villa for less than half an hour.

Wearily Tullus mounted his horse once more.

'Now, beloved Drusilla,' he thought, 'it's home at last.'

They rode up the valley to Florentia, crossed the bridge and headed north. Tullus's horse, long familiar with the road, quickened pace and laboured eagerly up the steep incline to Faesulae. Passing through the town, they headed east. From the high ground they could see the villa looking tiny in the hills. Turning north, Tullus and his party descended to the lower ground. The villa was now hidden. Then, climbing once again, they joined the mud-and-stone road used when travelling to Ravenna.

Tullus's horse broke into a trot and suddenly, round the side of the hill, the fortress villa stood before them. Unusually, a figure was moving on the turret and the heavy courtyard doors were shut. Tullus smiled knowingly. His agent Rufus was taking no chances. He knew, of course, for Valerius had received the fateful news from Drusilla.

As he watched, a blast of chill wind made his eyes water. Then the heavy doors swung open, and there were Drusilla and Valeria, with Rufus in attendance, proceeding to the open ground to meet them.

Because of young Thulwin and the escort, the family greetings were hedged with formality.

'Valeria, you remember your friend, don't you,' Drusilla prompted.

'Yes, Mother.' The wide eyes of the five-year-old gazed up at the tall youth. 'Hello,' she said.

Not knowing what to say, young Thulwin shifted on his feet.

'It's chilly, my dear,' Tullus said, covering the youth's embarrassment. 'let's go inside.'

Immediately they were alone and the doors were shut behind them, Drusilla rushed into her husband's embrace.

'Marcus, beloved Marcus.' Her arms held him tightly. 'I've missed you terribly.'

There was desperation in the way she clung to him.

'What are we going to do?' Her whispered words were urgent.

'I don't know, Drusilla,' he admitted.

'Thulwin's coming in a few days to collect his son,' she said flatly. 'Oh, Marcus.' The words suddenly exploded. 'I hate it when we're parted!' Tears were in her eyes.

'My beautiful, darling Drusilla,' he said slowly, holding her very close. 'This is a time to trust, to trust totally.'

ooo

The gossip of Ravenna rarely failed to echo in the quarters of the Royal Guard. In many cases it was the guards themselves who were the source of rumour, for their Palace duties gave them ample scope to see and hear and thus to speculate.

There were facts, of course, that all could observe: the King's failing health, his dark moods, the cautious ways of Cassiodorus and the growing influence of Cunigast and his allies.

The fall of Boethius still occupied the guardroom theorists. Most believed that he had lost a power struggle with Cyprian and that Cassiodorus had quietly seized the prize. Some dwelt on the charge of sacrilegious acts, but most agreed that he deserved his fate – anyway, he was a Roman.

During all this Theodis kept silent. There was little point in speaking, for his fellow guards saw him as a Roman-lover and any attempt to defend Boethius would have courted further jibes. Also it was dangerous, as telltale ears were everywhere.

Theodis was saddened and disillusioned. How could the great King accept the lies of men like Opilio and Gaudentius who had been banished for their countless frauds – and Basilius, another of Cyprian's so-called witnesses; a man previously dismissed from Royal service and desperate to redeem his debts? Justice and honour had died and the great King's days had withered. And Cassiodorus, he thought disdainfully, the new Master of Offices. He saw the bent and busy figure often but he saw no honour in him. To him, Cassiodorus was a time-server and greedy for promotion, no matter what the price.

Theodis confided in no one and his sense of isolation grew. In this state his thoughts continually turned to Faesulae, to Anna and the Count. The free air of the villa beckoned strongly.

Anna was very dear. She was part of him. It was typical of Theodis that he had resolved not to marry while she lived. For him, it was the honourable course, but he was tired of his lonely life and the mistresses who came and went.

There was little hope of getting leave. The orders of Triguilla had doubled the Palace guard and all were on special alert – against a Roman reaction, it was said. Nonsense. It was posturing and little else, yet it kept Theodis and his fellow guardsmen tied to duty. The Twins, however, had remained at Faesulae, a fact of no small consolation to Theodis, as it meant that Tullus still retained the Royal favour.

His belief in Tullus's security was rudely shattered early in December. The Twins had been recalled. He was at once alarmed, but whom could he trust? He had lost confidence in Cassiodorus. There was only one man he felt he could approach, a man he trusted fully – the Count Thulwin. But was he in Ravenna? Some said that, after quarrelling with Triguilla, he had left the town in plain disgust, while others held that he had had a fearsome row with Cunigast. But all agreed that he had lost his influence with the King. Theodis waited until one day he learned that Thulwin was in residence at his villa. At once Theodis resolved to contact him.

Theodis introduced himself to the villa guard and without delay he was taken to the Count. With due deference, the Royal guardsman paid his respects. He had always looked on Thulwin with a kind of awe.

Pointedly, Thulwin confined the conversation to the subject of the Royal Guard while the servants were present. Theodis was offered wine in a finely-wrought cup. This was an honour, a mark of friendship.

Slowly, Thulwin escorted his guest into the large garden enclosed by the rambling villa. There, well clear of servants, he stopped. Dusk was settling and the lamps were being lit. For a while both men were silent.

'Well, Captain?' Thulwin prompted, using the title given to him by the Tullus household.

Thulwin listened with his characteristic reserve to the guardsman's fears. His response was brief. He would see to the matter, and Theodis had no doubt that he would.

'I'll be with the Count in two days' time and I'll tell him of our meeting. He'll be grateful.'

Again the conversation turned to Army matters. Clearly Thulwin was avoiding current issues, yet Theodis felt compelled to ask about Boethius.

'What will happen to the great Senator?' he questioned.

Thulwin shook his head.

'Let's say he's not in immediate danger.'

Thulwin looked fiercely at the tall guardsman.

'Captain,' he said forcefully, 'Ravenna is mad with rumour and suspicion. Keep your own counsel.'

'Yes, Count.'

The meeting was over.

Theodis rode back through the dimly-lit streets to the guard quarters. The horse held its head high, fearful of every shadow. There was a moon, enough to travel on the open road, and the urge to ride away towards the hills was strong. Yet he kept straight for the palace. He was a Royal guardsman.

ooo

The arrival of Valerius and Poppea at the Villa Tullus was quickly followed by that of Cornelia and Atticus. The arrangements for their stay kept Drusilla busy, and as well as that, there was the presence of young Thulwin.

Tullus was grateful that his wife was fully occupied, for the arrest of Boethius had shocked her terribly. What was more, it linked too easily with the horror suffered in her youth. Because of this, he did not tell her that the Twins had been recalled. The fire of her distress was burning quite enough.

For his own part, Tullus was undecided. If he did nothing, how could he live with himself? How could he cower in his villa, fearful of the morning? Yet a false move could be worse than useless, knowing, as he did, the King's irrational state. Moreover, he had to consider Drusilla and the family. That was a paramount restraint. Meantime, though, there was little he could do until he spoke with Thulwin. The Count's news and advice would be invaluable. As it happened, Thulwin arrived much earlier than expected.

Thulwin first embraced his son, while making jokes about the youth's presumed excesses. Then, with equal predictability, Drusilla defended her young guest, but the humour was a surface gloss, for beneath the adult banter anxious questions waited. Prevarication, however, was not in Thulwin's nature, and within a short time he and Tullus were walking, deep in conversation, in the cold and dull December afternoon.

'They're afraid to execute him,' Thulwin said bluntly. 'Even Triguilla sees the danger of reprisals against the Arians in Byzantium.'

'Surely his arrest was provocation enough!'

'Yes, but if Byzantium values the noble Senator's life, they'll restrain themselves and leave their Arian citizens alone,' Thulwin countered.

'The factions in the city are beyond restraint,' Tullus said with knowing pessimism. He sighed. His hostage fears were realised.

Thulwin did not respond directly, but proceeded to list the witnesses arraigned against Boethius.

'Opilio!' Tullus exploded when the name was mentioned. 'He's a drunken rat!'

'That may be so, but the Senate have endorsed the charge of treason,' Thulwin said bluntly.

'Symmachus predicted that,' Tullus returned. 'One whiff of fear, he said, would be enough!'

Thulwin nodded. He understood completely.

'Your friend Theodis called on me, anxious for your safety,' he stated, shifting the direction of the conversation. 'The faithful Twins, he said, had been recalled, and he felt that you were vulnerable. He was right, you need protection.'

'We have the soldiers from Florentia ...'

'For how long?' Thulwin interjected. 'You know as well as I do that the role could quickly change.'

They stopped their slow progression, turned and headed back towards the villa. It was both damp and cold.

'Tullus, I'm leaving you a six-man guard,' Thulwin said abruptly.

Tullus stopped, showing obvious gratitude. He had not expected such generous support.

'My heartfelt thanks, sir – but such a gesture could be used against you at the court. Remember, Boethius has been my guide and mentor. Drusilla and I were married at his palace, as was our daughter. Your enemies could throw it in your face!'

'Just let them try, by God!' Thulwin growled.

They walked on in silence. The cold, damp air was heavy and the wind had died. Nature seemed lifeless and suspended.

'How is the King?' Tullus asked.

For some time Thulwin did not answer, and when he did he responded to the hidden question.

'Don't go to Ravenna to plead for Boethius. It would achieve nothing. Indeed, if anything it could make things worse.' He shook his head. 'The King is not the King we knew. He lightens in the morning sometimes, but the afternoon is dark. Then he sits staring straight ahead – his neck jutting forward. He still retains his common sense, but there are certain subjects on which his mind is closed – Boethius and the Senate being one of them. Tullus, it's a tragedy, like the ancient theatre where mortals are the hopeless puppets of the gods.'

Momentarily Thulwin screwed up his eyes as if in pain. 'I should not speak about my lord like this. Understand, it's not in hate ...'

'I understand, but what a tragedy, what a waste, for the great King and the Senator could have worked a miracle. Let's pray our Royal lord regains his former state!'

Thulwin nodded, and once more the conversation lapsed. It was growing colder and they quickened pace.

'My son-in-law Atticus wants to visit Albinus ...'

'Cornelia's husband!' Thulwin reacted vehemently. 'Keep him away. He will only put himself in danger. Tell him I forbid it. Say anything, but do not let him go. I will not have the daughter of Arria suffer!'

Again Tullus stopped. He looked straight at his tall companion, but when he made to speak, emotion forced him to be silent.

They continued on towards the villa, each lost in his own thoughts.

'How has my son behaved?'

'A fine young man, sir – he has an unquenchable thirst for knowledge. He's a great favourite with little Valeria. She follows him everywhere and looks up at him with her wide, innocent eyes – and when he's with my father-in-law Valerius, they have to be reminded when to eat!'

Thulwin shook his head in disbelief.

'What do they find to talk about?'

'Plato. When it's Valerius, it's always Plato!'

Again Thulwin shook his head.

'Last year it was hunting – there was nothing but hunting! This year he can't stop talking. He'll never be a soldier!'

Tullus laughed. He could not help himself, and the tall Goth looked on uncomprehendingly.

'Sir, may I make a suggestion? Look at your mirror image and then at your son – he is your double. He walks like you. He rides like you, and when the time is full he'll lead his men like you.'

'My nerves were toughened on the battlefield – blade to blade. My mind was never softened by philosophy!'

Tullus knew his friend was serious but he refused to hold his tongue.

'Sir, fearlessness is as necessary to the seeker of truth as to the warrior.'

'You're as blunt as the noble Symmachus.'

'Almost,' Tullus returned with humour.

They fell silent, for the name of Symmachus was inseparable from Boethius.

'What can I do? I must do something!' Tullus said desperately.

Thulwin knew exactly what was meant.

'There is nothing – nothing you can do – but I might get you permission to visit the noble prisoner. Don't ask me how.'

'That would be a blessing.'

'Tullus!'

'Yes, sir?'

'This conversation never happened.'

'My lips are as a clam upon a rock.'

OOO

Thulwin and his son left the Villa Tullus in time to reach Florentia by nightfall. As usual, father and son rode together.

'I heard you were with the Senator Valerius almost continuously for the last two days or so,' Thulwin began. 'I hope you didn't make a nuisance of yourself.'

'No, Father.'

'Whence all this sudden interest in philosophy?'

'Not sudden, Father.'

'Well, I'm not sure. I think a tour of duty in the border areas is needed. It will stiffen you, for Ravenna's only a parade ground.'

Young Thulwin knew it was useless to argue with his father. In any case, the prospect of duty on the borders was exciting.

OOO

# CHAPTER SIXTY

# TICINUM

At the end of December, Tullus received an official despatch from Cassiodorus, the Master of Offices, giving him permission to visit Boethius. Tullus assumed it was the work of Thulwin, but how? Why had he been given permission when Symmachus and Rusticiana had been barred?

Drusilla was almost sick with worry as she watched her husband leave for Ticinum. She tried to conceal her rampant fears, but her father, still resident at the villa, was not deceived.

'Don't worry, my dear,' he said, trying to reassure her, 'it will be all right – it always is with Marcus.'

'I know, Father, but this time it's dangerous. He should have taken more guards …'

'No! Marcus was right,' Valerius interjected. 'Two guards are manifestly modest, whereas more could be viewed as provocative.'

'And Cassiodorus,' Drusilla pressed, 'can we really trust him?'

'Thank God for Cassiodorus, my dear. That's my opinion, and I know that Marcus thinks the same. I would wager that he's working hard behind the scenes. Politics is his element. He could walk across a swamp and keep his feet dry.'

'I find him difficult to credit, Father. He praises monsters with his so-called eulogies.'

'Perhaps he hopes they'll hear and then reflect their new-found image. I know, my dear, such dissembling is difficult to take, yet many say that but for Cassiodorus, half the Senate would be locked up in Ticinum.'

OOO

The document permitting Tullus to visit Boethius was valid for only one occasion and Cassiodorus had made it clear that further visits would require a fresh approval. He also requested a signed report on Boethius's prison conditions. This puzzled Tullus. Did the Palace want an independent voice to placate a restive church? With the present state of things, such an answer seemed bizarre.

On arrival at Ticinum, Tullus went directly to the fortress where

Boethius was imprisoned and, being expected, he gained access immediately.

Leaving his escort with the horses, he went inside. There, grim-faced and tense, he waited while two soldiers were briefed to take him to the Senator.

With one soldier in front and the other behind he was escorted down a bare-walled corridor. Although the light was dim, Tullus noted every detail: the low arch of the ceiling, the broken lamp-brackets and the dirty, uneven floor. Soon they stood before a metal-studded door. A key turned noisily, the door creaked open and there, seated at a table, was the Senator Boethius.

'Tullus!' he exclaimed. 'This is a wonderful surprise.'

They embraced.

'I'm a bag of bones, Tullus, and my odour – you must excuse my unwashed state.'

Tullus made no comment. He was too moved by the awful reality.

'I know it's not Elysium, but I have a chair, a table and a flow of warm air from the boilers.'

'Who gave you the table, sir? It looks a stranger to this place.'

'The monks – friends of Cassiodorus.'

'Cassiodorus!'

'Oh, yes. Don't underestimate Cassiodorus. He could wring concessions from a scorpion!'

'I know, and he's been a constant ally, but, sir, he took your post with little hesitation. Is power so sweet a thing?'

'It's not like that, Tullus,' Boethius answered quietly. 'For Cassiodorus it would be God's will that he took the post ...'

'But how can he serve the gross injustice ruling at the court?'

'It's God's will that he labours in a barren vineyard. That would be his viewpoint,' Boethius replied calmly.

Tullus sighed, looking down at the rough stone slabs that made the prison floor.

'Sit down, Tullus,' Boethius said, indicating the chair, as he perched on the edge of his bed.

'The smell of bad drains is the so-called privy. It's better than it was, thank God. The monks have done wonders. I hope it's not too oppressive.'

'There must be something we can do. This indignity is beyond ...'

'No, Tullus,' Boethius rejoined quietly.

Tullus did not argue; instead he asked about the prison food and learned that the Senator's meals were regular, now that the monks had taken charge.

319

'What happened before, sir?'

'Initially I was treated well, but sensing things would change, I sent Rusticiana south – luckily I had a convenient pretext. What happened next is best forgotten. But tell me, what of my beloved wife, and that mirror of virtue, my father-in-law?'

Tullus related the details of his meeting with Symmachus in November. There had been no further contact, except that Drusilla had offered the hospitality of the Villa Tullus to Rusticiana.

'Nothing was put in writing,' he assured Boethius, 'but just before I left a churchman arrived, relaying the thanks of your wife and the message that, at present, she would be staying with her father.'

Boethius rose, taking the few steps to the end wall. There he gazed upwards at the light filtering through the grille.

'The Goths will never allow my father-in-law to visit me,' he said. 'They'd suspect some plot.' He swung round to face Tullus. 'My wife must not travel here to see me. She'd be distressed beyond endurance by this place – anyway, there's little chance that she'd be given leave. Tell me, Tullus, how did you get access?'

'Thulwin promised to speak.'

'He's your friend, I know, but he's only one voice.'

'There's another fact that might explain matters – they asked me for a written report on your prison conditions.'

'Ah! now it's clear.'

'Emissaries from Constantinople have arrived, or will be arriving. They'll be full of protests and a favourable report about prison conditions, signed by Marcus Tullus, would be well received by the nephew of Justin. That must be the answer.' Boethius smiled. 'I sense the deft hand of Cassiodorus '– it certainly explains the presence of the ministering monks.'

'There may be some compromise afoot,' Tullus said hopefully.

'Perhaps.' The Senator's voice was barely audible.

Boethius sat with his head bent forward, his elbows on his knees, hands cupping his chin.

'Don't forget Cyprian. How would he feel if I were free to expose the fraud of his witnesses – his brother Opilio for one. Cyprian will not advise the King to compromise. We can be sure of that!'

'There's Cassiodorus, of course,' Tullus suggested. 'After all, he's Master of Offices.'

'Yes, there's always Cassiodorus,' Boethius echoed, but the sound of hope was absent.

For a time both men were silent. The stillness deepened. It was always thus with Boethius, Tullus thought. Then he noticed paper and writing materials neatly placed on the table.

'You have been writing, sir.'

'Oh, yes – it's my consolation.' Boethius smiled. '*The Consolation of Philosophy* – and it's practical! For in this narrow, stone-locked world there's no pretence.'

'Have you written much?'

'Yes, since I've had the means to write – it occupies the mind.'

'Sir, give your writing to the monks. In their safe-keeping your Consolation will comfort many.' Tullus was amazed, for it truly seemed that someone else had spoken.

'Your confidence is flattering, Tullus, but you haven't read a word ...'

'Give it to the monks,' Tullus interjected, 'lest some suspicious Goth consign it to the flames!'

'I will obey,' Boethius laughed, before briefly outlining the content of his work.

'The question,' he said simply, 'is just this. Why do I grieve about the loss of worldly honours when I've known and taught that they are passing things? And happiness, why do I seek it outside when I know it is within? For who can rob us of that inner bliss other than ourselves?'

'It's not easy, sir,' Tullus responded, getting to his feet and pacing the narrow length of the cell.

'Is there any news of Albinus?' he asked.

'No, but I suspect our fates are interlocked.'

'I see,' Tullus murmured, sitting down again; there was so little to be said.

'Are you allowed exercise, sir?'

'Yes, I have my daily measure. At first two guards escorted me – now there's only one. He's friendly. I speak his language and he likes to talk. So my spells of exercise are generous. Things could be a lot worse, Tullus.'

The key turned loudly in the lock and the door creaked open. A soldier stepped forward and spoke briefly to Boethius.

'Apparently we've had twice the official time,' Boethius related to his visitor. 'Sometimes I think my jailers dislike prisons even more than I!'

They embraced, and again Tullus was aware of his mentor's frailty. Boethius had never had a soldier's figure, but now the Senator was grey and old before his time – worn out by overwork, and now this fate.

'I will return, sir,' Tullus said firmly.

'Love to my wife and honour to the noble Symmachus.'

The door closed.

Tullus felt completely impotent. A tiny piece in some large game he did not understand and could not alter. Once outside, he briefly thought of visiting the monks who were befriending Boethius, but the impulse was dismissed. The arrangements were working well and it was best to leave them undisturbed.

OOO

# CHAPTER SIXTY ONE

# BEYOND BELIEF

It was unnecessary, Cassiodorus had written, for Tullus to deliver his report in person, and, knowing Cassiodorus, Tullus took this as an order, so he sent it to Ravenna with two of Thulwin's men.

His message was not critical. Judging this to be counter-productive, he confined himself to a factual survey of conditions. He did make one suggestion, though: that the ex-Consul be moved to more spacious quarters – not an insignificant request, and one he hoped would not provoke reaction.

Thulwin's guards returned with a brief acknowledgement. His suggestion had been noted, Cassiodorus wrote, and the request for a further visit would be considered. Weeks passed before Tullus learned he was to visit the prisoner in April and report a second time.

April came and once more Tullus went to Ticinum, where he found the Senator's conditions much improved. No doubt the Master of Offices had been working hard behind the scenes. Tullus was greatly heartened. He was also pleased to learn that Boethius's writings had been handed to the monks. They, now, were the guardians of his *Consolation*.

In late July permission was given for a third visit, when he found the Senator in good health, but the banishment from Rome, his wife and the company of like minds was bitter. Yet the signs were hopeful. Indeed, Tullus had convinced himself that some mitigation of the Senator's sentence was probable.

As before, he reported his findings to Cassiodorus and sought approval for a further visit. The reply from Ravenna was, as usual, delayed. Tullus thought nothing of this, and when the messengers eventually arrived he opened the official roll with routine ease.

Shock drained the colour from his face.

'Is there a reply, Count?' asked a Royal guard in halting Latin.

'What?'

'A reply, sir.'

'No reply.'

Boethius was dead – executed by Royal command. It was madness beyond belief.

Tullus stood rooted to the spot while questions came at him like arrows. What had happened? Was it Byzantium's arrogance? Where was Thulwin? Was the King insane – a tool in the hands of Cyprian and Cunigast?

If the Goths could execute Boethius anything could happen. His thoughts ran on. Who would be next? Cassiodorus? How secure was the careful Master of Offices? The world was dark and dangerous. He must warn Cornelia, Atticus and Valerius. They had returned to their estates in the spring, hopeful that the dangers were receding, but the sooner they were back again behind the fortress villa's walls the better. God help Rusticiana, he thought wearily.

One of the messengers cleared his throat loudly.

'Count, we were ordered to proceed to Florentia.'

Tullus quickly came to himself. He knew the men before him, for he had seen them often at the Palace.

'Guardsmen, no matter how terrible your tidings, you cannot leave without refreshment – come!'

OOO

After the messengers left, Tullus went to his wife's rooms. He dreaded telling her the awful news, but when he did she responded stoically. To her the Senator's imprisonment had been the major shock and since then she had prepared herself for the worst.

'Marcus, I kept it from you,' she said. 'I never shared your sense of hope.'

That night Tullus slept little.

Until now he had been circumspect in the use of Thulwin's guards, but when the morning came he threw such caution to the winds. Messages had to be sent to Atticus in Umbria, Valerius west of Florentia and Symmachus in Rome, offering to all the Villa Tullus as a refuge, though he doubted that Symmachus or his daughter would leave Rome. If anything they would show defiance in the face of such an outrage.

Rufus was entrusted with the calls at Umbria and Rome. He had two guards, while another trusted servant, with one guard, was sent to the villa of Valerius, but he returned within the day, his mission unfulfilled. The Senator had gone to Rome. Tullus cursed inwardly, for he had no alternative other than to send his valued servant to Fidenae.

After five days Cornelia and Atticus arrived, and four days later Rufus returned from Rome. The Lady Rusticiana was grateful, the Senator Symmachus had told him, but both he and his daughter intended to remain in the city.

Another four days elapsed before the servant and his guard returned from Fidenae, but still without Valerius. The Senator and his lady had gone south to Beneventum a day or so before to visit friends. The agent at Fidenae promised to send a messenger. It was less than satisfactory, but Tullus held his peace. The servant had done his best and so would the agent. It was a pity Rufus had not called at Fidenae, but then, there was no need to.

In mid-November two monks arrived from Ticinum. They had walked all the way, carrying the manuscript of Boethius's *Consolation*.

'It was his will that you receive this, sir.'

Tullus afforded them every honour, and during their stay the aged Philippus, the one-time slave bought in the marketplace at Faesulae, began to copy the last writings of Boethius.

From the monks Tullus learned about the Senator's barbaric death. Soldiers had arrived from Ravenna with the order of execution. Brutally they seized their victim. To them the Senator's rank and dignity meant nothing. First he was tortured, then, mercifully, the club fell. His jailers, who had grown to like him, said he gave no cry of pain. The monks had many reminiscences – his jokes, his casual asides – but what impressed them most was the great man's equanimity. It was nothing less than saintly, they maintained. His death had been a glorious martyrdom.

Tullus kept the villa in a state of constant vigilance and had scouts as well posted on the roads. He fully expected trouble, for he sensed that Cunigast and his allies now controlled the Gothic Council. Indeed, this was confirmed in a brief note from Theodis, delivered by the hand of an old, grey-haired priest on his way to Florentia.

December came and still there was no word from Valerius. Tullus was concerned, more so than his wife, for Drusilla judged the lack of news against her father's known vagueness. But as Christmas approached she, too, began to worry. Word came, however, just as Tullus was planning to send another messenger. Valerius had taken ill at Beneventum and would be resting there until the new year.

OOO

Christmas at Faesulae was overshadowed by the tragedy of Boethius, concern for Valerius and the overall uncertainty. Tullus felt himself isolated and vulnerable. The bulletins from Ravenna had stopped and Theodis, always a source of news, was confined to palace duty. Again, Symmachus would not commit himself in writing. Only the Church remained. But their clergy saw their own affairs as news, and Tullus felt that fact was often mere opinion. Yet the all-pervading Church was an efficient medium of communication.

Through this mediumTullus learned how Symmachus had denounced a silent Senate for their sycophantic part in the condemnation of his son-in-law. Tullus winced when he heard the news, for he feared the noble Senator had rashly compromised himself. Nevertheless, he understood Symmachus's frustration. Silence had become unbearable.

OOO

# CHAPTER SIXTY TWO

# THEODIS

The Palace guard had been doubled – even trebled at times – since Boethius's arrest, and after his execution concern for security had become obsessive. Theodis rarely saw the King, but others said that he was fearful, narrow and suspicious. The Royal guardsman could scarce believe his lord had sunk so low. Indeed, he blamed the Palace officials: they were the authors of this madness, Triguilla in particular.

Theodis did not blame Cassiodorus, but saw him as a man ever ready to obey the fickle Palace will. The gaunt Master of Offices was always in a hurry and always wore a troubled aspect, but he rarely passed Theodis by without some hint of recognition. Theodis, though, remained disdainful. To him, Cassiodorus was a usurper. The rightful Master of Offices was dead. Theodis's mistrust was further fed by the growing alliance visible between Cassiodorus and Cyprian, the very man who had destroyed Boethius.

Palace politics were ever moving and one obvious change was the cooling in relations between Cyprian and Cunigast. The hearty greetings in the hall, the loud laughter, all had stopped, and it was also clear that Cyprian had distanced himself from Triguilla. Theodis did not understand the shifting sand of Palace politics, but guardroom gossip said that Cyprian had quarrelled with the reckless Goths. They had gone too far and Cyprian had been furious.

The meaning of this became tragically plain in mid-February when Symmachus, father of the Senate, was paraded through Ravenna as a traitor. Politically it was an act of gross stupidity, for nothing was more certain to alienate the Roman people. The populace looked on, sullen and resentful, as Symmachus, the father of the ancient Senate, upright and grey-haired, a very Cato, was arraigned before them. Only the powerful presence of the army held rioting at bay.

Theodis saw it all. He was ashamed for his race, yet most of his fellow guardsmen did not seem to care. It was assumed that Symmachus deserved his fate: after all, he was the father-in-law of a traitor. There were some who, struck by the nobility of the prisoner, were doubtful and uneasy. Even so, Theodis felt isolated for, excepting the Twins, there was no one he could talk to. Whom, in authority, could he trust? Thulwin was in Gaul and Ibbas in Hispania. Indeed, both men had been absent from Ravenna for some months. Many believed that they had left in sheer disgust, while others, the majority, felt they had been simply outmanoeuvred and sent away where they could cause no trouble to the ruling party. There was another view, however, and one for which Theodis had some sympathy. It was said that neither man, especially Thulwin, could bear to watch their failing King.

The day the news broke that Symmachus had been executed, Theodis received the Royal command to proceed to Florentia and arrest the Senator Valerius. For this detail he was given five men, including the Twins. That night, Theodis did not sleep at all. In the morning he protested to his commander, but the Royal writ could not be broken. He was told that Valerius was travelling north to his villa and would be there within the next few days.

In a daze he set about his preparations and at midday he left, leading his troop on the old familiar road towards the Arnus valley. He rode hunched and silent, his mind in hopeless turmoil. There was no rest. He could not do this thing. It was abhorrent, yet he could not break his oath.

Step by step his horse moved on.

'God help me!' he shouted inwardly.

The Twins rode on either side of him. He knew that they would follow his example and their furtive glances were impatient for a lead. But what could he do? He had his orders, and to disobey a Royal command was tantamount to treason. Yet thoughts of disobedience and desertion persisted, even though he knew them to be fantasy, for such a licence was against his nature and his training.

There was no sense of fantasy when his mind turned to the Villa Tullus. How could he ever visit there again? It would break poor Anna's heart, but rivalling his concern for her was the imminent plight of Poppea. Sweet, gentle Poppea, devoted to her lord – the tragedy would kill her.

'God help me!' his lips repeated noiselessly. Then, in a sudden involuntary movement, he straightened up. Powerfully and undeniably the freeing balm of trust brought rest. All would be well, it said, and for a moment he was free. He sensed the air crisp and clear about him, and breathed deeply. It was a sign, he thought reverently. The Lord had given him a sign.

Behind, he heard the laughter of the three soldiers. They were not guardsmen, but who were they? Until that moment he had been too distressed either to know or care.

'Who are they?' he asked one of the Twins.

'They're the Palace Prefect's men.'

'Triguilla's men!' Theodis exploded. 'We are Triguilla's joke and that, by God, I'll not endure!'

He stopped and swung his horse round suddenly.

'Are you the Palace Prefect's men?'

The tallest of the three nodded.

'What did the Prefect tell you?'

'That's our business,' the same man returned.

'Is it?' Theodis snapped, purposefully gripping his sword.

The tall man grinned. He had the same drink-bloated face as Triguilla.

'We're here to see the guardsmen do their duty – *Captain*!' the mockery was blatant.

White with anger, Theodis nudged his horse forward. Distress and lack of sleep had driven him to the brink. Slowly and deliberately he drew his sword and pushed its point towards the smirking face. Closer and closer the sword-point edged. It quivered a little as his arm extended but it kept moving, forcing the soldier backwards on his horse. The mocking smile had gone.

'Get to the front where I can see you – all three of you,' he ordered. 'Move!'

Triguilla's men instantly obeyed. They were no match for the guardsmen and they knew it.

Theodis's anger soon subsided, leaving in its wake a sickening tiredness. His thoughts were bitter. He was the tool of the Prefect Triguilla's perversion. Such was the Royal command and such was his reward for all his years of loyal service. Yet he kept on riding, step by step and mile, by mile, towards his destination. He felt trapped, helpless, like a netted beast.

'Trust, Theodis, trust,' he whispered fiercely.

They stopped at the old inn that Theodis often used. To him the place was full of memories, most of which were centred on Anna. Indeed, her image seemed to float before his eyes. There was a hint of grey now in her long dark hair. Her oval face had grown more mature and sensitive. That had improved her. Otherwise she had changed little. Her eyes were a mystery, though. Sometimes they were good and sometimes poor. For a time they had improved but that trend petered out, leaving her a narrow field of vision.

Wine, weariness and the heat from an open fire were enough to bring much-needed sleep. Theodis lay against the high-backed chair. The taller of the Twins was stretched out on a hard, unpadded couch. The other Twin had found a heavy rug and was curled up on the floor.

About midnight all three were awakened by the sound of drunken shouting from next door. Triguilla's men were threatening the landlord.

Stiffly, and with undisguised annoyance, Theodis and the Twins stood up, opened the connecting door, then without a word began to strip the soldiers of their swords and daggers. They protested violently, but were too drunk to stand against the powerful guardsmen who dragged them outside to an unused stable.

Theodis was furious. They, the drunken swine, would sleep, but he had little hope of that.

Morning came at last, cold and wet and grey. With dread Theodis watched the light begin to grow. He stood up noiselessly, for the Twins were still asleep. Then with slow, stiff steps, he walked outside, unbolted the stable door and viewed the dark interior. The soldiers were still asleep and one was snoring heavily. He pushed the nearest one with his foot until he grunted into wakefulness. Then, spinning on his heel, he strode back to the inn where the landlord had a bowl of goat's milk waiting. It was still warm from the milking.

Theodis prepared for the day's journey in a daze. Yet beneath the glazed exterior he was explosive. Sensing this, Triguilla's men obeyed his every word, for after the night's hard drinking they had no wish to provoke him.

Theodis saw himself delaying his departure. It was a game of self-deception and he knew it. The time had come.

Except for giving the order to proceed, he remained tight-lipped. The Twins tried vainly to elicit a response but he was locked within himself, his look no different from the day before, except that he rode bolt upright.

At the turning for Faesulae his horse strained stubbornly to travel the familiar road. Absently Theodis pulled the left rein hard, directing the animal towards Florentia. All too soon, it seemed, his troop passed through the town. Still he had no plan, no clear direction. His mind was numb, drained by the nightmare of his situation, but his biting stomach pain betrayed his tension.

Keeping the river Arnus to their right they headed down the wide flood-plain towards the hills. Then with fateful inevitability the villa of Valerius became discernible.

When they arrived at the flat, gravelled area, Theodis sat for some moments without moving. The Twins looked across at him and he looked at them. Still no words were spoken. Slowly he dismounted. His heart was pounding. Even now he had no plan, no thought of what to do.

'Theodis!' one of the Twins shouted suddenly. 'Triguilla's men are heading for the villa!'

'What?'

Shocked into action, he raced up the steep path, past the statues of the Gracchi, his sword already drawn. At the top, before the portico, he was greeted by the screams of Poppea. One of the soldiers was dragging her from the villa.

'Let her go!' Theodis bellowed. The Twins were close behind.

'Yes, Roman-lover!' one of the soldiers sneered, their appointed leader; the one Theodis had clashed with the previous day.

'Let her go!' Theodis repeated, his voice shaking with rage.

At that the soldier smiled and drew his knife, holding it close to Poppea's throat. Cautiously his companions moved away.

'You're here to arrest Valerius,' the soldier taunted. 'Ask her where he is. You know the Latin, Roman-lover!' His smile exuded mockery. Maddened, Theodis moved closer, his sword-point poised.

'Touch me, guardsman, and you'll be branded traitor. All they need is an excuse!'

'Traitor!' Theodis exploded. 'Who are you to call me traitor? Let her go and draw your sword.'

Triguilla's man grew nervous. The smile had gone. Menacingly he moved the knife-blade closer to Poppea's throat. Theodis stared.

'If you so much as graze her skin, you die!' His words that came had chilling force.

Slowly the soldier edged backwards, dragging Poppea with him. Theodis followed, cat-like. Behind, the other two were held at sword-point by the Twins.

Suddenly Theodis's quarry stumbled and, out of balance, he let Poppea go, but the knife had grazed her neck and blood trickled from the wound. For a moment she stood frozen to the spot.

'Go into the villa, my lady,' Theodis said quietly, his gaze fixed on the sprawling soldier.

'Go for your sword!' he bellowed.

The man began to protest, fear and cunning competing on his face. Then his hands moved deftly. A knife flashed through the air. Theodis jerked aside. The knife just missed him, but found its home in the smallest of Triguilla's men, who at once collapsed.

'Your sword!' Theodis shouted.

For a moment the man cowered like a frightened animal, but he knew he had to fight. So with a sudden agile movement he leapt backwards. Theodis sprang after him and in a powerful swing the guardsman's heavy blade descended. Triguilla's man did his best to parry but it made no difference. The power and weight smashed on. Instinctively he turned his head away. It was too late. A deep red furrow opened in his cheek, carried down his neck and ended in his shoulder. He fell to the ground, screaming with fear. The pain had not yet registered.

In a frenzied panic he scurried backwards on all fours, his sword abandoned. Theodis picked it up and threw it at him. His panic increased. At last, breathless and sobbing, he reached the bottom of the rise where his horse was tethered. Desperately he untied the reins, all the while blood streaming from his face and neck. Then with the energy of fear he leapt on the horse's back and galloped off.

From halfway up the slope Theodis watched him go with plain disgust. He quickly turned towards the villa to see the Twins still holding the remaining soldier. The other man was dead.

'Strip him of his weapons,' Theodis rasped, 'and make him load his late friend on his horse. Then let him go.'

Nervously the remaining soldier unbuckled his sword-belt, his hands shaking visibly, as Theodis disappeared into the villa.

'Senator! My lady!' he called.

There was no reply. He called again. It was strange, he thought. Why had the Senator not appeared? All the commotion must have aroused him. Surely his hearing was not as poor as that.

The answer was on Poppea's face as she emerged from the library, tears streaming down her face.

'My lord is dead,' she said absently.

'Was it the soldiers? By God, I'll ...'

'No! Theodis, no! He's in the library, sitting in his chair as if asleep.' She looked up at Theodis in despair. 'Oh, Theodis, what am I to do?'

The tall, powerful guardsman was moved by her distress. Gently he put his arm around her shoulder.

'My lady,' he murmured, 'may I see the Senator?'

She nodded, much too overcome for speech. Slowly they walked into the library and there the body of Valerius was sitting, uncannily natural, behind his desk. Before him lay an open manuscript. Plato's *Parmenides*, Theodis noticed.

Theodis put his hand on Valerius's forehead. It was growing cold. Then he lifted one of the lifeless arms. It was not yet stiff.

'He must have died just before we came,' he said, almost inaudibly.

Slowly and deliberately Theodis got down on his knees and in a childlike, imitative way, Poppea copied him. The Goth bowed his head. In very truth the Lord had given him a sign.

ooo

To Rufus, high in the turret of the Villa Tullus, the wide dome of the stars seemed close and intimate. The night air was crisp, not cold, and the waning moon had yet to rise. In the distance he could see the dark bulk of Faesulae against the starlit sky. He peered into the black emptiness about the villa but there was no sign of movement. He yawned. The night watch was a tedious business. Then, down in the valley, in the direction of Faesulae, he saw two points of light. At first they seemed stationary, but he soon detected a slow progress in his direction. Suddenly one of the lights was moving faster – at the pace of a horseman, he judged. Purposefully he pulled the cord beside him and heard the warning bell respond below.

It was Tullus himself who climbed the turret steps. Rufus was not surprised, for ever since the death of Boethius the Count had been zealous in matters of defence. Rufus pointed to the approaching lights, explaining how they had separated.

'One looks a herald of the other – but who, Rufus?' Tullus was puzzled. He thought of Valerius and Thulwin, but they had no reason to travel at night – or had they? There was Theodis, of course, but he would travel from Ravenna, not Florentia. The slow-paced one was that of an oxen-cart. Then all at once the closer light disappeared behind the ridge.

'When an enemy strikes at night, surprise and stealth are his greatest allies,' Tullus reasoned.

'Yes, sir. A herald with a torch is neither owl nor cat.'

Nothing was added as the two men waited for the rider to appear above the ridge. And there he was, carrying his torch slightly behind him. All Tullus and his agent could see was a silhouette.

'My God ...' Tullus began, 'I think – it is – it's Theodis. There's something wrong, Rufus!'

He looked quickly round the walls below the square turret. Thulwin's guards were already in position. Then he descended the spiral steps.

Tullus waited for Theodis just outside the courtyard door. He stood quietly, stilling the speculation in his mind, a discipline Boethius had taught him.

Theodis jumped from his horse immediately he saw the Count, and without preliminary greeting told his story.

'Boethius, Symmachus gone, and Valerius marked to be a victim too! What has happened to the King when such a madness rules?'

'Corruption rules, sir, not the King,' Theodis answered fiercely. 'Count,' he added, 'I must go back to the carts. We need two horses and some ropes. The cart with the body of the Senator may make the hill, but I doubt the one with the household valuables and the statues will.'

'Statues!'

'Yes, sir, the Gracchi. The Lady Poppea pleaded with me to bring them and I didn't have the heart to refuse.'

'You avoided Florentia, I suspect.'

'Yes, Count, I crossed by the raft ferry downstream from the Senator's villa.'

'That's a long and weary way.'

'I had no alternative. The wounded soldier might have reached Florentia and spread his lies about the garrison. And there's the other one with his dead companion. Why, even now they may be after me – they'll come here!'

'Let them!' Tullus growled.

'I must go, sir ...'

'Right. I'll send three of Thulwin's guards to follow you.'

'Thulwin's men?'

'Yes. The Count left six of his best men. Part of your doing, I believe.'

The guardsman did not respond but leaped onto his horse and was gone.

Tullus watched him go before returning inside. There was no energy in his step. His friend and father-in-law was dead. He found Rufus waiting in the middle of the courtyard and gave him his instructions. Then he walked slowly to his wife's rooms.

Drusilla was studying a manuscript when he entered.

'Is there something wrong, Marcus?' she asked. His face told all.

'Yes, my dear. Come and put your arms around me.'

She rose and came to him and for a moment they held each other closely. Gently his hand drew her head against his chest.

'It's Father,' she said suddenly, jerking her head back.

'Yes, Drusilla, it's your noble and learned father,' he responded quietly. Then he told her what had happened and her tears ran freely.

'He had a blessed end,' she said eventually.

'Thank God he cheated Triguilla and his brutish allies,' Tullus said evenly. 'Alas, his friend, the noble Symmachus, did not have that fortune.'

'Symmachus!' Stunned, she drew back.

'Yes, Drusilla – executed. The act of a suspicious tyrant – what insanity has possessed the King?'

'Poor Rusticiana – what will she do?'

'Theodis said the Pope had given her protection.'

'And Poppea – what will she do? She'll break her heart!'

'She'll need something to focus her devotion – otherwise she'll not last long.'

ooo

334

The two heavy carts arrived well into the night hours, both drawn by pairs of oxen, and both driven by the Senator's servants. The horses that had helped to pull the second cart stood listless, their ropes loose. Instinctively Thulwin's men formed a protective semi-circle.

Tullus stepped forward and helped Poppea and her personal attendant to alight. In doing so he glimpsed the prostrate body of Valerius, lifeless, but dignified in repose. It was a shock.

Drusilla was at her husband's side and immediately embraced the small, forlorn figure of Poppea. Then, with her arm still firmly around her, she walked towards Theodis as the guardsman was dismounting.

'Thank you, Theodis, you have been magnificent,' she said quietly. Her concern for Poppea had calmed her.

'My lady.' Theodis bowed.

For a moment her face lit with a smile. Then slowly she turned and, still holding Poppea tightly, walked through the courtyard gates and into the villa.

Theodis felt himself dismissed. His job was done, and leaving the confusion of men, horses and oxen, he made at once for Anna's quarters.

Quietly he trod the corridor to her room. He wanted to surprise her. As he drew close he could hear her talking to Valeria.

'You should be in bed, young lady.'

'No, nurse – Papa said I was to keep you company until the Captain came. You like the Captain?'

'Yes.'

'And the Captain likes you.'

'I think so.'

'You should get married,' the little girl said lightly.

Anna laughed.

'Where do you get such ideas?'

'Papa and Mama like each other, and they're married.'

'That is so, my dear, but a lady must wait until she's asked,' Anna said softly.

'Your waiting has ended,' Theodis boomed from the door.

The little girl looked up at Theodis as he stroked her hair. Then, with instinctive discretion, she skipped off down the corridor.

'Theodis, you're back,' Anna said, to cover her embarrassment.

'Anna, your waiting has ended,' he repeated, and without hesitation he lifted her from her couch and embraced her tightly.

'Theodis, oh Theodis,' she whispered. All reserve had gone.

'We're going to be married,' he said fiercely. 'I don't care what dogma you believe!'

'Your oath, Theodis?'

'What oath have I?' he countered. Bitterly he described the happenings of the last two days.

'No matter what, you still are bound by oath.'

'We'll work something out, Anna.'

'Let it be soon, Theodis – please God, let it be soon.'

They sat down on the couch together, his arm around her.

'Peace, peace at last,' he murmured.

'Where would we live, Theodis?' she asked softly.

'I don't know – somewhere near the Count.' He was almost inaudible.

'I should like that,' she said, but there was no response. He was asleep. Poor Theodis, he had had little or no rest for the past two days. Disentangling herself, she lifted his long legs onto the couch. Lovingly she adjusted the cushions and tucked a blanket round his prostrate form. Then she stood back and looked at him. Her sight was good tonight. Suddenly she remembered Poppea and the Countess and a wave of guilt came over her. Her happiness seemed indecent. But that was silly thinking – so the Count would say.

Carefully she made her way down the dimly-lit corridor. She felt compelled to pay her respects. Poor Poppea, the Senator had been her life.

OOO

# CHAPTER SIXTY THREE

# THE GHOST OF SYMMACHUS

They buried Valerius close to the rock outcrop above the villa where Tullus and Drusilla often sat on summer evenings. Poppea lived through the days, listless and absent-minded. In her own room she would weep when memory overwhelmed her, yet in company she barely showed emotion. Her grief was private. Much too private, Tullus thought, and she was growing thin.

One evening after supper Tullus expressed concern for Rusticiana. He addressed his words to Drusilla, but the real target was Poppea. His intent succeeded for, days later, she voiced the wish to join her former mistress. At last she had new purpose to her life.

Tullus knew an escort would be needed for Poppea's journey. He was reluctant, though, to spare the men. Yet if she was to go to Rome he had no option. It was awkward. Indeed, his impulse to awaken Poppea to the awful suffering of Rusticiana had been without prior calculation, but now that Poppea had responded he could not bring himself to thwart her fragile will.

Tullus was troubled, for no matter how he moved he faced real danger. Ultimately he could not stand against the Gothic nation. The fortress villa might delay but that was all. There was Thulwin, of course. Indeed without the Count he would be naked to the Gothic rage; but where was Thulwin?! Again, he had Theoderic's pledge, given before the second journey to Byzantium; but was the monarch in a fit state to remember?

The Goths would come, he had little doubt of that. They would be sent to bring in the 'deserters', Theodis and the Twins. It was predictable.

Theodis had offered to leave so as not to implicate the villa, but Tullus told him not to be an idiot. Orders would be out for his arrest , and to get to Pisae would be lucky, never mind the present camp of Thulwin. In any case the current Gothic council did not need excuses to attack the Villa Tullus. Their whim would be enough.

Tullus needed all the men he had, yet Poppea's emaciated looks were pressing; so, too, was his real concern for Atticus and Cornelia. They had returned to Umbria after wintering at Faesulae and they were vulnerable. The connection with Albinus and indeed the Villa Tullus, now harbouring 'deserters', could prompt vindictive action. Yet the fortress villa, being under threat, was no place for his son-in-law and daughter.

Eventually Poppea left with three of Thulwin's men and with Rufus as her guardian: the perfect choice, for he was a caring and compassionate man by nature. In her old age Julia had been fortunate.

Rufus was to convey the sympathy of the Tullus household to the widow of Boethius and explain the situation at the fortress villa. Hospitality was best suspended for a time.

On his journey back he was to call on Atticus in Umbria and, as with Rusticiana, tell him that the Villa Tullus was attracting trouble. Two of Thulwin's men were to remain in Umbria as guards. It was better than nothing, Tullus said tersely to his agent.

'And tell my son-in law to keep a lookout on the access roads, and in case of trouble use Thulwin's name. Emphasise that, Rufus, for the Count has pledged himself to their protection.'

On returning to Faesulae with the remaining guard, Rufus was instructed to be circumspect. If the villa was surrounded and in a state of siege, he was to turn away and seek out Thulwin: a dangerous mission, yes, but vital.

Tullus had already sent a messenger to Genua with this purpose – a Gothic friend of his from Faesulae. In fact, Tullus was desperate for the Count's return. Only Thulwin, Tullus felt, could stand against the Gothic council and only he could clear the names of Theodis and the Twins.

Tullus had managed to persuade the Florentia garrison commander to suspend charges against the Royal guardsmen pending Thulwin's return. But the Florentia officer was a known moderate. Ravenna, though, was quite another matter; but even there he had an ally, Cassiodorus. Only heaven knew his plans.

The threat from Ravenna first showed itself a few days after Rufus had returned from Umbria, when six soldiers drew their horses to a halt before the courtyard door. Their leader was elaborate in his deference to the Count and Tullus was immediately suspicious, a mood confirmed as he read the message handed to him. The Royal guards were commanded to present themselves in order that their names be cleared. The roll carried the Royal signature, but who had held the golden stencil for the King?

When informed, Theodis was prepared to comply. It would take the pressure off the fortress villa. But Tullus rounded on him.

'Stop thinking with your heart,' he snapped. 'I'll tell them that you'll present yourself when escorted by Count Thulwin.'

The leader of the troop accepted the reply without the slightest protest. Very civilised, Tullus thought cynically, as the horsemen rode away.

'They'll be back,' he said to Rufus, who was standing by his side.

His prediction was confirmed when the same officer returned with twenty men. This time his orders were aggressive. He was forbidden to return without the guardsmen, and the Count as well, he added.

Tullus's reply was similar to the first occasion. Neither he nor the guardsmen would leave the villa except escorted by Count Thulwin. The troop leader showed no aggression and, as previously, bowed politely before returning to his men. It had all been like a ritual well-rehearsed. Nevertheless, Tullus was worried, very worried, for the logical conclusion of a stand against the Palace did not bear inspection. Indeed, what could happen to his graceful wife made him shudder visibly. In truth, his stubbornness could only purchase time – time for Thulwin to return.

A day passed, and another, yet nothing happened. The soldiers lolled about the villa in the Easter sunshine, seemingly uninterested in the villa guards watching from the walls and turret. Some played dice and some appeared to sleep all day, while others groomed their horses constantly, or so it seemed.

On the third day a fight broke out amongst a group of soldiers, but the officer quickly intervened. A gambling row, Tullus guessed.

'What a waste of time,' he grumbled to Theodis as they stood together on the turret. 'look about us, the vines are begging for attention.'

Theodis smiled to himself. It was the Count's way of covering his concern.

'Yes, it's tiresome, sir,' he rejoined

'Tell me, Theodis,' Tullus said, pointing at the soldiery below. 'If you were their officer, what would you do?'

'I would ask for reinforcements and make the outcome of resistance obvious. What's more, I'd have a tree felled to fashion as a battering ram; again, I'd make this visible. With such a show of strength I'd hope to force an end, aided by some compromise that would protect the women.'

'Yes, Theodis. Did you have to be so honest?' Tullus growled. 'Well, at least they haven't felled a tree!'

'Yes, that's a puzzle, sir. They must be waiting for orders. It's the only explanation.'

'And those orders could arrive at any time. God above! Where is Thulwin?'

'We may have to wait some time …'

'You are a comforter today, my friend,' Tullus interjected. 'Well, I'm hopeful. I have to be! I'm gambling on one thing. I'm gambling that the death of Symmachus will have stung him. He admired Symmachus and liked his soldier-like nobility. He'll be outraged.'

'I hope you're right, sir – for the time may well be short.'

'How long could we hold out?' Tullus asked quietly.

'With these twenty,' Theodis said, pointing disdainfully, 'a long time. Double their number and add a siege ram – well, sir, not long.'

'Men can face their end with a certain resignation, but when they can't protect their womenfolk …' Tullus shook his head.

ooo

Since the death of Symmachus, Cassiodorus had become more bent and worried, yet the familiar figure with its familiar stoop excited few reactions. In fact, his unobtrusive ways proceeded, as it were, unseen.

Cyprian, however, saw through the public mask of the cautious official, but said nothing. Cassiodorus would always compromise and therefore posed no threat. In any case Cyprian and his pro-Gothic friends were supreme; and were there any rash enough to cross the man who had destroyed Boethius?

Cyprian's thoughts about Boethius remained dismissive: the great philosopher, the man who ever talked about the truth and never compromised. Where had it got him? One thing was clear: the court was a happier place without him.

Cyprian's power was rising and the thirst for power still drove him on, yet the clever Referendarius was not a man at peace.

He had two sons; 'eagles', Cassiodorus called them. Cyprian had a father's pride but it hurt to see their mother's breed in them.

Often he recalled the days before his own mother's violation. The days of Poppe, when his heart was fresh. She was free now, but it was too late. Poppe was with her old mistress Rusticiana, the widow of Boethius, the man he had destroyed. It was all too late.

Such were his thoughts as he made his way along the ill-lit corridor towards the rooms of Cassiodorus. He had received a summons, or rather a suggestion to pay a visit when it was convenient. It was typical Cassiodorus and, sensing urgency, Cyprian had responded instantly.

He was greeted in the usual confidential way. Elaborate thanks was heaped upon him for his prompt response, while all the time he waited. Cassiodorus, he thought, had the story-teller's art of building up suspense.

'News has just arrived,' the Master of Offices began. He paused, tried to straighten himself and breathed deeply. 'It's in your interest to know that the Counts Thulwin and Ibbas are converging on Ravenna.'

'With their armies?'

'We don't know – the detail is scanty.'

'That certainly explains the strange behaviour of Cunigast. Just now he rushed past me like a charging bull – full of panic, no doubt!'

'Well, my noble sir, if I may be so bold, you too could have some cause to be concerned.'

'Surely this is a Gothic matter – a power struggle within their council.'

'Well, sir, Thulwin opposed the arrest of Boethius ... not to mention his execution ...'

'Boethius was a fool,' Cyprian reacted. 'He met the end of fools.'

'You and I hold differing views on that.' The quiet voice of Cassiodorus contrasted sharply with Cyprian's indignant and self-justifying tone. 'But, sir,' the calm voice continued, 'we do see eye to eye when it comes to Symmachus.'

'Yes, that was stupid. The father of the Senate. It's built a wall between the Roman and the Goth.'

'Indeed, noble Referendarius, and your stated views may help you when the powerful Goths arrive, for Thulwin admired Symmachus. Now, there is another course of action that could put you in a favourable light.'

'What's that?' Cyprian asked sharply. He knew Cassiodorus's words were logical, but he resented them.

'The move against the Tullus household will enrage Count Thulwin, and as for sending the guardsman Theodis to arrest Valerius – well, sir, that will make things ten times worse!'

'Triguilla thought that that was funny. He roared with laughter at the thought of it. I opposed him, saying that Valerius was just a lackey, but it made no difference.'

'He may not laugh so loudly now.' The voice of Cassiodorus grew quieter. 'Noble Cyprian, if we were to send a message to the soldiers at Faesulae to halt their action pending further orders, shall we say. It would stop immediate trouble and would be looked upon with favour by Count Thulwin. Your name supporting such a move would be to your advantage.'

Cyprian nodded pensively.

Cassiodorus did not say, however, that he had already sent a message to the soldiers.

'There is one sovereign fact you have not mentioned,' Cyprian said in his quick way. 'The King – what if he recovers from his isolated state?'

'Well, sir, if I were Cunigast, I'd be worried.'

'The King will never touch him or Triguilla,' Cyprian returned. 'He knew their fathers and their fathers' fathers!'

341

'Perhaps you're right.' Cassiodorus nodded ponderously.

'I think the King's improving,' Cyprian said lightly, looking sideways at the tall official. 'He seems to have a better grasp of things.'

'Do you, sir?' Cassiodorus said innocently.

'The story goes that he's troubled by the ghost of Symmachus.'

'He may well be.' The reply was just audible.

OOO

The sky was overcast and the wet paved road was like a river. It was growing dark and the tall figure of Thulwin, accompanied by the broad, bull-necked Ibbas, looked phantom-like in the deepening gloom. Both generals had left their armies within two days' march of Ravenna and were proceeding with a modest bodyguard towards the city.

Ibbas would have marched his army to the gates, but Thulwin's view prevailed. The debate had been prolonged, but once a clear decision had been reached it bound both men.

Thulwin had agreed to seek an audience with the King, while Ibbas rested at his villa just outside the walls; from where he could respond to any call for help. But Thulwin did not fear the Gothic council; to him, the rats would flee the sinking ship.

It was almost dark when Thulwin and his bodyguard arrived at the Royal Palace. Dismounting, he proceeded with two of his most trusted men. The Royal guardsmen froze at his approach, for Thulwin was both famous and respected. There was no one to be seen except the guards, no one to act as herald of his coming but he sensed that hidden eyes were watching. At the threshold of the King's quarters he left his two-man escort and continued on his own until at last he stood before the Royal chamber.

With due ceremony he asked to be announced. The guard obeyed and at last the doors swung open.

Thulwin's gaze immediately fixed upon the King. He was on his feet and slowly descending from the dais, closely watched by an attendant. Some of the lesser members of the Gothic council were present but there was no sign of Cunigast or his allies.

'Thulwin, my friend, I've missed you.'

'And I you, my lord King.'

The two men embraced.

For Thulwin, the bitterness that had festered deep within his being melted. How could he be angry with the great King? He watched as Theoderic dismissed his attendants with the same familiar gesture of

impatience that he knew so well. The King seemed to be his old self, but he was bent and old in body. That was very plain.

Briefly the monarch and his general stood facing one another, the atmosphere uneasy.

'What happened, my lord? Why was the noble Symmachus executed?' Thulwin asked bluntly.

'Are you against me too?'

'Never, my lord, I speak with all respect.'

'Protect your own race, Thulwin – don't meddle with the treachery of Romans!'

'Symmachus was a very Cato, sir. He knew no treachery – you were ill-advised!'

'Are you telling me my judgement was at fault?' the King barked.

'You were ill-advised,' Thulwin repeated calmly, even though his heart was thumping hard. 'You were unwell, my lord, and men who have abused the human form whispered poison in your ear.'

'Can I not hear? Is the King deaf? Who says the King was ill?'

'I, my lord,' Thulwin said plainly. 'I saw your illness with these very eyes and heard the harshness in your voice issuing like a stranger from your lips. Men took advantage of your state.'

'Advantage!' Theoderic bellowed. 'It is you who take advantage. You, whom we treated as a son. You have ...'

Suddenly the King wavered on his feet.

'My lord!' Thulwin's hand shot out to steady him.

'The seat, Thulwin,' Theoderic muttered, pointing to the ornate chair beside the dais. He sat down heavily.

'Shall I call the physician?'

'No, Thulwin,' the King growled.

Thulwin sat down on the steps beside the dais. It was not right to stand too tall above his lord. The eyes of King and general met. Neither flinched. Then the King's gaze clouded.

'Last night my sleep was much disturbed,' he said wearily, looking at the floor. 'I saw the stern face of Symmachus with his eyes aflame. God, my God, what have I done?'

'Others did it, sir.'

'I gave the order, Thulwin, that I can't forget.'

Suddenly Theoderic grasped his general's arm.

'Pray, my friend, pray that God may give me rest from this!'

Thulwin could not think of anything to say. His heart was much too full. For a time both men sat in silence, then slowly Theoderic lifted his head.

'It's time to take some rest,' he said quietly. 'Come and see me tomorrow. Kings should have honest men about them.'

Thulwin helped the ageing monarch to his feet and they embraced again.

Thulwin's step was heavy as he walked away, his mind dulled by the tragedy of his lord. Because of this he did not see Cassiodorus at first; in fact, the Master of Offices was almost upon him before he recognised the familiar figure. What did the old fox want? he asked himself impatiently.

'Count, I am glad to see you,' the Master of Offices began in his usual confidential way.

Thulwin nodded warily.

'Our mutual friend Count Tullus is in trouble.'

'What is it? Tell me!' Thulwin said urgently.

In whispered tones Cassiodorus related the whole story of Tullus and the captain of his guard, including the conversation he had had with Cyprian.

'Now I know why Tullus holds you in respect,' Thulwin said plainly. 'You have done well, Master of Offices.'

'Will you act, sir?'

'Of course!' Thulwin reacted as if the question was an insult. 'I will leave for Faesulae tomorrow,' he added mildly. 'You have done well,' he repeated, before striding from the hall.

Outside, his bodyguard were waiting and, without speaking, he mounted. Then he headed for his villa. His men carried torches, giving the illusion of a misty, walled cocoon in the dark and dismal night.

Thulwin's mind was busy as he rode through the ill-lit streets. He would see the King in the morning and then report to Ibbas; following that he would set out for his son and his waiting army. Once arrived, he would dismiss the soldiers and send them to their families. A standing army was a costly creature. He would need thirty men, though, mounted men to confront the soldiers ringed around the Villa Tullus.

Thulwin felt it probable that the King was ignorant of the moves against Count Tullus. Possibly he knew about the summoning of the guards, but not about the twenty soldiers sent to force the issue, for the King had sworn not to harm his 'man from the north' and he never broke his word. It was, as Cassiodorus had suggested, the work of Cunigast and Triguilla. He should never have abandoned the Council to their mercy. Yet there was little, at the time, he could have done, for a year ago Theoderic's mind was closed to reason. Then Cunigast had been popular, with his grand, expensive promises yet to be revealed as false. Now it was different.

Ravenna was tired of him and his self-seeking friends. It was time to clip their wings. As for Triguilla, he thought disdainfully – to be chained in a bear-pit was the Palace Prefect's due.

The behaviour of Cyprian was strange. The ever-charming gloss covered an astute mind. But why had the enemy of Boethius spoken in defence of Symmachus? Thulwin was suspicious. He had never trusted Cyprian. The Referendarius was far too clever for his liking.

OOO

# CHAPTER SIXTY FOUR

# RELEIVED

The landlord of the ramshackle inn used by Theodis on that nightmare journey to Florentia was frightened when he saw the approaching soldiers. There were thirty at least, all mounted, and they could wreck the place, but riding with his fear was high excitement. There could be trade, good trade. It all depended on the officer, so when he saw Count Thulwin his heart leapt in anticipation.

'Pray God he stops,' he whispered as he stood, his squat form straining forward while he watched the mass of riders labouring up the hill.

'Wife!' he shouted, 'the Gothic Count is coming! – the friend of Tullus.'

His hopes, mountainous in proportion, soon shrank when Thulwin told him he was only stopping long enough to give the horses water. Yet there was time enough to serve the Count and his young companion with the inn's best wine.

'By our Christian God,' he burst out as he offered the young man a brimming cup. 'I didn't recognise you, my young sir – you're as tall as your father!' The landlord's genuine surprise cut through his play of servile deference, and Thulwin's smile reflected this.

'Landlord,' the Count said directly, 'did soldiers pass this way – say, seven days ago?'

'A troop of twenty, your honour.' The breathy mode of deference had resumed.

'What was their leader like?'

'He was all right, your honour, but his men were rough – broke the chairs and table, they did.'

'Were you paid for this?'

'No, your honour.' The landlord's hope for redress was barely disguised.

'Pay him,' Thulwin said abruptly to his son. Then he turned away to watch his men, now busy with their horses. The relationship between a soldier and his horse was strong. There were few exceptions. Indeed, Thulwin could recall tough men, hard men who could look upon the heaped result of slaughter with a frozen eye, yet when their horses died

346

they wept like children.

Thulwin's own horse was magnificent, but he had never chosen quite as well as Tullus. Claudius, for one, was almost human.

What had Tullus done with his animals? he wondered as his mind focused on the besieged villa. Marcus Tullus would have thought of something. In fact Thulwin was not overly concerned about the situation at Faesulae, knowing that the Royal guardsmen and his own six men were more than able to withstand attack. Nevertheless, he was not complacent, and even if he had been slow to move, his son would soon have goaded him into action.

Young Thulwin's anger had exploded when he heard about the move against the Villa Tullus. It was a seat of learning, he reacted. Thulwin liked his son's keen spirit, but he did not understand his way of thinking. He had always asked awkward questions and after meeting with Valerius he had become nonsensical. Yet Thulwin was not over-critical, for his son had proved himself with honour on the borders. No doubt the young man would soon grow out of his philosophy.

As soon as the horses were watered, Thulwin took to the road, with father and son leading the vanguard. They trotted sometimes when the ground was level; otherwise the pace was steady. They rarely spoke, except to estimate the time, but as they rounded the familiar hill that heralded the villa, young Thulwin broke his silence.

'We have done great wrongs, Father.'

'What do you mean, son?'

'Boethius and Symmachus – we have butchered the best.'

'Yes, my worthy son. The great King has soiled his reign. This, alas, he knows too late.'

'What happened?'

'God knows, my son. Only He knows all the truth.'

As the villa came in sight, shouting echoed round the hill. They had been recognised, not only by the villa guards, but also by the besieging soldiers who were frantically ordering their ranks in clear submission.

Thulwin sent his son to dismiss the soldiers and despatch them to Florentia, while he himself headed for the villa. As he approached, the heavy double doors swung slowly open, revealing the lone figure of Tullus striding towards him with the unmistakable, but stiffly-moving bulk of Claudius following behind. Obviously Tullus had kept him in the inner courtyard.

'Claudius is ever living.' A smile accompanied Thulwin's words.

'And Tullus is ever grateful. Thank God it was you who rounded the hill!'

'There's been no real danger for the past six days or so – thanks to the Master of Offices for, hearing that Ibbas and myself were on the way, he sent restraining orders to the besieging soldiers and persuaded Cyprian to add his signature.'

'Cyprian!' Tullus reacted.

'Yes, Cyprian – apparently he spoke for Symmachus ...'

'And Cassiodorus deftly used this to advantage.'

'Yes,' Thulwin added, 'he measures every move ...'

'To a featherweight,' Tullus added. 'But we are grateful to him, very grateful.'

Moving closer, Claudius nudged Thulwin gently with his nose.

'You're approved of!' Tullus smiled.

'What did you do with the other animals?'

'They're in the valley below. I dispersed them after the first "visitation".'

A pause heralded the dominant issue.

'Great wrongs have been done, Tullus,' Thulwin began, echoing his son's words.

'Terrible wrongs – what has happened to the King?'

'He wants to see you,' Thulwin returned, not answering the question.

A look of caution froze' on Tullus's face.

'It's all right – his black, unreasoning mood is past,' Thulwin continued quietly. 'But he's greatly disturbed. His remorse is bitter, especially in the case of Symmachus.'

'Strange how the death of Symmachus has cut deeper than that of Boethius.'

'Venerable age was violated.'

'There's more to it than that. Somehow it's been accepted, I mean the execution of Boethius, as if it were the call of fate.' Tullus bowed his head. 'When does the King want to see me?' he added.

'As soon as possible.'

'I see,' Tullus said pensively. 'And what of Theodis? Is he still in danger?'

'Not if I know it, by God!' Thulwin barked. 'It's the Palace Prefect's men who need to fear!'

For a moment the two friends stood without speaking while all about them sounds of men and horses filled the air. Claudius still stood close to Tullus; his fellow creatures had not lured him from his master's side.

'There's one question,' Tullus said, looking straight at Thulwin. 'Boethius was held for almost a year. Why was he suddenly killed?'

'Byzantium – harassment of the Arian population there. The King was enraged and Cunigast and his allies did the rest.'

'And Cyprian as well, no doubt – it's as I thought. He died the hostage of East-West politics. What a shameless waste!'

'Tullus,' Thulwin interjected, 'the Countess and your daughter are coming.'

Tullus turned to see Drusilla smile with the familiar light that he had never ceased to wonder at. Thulwin bowed, spoke of his outrage at the siege and then expressed his sorrow at her father's passing. Drusilla then responded with her usual grace and dignity.

Valeria was at her mother's side, gazing at the figure of the Gothic Count.

'Where is my friend?' she asked directly.

Thulwin bowed low.

'Young lady, your friend is here, but you'll not recognise him, he's …' Thulwin indicated his son's height roughly with his hand.

'Grandfather said he was tall inside.'

A surge of emotion almost overwhelmed Drusilla, but she managed to contain it.

'Your friend is close on seventeen, my dear,' the Count was saying.

'And I am nearly seven,' Valeria responded brightly.

The three adults smiled.

'Well, Count,' Tullus said firmly, 'I will tolerate no refusal, nor any hurried departure for Florentia – you're staying with us.'

'My son had hoped for such an invitation,' the Goth admitted.

Once Thulwin had agreed to stay, he dismissed most of his men; they could easily be recalled. Yet he still retained a hand-picked guard of twelve.

During the next few days the villa staff became accustomed to the presence of the Gothic Count. He was dignified, formal and more distant than his son, they judged, and his wants were modest. In the morning he would ride alone, but two of his men were never far away.

'I told them not to follow, but they're always hovering and watching. It's an insult to your hospitality, Tullus,' Thulwin grumbled.

Tullus shook his head.

'Be grateful, sir, for loyal men. Remember, Triguilla and Cunigast will be boiling with resentment and to strike here would accord with their perversity.'

'The rats are in the drains, Tullus,' Thulwin said disdainfully. 'Now, to change the subject; what do you think of the Royal daughter – mother of the future king?'

'Amalasuentha.' Tullus pronounced the name pensively. This was the herald of the dreadful question – what would happen after Theoderic?

'Well, Tullus?' Thulwin pressed.

'She tries to emulate the Roman ways and it pleases neither Goth nor Roman.'

'You're right,' Thulwin reacted with passion, 'and the Royal heir is too much in his mother's company. A future king should never learn a woman's habits.'

'He's just a boy, sir.'

'Even so, he needs strong company.'

'Yes, but not the company which, pretending manliness, would have him swilling wine before he's ten!'

Thulwin nodded. The danger was real enough, especially if the Royal youth were headstrong.

'The future is uncertain,' he said quietly.

'It always is,' Tullus was about to say, but he held his tongue.

Tullus's conversation with Thulwin centred mostly on politics, but with his son it was history and philosophy, and Boethius in particular. Tullus was tempted to show him the text of the *Consolation*, yet he refrained. It was not the time. Moreover, the *Consolation* had a political content and it would be clearly wrong to burden either Thulwin or his son with the knowledge of its presence. This reservation aside, Tullus answered the young man's questions with unflinching directness.

On the second morning following Thulwin's arrival, Tullus went out early to inspect his vines and olives. It was not long, though, before the young man sought him out.

'What did the philosopher Boethius hold most dear?'

'The truth,' Tullus returned from his crouched position amongst the vines.

Thulwin's son stood pensive for a moment before sitting down beside him.

'The Senator Valerius maintained the truth was single – one – but ,sir, people say that this is true, that that is true; they say that many things are true!'

'There are many facts, yet truth itself remains the same,' Tullus responded.

'People say that only their beliefs are true,' young Thulwin pressed.

'The roads to truth may differ but truth ...'

'Remains the same,' the young Goth interjected.

Thulwin's son fell silent and Tullus stretched himself full-length between the vines, his hands behind his head. The sun was warm, the air fresh and the young vines green and growing. It was a beautiful morning. In an instant memory flashed him back to Britain and how, in a similar way, he had been wont to lie extended on the southern slopes that looked across the sea to Gaul. He had been a young man then and in that youthful time the girl to whom he was betrothed had died. Then had come the years of anarchy – restless, troubled years. The marauders came mostly from the sea, and for some time the Tullus villa managed to escape. Thank God his parents had not lived to see it, for when the raiders struck they left a smouldering ruin.

'Sir,' young Thulwin started, interrupting his reverie. Tullus sat up abruptly. 'If the truth is always the same – oh, I can't – my mind is stretched beyond itself.'

Tullus laughed and Thulwin's son continued.

'If truth is always the same, then the truth about everything must be the same – what is that truth?'

'You never leave the eagle's eye!' Tullus exclaimed. 'Where did you learn to think like this?'

'Father's old scribe – and the Senator Valerius. But, sir, the answer – what is that truth?'

'In terms of number, one. That's the theory. Knowing it is quite another matter.'

'That's what the old scribe and the Senator said, but sir, how can it be? I mean, who am I, and who are you, if there's only one?'

Deliberately Tullus lifted two pieces of earth and held them up.

'I see, there's only one earth.'

Tullus stood up.

'Look at the scene before you, the vines, the trees in the distance, the olives, rows of young plants close to the villa – what strikes you?'

'It's all very alive, sir.'

'Yes, that's evident – what do you know about this life? What do you see in all these plants and trees – and animals?'

'It seems obvious, sir. There's one life, but ...'

'Our friend "but",' Tullus smiled, then his look turned serious. 'Boethius said, "Human perversity makes divisions of that which by nature is one and simple, and in attempting to obtain part of something which has no parts, succeeds in getting neither the part – which is nothing – nor the whole, which they are not interested in".' Tullus had quoted from the *Consolation*.

'I understand and I don't understand,' the young man responded with animation.

'Your father's coming,' Tullus said pointedly, looking in the direction of the Count's approaching figure.

The young man was disappointed that the conversation had to end, but he respected his father too much to let his feelings of frustration show.

OOO

Below in the open ground adjacent to the inner courtyard, Drusilla and Anna were walking arm-in-arm, with Valeria skipping beside them. Drusilla could see her husband on the higher ground in conversation with Count Thulwin and his son. Marcus was his old self again, she thought. Indeed, two good nights' rest had worked wonders, for the strain of the siege had been terrible.

Behind her she heard the sound of an approaching horse, and turning round she saw the rider stop. He had come from the direction of Faesulae and she assumed that it was yet another messenger for Thulwin.

'Where is Theodis this morning?' she asked Anna.

'He's in the valley, my lady – helping to bring the horses back.'

'He looks very relaxed – still determined to be married?' Drusilla smiled.

'Yes – he says he wants to see the Count's friend south of Rome.'

'Martin!'

'Yes.'

'I sense you have some doubts about this, Anna.'

'It's his oath, my lady. He says he has no oath, maintaining it was broken in Ravenna when they sent him to your father's villa.'

'I well appreciate his feelings,' Drusilla said quietly. 'Yet, like you, I can't see how he can escape his pledge. Don't worry, Anna, I'll talk to the Count.' But even as she spoke she knew her words were hollow, for while Theoderic lived Theodis was a prisoner of his guardsman's oath.

'The rider's message must have been for us,' Drusilla reacted as Rufus approached, the note of anxiety not disguised.

'It's from Umbria, my lady,' Rufus announced, handing her the roll.

Drusilla quickly read the contents.

'Cornelia is expecting,' she said without apparent emotion. 'Rufus, you'd better tell the messenger to wait.'

Anna was at once excited, but she could see her mistress was concerned.

'Is there anything wrong?' she asked hesitantly.

'Atticus is thinking of moving to Constantinople. He says Italy's no place to bring up children.'

'Cornelia would be lost to us. It would be like ...'

'Don't say it, Anna,' Drusilla interrupted. 'Anyway, there's nothing we can do. Cornelia must follow her husband, and in truth he may be right.'

Cornelia was not Drusilla's blood, but she was no less dear. In those early days when Marcus had been distant, Cornelia had received the fullness of her love, and a deep attachment had been forged.

Drusilla's heart was heavy, for after losing her father, the plans of Atticus heralded a second blow. Moreover, she knew that one day Valeria would marry and would also leave. Then, if God spared them, Marcus and herself would be alone, and then – God! she could not think of it. But such was the destined way of all things born. Dear Father, are we the shadow shapes of Plato's cave? The light, never the shades, you would have said.

When Drusilla managed to speak to her husband privately, he listened to the news about his daughter with reserve; the memory of her mother's death was close.

'She should be in your care, my dear,' he said eventually. 'That is, if Atticus agrees.'

'He will – but what about Constantinople, Marcus?'

'I don't like it – yet if I were Atticus I would make the same decision.'

'It's a pity,' she said sadly.

'Come, let's have a walk around the villa. Last week's mess is almost cleared,' he said quietly, alerted by the sound of his wife's voice. It was the note that parented depression.

He held her arm tightly as they walked from the inner courtyard past the open double doors. Turning right, they then proceeded slowly, stopping with each servant that they met. Drusilla's mood grew lighter, and Tullus thought of Cornelia. Please God, let the birth be trouble-free.

'Old Philippus has almost completed the second copy of the *Consolation*,' Drusilla said suddenly. 'What do you propose, Marcus?'

'We ought to deliver the original to Rusticiana. After that – well – there's Byzantium and, of course, the Church. We'll have to be careful, for as you know, names are mentioned in the text.'

'Marcus, look!' Drusilla exclaimed.

At once his gaze followed her pointing finger to where Valeria and young Thulwin stood before the grave of Valerius, his daughter's smallness looking comical beside the tall young Goth.

'It's beautiful, Marcus,' Drusilla said, clasping her husband's arm.

As if drawn, Tullus turned to see Count Thulwin also watching. Their eyes met, their thinking naked in the air. There was something strangely fateful in the scene that they had witnessed, and both could see the seeds of tragedy.

Without thought, and beyond mere reaction, Tullus smiled. At that moment Goth and Roman were as one.

OOO

# CHAPTER SIXTY FIVE

# LEAVE PAST DEEDS TO GOD

Early on the fourth morning after Thulwin's arrival, Tullus set out for Ravenna in the company of Count Thulwin and his son. They broke their journey at a country villa owned by one of Thulwin's friends. But a late start in the morning meant they only reached the Gothic capital at dusk.

Tullus was the honoured guest of Thulwin at his villa. He was treated as a Roman would expect in every detail, but if he hoped at last to meet Count Thulwin's wife, he was frustrated.

'Mother is, as usual, in Verona,' Thulwin's son explained. 'She doesn't like the bustle of Ravenna.'

In the morning Tullus set out to see the King, passing through the now familiar streets towards the palace. At last he reached the packed reception hall with all its air of chaos.

The Royal guards snapped to attention as he approached. He was well known and he was respected. Then, as Thulwin did, he stood before the double doors waiting for the summons.

The King was on his feet when Tullus entered. Their meeting was warm but Tullus was shocked. Theoderic had greatly aged.

'There's an old, quiet mare waiting in the courtyard for a tired king.' The monarch's voice was still strong. 'We'll go riding as we did in happier days.'

It was a beautiful morning and the park smelled fresh. The King rode slowly, remaining silent for some time. Tullus waited; it was not his place to speak before the King.

'I feel you think your King a friend,' Theoderic began. 'Am I right?'

'Yes, sir.'

'Why, Tullus? Why, when I've butchered your friends?'

'You were not yourself, my lord.'

'That's what Thulwin said, but I knew, Tullus, and at no time was that knowledge absent. I knew what I was doing.'

'But it was faint, and the pall of your sickness was heavy – and also, you were goaded by Byzantium.'

'You're generous, Tullus, but Theoderic can't be generous to himself. I've killed the men I honoured most!'

'There were those who ill advised you, sir.'

'Such men have always been about the court,' the King countered.

'You've ruled with honour all your life and now, because your illness dulled your sense...'

'Tullus,' the King barked, 'I killed two men – good men – at night they stare at me – my sleepless hours are many.'

'My lord, leave past deeds to God.'

'How can I, Tullus?! My stabbing thoughts are with me day and night, and when I dream! – God save me – and you ask me to forget!'

'No, my lord, to trust! Leave past deeds to God and trust!'

The King did not respond and Tullus held his peace. They rode on down a narrow passage flanked by trees and the Royal guards grew nervous, knowing an assassin's arrow could have easy cover, but when they reached the open ground again the guards relaxed.

'Tullus, what do you think of the Pope?' the King asked bluntly

'I've never met him, sir, but all reports maintain he leans towards the East and is much respected in Byzantium.'

'I'm thinking of sending him to Constantinople to demand – no, that would be stupid – to plead for tolerance, as mob violence against our Arian brothers still persists. How would your friend Justinian react to such a visit?'

'He would welcome it, and would use the Papal presence to demonstrate the unity of East and West. The Arian question would take second place. I doubt if you would like it, sir.'

'You're right, Tullus,' the King growled. 'I'd find it hard to bear. Would it work, though? That's the question. Would it help the Arian families?'

'Much would depend upon the Pope's intention,' Tullus responded.

'That's the trouble, Tullus. I don't trust him!'

The sound of the old lion was still there.

For a time they rode in silence.

'The problem is, Tullus, after the past year, who trusts me?' The King's voice had changed. The pain was unmistakable.

'Leave past deeds to God, sir.'

'Damn you, Tullus!' Theoderic growled, but his eyes were friendly. 'I like your horse,' he added firmly. 'What do you call him?'

'Titus, my lord.' Tullus did not like to say that the King had seen him twice before. 'He's getting old. The journey from Faesulae was almost too much for him. Anyhow, I'm training another at present.'

'What will you call him? I like your names.'

'Britannicus.'

'Ah, the man from the north has not forgotten his roots. What was the name of the other horse you used to have?'

'You must mean Claudius – he's still about the villa.'

'Claudius – yes, I remember you never used to tether him.'

'That's true. If the reins were left about his feet he wouldn't budge. But he's getting very stiff. Dear God, I hope I never have to put him down.'

'Are they all soft-hearted in Britain, Tullus?'

Horses were Theoderic's favourite subject and the Royal stables the source of many stories. The King's spirits improved as the morning progressed, yet no mention was made of events at Faesulae.

'You've been a tonic, Tullus,' the King said on parting. 'We'll meet again tomorrow, same time, eh?'

'Yes, sir,' Tullus acknowledged. Unflinchingly their eyes met.

'Leave past deeds to God,' Theoderic repeated gently. 'You see, I have remembered!'

Tullus felt great affection for the old Goth as he rode along the streets to Thulwin's villa. The King's black anger had destroyed both Boethius and Symmachus, yet he could not hold a grudge. It was strange, for the savage end of the two great senators still outraged him.

It was a tragedy worthy of the ancients. The scale was large, but had the tragedy a purpose? Was it the call of fate? Socrates had been condemned to swallow hemlock. Zeno had been drutally destroyed and, of course, Christ crucified. Even Cicero and Seneca had had their lives cut short. The words of truth were potent and those who uttered them became the hated enemy of ignorance. Yet the work of these great souls lived on and, for Boethius, there would be his writings, not least his *Consolation*.

From the very beginning, Tullus had viewed the prison writings of Boethius as a future force. They had the practical immediacy of a prisoner; and again, the manuscript was short, succinct and shining with the words of Plato.

Plato might be shunned by pious Christians in the future, not to mention now, but a Christian martyr would be read, and Boethius was a martyr. Indeed, this claim was on the lips of every Roman churchman. For these reasons Tullus was determined that the writings would be safely guarded. Philippus had made two copies and was busy with a third. They would need safe keeping, but whom could he trust? Boethius's scathing denouncement of his enemies and of rapacious Gothic greed would not make welcome reading in Ravenna.

Unexpectedly, a solution arose from his meeting with the King on the third day when, after a period of reminiscences, Theoderic broached the serious matters on his mind.

'Count,' Theoderic began gruffly, 'I want you to go to Hispania and to southern Italy. Let them know Theoderic's writ still runs – you have your contacts there.'

'Yes, my lord,' Tullus responded formally. It was the perfect way to pass on copies of the *Consolation*, though the prospect of the tiresome journeys was oppressive.

'The reports say that the prisoner Boethius was forever writing. Is that right?'

'Yes, sir,' Tullus said with shock.

'Are names mentioned, Count?'

'It's almost all philosophy, sir.'

'I know, but are names mentioned?' Theoderic pressed, his stare relentless.

'He denounced his enemies, sir.' Tullus heard his voice grow hard with tension.

'And the King?'

Tullus sat as if frozen. His mouth was dry and the King's eyes seemed like arrows.

'My lord, he was sparing with his words. He did say, though, that you were set against the Senate. If there's more, I can't remember,' he concluded, his voice strained and anxious. Confiscation was all too probable.

The King's stare relented and he bowed his head in thought. Slowly his gaze lifted.

'Part of me would have the writings burned, but the other part, the part that values friendship with the noble Thulwin and yourself, says otherwise. So let the writings of the great Anicius be.'

Tullus's relief was visible.

'That pleases you, Count.'

'Very much, my lord.'

'Good, but keep the writings secret till we've gone.'

'My lord, I hope that many years will pass before...'

Theoderic waved his arm impatiently.

'Be practical, Tullus!' he growled, but the sound was not unfriendly.

They rode for quite some time until, without warning, the King lurched to the side.

'My lord King!' Tullus reacted.

'Old age, Tullus, old age,' the monarch grumbled. 'It's time to return.' A dogged expression had replaced his look of ease. 'There was a Roman priest,' the King continued, 'who converted to the Arian church to further his ambition.' He paused and looked at Tullus. 'I had him clubbed, for his behaviour was an insult to our faith.'

Tullus was immediately apprehensive. What was the King trying to say? Was the harsh story a direct, unsubtle warning? Was the King's unsteadiness on his mare a herald of his illness?

'Our justice has been sudden,' Theoderic declared. 'last year, alas, it overspilled. A bitter year – a poisoned harvest, Tullus. But, Count, know this. Theoderic is a Goth; the noble Thulwin is a Goth. Our numbers are not Empire-large. I knew Triguilla's soldier father and Cunigast's as well. We are a swelling family united by our Ostrogothic roots and faith. To fight amongst ourselves would bring us ruin. The King is careful, therefore, when he passes judgement on his peers. Boethius knew, of course, that we were lenient on our own, and it outraged him.'

The King paused and glanced across at Tullus.

'Triguilla is a fool and yesterday I told him so. I should put him down the mines, but that would be a slur on his father's name. Never mind, he treads with caution nowadays, and well he should, for if, by God, your family or the guardsman had been harmed...' Theoderic did not need to finish. He breathed deeply, as if to gain energy.

'What an indignity,' he grumbled. 'Even talking tires me. Come tomorrow, Tullus – early. Then you can return to Faesulae.'

ooo

# CHAPTER SIXTY SIX

# THE SLAVE

Tullus felt exhausted as he made his way to Thulwin's villa. It had been an awkward morning, for the questions on the writings of Boethius had been unexpected and a shock.

There was an element of caprice about the Crown, and the man who took the King for granted was a fool. Indeed, the interview just past had been an object lesson on that very point. Yet Tullus still enjoyed Theoderic's favour.

He looked about him; he was tired of thinking. The streets were busy and the crowds pressed close. Shuffling towards him he could see a line of prisoners tied neck to neck, just as Valerius had been all those years ago. Were they criminals or victims of some border clash? Perhaps amongst their number was a man who, like Valerius, had been driven off his property by greed.

The line of drooping men drew closer, their abject state a vivid contrast to the well-fed man in charge: a slave-merchant, no doubt, making Tullus feel the prisoners were not common criminals – for who would want to buy a villain?

Suddenly he was back in time, crouching with the figure in the tree just north of Turones. Below was Clovis with his army, the threat of death or slavery well-near certain.

He had almost passed the prisoners when one of them glanced up. The look, though brief, was simple, clean, yet startling in its plain humanity.

'Stop!' Tullus's powerful voice loomed out above the bustle of the narrow street, and voices dropped to whispers.

'It's the Roman Count,' the whispers said, 'the man from the north.'

Tullus pointed.

'That man – how much?' he questioned in the Gothic tongue.

The merchant bowed and gave his figure.

'I have no desire to buy the street!' Tullus barked. His two-man guard moved closer. 'How much?'

He sat impassive while the merchant dropped his price by half; old Philippus had been bought on impulse. Eventually a deal was struck and the long end on the neck-rope handed up to him.

'Cut him free,' he ordered angrily. 'And his hands!'

'He'll run away, your honour,' the merchant protested.

'I'll risk that!' Tullus snapped.

He nudged his horse and it started slowly forward, the slave following, dazed and uncomprehending, while all about them sudden noise erupted like a dam released.

At Thulwin's villa Tullus left the slave with servants while he sought out Thulwin's son; the Count was at the palace.

Tullus and the young man ate together and the conversation never flagged. History was the subject, but Tullus had to cut their meeting short to keep a prior appointment with Cassiodorus.

The villa of Cassiodorus was close and Tullus covered the distance quickly. The Master of Offices had just returned after a few days at a nearby monastery. The first time he had felt able to vacate his post in eighteen months, he said to Tullus.

Tullus heaped praise on the tall public servant.

'I'm certain that your intervention saved lives at Faesulae.'

'God's work, Tullus – not mine,' Cassiodorus responded with slow deliberation.

Soon the subject of Boethius grew to dominate the conversation.

'Boethius had many enemies,' Cassiodorus said quietly. 'The ambitious, including Cyprian, were jealous of his ability; the greedy were envious of his wealth and furious at his attacks on their fraudulence. And his great learning provoked a ...'

'Sly resentment,' Tullus interjected. Those were his own words.

Cassiodorus nodded in his usual confidential way.

'I do believe the King himself was jealous, even fearful, of the Senator for, as you know, Boethius could be a powerful presence ...'

'He was imprisoned for a year, sir,' Tullus interrupted. 'What really happened?'

'Officially he was a hostage against the ill-treatment of the Arians in Constantinople. Unofficially – I'm not so sure.' Cassiodorus sighed. 'I strongly feel the King had doubts about the accusations levelled at Boethius. He held back, and even at the end he was reluctant, but the constant jibes of Cunigast and the poisoned words of Cyprian kept him fearful. The King was not himself. That was the matter of it. Who ever heard of Theoderic being fearful?'

'No one!' Tullus affirmed.

'It was the anti-Arian measures in Constantinople that eventually tipped the scales. The King became possessed; a black fury, I would call it, and it continued; by God, it did! Ravenna was a dangerous place, and how Cyprian survived I am at a loss to know, for he spoke for Symmachus.'

'Cyprian was ever complex,' Tullus mused aloud.

'You're right, my friend. He has a ready wit, but when I look at him I see a lonely man.'

Cassiodorus sighed.

'The cloister beckons, Tullus. I've established a community on the family estate at Squillace in the south – how I long to be there!'

'What's stopping you, sir?'

'Difficult times, Tullus, difficult times. God will tell me when to go.'

Tullus wanted to speak of the *Consolation* and to ask if he might leave a copy at Squillace, but he hesitated. Cassiodorus could keep a secret, there was little doubt of that. But his friend was Master of Offices and, as such, was in constant contact with the King. Theoderic could ask questions, and misunderstandings could arise. Caution was the better course. Moreover, he genuinely wanted to obey the King's desire for secrecy. So he held his peace.

The two men talked until the sun was low. Then Tullus took his leave and made his way to Thulwin's villa.

OOO

The next day, after a brief and friendly meeting with the King, Tullus set out for Faesulae. Riding with him were three of Thulwin's guards and the newly-purchased slave, now in a clean tunic, his hair cropped short – a routine precaution against lice.

The slave was Latin-speaking and showed Tullus every respect, but in the presence of the Gothic guards he displayed a clear aversion. The potential for trouble was evident and Tullus was quick to act. At first the slave was stubborn and did not want to speak, but when he did his pent-up feelings burst with torrent force. All the able-bodied in his village had been put to slavery and his wife and child snatched brutally from his arms.

'The work of the Goths,' he said with savage bitterness.

'Where is your village?' Tullus asked.

'In the hills north of Verona.'

Tullus looked intently at his newly-purchased slave. He was a man of medium build; his hair was fair and his eyes blue. Armies had swarmed over his native hills for generations. Only God knew his origin.

The slave's story was pitiful, but hillmen were not angels.

'What provoked this outrage?' Tullus asked sharply.

'Some Goths were ambushed,' the slave said briefly. His accent was difficult to follow.

'And more than once, I suspect,' Tullus responded knowingly. 'And no doubt you, in your turn, thirst for vengeance.'

'It's my duty!'

'Duty!' Tullus exploded. 'You're a human being with a duty to be human – not a savage!'

The slave was too startled to react and the Gothic guards drew close.

'I pulled you from that line of misery because of the humanity in your eyes,' Tullus continued fiercely. 'Now you talk of vengeance. Swear by the living God that you'll renounce this madness – swear!'

The slave, awed by his master's power, obeyed.

'Remember your oath,' Tullus barked.

'Yes, my lord.'

'Come, ride with me,' Tullus added in a gentler voice. The guards relaxed.

Tullus was uneasy. He had purchased trouble, for even though the hillman slave had pledged his oath, the call for blood would still be burning. The trouble was compounded by the imminent journey to the south. What could he do with him? To leave Rufus with the problem would be irresponsible and to sell him was against his nature. There was only one solution. He would take him on the journey. That way he could be watched.

'What is your name?' Tullus asked abruptly.

'Petrus, sir.'

'What age was your boy when the Goths came?'

'Ten.'

'When did it happen?'

'Last full moon.'

'I see,' was all that Tullus said. His eyes looked straight ahead, his features frozen as he thought of Drusilla and those early, anxious days when most had thought her lost or dead.

'Petrus,' Tullus said gruffly, 'when we get to the villa, give your story in detail to the scribe Philippus. We can make enquiries.'

'Philippus,' the slave mouthed. His eyes widened and the sagging heaviness about his face dissolved.

'You'll try and find my wife and boy?' his voice caught between surprise and animation.

'I'll ask my Gothic friends.'

'Alas, my wife.' The slave's voice saddened. 'She was not strong.'

The conversation stopped and Titus quickened pace. He was a home-bird.

'You'll not get home tonight, old son,' Tullus muttered, patting the horse's neck. 'We'll have to find an inn. Well, Titus,' he added, 'this is your last journey. From now on Britannicus will search the corners of the Empire.'

OOO

Drusilla was waiting to greet her husband. She was radiant.

'All went well, Marcus?' she whispered when he dismounted.

'Yes, my dear,' he replied with equal quietness. They were before the servants.

Suddenly from the open courtyard Valeria came running. Impulsively she rushed into her father's arms, and he hugged her tightly.

Petrus sat on his horse, tears streaming down his face. The image of a happy family was too much for him. Enthralled, he watched his master greet his staff, in particular three tall men – Gothic guards – and a smaller, broad-shouldered Roman. To judge by the friendly laughter, the bonds were close. Then the Count pointed in his direction.

'Rufus,' he said to the broad-built Roman, 'we have a new man – Petrus.'

'What is your work, friend from the hills?' the Count called out.

'A horseman, sir.'

'A welcome arrival, Rufus,' Tullus said firmly.

'Yes, Count.'

Petrus sat as if mesmerised, until the broad-shouldered Roman approached.

'Where are the slave-quarters, sir?' he asked as he dismounted.

The Roman puckered his brows.

'We know no slaves here at the Villa Tullus,' he said, the note of indignation undisguised.

OOO

That evening Tullus and his wife made their way, as was their habit, to the bench-seat on the outcrop just above the villa.

'Who is the new man? Another of your strays?' she jested.

As he described the purchase in the street she chuckled.

'Underneath your upright soldier's looks you're just a soft-hearted Briton.'

He laughed. 'That's what the King said.'

He felt her shrink with aversion.

'What's wrong, Drusilla?'

'Marcus, I know you like the King, you always have, but I can't forget the brutal end of Symmachus and Boethius.'

'Neither can he!' Then he described the meetings in the park.

'You're concerned, Marcus.'

'I am, Drusilla dear. There's no point in denying it. When I first met the King he was a rock of common sense. Now his powers are failing. True, he has recovered, but for how long? There's one blessing, though: Thulwin's at his side.'

Having reached the outcrop of rock, they turned and looked over the villa below towards Faesulae.

'I love this place,' she murmured softly.

'Don't get too attached, my dear,' he said with equal gentleness.

'Oh, Marcus, no!'

'Uncertain times lie before us, Drusilla.'

They sat down on the weather-worn wooden bench and he took her hand in his while she, moving close, buried her head against his chest.

'After all these years we're still like lovebirds,' she whispered wistfully.

'We're mental cases,' he said gruffly.

'Marcus!'

'My lady is beautiful in looks and nature,' he said tenderly.

'And my lord is good.'

She reached up and kissed him on the cheek.

'You didn't say that I was handsome,' he said, nudging her playfully. 'Come, Drusilla, it's getting dark; we'd better wander back.'

As they made their way down he told her of the journeys now before him. He felt her stiffen: she hated the long weeks of waiting, but when he said he would be visiting Rusticiana and Poppea she brightened.

ooo

# CHAPTER SIXTY SEVEN

# AMBUSH

Ten days after his return from Ravenna, Tullus left for the south, accompanied by Theodis and the Twins who, owing to the influence of Thulwin, were all but permanently assigned to the Tullus household. At Florentia he acquired three supplementary soldiers. So, with Petrus the hillman travelling as a personal servant, the total number, himself included, was eight.

Tullus had left the villa guarded by six of Thulwin's men: the three who had escorted him from Ravenna and the three who remained following the siege. All this had been arranged at Ravenna. Tullus had grumbled at the need for such arrangements, but he knew too well that they were necessary, for Triguilla and his friends were smarting with resentment.

Immediately he arrived in Rome, Tullus went to the villa of Symmachus, where Rusticiana and Poppea were in residence. The wealth of the Senators had not been wholly plundered.

The initial meeting was not easy, for Tullus's very presence was a reminder of old and happier times. He found the ladies better than he had expected, and busy in a practical way with charitable works. Tullus concluded that their compassion for the suffering of others was blessing them as well. Later, in a private meeting with Rusticiana, he told her of his conversation with the King. She, like Drusilla, shrank at the sound of Theoderic's name. She listened to the full tragic story, but trust had been destroyed. There could be no forgetting. It was indeed a tragedy. At length he told her of his meetings with her husband and how the monks had marvelled at his equanimity. Then he talked about the Senator's writings and how he had delivered the *Consolation* into the care of the old Anician agent with strict instructions that only she had access. Tullus was adamant that the King's will should be obeyed, warning that a breach could lead to confiscation. Rusticiana assented.

'My late lord would have had it so,' she said quietly.

After leaving the villa of Symmachus, Tullus headed straight for the Via Tiburtina and for Sublaqueum. The famous road was still in serious disrepair. Nothing had changed, it seemed, nothing at all. The crumbling villas in the hills, the one-time pride of senators, remained neglected. He looked about him. Never would he pass this way again. The thought was sudden, like a judgement.

At Sublaqueum there was no neglect. On the contrary, evidence of patient industry was everywhere. The community was clearly prospering, but their very success had bred resentment at the local church. It had focused on the Father Abbot, Brother Maurus said, and he feared the Abbot might consider it his duty to move on.

Brother Martin spent the evening with his old friend Marcus Tullus. They walked and talked, Martin of his teacher Benedict and Tullus of the Senator Boethius. So the conversation was confined, except when Martin asked about the Tullus family. Indeed, the ways of the monk and the Count had little in common, yet they were bound by mutual respect and shared experience. Tullus marvelled at Martin's quiet serenity, the same serenity he had witnessed in the Hermit of the Rocks.

Theodis also spoke with Martin. Tullus guessed the subject to have been his hoped-for marriage, but the guardsman ventured not a word.

Tullus and his escort stayed overnight, and in the morning, after paying their respects, they journeyed south.

In time they reached Beneventum, where Tullus met old contacts. It soon became apparent that attitudes had changed. True, he was treated with respect, yet he felt his words would be ignored. He was the King's man, but most knew, or had heard the rumour, that Theoderic was fading. They would prevaricate and delay reform, knowing well that change was in the air.

The nagging sense of being ineffective was disturbing. Otherwise all was going well. The hillman Petrus, who had proved himself a cook, was joking with the guards, his bitterness forgotten. It was hot, of course, but generous midday stops relieved fatigue.

It was south of Beneventum that Theodis began to act nervously.

'We're being followed,' he asserted.

'By what? A farm cart!' Tullus countered.

'Count, I'm serious!'

Tullus turned and scanned the road. Riders were following, but that was not unusual.

'We've travelled this road a number of times,' Theodis said earnestly.

'Yes, Theodis,' Tullus sighed with exaggerated patience.

Undeterred, the guardsman described the road ahead. It turned back, U-shaped, on itself around a jutting spur of high ground. A following enemy could easily climb the spur and then, with ample time, await its victim. The area was well wooded, giving excellent cover. It was the perfect ambush site.

'The sun has gone to your head, Theodis. We're armed to the teeth. What self-respecting bandit would attack us? Such men go for easy targets.'

'I didn't say they were bandits, sir. Look, they've vanished!' He pointed vigorously.

Tullus checked. There was sign of neither man nor horse. Certainly their move had been deliberate, for the road cut into a slope, making their passage difficult whichever way they went. Theodis's suspicions could be legitimate.

'There's something more you haven't told me, for you've been agitated for some time.'

'Yes, Count. In Beneventum we kept meeting a party of four men – Goths, but from a clan of vicious reputation. One of them came up to me and praised your horse Britannicus. I don't trust them, sir, and I'll wager ...'

'What are you trying to tell me, Theodis?'

'That they're assassins!'

'That's what I thought. You're sure of this?'

'I'm as sure as I can be, but there's only one way we can prove it ...'

'By stalking them,' Tullus interjected.

'With your permission.'

'You have it!'

They rode on, giving the impression that all was proceeding normally, but when they rounded the tip of the spur, they stopped.

'If I'm the target, who in God's name thinks I'm worth the trouble?' Tullus burst out.

'It's not a trouble, Count, for those who seek revenge. Remember, sir, the fortress villa stood against the Palace Prefect's will!'

'I know – you're right – I warned Count Thulwin of this very danger. Well, if they're after me, they're after you as well, *and* the Twins. But, Theodis, why so far away? why here? They could have picked us off much nearer home.'

'And attract suspicion. No! But here it can be blamed on bandits. In his rage the King might raze a village, but that's all that would happen.'

'All!' Tullus exploded.

'It's a harsh world, sir!'

'By God it is!'

The short halt over, they retraced their steps along the road towards Beneventum, keeping close to the hill in order to avoid detection. With little trouble they found clear evidence of horses' hooves imprinted on the steep incline.

Theodis insisted that only he and the Twins should proceed. More men would destroy the element of surprise. He needed Petrus, though, to bring the horses of their four pursuers to the road. They would be on the top somewhere, ready for a quick escape along the ridge. The whole affair was simply read, Theodis emphasised.

Tullus waited with the three remaining guards, his agitation rampant. An age seemed to come and go, before a grinning Petrus all at once appeared with the four horses, their legs stretched rigid as they slipped in jerky movements down the slope; they were not easy to control, but Petrus had the knack.

Again they waited. Time dragged endlessly. It was hot and no one spoke, but all were anxious, their grim-faced looks a clear reflection. Suddenly Theodis and the Twins were on the slope above them. 'It was the men we saw at Beneventum,' Theodis boomed. 'We've paid their wages, sir, but not in gold! You'll see them when we travel round the spur.'

When they reached the fateful spot Tullus quickly dismounted. The bodies lay where they had fallen but none carried any hint of identity. It had been the same with the horses. He looked around him. Their enemies had been waiting near the road and each had arrows at the ready.

'But for you, Theodis ...' Tullus began, but he did not finish. 'Dear God, if this can happen while the King's alive, what will happen when he's gone?'

ooo

It was six weeks before Tullus completed his mission and returned to Ravenna. On arrival he went straight to the Palace. In the main hall he hesitated and, instead of going to the Royal chambers, he turned back, obscuring himself behind the pillars. Almost at once he saw the man that he was looking for, the Palace Prefect, Triguilla.

Immediately he moved to confront the Gothic nobleman. Triguilla had not seen him and turned quickly on hearing the approaching footsteps. His look of shock was obvious.

'Marcus Tullus!' he exclaimed.

'Shocked, are we, Triguilla?' Tullus barked, his stare focused on Triguilla's face.

'About what?'

'I think you know, Prefect. I would like to tell you we have evidence – convincing evidence. Your men were very foolish.'

Triguilla began to bluster.

'Don't be troubled, Prefect. The evidence is in good hands – a high-born Goth and a Churchman much trusted by the King.' Tullus had assumed a soothing tone. 'However, if any "accident" should happen to myself or my guard captain, my friends could feel it right to see the King.'

'I – I don't know what you are talking about,' Triguilla blustered on.

'Prefect, I'm glad of that,' Tullus responded mildly. Then, with due formality, he excused himself and headed for the Royal chambers. He could not suppress the smile that played about his mouth. There was no real evidence, of course, but the bluff had worked.

The King was in good spirits, and Tullus's report was well received. Tullus suggested instant action on a series of matters in the south. Such efficiency would convince the waverers that the Royal writ was still the sovereign force. Theoderic took his Roman Count's plain speaking well, but his face darkened when he heard about the ambush. The news that the criminals had been Goths was far from welcome, and Tullus was not ungrateful that the King was short of time to question him. There was no evidence, and the assumption of banditry was best left undisturbed.

Although friendly, the audience was brief, as the King was busy with foreign delegations. So, tired, and glad to be released, Tullus set out for Faesulae.

ooo

# CHAPTER SIXTY EIGHT

# THE WEST – AD 525

For Tullus and the Royal guardsmen summer at the fortress villa was happy and restful.

The Twins had their 'wives' at Faesulae and were the butt of many jokes. Theodis, walking arm-in-arm with Anna, was a common sight and, plain to all, Drusilla was delighted by her husband's company.

Theodis had seen Brother Martin and made no secret of the fact. When Tullus reminded him about his binding oath he waved the difficulty aside. It was wilful ignorance, but Tullus knew the coming journey to Hispania would keep him occupied.

At the end of August Cornelia arrived for the final months of her pregnancy, and two weeks later Tullus left for the west. Grandfather, he told his daughter, would have her very much in mind.

Tullus entered Narbonensis at the end of September. With him were three Royal guardsmen, Petrus the hillman, who had proved himself an asset in the south, and the same three soldiers from Florentia.

At the garrison of Narbo Martius he doubled his escort, but he did not leave immediately, as permission from Barcino was required before he could proceed.

Indeed, he was acting very much the part of an ambassador, for Theoderic's general had assumed the mantle of a regent. Yet the general still paid homage to Ravenna, and Theoderic thought it best to let the matter rest.

Tullus, of course, had no wish to upset any political balance and his message to the Ostrogothic general was deferential. He desired, he said, to bring the King's good wishes, and he hoped to visit some old friends. These he listed, so that all was open.

Marcus Tullus was well received in Hispania, for his name was famous in the land. First he visited Barcino, then he journeyed inland to Caesaraugusta, where he left a copy of the *Consolation* in discreet hands. Following this, he made his way to Ilerda to see Osca, only to learn that his friend had died the year before. Saddened, he began the journey back to Narbo Martius and to Italy.

He had found Hispania well-ordered, in the sense that Theoderic's general punished crime with strict severity. This kept discipline, but Tullus sensed a lack of real stability. Too much rested on the shoulders of one man. It was not unlike Italy, where the King's masterful rule still kept the peace and where anarchy was kept at bay more by the force of Theoderic's will than the working of the law, for the ancient institutions that had held their course through many tyrannies were very weak.

Boethius had worked tirelessly to redress this situation and to uphold the Senate.

The Roman Senate was, to many, a near mystical institution and, for all its failings, it still pronounced the law. It also embodied a system of government. This was what Theoderic did not seem to understand. To him, the Senate was a rival or a tool, but not a partner.

After returning his supplementary guard to the Narbo Martius garrison, Tullus headed east. When he reached Italy he rode north to the Via Emilia and then towards Ravenna. He was exhausted. Grey hairs were telling, he confided to Theodis.

Once through Ravenna's gates, Tullus made straight for Thulwin's villa, where he found the Count at home. There he learned the Pope had gone to Constantinople, but the news filtering from the Eastern capital had enraged the King. It was as Tullus had anticipated. Justin had exploited the Papal presence to the full in a grand pageant of Church unity. Concessions had been gained for the Arian population; even so, the unmitigated arrogance of the dominant church had infuriated Theoderic.

It was now early December, but the weather was still mild. So when Tullus saw the King their meeting was, as custom ruled, within the forest park. Theoderic looked frail, and his posture had deteriorated further, but his mind was clear.

At first the King seemed more interested in Britannicus than the journey to the west. 'A magnificent animal,' he kept repeating. Soon, of course, the subject of Hispania arose. Tullus described the instability he had sensed beneath the surface. There was an imposed order rather than the rule of law. The King, however, did not seem to grasp the point.

'Either a king rules or he doesn't,' he responded with finality. 'Tullus, you were right about Byzantium, but it's hard to bear; by God, it's hard to bear!'

As the audience continued, Theoderic made it obvious that he did not want to dwell on serious matters. He was with Tullus, his friend from the north, and he wanted to relax. Yet the time spent in the forest park was short. There was much to do.

'I miss Eutharic,' he said wearily as the meeting drew to a close. 'He should not have died.'

Tullus remained silent. He anticipated a further audience. Instead, he was released.

'Go back to your villa, Tullus. Your lady will be waiting.'

OOO

# CHAPTER SIXTY NINE

# THE POPE'S RETURN

A few days after Tullus returned to Faesulae his daughter was delivered of a baby boy. The birth was premature and old worries stabbed sharply, yet all went well.

Cornelia stayed at the Villa Tullus until Easter when she returned to Umbria. Predictably, her son was christened Marcus. But there was a shadow clouding the family happiness, for Atticus was still determined on the move to Constantinople.

Shortly after Cornelia left, Thulwin's son arrived with twelve of his father's guard. They were, as always, well provisioned, and no undue strain was put upon the villa staff.

The young man openly admitted that he had come for company and had volunteered to be his father's messenger for that purpose. There was no one in Ravenna he could talk to, he maintained.

There were three rolls from the Count: one a domestic matter relating to Petrus the hillman and two concerning issues of state.

Tullus had enquired about the family of Petrus and the news received was stark and brief. The wife was dead, but the son was alive and could be bought.

There was nothing brief about the rolls dealing with matters of state. Firstly, and in some detail, Thulwin described the King's distress over his sister – the widow of Thrasamund, King of Carthage. Bitter rumours had reached his ears that she had been murdered, together with her guards. He had just learned of his sister's imprisonment when at Genua, and since then he had called for compromise. Indeed, there was little else he could have done, with the Great Sea as a barrier, and more especially with his sister's life a hostage to retaliation. Now, if the cruel rumours were correct, the King would feel himself released from such restraint. In fact, shipbuilding was already under way.

The whole sad business, Thulwin emphasised, had further wearied Theoderic. Once more the trouble was religion, with the King's sister, a symbol of her Arian faith, in opposition to the Vandal King, a new and passionate convert to the Orthodox persuasion.

The second major item again concerned religious troubles. This time it was the Pope's mission to Byzantium. Pope John had gained concessions; not all the King's demands, but nonetheless, concessions.

The ostentatious displays surrounding the Pope's visit, though hard to bear, had been accepted by Theoderic as inevitable. Now Pope John, having spent Easter in the eastern capital, was journeying back to Italy. He was due in Ravenna in mid-May, when Theoderic planned to greet him in the great hall of the Palace, and the King expected his 'man from the north' to be present.

OOO

The great hall of the Palace was alive with the flickering light of many lamps. The dais with its empty throne stood at the end nearest to the Royal chambers. For an hour the Gothic Council had been gathering, together with the palace officials. Most stood in groups, talking busily, while close by attendants hovered. The bent figure of Cassiodorus was in their midst, looking anxious. Perhaps he sensed some undercurrent. There was a rumour circulating that the Pope was ill. How ill? No doubt the tall official knew. Tullus himself was placed beside the throne, an honoured position. There was purpose in his placing, though, for the Byzantine officials who had escorted the Pope would be near to him: the man who knew Justinian.

Standing to his right and beside the throne were two Arian clergy. Theoderic had restricted their number because of Roman sensibilities. One of them, a man that Tullus knew, turned to him and smiled. Indeed, he mostly found the Arian clergy friendly. He was, of course, well favoured by their monarch and that, they doubtless felt, was good enough for them.

There were no smiles for Tullus when the Roman clergy entered. Their looks were cold. He had opposed the Church during the anti-Jewish riots and had humiliated the Deacon at Fidenae – now an important official at the Papal court. These events had moulded attitudes. Even his closeness to Boethius and Symmachus – seen as martyrs – and to Cassiodorus, a church favourite, made no difference. Tullus was a friend of heretics.

Heralded by trumpets, the King entered, followed closely by his daughter Amalasuentha and her young son. To Tullus it was a glimpse of things to come, and it was disquieting. How could Amalasuentha control the powerful jealousies playing in the Gothic Council? Furthermore, she was a widow, and an indiscreet choice of partner could be disastrous. The future troubled him, as it did Thulwin.

As the King took his seat, the trumpets sounded again. This time they heralded the Pope.

The Father of the Roman Church walked slowly. To his left was

Thulwin, who had welcomed the Pontiff on Theoderic's behalf. Behind and to the right were three close Papal aides, and amongst their number was the one-time Deacon of Fidenae; the embodied voice of reason, Tullus grated cynically. The Pope would hear of little tolerance from him. How could such men rise within the Church?

The Pope looked very ill. So much so that he appeared more corpse than man. He walked stiffly and unnaturally erect, his mouth twisted, giving an unfortunate supercilious impression. He stopped, and his advisers closed about him.

Slowly the King descended from the dais, bowing formally in the manner of the Goth, but the Pope stood unresponsive. He looked confused; much too ill, it seemed, to know what he was doing. It was cruel, nothing less, for his advisers to have compromised him in this way.

One limp hand half raised, as if accepting homage, was the only gesture that he managed. To Theoderic it was a gross insult. He did not see a dying man but only Roman arrogance.

At that moment Cassiodorus stepped forward, hoping to solve the impasse. If anyone could repair the situation it was he, but the King brushed the tall official angrily aside.

Theoderic was white with fury. Awkwardly he turned and ascended the dais. He sat down heavily. There were no words, but the warning signs were obvious; his jaw jutting forward, his eyes staring fixedly before him.

Suddenly the silence was broken by one of the Pope's advisers.

'The Supreme Pontiff,' he said, in a voice resembling a chant, 'wishes to progress to Rome.'

'No!' Theoderic thundered. 'The Bishop of Rome will remain here in Ravenna at our pleasure!'

Having pronounced, the King rose abruptly and left the hall.

Suddenly everyone was talking. Tullus was blunt with the Byzantines standing close to him. The King had been insulted and the Pope had been too ill to know his mind. His three advisers were to blame. The travellers from Constantinople listened respectfully, for Tullus was Justinian's friend.

'Don't worry, Marcus Tullus.' It was Cassiodorus.

'The Pope's advisers are either blind or mad,' Tullus blurted. 'Why did they allow the poor man to attend?'

'Apparently the Pope insisted ...'

'And they heeded him!' Tullus reacted. 'That was not obedience, it was idiocy!'

'Byzantium has gone to their heads,' Cassiodorus whispered. 'They were entertained beyond their wildest dreams.'

'Damned fools,' Tullus muttered.

'John is dying,' the whispers continued. 'Before long we'll have another Pope and then a new-found nest of bees will buzz around the honeypot.'

For a devout churchman like Cassiodorus it was strangely cynical. Tullus said nothing and the Master of Offices slipped away with a lightness surprising for a large man. Tullus stood alone amidst the storm of noise; not for long, for Cyprian was approaching, his smile as herald. Tullus did not respond, for when he saw Cyprian he saw the destroyer of Boethius.

'The King wants to see you, Count,' Cyprian said in a friendly way.

'Now?'

'Yes.'

'Lead the way, Referendarius.'

Cyprian was ageing. The once quick, slim figure was quick and slim no more. His body had broadened out and his gait had now acquired the measure of a court official, but there was a dullness in his step that was not due to age.

'How is Rufus?'

'As ever, solid and reliable.'

'He was good to my mother.'

'He was.'

The brief exchange was full of undercurrents. Cyprian wanted to talk. He was reaching out for friendship, but the wrongs against Boethius rose in protest.

'Count, we need your opinion,' the King called immediately the double doors swung shut.

'My lord,' Tullus responded, bowing low.

'We have been grossly insulted, and such an insult cannot pass unpunished. We have a mind to lock this Pope in prison. What is your view, Tullus?'

Tullus glanced at the ring of Councillors; Thulwin, Ibbas, Triguilla, the Arian bishops and Cassiodorus were amongst their number. All were waiting, like the King, for his reply. He swallowed hard.

'If you confine the Pope, even in the gentlest way, there will be trouble in the streets, and should the Pontiff die it will be said you starved or poisoned him.'

'You're right, Count,' Theoderic reacted with frustration. 'But we cannot overlook this insult and let the Church's arrogance prevail again. Our patience is about to snap. And those three advisers – bishops, no less – the only souls they cared for were their own!'

'One of them was the former Deacon of Fidenae, my lord,' Tullus prompted.

'I remember – I remember well. Tullus, you made him Bishop.' The King smiled briefly. Then instantly he was serious.

'If we do nothing the Church will claim a victory and if we confine the Roman Pope they'll trumpet martyrdom; but we've already spoken, and our word must be obeyed. We'll keep him at our pleasure and release him soon.'

There were general murmurs of approval and then the King turned to Thulwin and Ibbas. Carthage was the subject.

'Our sister's death must be avenged,' the monarch growled.

ooo

The Pope died a few days later, and rumours spread maintaining that he had been starved. There were riots, and wild stories spread from lip to lip that John had died in fetters. To Tullus, it had been predictable.

The King's mood was one of disillusionment. His policy of co-operation lay in ruins, yet he was determined to influence the election of the future Pope. There were jealousies to exploit. There were always jealousies in the Church, the King had muttered to Tullus, adding that his daughter needed someone she could work with. The implication was obvious. The monarch felt his time was short. In fact, it seemed to Tullus that all the King could see was death and dissolution. Nevertheless, Theoderic's pace of work continued unabated.

As well as the Pope's election, the planned attack on Carthage was continually on his mind. The difficulties were many, but nothing would induce him to defer his preparations.

Loud in support of the attack was Theodahad, his sister's son by her first marriage. Celebrated for his learning, he loved to talk, but he did not love to dip into his coffers; indeed, his avarice was rampant. The King had little time for him, and was never slow to thwart his selfishness.

Tullus detested him and his so-called learning. He was a fraud, whose greed caused endless trouble, especially in Tuscany, where his lands were mostly situated. But Theodahad was much too cunning to disturb his uncle's Roman friend. Marcus Tullus was left in peace, except for the earnest philosophical discussions Theodahad affected.

Young Thulwin, Tullus recalled, had summed up the Royal nephew well. 'When Theodahad spoke of Plato's *one*, Theodahad meant Theodahad.'

It was therefore with some annoyance that Tullus caught up with

Theodahad's slow and ostentatious progress on the journey back to Tuscany.

Though loath to waste time, Tullus stopped and dismounted, deeming it prudent to be civil to the wealthy Goth.

'Ah, the philosopher of Faesulae,' Theodahad hailed grandly.

'Tullus is a farmer, sir.'

'As modest as Socrates. Your horse is magnificent,' Theodahad continued. Then a minstrel began to sing. The pretension was laughable.

Suddenly Theodahad became confidential.

'What do you think of Amalasuentha?'

'She has her father's good sense,' Tullus responded cautiously. One thing was certain, he was not going to unburden his thinking to Theodahad.

'She has indeed, but, noble sir, she is a woman,' the King's nephew whispered loudly.

'Indeed, and with becoming looks,' Tullus reacted bluntly.

'You are cautious, sir, but Theodahad is not. He will be rash and speak his mind.'

That will be the day, Tullus said silently.

'A woman cannot rule.' The Goth grew more confidential. 'Thulwin should be regent until her young son comes of age. Many think like me. Many think he should be king, but Thulwin will not have it. Can you persuade him, sir?'

'Thulwin thinks for Thulwin,' Tullus retorted.

'His son might be ambitious?'

'My lord Theodahad, let this be clear. I have no part to play in Gothic politics.'

Theodahad frowned.

'You will say nothing to my uncle on this matter. In fact, I know that you will keep your silence, for any breath of this would compromise the noble Thulwin.'

Theodahad was cunning.

The conversation reverted once more to pleasantries. Theodahad had been reading Virgil, he said, and had many questions. Deferentially he entreated Tullus to call at his villa, where they would have ample leisure for literary discussion. Tullus played the game of courtly thanks, but he had no intention of visiting Theodahad. He did not trust him.

With due ceremony Tullus extracted himself. Thankfully he mounted his horse. Then, as if sensing his master's mood, Britannicus surged to a gallop, and in no time Tullus and the three Royal guardsmen had left the cart and company of Theodahad behind.

OOO

# CHAPTER SEVENTY

# THE LAST SUMMONS

The new Pope was elected in July. He was the candidate the King had backed, and Tullus guessed Theoderic's will had not been over-troubled with discretion.

About a month later the evening peace of the Villa Tullus was shattered by two hard-riding guardsmen. Their message was both brief and stark. The King was dying and was calling for his Roman-from-the-north. The signature was that of Cassiodorus.

There was a full moon and Tullus resolved to leave at once. On this final summons he was determined not to fail the King.

Drusilla watched her husband ride away as she had done so often, but usage did not make it any easier. The anxiety and the waiting were just the same, and if anything it was worse, for she knew Theoderic's death would herald much uncertainty. For her, the years of stability had ended with Boethius's arrest; now the very ground was shifting.

Fortunately she was fully occupied. It had all happened apparently by chance, when one of the servants had asked if her daughter could be taught to sing. Drusilla had agreed, but she soon discovered that the child had further needs: reading and writing in particular. Then there was another pupil, and another, this time all the way from Faesulae. Marcus had encouraged her and had built a small schoolroom by the outer courtyard. Presently the numbers were twelve.

The parents' gratitude was moving. Drusilla asked no payment, yet gifts were pressed upon her: wood carvings, metalwork, embroidery – the work of loving hands.

From the beginning, the Church had been invited to participate. Marcus had urged the move, knowing that, if excluded, they would become suspicious. It had proved a prudent step, for the villa school was prayed for from the altar steps. Fortunately the antagonism Tullus had experienced in Rome and Ravenna was nowhere evident at Faesulae. The Count and Countess were regular churchgoers and generous patrons.

ooo

The night ride to Ravenna was slow, for the horses were nervous and shied at every shadow. When they reached the inn amongst the hills they rested for an hour before continuing. The dawn broke when they were well short of Ravenna, and with the light the pace grew quicker. By mid-morning they reached the gates of Theoderic's capital.

A crowd had gathered round the Royal Palace. Most were Goths, their mood subdued, and as Tullus and the guardsmen approached their ranks soon parted.

'It's the Roman Count – the man from the north,' one whisper said.

'They say the King loved him like a son,' said another.

Tullus displayed no reaction but dismounted quickly and strode to the Palace. He was expected and doors opened instantly at his approach. Outside the Royal quarters he was met by Cassiodorus.

'Thank God you're here, Tullus – he's very low.' The confidential manner, for once, was absent. 'He's seen his Council and lectured them on tolerance. He's also told his daughter publicly to co-operate with Constantinople, and his grandson, the future King, has been presented to his peers. All this, all this, Tullus, and still he calls for his man from the north. You must have ridden through the night, for we didn't expect you until the afternoon.'

'Where's Thulwin?' Tullus asked.

'Behind you.'

Tullus turned. His friend was fast asleep, his head against his chair.

'He's been with his Royal lord all night,' Cassiodorus explained with some indulgence. 'Come,' he added, turning to the double doors. 'I'll announce you.'

'Tullus,' the King called as he entered. The voice was weak but unmistakable. 'What kept you?'

'My lord King, I came as quickly as I could.'

'Come closer, Count.'

Tullus obeyed, and Amalasuentha, who was sitting at her father's side, withdrew discreetly. Tullus bowed in acknowledgement of her discretion.

'No park today, Tullus.' A gruffness covered the King's emotion. Then, almost fiercely, he gripped Tullus's arm.

'The night before we took to bed, we dined, and on the table was a fish.' The King stared intensely. 'It had the eyes of Symmachus, and all the while its teeth were waiting for revenge.'

'My lord, fish are fish and Symmachus is dead.'

'It had the eyes of Symmachus,' Theoderic insisted.

'The fever of your illness, married to your self-accusing thoughts, but not the eyes of Symmachus!'

'I'm dying, Tullus! I want to know the truth!'

Tullus swallowed hard. It was no time for self-consideration.

'The soul that turns to truth is loved by truth.'

'I would turn, friend from the north.'

'Then love the truth, my lord; the images of gaping fish are lies.'

'What is the truth?'

'The light within the soul,' Tullus heard himself reply. 'Surrender to that light, my lord.'

'And love the truth,' Theoderic mouthed. Weakly, he beckoned his daughter, and Tullus called at once for Thulwin. With discretion, the Arian Bishop, who had been waiting on his Royal lord, approached.

'I feel my body letting go of life,' Theoderic whispered.

Thulwin entered and the King looked up.

'I'm going.'

He sighed and his body sagged heavy on the bed.

'It's over,' Tullus said gently.

Amalasuentha began to weep.

Moments later, Cassiodorus entered with the physician, and death was immediately confirmed.

For a short time the Master of Offices stood reverently before the body of his earthly lord. Then he turned to Amalasuentha and bowed.

'I am your servant, Madam.'

OOO

# CHAPTER SEVENTY ONE

# BROTHER MARTIN

The round face of Brother Martin streamed with sweat. It was very hot and his rough-spun habit hung heavy on his shoulders. He sat down. A snake slid by and he looked at it with compassion. No arms, no legs, he thought with sadness. The snake passed on.

Beside him a grove of olive trees looked cool and inviting. God always provided, and soon he was stretched full length beneath their shade.

When he awoke, two toothless men, field workers, were looking down at him.

'Are you well in body, holy Brother?' one asked.

Martin nodded.

'But I'm thirsty,' he stated. 'Is there a well nearby?'

'We have what a well is jealous of!' the other said, offering his wine-bag.

'All Tuscany is generous!' Martin smiled. 'I'm looking for Marcus Tullus. Is his villa close?'

'The Roman Count! There, on the hillside opposite. There's his place.' The man who had offered the wine-bag pointed.

'Is Marcus Tullus well in health?'

'Oh, yes; he's out amongst his vineyards, even on the hottest days. All that is his.' The arm swung grandly in an arc.

'The old heretic has been good to him,' his companion added.

'Who?' Martin asked.

'The King.'

Martin did not respond but watched the two men closely. Years of labour were written on their faces. The curse of Adam, he concluded. Both men were thin, one being taller than the other.

'You work hard,' he prompted.

'Too hard, Brother. We work for the church up there in Faesulae,' the taller man responded, jerking his head back in the direction of the town.

'But it's a safe job,' the other labourer added.

'Do they pay well?'

Both men laughed loudly.

'We're labourers, holy Brother!' the smaller man said cynically. 'You know the Count, then.'

'Since a boy. Marcus Tullus is blessed – the Christ walks with him.'

The wine-bag was passed in silence, before the tall man spoke again.

'The mad priest screams that Tullus is a heretic.'

'But he's mad, Paulus,' his companion objected. 'He's not a priest, reverend brother. He lives up the hill near the old temple. He's got a hut there. The Count stopped the stoning of a girl he had denounced. Now he hates the name of Tullus.'

'The man who harbours hatred does not know the Christ,' Martin said quietly.

'There are many who believe on him,' the tall man persisted.

Martin shook his head sadly.

'He'll not die well,' he said.

'Here comes trouble,' the tall man groaned.

'Is it your boss?' Martin questioned mildly as he watched a broad-built man approach.

'These men should be working, Brother,' the man said bluntly.

Martin stood up as the two labourers hurried off.

'It was my fault, sir,' he said, watching the aggressive face.

The overseer grunted and still Martin watched.

'There's pain on your face, my friend,' he said.

'What is that to you?' the overseer said harshly.

'Your pain is my pain,' Martin responded simply.

'You don't know my pain.' The overseer's voice was forced and brittle.

Martin's gaze was steady and uncritical and the overseer's cry for help no longer could be silenced.

'My wife – she's –' His voice cracked.

'Take me to her, friend.'

The man obeyed, and Martin followed his heavy form as he laboured up the hill towards the town. Soon Martin found himself within a small house built against the hillside. It took a moment to become accustomed to the gloom, but the overseer's wife saw the habit of the monk immediately.

'I don't want to die,' she moaned, her prostrate body shifting weakly.

'The Christ is with you, have no fear. He's in the very air about you. Rest, sister,' Martin said gently. 'Some spring water,' he asked, addressing the overseer, who at once rushed out to fetch it.

Two hours later Martin emerged into the sunlight. The woman's fever had abated and the overseer was calling it a miracle.

It was late afternoon and the oppressive heat had waned. Martin walked at an easy pace and soon reached the valley below Faesulae. He continued on his way until he heard a noise above the movement of his habit. He turned and there, looking up at him, stood a very mangy dog. Its sad eyes expected the habitual rejection, but Martin patted it and the hairless, bony tail wagged vigorously.

'What's happened to you, old friend? Have you lost your master? I have no food, you know!'

The tail still wagged and Martin carried on, with the dog following behind. The area was well husbanded, like Sublaqueum, he thought, as he walked along the hard-baked, stony road.

To his left, on a platform of higher ground, he came upon a row of dwellings, their gardens measuring their distance from the road. Womenfolk and some old men were busily at work. Martin greeted them in turn, and at the last garden plot an old, bent man, glad to seize a rest, looked up.

'Going far, Brother?'

'The villa of Marcus Tullus.'

'That's not far, just beyond the ridge,' the old man responded, raising an arm to indicate the direction. 'You'll not see the Count. He's in Ravenna. Would you like some wine, Brother?'

'I can't, not until my friend here has some food,' he said, bending down and patting the dog gently.

'Don't worry about him. He's been scrounging food for days. The children chase him.'

'He's hungry,' Martin returned simply.

'Here, son!' the old man called to the boy playing close by. 'Get the dog some scraps.' Then he sat down awkwardly and Martin joined him.

The old man peered at Martin closely.

'I'm sorry for staring, but my eyes are not so good,' he said, shaking his head.

'Can I look?'

Moving closer, Martin gazed intently at the old man's eyes, his hand resting on the wrinkled forehead.

'You have a healing touch, reverend Brother.'

'People tell me so. Your eyes are dulling. I'll bring herbs.'

'Thank you, Brother ...'

'Martin.'

'Martin! You're the Martin ... everyone at the villa has heard of you. The Count himself has told me stories of his journeys in your company.'

Martin laughed.

'We must drink! Where is that boy?' the old man said impatiently.

'Here he is,' Martin answered as the boy raced up to them.

'He's mangy!' he reacted, throwing down the scraps before the dog and running off again.

'Now we can drink,' the old man said with satisfaction. 'It's well diluted,' he added, wiping the mouth of his wine-bag with some of the grass before handing it to Martin.

'Will Marcus Tullus be long in Ravenna?' Martin asked as he handed the wine-bag over.

'I don't know. Rufus, my son-in-law, will know.' The old man's voice dropped to a mutter as if he were talking to himself. 'You see, the King has died and the Count will stay for the burial. So there's no knowing how long he'll be.'

'I'm sorry to hear about the King. Marcus Tullus liked him.'

'And he liked Marcus Tullus.' The old man had clearly brightened and the two continued talking, sitting on the hard, dry ground until the sun began to drop.

'You'd better go, Brother Martin. The Gothic guards get edgy when it's dark.'

'Guards!' Martin repeated.

'Oh, yes, the Villa Tullus is always guarded. It's the tall Count's men at present.'

'The tall Count. Thulwin, you mean? I met him when I was a boy.'

'I know, I know the story,' the old man responded, patted Martin's arm. 'You'll visit me again, I hope.'

'Yes, I promised you some herbs.'

'Of course! The memory's not the best, but never mind.'

They parted, and the bent figure remained watching until Martin and the dog disappeared behind the ridge.

OOO

# CHAPTER SEVENTY TWO

# A NEW ERA

The state burial of the King and the noisy Gothic Council meetings were over. Ravenna was quiet and, to Tullus, empty. The Great King was no more.

Thulwin had left for Verona: an escape, Tullus concluded. The same mistake he had made during the King's dark months. Thulwin's place was in Ravenna, where his word in Council would be heard, and where Amalasuentha could easily consult him. Unfortunately, though, there were strong divisions between him and the young King's mother. Amalasuentha saw Thulwin as hard-headed and backward-looking; while he saw her as a betrayer of the old traditions. There was little room for compromise, for Thulwin was Thulwin and Amalasuentha was the daughter of her father. The trouble was, his absence gave Theodahad full play. There was always Cassiodorus, of course, and as long as she needed his advice, all could be well.

In Theoderic's will, Tullus had received three parcels of land bordering on his estate. As ever, the late King had been generous. It was a princely gift, but one that Tullus felt would be a fitting recompense for Theodis and the Twins who, using age as an excuse, had not renewed their oaths.

Theodis was now free to marry, but in this freedom doubts began to prey. The attachment to his faith was strong; feelings that had fed upon the strong emotions running at the great King's burial. Yet he was resolved to marry. Nothing would stop him now, though he still hoped for another sign, something to resolve all doubt; something to end the battle of conflicting loyalties that had troubled him so long. But he did not mention this to Tullus. He knew better.

Although he would never have admitted it, Tullus too was looking for a sign; for the ever-nagging question – should he move to Byzantium? – was unresolved and hanging heavy on his mind.

The safety of his wife and daughter worried him. The years were marching. What would happen if he were taken? What would happen to Drusilla and Valeria? These questions had often troubled him, but with the death of Theoderic and the imminent departure of Atticus, they were urgent.

Constantinople had much to recommend it: a stable system of government, the promised presence of Atticus and, he hoped, the protection of Justinian; whereas Italy was facing a period of great uncertainty. Without doubt logic pointed to the East, but Tullus knew that his decision was not bound by logic only. It was not so simple, for the greater family, even the animals, had to be considered. Then there was Drusilla's school – not an unimportant factor – and the strange, unplanned gathering of men who had fastened on regular meetings at the villa. Men of like mind, hoping for the fumes of Delphi, he said jokingly.

With this in mind, narrow family concerns seemed grossly selfish. Yet the misgivings that he held about the future circled in his mind continuously.

Thulwin, of course, would protect his family, he was sure of that; but Thulwin was at odds with the Queen Mother, Amalasuentha, and such rifts were dangerous. In his own audience with the Queen, Tullus had been treated with respect, even deference, yet there had been no commissions. This had surprised him, for at such a time of change he had expected to be used. Moreover, his known friendship with Justinian made this logical. Yet nothing happened.

The answer was simple, he concluded. The Queen had her own friends and preferences, and his closeness to Thulwin might well have been an issue. It was a new era and the time of easy access to the Royal presence was no more. He was not unhappy that the long, tedious journeys were over, for at times he felt as if a lifetime had been spent on horseback. Nevertheless, the lack of Royal contact left him with a sense of isolation.

This sense of isolation grew when, the formalities of the King's will completed, Tullus rode from Ravenna with Theodis and the Twins. Even Thulwin seemed shadowy. Suddenly Tullus thought of Thulwin's son. It was fresh and unexpected. He had a new and powerful ally after all; someone he had strangely overlooked. Indeed, during the past month in Ravenna the youth had been his constant companion.

The young man had all the dignity of his father. Service on the borders, where skirmishes were a constant danger, had matured him without brutalising his nature. Unusually for a young Goth, his drinking habits were moderate. Excesses were rare and, like the Count, he tended to keep his own council. Indeed, father and son were very much alike.

Undoubtedly, young Thulwin greatly respected his father and the father loved his son. Thulwin might grumble publicly about the boy's pursuit of learning, but privately he welcomed the serious turn of mind. As long as his noble son remained a Goth and not some half-baked Byzantine like Theodahad, he would be satisfied.

So far all attempts to marry the young man had failed. Betrothal had been fixed on two occasions, but both girls had died.

'He'll marry me to some doe-eyed empty-head who doesn't know a word of Latin,' young Thulwin had complained to Tullus, who could see the young Goth viewed the whole affair with total cynicism.

Thulwin's son had left Ravenna a few days earlier, and Tullus had invited him to Faesulae when his business was completed. The invitation was eagerly accepted, and it was no surprise when they met up with him watering his horses at the inn amongst the hills. So from there they rode together on the last miles of their journey to the fortress villa.

OOO

# CHAPTER SEVENTY THREE

# GROWING REPUTATION

Tales of wonder began to follow Brother Martin from the first day he set foot in Faesulae. The overseer's wife was cured. The mad 'priest' had dashed himself against the rocks; he had not died well, as Martin had predicted. And all could see the one-time mangy dog was covered with a glossy coat. Martin was the talk of Faesulae, yet he came and bowed before the clergy there with all humility. The Church could see no fault in him.

Drusilla watched the progress of her husband's friend with some bewilderment. There was no doubt that Martin had rare qualities – his aura of peace, his intuitive perception and his unpretentious humility. There was an openness about him, an innocence; yet no one could have called him foolish.

There was one strange instance, when Rufus talked about his former mistress in her final years. Then, for a moment, Martin had been flustered.

'That brings me joy. The Lord's ways are gracious,' he responded gravely. His words were clearly genuine.

The incident had passed as if it had never been, but Drusilla knew that Rufus knew the secret of the blush on Martin's face.

Martin had no plans. Go north, his master had instructed him. God, he said, would tell him where to stop, and Martin had, of course, obeyed. Only his wish to speak to Marcus Tullus and the memory of his conversation with Theodis had pointed a direction. When he heard that Tullus was in Ravenna he waited, for there was no reason to move on. However, in the waiting he had become a very prophet in the eyes of many.

Drusilla watched his reputation grow. Every word, every step just happened. There was neither plan nor aim. He sought no honours, and the myths that grew about him came from other lips.

Rufus had found him a deserted hut some two miles from the villa. It was a place of solitude and there both young and old would go to seek his blessing. Some were cured of illness, yet Martin claimed no miracle. Their faith in Christ had cured them, he maintained.

Many of the villa staff were drawn to him. At first, Drusilla was concerned, but when she learned of Martin's ways she was relieved. There were no harsh directives. His teaching was gentle, but when it came to those who asked to join his solitary life, there was no compromise. Martin's rule was strict. It was a needed test, he said, in preparation for the rule of Christ. It was also practical, for a soft monastic life served little, other than escape from duty in the harsher world outside. Most of Drusilla's information came from Rufus. He, from the beginning, had acted as protector to his master's friend. But Rufus did not join the ring of men who sat in circle form about the monk.

Martin had reached the villa two days after the news of Theoderic's death. Now, within the period of a month, he was established. His success had been remarkable, though success was not the word he used. It had simply happened.

Clearly, to many, Martin's ways were quite miraculous. This was certainly Anna's view. He was the very one Theodis had made contact with, the one to bless their union. Their marriage had to happen; it was God's will.

OOO

# CHAPTER SEVENTY FOUR

# VALERIA

Drusilla received two messages from her husband by way of the Army at Florentia. On the second occasion she reciprocated, hoping that the soldier could arrange a prompt delivery to Ravenna. Her message carried the news of Martin's arrival, but the garrison post was irregular and Tullus failed to receive it. So when he and Thulwin's son arrived the news was fresh. Theodis, for one, was dumbstruck. It was the sign that he had prayed for.

The obvious joy of Anna and Theodis and the presence of young Thulwin seemed to charge the villa with energy, and in the evening the mood was one of celebration. Not surprisingly, the talk focused on the subject of Martin, and Tullus was pressed to tell the story of the early years.

Slowly he spun the tale about the Hermit of the Rocks, the Greek islands and Justinian, the journey home to Italy, the bitter sea voyage and the old, bent monk within the burnt-out village. The room grew still when he described the rescue of Valerius, and finally he spoke of Sublaqueum and its Abbot.

The young Goth, who had heard of Martin from his father, was fascinated and asked if he might visit him.

'Tomorrow morning we can go together,' Tullus responded.

'Can I come, Papa?' Valeria asked excitedly.

Tullus smiled.

'You can ride with me on Britannicus.'

'Britannicus! Oh, Papa!'

OOO

The sky was cloudless and the air, still damp with dew, was fresh as they set out. The morning light was magical and the colours of the autumn shone.

Valeria was bubbling with happiness, for riding with her father on Britannicus was a treat. Like Titus, Britannicus was a powerful animal, yet he walked with care, sensing, no doubt, that he had a tender load. Claudius had been like that too, Tullus mused, but old Claudius was gone. He had died soon after his master had left for Ravenna: the same day as the great King. His heart had given up, they said.

'Papa!' Valeria called, bringing her father back to the present. 'Is Martin going to stay?'

'He will wait on God's direction.'

Suddenly she threw her hand up exuberantly.

'Careful, my dear,' Tullus cautioned.

'He should stay here – this is a happy place,' she pronounced, while laying her head flat along the horse's mane, her arms pressed tightly on each side of his neck.

'Oh, Britannicus,' she sighed. Her joy was brim full.

Young Thulwin looked across and smiled.

OOO

Martin's hut was no longer the isolated dwelling on the hillside that Tullus had remembered, for beside the lonely shelter two other box-like structures had been added: the work of Rufus and the villa staff.

The hill was partly wooded, so fuel was plentiful, and at its foot a stream flowed abundantly and clear.

Young Thulwin watched intently as they approached. He had seen such communities before and had respected their sacrifice, though he felt little affinity with their way of life. He could not understand their intense personal faith, yet it was the chosen path of a growing number, even amongst his own Gothic kin.

They stopped about two hundred paces short of the buildings and Martin's approaching figure. Thulwin immediately dismounted and lifted Valeria from her father's horse.

'Stay with me, Valeria,' he said gently, 'while your father greets his friend.'

'Yes, Thulwin.'

She stood quietly while the two guards who had been following came forward to hold the horses. Then, when she could see her father and Brother Martin talking, she sought Thulwin's hand.

He looked down at her small form and smiled.

'You're right, Valeria, we can go now.'

'Ah, the angel from the villa.' Martin beamed as Valeria approached. 'You are thrice blessed, Marcus Tullus.'

'I know,' Tullus responded.

'I was told I would recognise you, sir,' Martin continued, addressing the young Goth, 'and I do! You can only be the son of the great Count, for after all these years I can still remember his strong features.'

'He still remembers you.'

'But has he forgiven me for running away?' Martin retorted, while laughing heartily.

They talked easily, until eventually Martin and Tullus started slowly towards the three huts of the fledgling community. Thulwin and Valeria walked behind.

'You're growing, Valeria,' he said as he helped her over some rough ground.

'I'll soon be eight,' she said chirpily. 'Eight and eight are sixteen; Mother's teaching me to count. Thulwin, I wonder what I'll be like when I'm sixteen?'

'Don't ask silly questions, Valeria,' he said roughly.

She caught his hand and tugged gently.

'Why are you angry with me, Thulwin?' she asked, puzzled by his mood.

'Valeria, I'm not angry with you. You'll be like your mother, gracious and beautiful. Now, did you enjoy your ride on Britannicus?'

'Oh, yes.' Her wide eyes looked at him, but she said no more. Instead, she lifted her hand toward his and they walked on, following her father and Martin. Almost at once her hand slipped away.

When they reached the small community it was clear that the huts were roughly primitive and little more than hermits' cells. They had everything they wanted, Martin said. Tullus, however, looked forward to the time when a refectory, a guest-house and a basilica would crown the site. Thulwin smiled. It was as the Countess had predicted. Her husband would not rest until he had built a monastery.

Thulwin was pensive on the way back to the villa, for Valeria's innocent question about her age had opened a painful area of mind. His father was determined on his marriage, and soon some high-born creature would be chosen as his bride. Then the hope for sons would permeate the family. It was all inevitable, but he would still visit the Tullus household. He could not see that ending, for the Count was the only one he knew who could answer all his questions. He was drawn to Faesulae and, if death should rest awhile, the Count and Countess would grow old and at their side their daughter's beauty would be like the sun. It was all so damned predictable, he thought.

He turned his head towards Tullus, and without his bidding the words were on his lips:

'When you love the best, how is it possible to compromise?'

'Truth is without compromise, Thulwin, but it has no burden of possessions.'

'Sir! That's hard.'

'It's true!'

'Then what of fortune?'

'Boethius wrote about this at length – in prison, so it wasn't dictated from an easy couch. All fortune, he said, was either meant to reward and discipline the good or to punish or correct the bad. I'll get old Philippus to look the passage up.'

'Philippus is eternal, sir.'

'Yes. I suppose when you copy the words of Plato and Boethius for years, as he has done, it must have an effect.'

'Papa,' Valeria called out, 'look, there's Mama coming.'

'So she is. You have good eyes, my dear.'

They continued to ride for a little before Tullus drew Britannicus to a halt. Thulwin dismounted first and again lifted Valeria to the ground. At once she ran off to her mother, with Tullus following. Thulwin waited for the two guards to catch up and handed them the reins of his restless horse.

'What about the Count's horse?'

'Don't worry about Britannicus – he knows where to go.'

Slowly he began to walk towards the villa. Ahead of him Valeria was walking between her parents. Suddenly she turned and came towards him.

'I think Mama and Papa want to be alone,' she said.

'That's perceptive of you, Valeria.'

'Are all marriages happy?' she asked impulsively.

'No, Valeria,' he said gently. He knew she was watching him.

'I think you're unhappy, Thulwin, but it's all right, you'll be happy one day.'

At once she skipped away towards the villa.

Her words echoed strongly in his mind, and he knew he would never forget her strange prophecy.

ooo

# CHAPTER SEVENTY FIVE

# THE LAST JOURNEY

In the spring of the year following Theoderic's death, Theodis and Anna were married at Faesulae. It was very much a family occasion, with Cornelia travelling all the way from Umbria to rejoice with her beloved nurse.

Despite everything, it had happened, Tullus thought as he watched the couple at the altar. But he knew Theodis was indifferent to the ceremony. It was Martin's blessing that the Arian guardsman trusted.

Anna held firmly to her husband in the dim interior of the church; her hesitant steps contrasting with the power and confidence of Theodis. It was very moving and the tears of both Drusilla and Cornelia were the proof.

OOO

The day after the wedding a priest and his attendant called with news from Cassiodorus. There was nothing written, but, by word of mouth, Tullus learned that the Emperor Justin was seriously ill and had co-opted Justinian as his colleague. So with Theoderic gone and Justinian poised to mount the throne, the world had changed indeed.

It was late August when further news was received, this time from Atticus, newly arrived in the city. Justin had recovered, but for a few months only, for on August 1st he had died: an old campaign wound, Atticus explained, an ulcer of the foot. Justinian was now sole master of the Empire.

Atticus, it seemed, had quickly settled in Constantinople and was full of admiration for the new Emperor. Justinian, he wrote, was easily accessible, highly intelligent and master of his temper. He worked long hours and was temperate in his habits. Nothing seemed to escape his notice and Atticus was certain that a great age lay before the Empire.

Atticus also enthused about his position with the lawyer Tribunian: a great man, he wrote, who knew the ancient teaching. The task before them was high and challenging, for the whole area of the law had to be reformed and codified. Such was the Emperor's will.

Tullus was relieved that his daughter, Atticus and his grandson were all well and obviously established. Clearly their move to Constantinople had not been regretted. No doubt being the son-in-law of the Emperor's friend had helped, but Atticus would have to prove himself. Justinian was not one to suffer fools.

It was plain from further letters that Atticus had frequent contact with the Emperor. Indeed, one roll quoted Justinian's own words. 'Tell Tullus,' it read, 'to stop masquerading as a farmer. His work is here!'

Tullus, however, had made his decision. He could not ignore the duties that had risen about him in Faesulae. There was Drusilla's school and the growing group of 'hard-drinking philosophers' who met monthly at the villa. Some even made the journey from Ravenna. Furthermore, there were the faithful villa staff and now, of course, there was Martin. Martin needed space and peace to grow and Tullus feared that, in his absence, a land-hungry Theodahad would sweep the small community aside. Added to this, the rule of Amalasuentha had started favourably, her goodwill towards the Roman people evident in the formal restoration of the Anicius lands to Rusticiana. In short, the order of the State was holding and Tullus felt it safe to stay.

Tullus was especially relieved that the strained relationship between Thulwin and the Queen had eased. In this Amalasuentha had shown considerable sagacity. What pleased Tullus most was the title of Patrician with which Thulwin had been justly honoured. This was the gift of the Emperor, but there was little doubt that the Queen had made the recommendation.

Tensions remained, however, and as the months, and then the years, slipped by, resentment of her Romanised reforms began to grow. They were much too hasty for her old-established peers, who saw the vigour of their warrior culture now at risk, believing comfort-loving Roman ways would sap their manliness. Tullus understood their point of view, as Rome herself had withered in this way, but he did not understand their attitude to education. The cultured Roman stoic was neither coward nor weakling on the battlefield. Education had not softened him. This the Gothic peers did not appreciate. Indeed, the Roman education of Amalasuentha's son enraged them. The King of the Goths, they proclaimed, was primarily a soldier, and if the Queen's son feared his tutor's strap, how could he look upon a sword or spear? To Tullus this was nonsense, yet he feared his friend Count Thulwin was mixed up in it. The Count had never been at ease with Roman learning and never felt it fitted with a soldier's ways, but at their first official meeting Tullus well remembered how the Count had quoted Seneca. Nothing was quite what it seemed.

Agitation amongst the Gothic nobles continued to mount. Eventually, to keep the peace, the Queen released the young King to the company of his peers. The result was disastrous, for the youth's weak and degenerate nature soon succumbed to precocious debauchery, thus undermining his health.

The Queen's concessions did not satisfy her nobles, for the opposition, once aroused, soon found other disaffections. Rumoured plots against her person made her fearful; so she resolved to act. First she sent her main opponents to the northern frontier; then, when their alleged intrigues persisted, she simply had them killed.

Tullus heard these brutal facts from his Ravenna friends during one of the monthly gatherings at the villa. He was at once concerned, fearing that both Thulwin and his son were also on the northern borders. Tullus had not seen the son of Thulwin or his father for at least two years. His young friend had written, though, telling of his marriage and how his father had been greatly pleased. The Count had also written, using his Latin scribe. He seemed to be forever on the borders. But was it by his own design? Or was it Queen Amalasuentha's will? The question was, where in God's name was he now? and was he safe?

His fears, alas, were tragically confirmed when Thulwin's son rode specially to Faesulae with the awful news of how his noble father and his guards had all been slaughtered in a border ambush. Their bodies had been stripped of armour and their horses taken. It all pointed to a raiding party from the hills, but such effects could be contrived.

Young Thulwin blamed the Queen. His father never would have fallen to simple hillmen. She was the author, he maintained, and thoughts of vengeance possessed him.

"'Vengeance is mine; I will repay'". Tullus almost shouted the Biblical words, but the young Goth did not want to listen.

'What man could let this rest? I cannot do it!'

They were before the courtyard door where the new Count Thulwin had dismounted, but Tullus did not take his visitor inside. Instead, he led him quickly up the hill towards the grave of Valerius. Tullus pointed vigorously at the marble stone.

'What would he have said?' His words were clipped and sharp.

Thulwin's son was silent.

'Thulwin,' Tullus continued, 'do not soil your soul with vengeful killing. Such punishment is meted out by God. If it were not so, justice would be flawed, and that's impossible.'

Still the young man held his tongue, but he was thoughtful. Everything the Count had said was true.

They walked slowly down the hill and at the bottom they were met by the Countess and Valeria. Tullus immediately broke the tragic news. Drusilla was deeply shocked, and Valeria, now almost fifteen, looked at Thulwin's son with open sympathy. The young man was moved, but he felt embarrassed by Valeria's beauty. Shifting awkwardly, he turned to Tullus.

'Count, I will take your advice.'

Thulwin stayed overnight and left early in the morning, ill at ease, for the vision of Valeria's loveliness troubled him. They were close, he knew that, but he also knew that in Verona his wife and child awaited his return.

OOO

For a time Amalasuentha was supreme. Then, in October 534, the young king died. With this her regency ended, and her legitimacy as a ruler was in question. How could a woman lead a warrior race? The old problem was pressing once again. Amalasuentha, though, enjoyed her role and could not bear to give it up. So burdened, she made the fatal blunder of inviting Theodahad, her cousin, to be King – provided she retained the reins of power.

When he heard the news Tullus was appalled. Theodahad was a fraud and his elevation folly. Within a year, he told Drusilla, Amalasuentha would be dead.

Tullus's prediction was proved correct. The Queen was murdered, and in 535 the reign of King Theodahad began – nine years after the death of Theoderic.

Goths and Romans alike were shocked by the murder of Theoderic's daughter, and Justinian's messenger said the crime meant war without a truce. Theodahad, desperate to avoid hostilities, maintained it had been done against his will, yet he continued to honour the assassins. Tullus did not know the full story; the days when Cassiodorus sent his bulletins were over, but he suspected the dissembling web spread wide, even to the very walls of Byzantium.

OOO

Marcus Tullus was sixty-five, yet he looked a man of fifty. Like Drusilla, he had little trouble with his teeth and his hair, though grey, was full. He led a busy, active life, but he shunned excess, especially in the hot days of the summer. In any case, Rufus was more than capable of running the day-to-day estate matters.

Valeria was now seventeen and a joy to both her parents, but she was a worry too, for it was very much the time to think of marriage. Indeed, if anything it was overdue, but no matter how much her parents pondered they could not think of any suitor that they deemed worthy.

When Tullus mentioned the subject to his daughter she simply smiled a knowing smile, just like her mother and like someone who already knew her mind. It would happen in the good Lord's time, she said. God, she was like Drusilla. The same poise, the same inner strength and a wisdom, yes, a wisdom. He could find no other word for it. She could be stoical, too stoical, for then the headaches came with an accompanying sense of isolation. But, again like Drusilla, she would respond to humour, not a contrived humour; it had to be apt.

Just before the news of Amalasuentha's death Tullus decided to take Valeria to Rome. She could stay with Rusticiana and Poppea, he planned, see the sights of the city and hopefully meet some young man of recommended character. The proposal met with Valeria's enthusiastic approval, but not for the reason Tullus hoped. She longed to see the great buildings of the Empire, to visit the site of the old Villa Valerius and to see her grandmama, Poppea.

OOO

Tullus cancelled his plans to visit Rome on hearing of Theodahad's ill-gained power.

He did not trust the so-called philosopher. Theodahad was both craven and avaricious – a fatal combination in a ruler. He would bring chaos, and Tuscany would be the first to suffer. Marcus Tullus was worried, but a secret message from Cassiodorus, now Praetorian Prefect, gave him comfort. The message ran that Theodahad greatly feared invasion and was desperate to maintain good relations with Justinian, for, officially at least, the murder of Amalasuentha had outraged the Emperor. In the circumstances Theodahad dared not touch the coveted Tullus property, as the relationship between the man from the north and Justinian was well known.

Tullus knew, of course, that this advantage could work against him, as it would be logical for Theodahad to send him as an envoy to Byzantium. Tullus dreaded the command, knowing that it would be difficult, if not impossible, to refuse, and knowing it would leave his wife and daughter virtual hostages. As it happened, Theodahad sent his own paid sycophants, fearing, Tullus guessed, that the Roman Count would speak too plainly to

Justinian. Tullus was relieved, but he was not complacent, and once more scouts were posted to watch the approach roads.

Two months passed without incident. Then, one evening in late summer, the turret lookout reported a large troop of horse moving down the valley from the north towards Florentia. It was unusual, for garrison transfers were usually effected from Ravenna. The next morning a similar troop appeared in the valley, but this time they turned to climb the hill.

At once frantic activity seized all about the fortress villa. All knew their tasks, for old lessons had not been forgotten. Tullus made for the turret steps and half-way up he heard the heavy courtyard doors slam shut, but before he reached the top there was the sound of cheering. It could only mean one thing: Thulwin's son. And it was.

The young Count first apologised for the consternation he had caused. A mix-up, he explained. He had sent messengers who had gone mistakenly to the town of Faesulae. Tullus brushed the matter aside.

'I have brought my son, sir,' Thulwin said quickly as his attendants presented the boy. 'His Gothic name is much too long – his mother's doing. So I've given him a Roman name as well; it's Manlius.'

'In memory of Boethius,' Tullus mouthed.

The four-year-old bowed gravely before the grey-haired Count, who smilingly bowed back.

Thulwin laughed.

'I cannot claim spontaneity, sir – it was well rehearsed.'

'Ah! Here come the Countess and my daughter.'

Greetings were at once exchanged, and then without delay Thulwin explained the meaning of his visit.

He had been posted to Sicily by the King and wished to leave his son in the care of the Tullus household. He wanted the child educated, he said plainly, and the Captain, as he called Theodis, could keep him practised in the Gothic tongue. The boy had lost both mother and nurse within the past six months, he added with uncompromising bluntness.

Tullus looked at his old friend's son for a moment. Then, remaining silent, he put his hand on Drusilla's shoulder.

'Our home is your home, Thulwin,' he said quietly.

The young Count bent down and whispered in his son's ear. Shyly the boy moved across to the Countess and Valeria, bowing to each in turn.

Spontaneously Valeria fell to her knees, her hands held out in welcome. At first the child hesitated, but with Valeria's smile his shyness melted. Solemnly he moved forward, his step measured and unhurried. A Thulwin was a Thulwin, Tullus thought, even at the age of four.

The heir to the vast Thulwin estates had made ample provision for his son, a not unwelcome generosity as far as Tullus was concerned, as the Royal grant had ended with the great King's death. Furthermore, the young Count left twelve of his best men to supplement the ageing guard; again with adequate arrangements for their upkeep.

Thulwin's stay at the villa was short and by the early afternoon he left. Once he had disappeared below the ridge, Tullus, Drusilla and Valeria climbed to the turret and there, with the grandson of his old friend perched upon his shoulders, Tullus waited for the troop of horse to reappear.

'There's your father now – do you see? – I think he's waving.'

'Yes, sir – will he be gone long?'

'He will.' Tullus despised sentimental lies.

He let the boy down carefully from his shoulders.

'Come, young man. I'll show you the horses.'

Slowly they descended the spiral steps with Drusilla following, but Valeria remained behind watching to the last fading glimpse of the receding horsemen.

'I'm troubled, Marcus,' Drusilla said to Tullus later when they were alone. 'Valeria and the young Count – it was obvious, but all I see is tragedy.'

'Don't ask me to stand against it, Drusilla. I couldn't ...'

'No, Marcus.' She shook her head vigorously. 'I would never ask ... It's their religion ...'

'It's Sicily that worries me,' Tullus interjected. 'The threat of invasion by the Empire's mercenaries is all too real, and if it happens he'll be there.'

'But, Marcus, we can't dismiss the differences in religion – he's an Arian.'

'Young Thulwin doesn't care about such things, and neither does Valeria.'

'I know, Marcus, but the world cares, and he's a Gothic Count, even if you've made him Platonist!'

Tullus nodded.

'There's much, too much, alas, in what you say, but the truth is, Drusilla, nothing would please me more.'

She moved closer to him.

'I like him too. Let's pray that he'll be safe in Sicily.'

Tullus did not respond. He had no wish to disturb his wife, for he was pessimistic and dreaded the presence of the Byzantine army in Italy. The Goths were harsh enough, but the mercenary soldiers of the Empire would make a desert.

The fear of invasion was not idle, for Justinian's general, Belisarius, was active. Young Thulwin had told him that the Byzantine had taken Carthage – news not unwelcome to the Goths – and had received a triumph in Constantinople, an exceptional honour. But most were certain Sicily would be next.

OOO

The months passed, and soon a year, but no message was received from Thulwin. Tullus feared the worst, for he knew that Sicily had fallen and that Belisarius was besieging Naples. Indeed, rumour had it that the town was lost and that the Empire's Hunnish mercenaries had wrought a slaughter in the streets.

Bitter criticism of Theodahad was rife. He had done nothing to save Naples, and the Goths were outraged. It was only a matter of time, Tullus guessed, before Theodahad would suffer the same fate he had apportioned to Amalasuentha.

Again Tullus's prophecy was proved correct. The Goths elected a new king. His name was Witigis, a man of undistinguished birth, and not long afterwards Theodahad was assassinated. It was November 536 and Belisarius was on the way to Rome.

Tullus learned of these events with growing alarm. He had hoped that Witigis, who had married into the Royal family and was untarnished by the crime against Amalasuentha, would have been able to treat with Belisarius. This did not happen. The war was moving slowly and inevitably towards Tuscany.

In January 537, the children of Faesulae failed to return to the villa school. A message read that they were needed to rebuild the walls. The Goths were fortifying Faesulae. The same was happening in Ravenna. In fact, only one of his Ravenna friends had been able to attend the monthly meeting.

In February the weekly provisions for Thulwin's soldiers stopped. Not only that: Tullus was ordered to provide grain for the growing garrison at Faesulae. It was prudent to comply, but his grain stock was wholly insufficient. In time they would take Thulwin's soldiers, Theodis and the Twins. Tullus had no illusions. He could see that Faesulae was fast becoming a fortress and if the war continued, as he thought it would, warring armies would battle over it, leaving the surrounding countryside a wilderness. He thought of the olives he had planted twenty years ago, now mature – the waste, the awful waste. War was a fearful thing.

Tullus rode about his estate almost continuously. It was the old family land and he loved the place, but he knew it was the end. He would have to leave.

At the close of February he went to see Martin. There were eight small, box-like huts now, standing in a row. Nearby was a low, rambling refectory.

Wearily he dismounted from Britannicus. His heart was heavy.

The two friends embraced.

'Are you well, Marcus Tullus?'

'Just old and tired, Martin.'

'There's something else.'

'Yes. War is coming to Tuscany. It's as certain as the sun will set.'

'You should leave this place – your graceful wife, your lovely daughter and the Count's boy ...'

'I know, Martin. I should have left when the great King died.'

'No, Marcus Tullus. Now is the time to leave.'

'What will you do, Martin?'

Martin shook his head. He did not know.

'Any news of the young Count?'

'I fear he's been a sacrifice to war.'

'Somehow I don't think so, Marcus Tullus.'

Tullus looked at his friend closely. He had good cause to trust Martin's intuition.

'Dear God, I hope he's safe – at least for Valeria's sake.'

ooo

That night Tullus told his wife and daughter of his plans. Tomorrow he would tell the staff and start despatching valuables to Thulwin's estate north-east of Verona.

With her usual grace Drusilla rose from her couch and approached him. Gently she put her arm around his waist, while stretching her other hand out to Valeria.

'Marcus,' she said quietly. She could see that he was anxious for their sakes. 'Neither your daughter nor your wife have seen the city of Constantine.'

'Both of you are jewels,' he said with fierce intensity. But he was sick at heart. He slept little that night, and when he summoned Theodis and Rufus the next morning his mind was dull and heavy. He dreaded telling these two faithful friends of his decision, but when he did a burden seemed to drop from him. They had expected it.

Tullus invited both men and their families to travel with him and Rufus, in his frank, Tuscan way, said that many of the staff had guessed his plans and hoped to join him.

Though moved, Tullus was practical. For ten years there had been no Royal commissions. The Tullus wealth was vested in vines and olives, and the estate was worth little, with war about the town of Faesulae presumed a certainty. There was some Valerian plate which had been hidden and retrieved by Valerius; otherwise the villa coffers were low. All he could offer the staff was a destination – Thulwin's Verona estate. It was large, and he knew the father of the current agent from the old days.

'Is the journey's end to be Byzantium?' Rufus asked.

'If the war continues there may be little alternative; but could we pass safely through Dalmatia?' Tullus shook his head. 'Rufus,' he added forcefully, 'let's get to Verona first!'

The moving was a long, painful process, with time for carts to journey to Verona and return for more.

The day before they finally left, Tullus saw that Martin was provisioned. Otherwise there was nothing he could do. They parted without fuss. Martin asked about the young Count, and Tullus shook his head, indicating the absence of news.

'He'll turn up. He's like you, Marcus Tullus. The Lord has smiled upon him.'

The two men grasped each other's arm. Then Tullus mounted the ageing Britannicus and rode away without once looking back.

The next day Tullus and his family left the villa. He did not take the statues of the Gracchi. They were too heavy. So they left them standing, as they had for a decade and more, beside the grave of Valerius.

Anna, Theodis's wife, was red-eyed. So, too, was Valeria, but Drusilla did not weep. Instead, a kind of numbness had possessed her. Then suddenly she thought of Rusticiana and Poppea. God help them. Marcus had told her that Belisarius had entered Rome and that the Gothic King Witigis was besieging the city.

ooo

Thulwin's villa near Verona was a huge, palace-like place: a one-time governor's residence. It was not empty, though, for the relatives of the young Count's late mother and wife had taken refuge there. None of them spoke Latin, and all resented, with some cause, that a Roman had been made guardian of the family heir.

For the first month or so the villa was crowded and the endless cries of children reminded Tullus of the tenements in Rome. The congestion eased, however, as, one by one, the Faesulae families found other accommodation.

There was ample work for the new arrivals, as most of the able-bodied Goths had been drafted to defend Ravenna. The question was, would Thulwin's soldiers and the former Royal guardsmen be drafted too? They had escaped the clutches of Faesulae, but would they be so fortunate with Verona? They had their oaths of loyalty to Tullus and the Count's young son. These had been used to block the draft at Faesulae but, as desperation grew, such oaths would stand for little.

Only Valeria managed to make real contact with the young Count's relatives, and in particular with one old widowed aunt. She had asked her, with the aid of Theodis, if she had any news about her nephew. The old lady had shaken her head, but she had smiled, and over the weeks a relationship began to grow. Valeria, in halting Gothic, was able to describe the old, well-tested friendship of her father with the house of Thulwin. In turn, the old aunt talked amongst her own, the stories spread and smiles became more general.

Thulwin's boy knew his relatives, of course, and was naturally free in their presence; yet he preferred the company of the Tullus family, even though the schooling disciplines were irksome. From time to time he asked about his father, where he was and when he would be back, but as no one could answer, the questions became infrequent. The memory of his father was becoming hazy.

There was nothing hazy about the missing Count in Tullus's mind. Every week he rode to Verona seeking news. He made regular enquiries at the Gothic garrison but the army, preoccupied by war, had little time for detail. In their eyes it was simple. The Count Thulwin was presumed dead; otherwise he would have sent a message.

There was never any lack of war news, or rather rumour, for the town buzzed with stories from the ancient capital. The siege of Rome continued, and Witigis, it was said, had destroyed the aqueducts, thus starving the grain mills of their power. Belisarius had countered with a mill-wheel poised between two boats on the flowing Tiber; Justinian's general was resourceful. In fact, for some, an air of invincibility had attached to his person and it was generally believed that Witigis's siege would fail. Such an outcome would save the city from the anger of the Goths, but other than that Tullus felt no cause for jubilation. On the contrary, the war was ruining Italy, and in many of the southern provinces agriculture had almost stopped. It was a disaster, not only for the native population, but for the Gothic army too. The facts were simple. The Goths could only live off the land, whereas the armies of the Empire could be supplied by sea.

Tullus knew that if the war continued, famine and disease would ravage Italy. He also feared the cruelty of the Goths, maddened by what they saw as gross betrayal, for every Roman had, at best, divided loyalties. Tullus took nothing for granted, and what was more, he did not trust the young Count's relatives, even though their smiles had grown warmer.

Christmas came, and still no news of Thulwin. Yet Tullus did not give up hope; after all, he himself had been missing for a year. But concern for the young Count's fate was ever close and pressing, and Valeria, though she did her best, could not disguise her anguish.

The anguish of the daughter was rivalled by her father's indecision. Tullus faced harsh realities and he had to choose alone. The dilemma seemed impossible to solve, for no matter how he looked at it, the danger seemed of equal force.

Reason pointed to the east, but once he started for Byzantium – given the miracle that Dalmatia was safe – he would risk denouncement by the Thulwin family, for, in taking the Count's son, he could be accused of his abduction. The response of the Verona garrison, especially to Roman rebels in a time of war, would be uncomplicated. But how could he remain in what might be a battleground?

It was an illusion to think the war was distant in the south. True, Rome was far away, but the Byzantine navy ruled the sea and could land soldiers on the northern coast at any time. In fact, he had heard rumours that Belisarius had promised to send men to Mediolanum. Furthermore, he could not ignore the recent arrival at Verona of a high-ranking officer known to be the nephew of Triguilla. Old scores could be neatly settled.

Drusilla heard the same news from the servants – Tullus would never have told her – and it disturbed her already agitated state. Her nightmares had returned, with the grinning face of Triguilla mixed up with the hated images of the Verona villa. Drusilla loathed the place: Thulwin's suspicious relatives, the cramped conditions and the lack of water – it was hell.

Tullus was concerned about his wife. She was losing weight and he feared the consequences of staying longer at Verona. She did not complain overmuch; that was her nature, but the discipline that restrained her also held her in a rigid isolation. Tullus did his best to ease the situation. He took her riding, though he sensed that she responded more from duty than from inclination.

It was his wife's misery that tipped the balance of decision. So, early in February, he sent Theodis and the Twins to scout the beginnings of a route towards the east and to find adequate places of sanctuary for the women and children.

The responsibility of sending the ex-guardsmen on such a dangerous mission weighed heavily on Tullus. It was a difficult time, yet he was comforted by the marked improvement in Drusilla's state now that she could see some hope.

At the end of February Tullus learned that a large number of the Verona garrison had been transferred to Ravenna. It was good news, as he judged a depleted force would be less likely to thwart his movements.

The news coincided with the return of Theodis and the Twins. All three were hopeful and Tullus decided to leave at once. He made no attempt to be secretive. Thulwin's relatives were not fools and Valeria, who had managed to penetrate the shell of their clannish circle, explained as best she could.

Only half the number that had left Faesulae decided to continue. Mostly, they included those whose children were the pupils of Drusilla and Valeria, as well as the young and unattached. There was the eternal Philippus, of course. How he had managed to cheat death so long was beyond Tullus's comprehension. Again, there was Petrus-the-hillman and his son, whose freedom Tullus had managed to purchase. Indeed, there were far too many. Food would be a problem, but with large barrels of flour in every cart and with olive oil and wine, they had the basics.

Thulwin's relatives affected a polite regret, and Valeria was confident that they would hold their peace. Even so, her father was uncertain. In fact, there were so many uncertainties that Tullus had the feeling he was travelling blind.

It was an anxious time as the long train of carts set out. But they were well protected, for Thulwin's twelve men were still in place; they had given their oath to protect the Tullus family. Of course, there were Theodis and the Twins, still a formidable trio, and also the young Tuscan men, together with the faithful Rufus. All were heavily armed. They could repel banditry, provided they were cautious.

They were very cautious, avoiding towns where possible. River crossings were difficult, as they always tried to find a ferry far from prying eyes. Theodis sent scouts in all directions. Nothing was left to chance. Progress was therefore slow, but after a week without incident their confidence increased.

The women slept inside the covered carts, the men below, with canvas as a windbreak. The nights were cold and conditions were anything but easy. Mercifully, though, Drusilla's nightmares stopped and a pioneering spirit had possessed her.

'At Verona,' she joked, 'I complained about the lack of water, while here I haven't had a proper wash for days. What strange perversity!'

'Not strange, my dear,' Tullus quipped. 'You are a woman.'

He ducked as Drusilla made to punch him in the ribs, and they laughed. Tullus was delighted at his wife's improvement. Indeed, her good spirits were infectious and inspired the womenfolk. This was a blessing, for it helped the men and made them more effective; they had to be, for the way ahead was fraught with danger.

On the tenth day out of Verona the ring of scouts was tested. A column of Gothic soldiers, they reported, was approaching from the south. Such an event had been anticipated and the plan devised was simple. Theodis would say he was escorting women and children and the elderly, who were escaping from a town threatened by siege. If pressed, he was to name the town as Faesulae. It was not uncommon for families of gentle birth to be given safe passage. The reason was practical – if not cynical. They left their wealth behind. Furthermore, all soldiers knew the fate of 'useless mouths', for when a siege began to bite, only those who fought were fed.

The young, able-bodied Tuscans kept well hidden in the dim interiors of the carts as the soldiers approached, but fears were soon forgotten when Theodis recognised the captain of the troop. He knew him well and had trained him as a young recruit. It was a fortunate meeting, for the young man gave Theodis valuable information. They would be wise, he cautioned, to avoid Salona and the adjacent fortress of the one-time Emperor Diocletian.

Three days later the scouts reported twenty horsemen approaching from the east – brigands, almost certainly. Tullus was alarmed but Theodis was dismissive.

'Stop the line of carts on the high ground where they are clearly visible,' Theodis suggested. 'The hope of plunder will be irresistible. They'll be drawn like bees to honey, and we'll be waiting.'

Tullus assented, and when the clash occurred it was little better than a massacre. Only a third of the outlaws escaped. The Goths seemed to treat the matter as a gentle exercise. They were a natural fighting force, he thought. All they needed was a leader.

As they neared Salona they came upon a burnt-out village. The following morning they found another had been fired. Clearly the Gothic officer's warning had been well advised.

In a wide arc they began to skirt the area, but the going was difficult, with roads little more than tracks. Progress was very slow, but at no time could they drop their guard, for the naked envy they encountered had a cunning that only force of arms deterred. The young Count's soldiery were essential.

Thulwin's boy enjoyed the drama; his great delight was to ride with Tullus on Britannicus, but mostly he sat beside Valeria in her cart. For Valeria the son was a sharp reminder of his father. When logic ruled, misery would engulf her, yet it did not last, for in her heart she nurtured hope. Somewhere, somehow, he was alive. Fervently she prayed that he was well.

The going was not easy and one small detour eventually took a day. What was more, the flour and oil were running low. Indeed, a general air of weariness had descended. Doggedly they struggled on, yet at no time did Theodis drop his guard, and scouts were always on the watch. But Theodis looked uneasy. The strain was showing. He knew too well the dangers that they faced.

They passed more burnt-out dwellings, then, all at once, it seemed, the countryside had changed. Not that the terrain had altered, but somehow there was a different feel. Both Tullus and Theodis, riding out in front, sensed that they had reached the Empire's border. If so, their troubles were by no means over, for they would have to treat with Byzantine officialdom, not to mention soldiery, and Tullus knew that with the presence of the Gothic guard it could be very awkward.

They had little time to wait for contact with the Imperial forces. As Theodis had sensibly predicted, there would be scouts well placed, for after all, it was the border.

The troop of soldiers that eventually confronted them were mounted archers – twenty-four in number.

Tullus had warned the Gothic bodyguard to be calm, especially in the face of provocation. It was sound advice, as the Byzantines immediately formed an aggressive arc, their bows loaded.

'Captain, we seek the protection of the Empire,' Tullus said respectfully.

'Many do, old man,' the officer returned indifferently.

'Do you know who you're speaking to?' Theodis exploded in Latin.

'I don't need a Goth to tell me,' was the quick response. 'Arrest these heretics!' he shouted to his second in command.

'No!' Tullus bellowed in Greek. The officer froze.

'It's I who give the orders,' he reacted. 'Who are you?'

The situation was tense, to say the least. Clearly the officer was not a man of towering intellect, but he would be quick to grasp the import of

Justinian's ring, given as a pledge of friendship in the early days.

'I suggest you read the inscription, Captain,' Tullus said quietly as he handed him the ring.

The officer peered closely.

'Petrus Sabbatius Just …' he said slowly, without finishing the Emperor's last name. He saluted stiffly. At once the situation was transformed, and within three days they were safely in Dyrrachium.

Tullus wrote immediately to the Emperor, asking formal permission to enter Constantinople. He also sent a note to his daughter and Atticus, and within ten days Justinian's reply arrived. It was couched in official language, with a few words added in the Emperor's hand: 'At last,' it read, 'after thirty years.'

While waiting at Dyrrachium, Tullus was bombarded with war news. Belisarius, it was trumpeted, had broken out of Rome and was heading up the coast to Ravenna. An Imperial force had been despatched to garrison Mediolanum. The news made him shiver. They had escaped, but just in time.

Still there was no news of the young Count. It was strange, for whether dead or captured, the name of Thulwin would have caused a stir.

oOo

The Via Egnatia was in good repair, much better than the first time Martin and Tullus had travelled its length. Broken bridges had been mended and many of the detours were no longer necessary. Yet it was a month before they reached the great walls of the capital.

Atticus, who had learned of their approach, was waiting with Cornelia and young Marcus. Emotions ran wild, and Anna wept joyfully as she held her baby, as she called Cornelia.

As the excitement subsided, Tullus became aware of his daughter standing quietly by his side. She had a lonely, distant look, a habit that was growing in its frequency, and he knew the cause. Gently he put his arm around her shoulders and drew her close.

'Atticus,' he called above the hubbub, 'the chances are remote, I know, but have you heard anything of the young Count Thulwin? He's been missing …'

'He's here! The young Count's here!' Atticus replied.

Impulsively Valeria buried her face in her father's tunic. She did not sob, but Tullus felt the dampness of her tears.

'How did he get here?' he asked, still holding his daughter close.

'Apparently he was captured before Naples. The name of Thulwin is well known and the Emperor was interested. So he was put on board a ship bound for the city. On the way the ship was damaged by a storm and had to seek harbour and repairs at some remote island, where the pace of work was somewhat slow, to put it mildly. Anyway, he eventually got here two weeks ago.'

'Is he well?' Tullus asked. His daughter stiffened.

'Oh, yes. He's at the Palace. The Emperor favours him. Rumour has it that he's taken an oath of loyalty – with one provision – that he's not required to fight against his own. Look, sir!' Atticus added, pointing to the white-robed guards approaching.

'The Candidati,' Tullus said in recognition.

'They're coming to escort you, sir – a rare honour for a private person.'

Tullus nodded. Justinian was honouring an old friend and he was grateful. Bending down, he lifted Thulwin's boy onto the broad back of Britannicus. He patted the animal. The old horse had done well.

'Now, young man, you will see your father soon.'

'Yes, sir,' the boy replied with a maturity far beyond his years, and for a moment Tullus felt that he was looking at his old benefactor, the great Count himself.

OOO

They were escorted to the villa within the walls, used to house the Emperor's guests, and while they were given leisure to rest, it was made quite clear that the Count and Countess, with their daughter, were expected at the Palace. In two hours' time a carriage would arrive for them. It did, precisely, with a message from Justinian carried by one Isidore of Miletus. They were to see the sights of the city before arriving at the Palace and he, Isidore, an assistant of Anthemius the architect, was to be their guide.

'You'll not recognise the city, sir,' Isidore declared. 'The new Temple of Divine Wisdom, Hagia Sophia, was opened last December. It's a wonder, and it dominates the city like a watch-tower.'

'When did the building start?' Tullus asked. They were standing in the large paved courtyard awaiting the arrival of the ladies.

'After the Nika revolt in 532.'

'Yes – there was some trouble in the Hippodrome then, I heard.'

'Oh, no, sir – much worse than that. The centre of the city was devastated. It was very serious, for both the Greens and the Blues combined against the Emperor!'

'Combined!' Tullus exclaimed.

'Yes, sir. The Emperor was punishing the licence of both factions impartially. The Blues especially didn't like it.'

'I wager they didn't! The news I received at Faesulae played the matter down. Even my son-in-law said little.'

'Perhaps he was being prudent, sir. It was a difficult time.'

Isidore bowed low as the ladies arrived and was clearly impressed by the beauty of the Countess and her daughter.

After a few brief pleasantries they started out. The villa was a full mile from the centre, and as they approached the mighty dome of Hagia Sophia began to dominate. Tullus was amazed at the changes in the city. The scale was vast, a reflection of Justinian's vision, but taxes must have soared to cover the expense; and there was the near-continuous war as well. The costs would be enormous.

The huge structure of Hagia Sophia was plain outside, but inside it was breathtaking. The great cross on a starry heaven shone from the summit of the dome. The ceiling was covered with pure gold and the answering reflections from the marble on the pillars and the walls were magical in the evening light. Silence was the natural reaction.

Eventually it was time to journey to the Palace. Valeria was visibly nervous, and Tullus put his arm about her.

'Don't worry, my dear,' he said. 'Just follow your mother's lead.'

'Thulwin may be present, Father.'

'Yes, if the Emperor wills.' So that was it. Thulwin, and not the master of the Roman world, was causing her unease.

Escorted by Isidore, they were directed to the Emperor's private quarters and, after the hardship of their flight from Italy, the surrounding opulence was dreamlike. Guards snapped to attention as they entered a large, ornate reception room, at the end of which double doors swung open. Before them were the Emperor and his Empress, Theodora.

Drusilla curtseyed, followed quickly by her daughter. Prompted by his wife's response, Tullus made to bow with due formality, but Justinian gestured him to stop.

'No more formalities, Tullus; these are our private quarters.'

The introductions proceeded in an easy, open way. The Empress did most of the talking. She was gracious and welcoming and her wit was quick and ready. But Tullus was grateful that Drusilla did not try to match her brilliance, for it was neither proper, nor indeed prudent, to eclipse the first lady of the Empire.

The Emperor's private guests were modest in number. Some Tullus had met before: his old friend Tribunian the lawyer; Anthemius the architect. There was an artist in mosaic design whose name he had forgotten and another face he could not name, a man familiar with the ancient modes of music. These were Justinian's artist and scholar friends, men outside the politics of Church and State, if that were possible. Tullus was surprised, however, that Thulwin was not present but, not knowing the details of the young Count's position, he thought it best to let Justinian raise the subject.

The Emperor and Tullus were standing apart and all eyes were upon them, expecting some pronouncement, but Justinian was in no mood for public statements. Instead he turned to Tullus privately.

'Tullus, you can't live on air.' It was typical Justinian, straight to the point. 'Tending a few vines and olives won't keep you going in this city!'

Tullus waited; there was little doubt that Justinian had already planned his fate.

'I'm putting you with the city planners. That will give you a revenue.'

'What can I offer, sir?'

'Common sense!' Justinian was impatient to continue. 'Your estate at Faesulae will be annexed and you'll be given comparable lands outside the wall and a town villa in case of danger.'

'But Atticus has a town villa, sir!'

'Tullus, for the sake of God, let me play the Emperor!'

The two men looked at each other almost fiercely.

'Remember we were friends before all this.' Justinian's arm swung round.

'I'm grateful.'

'I know you're grateful. Now, tell me about that miracle we both know – Martin!'

A smile spread across Justinian's face as Tullus told the latest tales of Martin's progress.

'We'll see that he's protected.' The smile continued. 'Think of him as a Patriarch – but they'd kill him. They couldn't stand a good man in their midst!'

'Sir, you've just described the tragedy of Boethius; all other causes were secondary.'

'A great tragedy,' the Emperor echoed. 'You'll be pleased to know his wife is well. She supported Belisarius wholeheartedly and was generous with the Anician wealth.'

Tullus nodded in acknowledgement..

For a moment they were silent, and Tullus could not help recalling how Theoderic had been goaded by Byzantium, but he kept his counsel.

'What would you do with the Goths, Tullus?' Justinian suddenly asked.

Briefly Tullus had a vivid recollection of the great King. He almost heard him speak.

'Have I a day, sir, or a month?!'

'Come, Tullus. You're a man of short sentences!'

Tullus smiled. Unlike similar situations with Theoderic, he felt at ease.

'With a general worth the name to lead them, the Goths would be a powerful force. Don't underestimate them, sir. Their best men have a nobility that I sometimes feel we have forgotten. Treat with them. Give them land to the north.'

'Good advice – if I could get the generals to follow it. Don't be mistaken, Tullus – Justinian's not all-powerful, especially when his generals play the king in distant lands. The Empire's full of Emperors!'

'But there's only one Justinian, sir!'

A brief smile played on the face of the Emperor.

Tullus looked across at his wife, standing tall beside the Empress. All the women about were bedecked with jewels, but not Drusilla. One ancient brooch with the letter 'V' inscribed on it and one gold bangle; that was all. As with the plate, both had been buried and recovered by Valerius. His gaze passed to Valeria, standing graceful like her mother, her eyes glancing frequently at the double doors as attendants came and went – anticipating, hoping, even fearing that the young Count might be next to enter. Close to Valeria was the dainty figure of Cornelia. Dear Arria, what would she have said if she had known her daughter would be feted by an Emperor? She would surely have approved of Atticus, Tullus mused, as he watched his curly-headed son-in-law busy talking to Tribunian. No doubt their subject was the law and the all-consuming task they were engaged upon, Justinian's new institutes. Atticus was well employed.

Again Tullus looked at his beloved wife and daughters. The family was united. It was all complete except for Thulwin; he was family even as it was – and Poppea, far away in Rome. Perhaps one day she and Rusticiana would make the journey to Byzantium.

Tullus was tired of standing, but there was no alternative while the Emperor was on his feet. He, like Tullus, had been scanning the assembled guests. Suddenly he beckoned one of the attendants.

'Where is the Gothic Count?'

'With the Excubitor Guards, sir.'

'He should be here.'

'Yes, sir.' The attendant bowed and hurried off.

This was the Justinian Tullus remembered. The driving impatience had not been lost.

'Atticus told me you had given the young Count a commission. I'm very ...'

'Yes, with the Excubitors,' Justinian interrupted.

'But his religion.'

'Religion! You should know the answer to that!' the Emperor shot back. 'He was fearless when I questioned him, yet measured and polite. He quoted Plato, Boethius – and as for Tullus – the Count said this, the Count said that! We talked for ages, much to the consternation of the guards, for he came to me a captive. But I ceased my questions when he quoted St Augustine on the one religion. You know the passage?'

'Yes – about the one religion that has always been, and which we now call Christian. It's a favourite of his.'

'Yes, but very controversial, Tullus, and it was recanted. He's like you. Church dogma doesn't interest him. But the Emperor can't take such a comfortable position. He must decide. So I warned him strongly to be discreet in public, for this city is not known for its tolerance. I also said that the Emperor Justinian was Orthodox and would not have his will ignored.'

The warning was not lost on Tullus. Constantinople was not Theoderic's Italy.

'His Latin's good,' Justinian continued, 'but he'll have to learn Greek. I like him; he'll be useful.'

'Here he comes, sir. I know the step,' Tullus interjected.

'He will be looking for your daughter,' Justinian said knowingly.

'And she for him,' Tullus responded quietly.

All at once the tall figure stood framed by the doorway.

'My God, he's like his father,' Tullus mouthed.

The young Count bowed towards the Emperor and his father's friend, but his eyes had found Valeria.

Tullus could see the Empress whispering to his daughter. The impish look was undisguised.

Slowly Valeria moved to meet the tall young Goth; a father's heart was beating for his daughter. Then Thulwin held his two hands out towards her and she did likewise in response. Firmly their hands entwined.

Tullus had no doubt that he was watching his future son-in-law, but this time the wedding would not be in the Anicius chapel. Briefly the loss of Anicius Boethius pained fresh and raw.

He turned towards the Emperor.

'The prison writings of Boethius were saved. I brought a copy for you. Isidore has it in his care; it's pure Plato.'

'A unique gift!' Justinian responded with surprise. 'How did you manage to preserve the manuscripts?'

Tullus outlined the story briefly.

'Another miracle! Tullus, I do believe that if an arrow-storm assailed your person you would emerge unharmed. What is your secret?'

'The only secret, sir – God's will!'

OOO

# THE LAST ROMANS

## CHARACTERS IN THE STORY
(H – historical; F – fictional)

| | |
|---|---|
| ALBINUS (H) | Senator of Consular rank – accused by Cyprian of treason |
| AMALARIC (H) | Son of Alaric and grandson of Theoderic |
| AMALASUENTHA (H) | Daughter of Theoderic |
| ANASTASIUS (H) | Eastern Emperor AD 491 – 518 |
| ANNA (F) | Nurse to Cornelia |
| ANTHEMIUS (H) | Architect of Hagia Sophia |
| ARRIA (F) | Impoverished gentlewoman, first wife of Tullus |
| ATHALARIC (H) | Grandson and heir of Theoderic |
| ATTICUS (F) | Husband of Cornelia |
| AUGUSTINE OF HIPPO (H) | Saint Augustine AD 354 – 430 |
| BASILIUS (H) | A Roman of doubtful reputation |
| BELISARIUS (H) | General of Justinian |
| BENEDICT OF NURSIA (H) | Founder of the Benedictine Order |
| BISHOP OF ARELATE (F) | |
| BOETHIUS (H) | Anicius Manlius Severinus – Philosopher, Senator, Consul and Master of Offices under Theoderic |
| CASSIODORUS (H) | (cAD 480 – c575) Minister under Theoderic |
| CORNELIA (F) | Daughter of Arria and Tullus |
| CUNIGAST (H) | Gothic Minister accused by Boethius of oppressing the poor |
| CYPRIAN (H) | Referendarius in King's Court of Appeal |
| DEACON OF FIDENAE (F) | |
| DRUSILLA (F) | Daughter of Valerius |
| EUTHARIC (H) | Husband of Amalasuenth |
| GESALIC (H) | Claimant to the throne in Hispania |
| HERMIT OF THE ROCKS (F) | |
| IBBAS, Count (H) | General of Theoderic |
| ISIDORE OF MILETUS (H) | Assistant to Anthemius |
| JOHN (H) | Pope (Meeting with Theoderic fictional) |
| JULIA (F) | Mother of Cyprian (Her family setting also fictional) |
| JUSTIN (H) | Count of the Excubitor Guards - elevated to Emperor |
| JUSTINIAN (the Great) (H) | Emperor AD 527 – 565 |
| MARTIN (F) | Boy servant and disciple of the Hermit of the Rocks |
| MAURUS (H) | Monk – disciple of Benedict |
| NARCO (F) | Servant of Cyprian |
| OPILIO (H) | Younger brother of Cyprian |
| PHILIPPUS (F) | Servant of Tullus |

| | |
|---|---|
| POPPE (POPPEA) (F) | Servant of Rusticiana – later, wife of Valerius |
| RUFUS (F) | Servant of Cyprian, later Tullus's agent |
| RUSTICIANA (H) | Wife of Boethius, daughter of Symmachus |
| SYMMACHUS (H) | Father-in-law of Boethius |
| THEODAHAD (H) | Nephew of Theoderic – becomes King |
| THEODERIC (the Great) (H) | King of the Ostrogoths |
| THEODIS (F) | Captain of Tullus's guard |
| THULWIN, Count (H) | General of Theoderic |
| THULWIN (Young) (F) | Son of Count Thulwin |
| TRIBUNIAN (H) | Lawyer under Justinian; President of Commission to review the Law |
| TRIGUILLA (H) | A Goth whose evil designs were frustrated by Boethius |
| TULLUS, (F) | The Man from the North Marcus Valerius |
| VALERIA (F) | Daughter of Drusilla and Tullus |
| VALERIUS (F) | Father of Drusilla; rescued by Tullus; becomes Senator |
| WITIGIS (H) | King of the Goths |

## HISTORICAL DATA

| | |
|---|---|
| c.454 | Theoderic (known as The Great) born |
| c.466 | Clovis, King of the Franks, born |
| 480 | Birth of Boethius, and of Benedict of Nursia |
| 481 | Reign of Clovis commences |
| c.482 | Birth of Justinian |
| 491 | Anastasius becomes Emperor |
| 507 | Alaric, Visigoth King, falls to Clovis, King of the Franks |
| 508 | Clovis nominated Consul by Anastasius. Thulwin deals blows to Franks and Burgundians |
| 510 | General Ibbas inflicts crushing defeat on Franks and Burgundians. Boethius made Consul without Companion |
| 511 | Death of Clovis, King of the Franks; riots in Constantinople (re: Monophysites) |
| 514 | Pope Hormisdas elevated |
| 515 | Eutharic marries Amalasuentha, daughter of Theoderic Some time between 515 and 522, riots occur against Jews in Ravenna in the absence of the King from the city, when Eutharic is left in charge. |
| 518 | Death of Anastasius – Justin elected; birth of Athalaric to Eutharic and Amalasuentha |
| 519 | Eutharic Consul |
| 522 | a) Sigismund the Burgundian King puts son to death – son was named Sigeric and was a grandson of Theoderic. b) Boethius's two sons made joint Consuls c) Boethius Master of Offices |
| 523 | a) Death of Eutharic b) Death of Thrasamund, Vandal king of Carthage; his wife Amalafrida (sister of Theoderic) taken captive, mid-523 c) Death of Pope Hormisdas - Pope John elevated d) Thulwin escapes storm e) Albinus accused by Cyprian of treason f) Boethius imprisoned |
| 524 | a) Anti-Arian edicts made in Constantinople b) Execution of Boethius |
| 525 | a) Execution of Symmachus b) Pope John sent to Constantinople – honoured by Justin |
| 526 | a) Death of Pope John (May) b) Death of Theoderic (August) c) Regency of Amalasuentha begins |
| 527 | Death of Justin – Justinian elevated |
| c.526 | Thulwin made Patrician |
| 528 | Benedict of Nursia moves to Monte Cassino |

| | |
|---|---|
| c.532 | a) Thulwin thought to have been murdered by order of Amalasuentha<br>b) Nika revolt in Constantinople (when Greens and Blues combined against the Emperor) |
| 534 | a) Death of Athalaric, boy King, son of Eutharic<br>b) Amalasuentha's regency ends; she offers Theodahad (Theoderic's nephew) title of King on condition that she holds in her own hands the exercise of government |
| c.535 | Amalasuentha assassinated - Theodahad King |
| 536 | a) Siege of Naples by Belisarius (Justinian's general)<br>b) Theodahad assassinated - Witigis king |
| 537 | a) Siege of Rome by Witigis<br>b) Hagia Sophia opened |
| 538 | Siege of Rome lifted |
| 539 | a) Siege of Milan by Goths and Burgundians – male inhabitants massacred<br>b) Faesulae probably taken about this time by Belisarius |
| 540 | Belisarius enters Ravenna |
| 546 | Rusticiana – possibly at the same time as Cassiodorus – may have travelled to Constantinople (Procopius) |
| ARIANISM | A Christian heresy which taught the divinity of the Father but not of the Son. |
| MONOPHYSITES | A heretical sect which taught that in the Person of the incarnate Christ there was a single divine nature; the orthodox teaching is that there is a dual nature in Christ, divine and human. |